Wizard Rebellion

Book Five

Intergalactic Wizard Scout Chronicles

Rodney W. Hartman

ISBN-13: 978-0-9982166-1-4 (R&K Publishing)

ISBN-10: 0-9982166-1-5

Cover Design by Angie Abler

Proofreading service by The Pro Book Editor

Books by Rodney Hartman

Intergalactic Wizard Scout Chronicles

Wizard Defiant	Book One
Wizard Cadet	Book Two
Wizard Scout	Book Three
Wizard Omega	Book Four
Wizard Rebellion	Book Five

DEDICATION

This book is dedicated to my stepson, Jake. I am very proud of you, not only as a son, but as a man. I thank God for allowing me the privilege of being a part of your life..

ACKNOWLEDGMENTS

I want to thank my wife, Karen Hartman, for putting up with my many hours locked up in my office writing. I also want to thank my son-in-law, Jonathan, and my daughter, Stephanie, for their timely advice and opinions. Finally, I'd like to thank Debra Hartmann (no relation) for her many hours of editing and proofreading.

CHAPTER 1

[*Begin Transmission*]

"Hurry!" shouted the deep-bass voice Emerald had come to love so well. It was the voice of her father. It was the voice of the dwarf king.

"They're in the western corridor," he said to the soldiers around him. "Keep everyone moving."

"They're in the eastern corridor as well," shouted a second dwarf who was dressed in dented and bloodstained, full-plate armor. "We're trapped."

"Most of our soldier's weapons can't harm them, sire," said a third dwarf wearing chainmail and carrying a large war hammer.

Emerald recognized the second and third voices as those of General Fenmar and Colonel Granos. She headed in the direction of their voices, struggling against the press of dwarves around her. She hated being a child. Everyone was so much larger than her, and they were all moving in the opposite direction. She needed to see her father. As she wormed her way through the panicking crowd, a flash of blue light caught her attention.

I know that blue, Emerald thought. *It's the gem in Thoagmar's Hammer. Where my father's hammer is, he'll be.*

Like a moth to a flame, Emerald pressed onward. Before long she caught sight of the well-muscled hand of her father, King Lokanstanos, rising above the heads of the crowd. His hand grasped the dark wooden handle of the king's magic hammer. She followed her father's arm downward, trying to glimpse his face, then lost sight of it when the crowd shifted. Emerald shoved against the crowd in frustration. If she was going to die today, she wanted to be with her father.

Renewing her efforts to move forward through the swell of bodies, Emerald followed the deep, strong voice of the dwarf king.

"This is it!" shouted her father over the cries of the milling crowd. "We make our stand here. Those with magic weapons protect our rear. Magic users line up at the front with me. Those without weapons get the children to the center and protect them as best you can. Move! Now!"

Rough hands of well-meaning adults shoved Emerald toward the center of the two thousand plus dwarves in the crowd. Other children congregated around her, carrying her along in their wake by sheer force of numbers. Many of the youngest dwarves were crying at the forced separation from their parents.

"No!" Emerald shouted as she struggled against the flow of children. "I want to stay with my father. I want to fight!"

The shouts and cries of the crowd overwhelmed Emerald's senses. With great effort, she forced herself to concentrate on the task at hand. She needed to find at least one of her parents. She wanted to fight. Since the path to her father was blocked, Emerald changed direction. Through force of will and a strength born of necessity, she bulled her way through the larger adults until she succeeded in reaching her mother, Queen Saphiria. She looked up at her mother with pride.

Queen Saphiria stood strong among the frightened crowd. Dressed in gold-trimmed armor embedded with the Holy Metal, she was surrounded by her shield-maidens.

Her mother looked every bit the warrior queen she was. Emerald sensed the ebb and flow of strong magic in the battle-axe carried by her mother. She'd often seen the weapon hanging on the wall in her parents' bedroom. The battle-axe had defended the Drepdenoris dwarves for over fifty thousand years. From the determined look on her mother's face, she was confident it would do so again this very day.

"Mother!" Emerald shouted over the fear-struck crowd. "Give me a weapon. I'll fight by your side."

For the first time in her life, Emerald thought she saw fear in her mother's eyes.

"Emerald, no!" said her mother in an unusually harsh voice. "Now's not the time for your arguing. I told you to stay with the other children. Now go!"

"But I want—"

A loud explosion silenced everyone as a flash of fire reflected off the stone walls of the dimly-lit cavern. The smell of brimstone assailed her nose. Her father's magic users had unleashed their spells.

The enemy must be close, she thought.

A series of smaller blasts followed as fireballs and lightning bolts leaped from the hands of the black-robed mages of her father. Emerald tried to follow the tracks of the magic to spy their intended targets, but try as she might, the attackers were out of her sight.

Why do I have to be so short?

"Stay strong!" shouted her father.

Even in their panic, the people responded to the voice of their king. Their shouts lessened as they strained to hear his orders.

"You're Drepdenoris dwarves," said the king. "Our halls have stood for fifty thousand years. They will not fall today. Stay strong, my soldiers! You are the dwarves of Drepdenoris. The winged devil Cancontus and his servants will rue the day they tested their strength against the halls of Drepdenoris. Stay strong, my brothers and sisters! Stay strong!"

Pride swelled in Emerald's heart as she sensed Power flow outward from her father to the dwarves around him. His Power linked with that of his subjects.

He's forming a Circle.

She felt her father's Power flow over her and her mother, continuing on to her mother's shield-maidens. The dwarves' Power responded to that of their king and boosted her father's strength while sending the Circle on to touch other dwarves in the crowd.

The strength of her father surged through the interconnecting lines of Power. Courage swelled within Emerald's soul as it did in the souls of the other dwarves around her. Many in the crowd began to sing the battle songs of old as the king's courage took hold. Buoyed by the strength of the Circle, their previous cries of fear were forgotten.

The Circle grew ever larger until it encompassed the entire crowd. Emerald had often heard tales of the kings of old and how they had formed Circles during times of darkest despair. Circles were the stuff of legends. The last one had been formed thousands of years in the past. The legend was happening once again, and she was a part of it. She wanted to fight. The Circle gave her the courage to fight. She feared no enemy; the Circle wouldn't allow it. She sensed the Circle giving her an unnatural strength as it flowed through her limbs. Her senses grew sharper. She instinctively knew her reflexes would be quickened when the need arose. She was part of the Circle.

A second series of explosions echoed throughout the chamber. The darkness momentarily gave way as the light from a dozen fireballs and lightning bolts flickered across the cavern walls. The spells of the dwarf mages seemed larger, more powerful than normal.

Even the abilities of the spellcasters are increased by the Power of the Circle.

Emerald heard the rallying cry of her father as he led his personal guard against the minions of Lord Cancontus. The sound of steel on steel echoed from behind Emerald. The sound was much too close. She turned in time to see the bloodied form of an armored dwarf rising out of the stone floor. He was almost translucent. The word 'vampire' echoed in Emerald's mind.

Before anyone could react, the dwarf-vampire grabbed a nearby child and sank his fangs into her throat. The young dwarf-girl screamed as those around her tried to pull the bloody vampire away from the child. The rescuers' hands and weapons passed harmlessly through the vampire's body.

Emerald remembered the stories of the elders. *The vampire is in the void. Only powerful magic can harm it.*

"Be gone, foul creature," shouted Emerald's mother. Her battle-axe rose, then sliced downward into the vampire's back. Even the void couldn't prevent the Holy Metal and the magic of the battle-axe from cutting the snarling vampire in half. The two halves of the vampire shifted back into the physical dimension and dropped to the floor.

The wounded dwarf-child fell to the floor, screaming. She thrashed and twisted about grasping her neck with both hands.

Then the screaming stopped. The child rose and growled at those around her. Her eyes shone with red fire. Long fangs glistened in the torchlight as the newly-formed vampire reached out to grab a child nearby. Before she could pull the screaming victim to her mouth, the battle-axe of the queen cut the child-vampire's head free of her body.

The intended victim backpedaled away from the blood spewing out of the headless corpse.

The dark form of another vampire rose out of the stone floor just behind the frightened dwarf-child. This vampire had the body of a human. He grabbed the child and tore out her throat.

Dozens of dark forms, both short and tall, began rising out of the stone floor. Others emerged from the walls of the cavern.

The jostling crowd knocked Emerald from one side to the other. The dwarves around her fought as best they could. The Circle gave them abnormal strength and courage. However, even the dwarves' enhanced abilities did no good without magic weapons. The vampires were in the void.

The dark shape of a human vampire dressed in rags rose out of the stone floor near Emerald. It made a grab for her, but Emerald was fast. She'd always been fast. Dodging the blood-thirsty monster's outstretched hands, she slipped to the side and began moving forward as fast as possible. She heard a scream as the vampire found another victim instead of her.

I have to find my mother, Emerald thought as she wormed her way through the milling crowd of dwarves.

Images of steel weapons slicing through the dark forms of vampires without effect assailed her senses. More often than not, any dwarf swinging a non-magical weapon quickly fell victim to their intended target. Within seconds, the downed dwarf was transformed into a new vampire who began attacking former friends.

I need a magic weapon.

Emerald sensed no weapon of magic within range that wasn't already in use by one of the dwarf defenders remaining. All her horror-stricken eyes could see were the forms of her friends and neighbors lying on the ground with vampires sucking at their bleeding flesh. Emerald knew the luckless victims would soon be rising to add to the carnage. Without the courage of the Circle, she would've fallen to the floor in fear.

Without warning, strong hands grabbed Emerald from behind and lifted her high into the air. Even with the courage of the king's Circle flowing through her, Emerald screamed and struggled to no avail. The hands grasping her were too strong.

"Take this," shouted a feminine voice in Emerald's ear.

One of the hands holding her let go and thrust a dagger into her right hand. Emerald felt the Power of the Holy Metal flowing through the blade. The dagger was magic.

With a sense of relief, Emerald realized her captor was shield-maiden Osglow. She'd always been kind to Emerald.

The shield-maiden lifted her higher into the air and tossed her toward the cavern wall. "Run! Live and avenge your people!"

Even as Emerald flew through the air, she saw a wave of dark forms overwhelm the shield-maiden and drag her to the ground. She hit the wall of the cavern and groaned as the air was forced out of her lungs. "Umph!"

Sliding down the rock wall, Emerald fell into the rushing waters of a small underground stream. The fast moving current carried her into a black opening in the cavern wall. All sight and sound of the ongoing battle between the dwarves and vampires disappeared. Her body was racked with the pain of a thousand icy knives as the cold stream swept her along its underground passage. Emerald tried to breathe, but couldn't force her collapsed lungs to draw air.

She struggled against the rushing water, but her battle was as hopeless as that of the handful of remaining dwarves against the horde of vampires. Despite the odds, Emerald continued to fight for her life. She had to; the strength of the Circle still flowed through her body. It wouldn't allow her to do otherwise.

Hope swelled in her heart. *My father must still be alive.*

The knowledge gave her mind an anchor point against the pain of the icy water. The strength of her father wouldn't allow her to give up.

Spots of red flashed before Emerald's eyes as her oxygen-starved brain began to shut down. Just before she blacked out, her head hit the ceiling of the underground passage. For a moment, her head was above water in a pocket of stale air. She reflexively drew in a gulp of the life-giving oxygen. All too soon, she was plunged back beneath the waters. Just as her head went below the water's surface, she felt the Power of her father's Circle disappear. Despair swept over her. Her parents were dead. Just as she prepared to give her own life over to the icy grip of the stream, she was thrust into the light of the sun. The stream dropped her into a swirling pool of water. She knew the place. She was in the Pool of Hope.

"Swim, girl," said a voice.

Emerald recognized the voice as her own. She swam. Just when she felt she could swim no more, her feet touched bottom. She fell forward onto her hands and knees and crawled out of the shallow water onto dry ground.

Emerald shivered, partly from cold and partly from fear. The sound of screams and visions of bloodied bodies fresh in her mind, she forced herself to stand. She had to keep moving.

There will be time to grieve later.

Suddenly, Emerald sensed the approach of pure evil. She stumbled into the forest. Half-running, half-crawling, she tried to put distance between her and the unknown pursuers. She knew she wasn't fast enough. They'd be on her in seconds. Spying a small clearing to her left, Emerald made for it. When she reached the center, she turned to face her enemies. She was the daughter of a king. She refused to go down without a fight.

Emerald shivered. *It's just the cold. I'm not afraid.*

Three vampires drifted into the clearing. One was short. He was a dwarf-child. Another was tall. He was an orc. His ugly form was made even more hideous by his red eyes and the long fangs protruding from his mouth. The last vampire was a human woman. She had long blonde hair. If not for her red eyes and fangs, Emerald thought the woman would be pretty.

"Don't worry," said the blonde vampire as she glided forward. "Lord Cancontus has need of you. I'll make your death as painless as possible. You'll soon be one of my disciples."

By the blood in the eyes of the child-vampire, Emerald knew the boy was newly formed. He appeared impatient, or perhaps the burning hunger of his new vampire form couldn't be denied. Whatever the reason, the child-vampire lunged past the blonde woman and dove straight for Emerald's throat.

Although the Power of the Circle no longer flowed through her, she didn't shrink away. Her mother was a queen. Her father was a king. She was too proud to do anything but fight. Emerald felt shield-maiden Osglow's dagger still in her hand. She brought it up and aimed a blow for the child-vampire's heart. The tip of the dagger struck a rib bone. Although the cold water of the stream had drained her strength, the momentum of the vampire's charge forced the tip of the magic blade past the rib and into the vampire's heart.

The momentum of the lifeless corpse knocked Emerald to the ground. Ignoring her pain, she rolled to her feet and came up in the fighting stance she'd been taught by her mother. She was a Drepdenoris dwarf. She would fight as long as she had breath.

Holding the dagger before her, Emerald faced her remaining opponents.

"Well, well," said the blonde woman. "Looks like we have a fighter here." Drawing a longsword from its sheath, the blonde vampire gave a wicked grin. "Come, little one. I'll show you how to use that little pig sticker of yours."

"No play," growled the orc in broken common. "I hungry. I kill."

The orc-vampire started forward with his well-muscled arms outstretched. He carried no weapon, but Emerald knew his finger-length fangs and razor-sharp claws were all the weapons he needed.

"Run, girl," said the orc. "I like when they run."

"Drepdenoris dwarves don't run," Emerald said in a voice brave enough to belie how she really felt. She might be young, but she was the daughter of a king.

The orc snarled and charged forward.

Emerald noticed the vampire's feet were bending the blades of grass as he came. *He's too confident.* She lifted the tip of her dagger to meet the vampire's charge. *He's not even in the void.*

Without warning, a series of red streaks passed over Emerald's shoulder and struck the orc in the chest, knocking him head-over-heels. She sensed powerful energy in the red streaks but dared not look to see from whence they came. The blonde vampire was too much of a threat.

"Didn't anyone ever tell you to pick on someone your own size?" said a voice.

The orc-vampire jumped up snarling with rage. Even as the vampire stood, the holes in his chest closed over and healed.

Emerald sensed both vampires shift into the void.

Not so confident now, are you? Emerald thought.

She didn't know who her unseen ally was, but the tide of the battle had shifted. She now had a slim chance of remaining alive.

The orc-vampire roared and charged forward again. Emerald could tell his path wasn't headed toward her. His target was located to her right rear.

The blur of a tall figure wearing black armor passed to her right and intercepted the orc. The armored figure swung a sword at the vampire's head. The sword had miniature red lightning bolts running up and down its length. The orc tried to dodge, but he was a little too slow. The tip of the red sword caught the vampire on the temple, knocking him to the ground.

Quick as a wink, Emerald dove on the orc and used her weight to drive her dagger deep into his heart. The orc-vampire was in the void, but it didn't matter. The Holy Metal penetrated the vampire's heart, releasing a spray of blood into the air.

Before the vampire could do more than scream, the mysterious figure's red sword struck three more times at his unprotected head. Blood splattered on both Emerald and her black-armored ally. The orc-vampire stopped moving. Emerald noticed blades of grass bending underneath the orc's body.

Well, he's not in the void now, Emerald thought. She pulled her dagger free of the vampire's heart to face the blonde woman.

The blonde vampire was still standing where she'd been when her companion began his charge. She held her sword out before her in a defensive position. The vampire didn't seem concerned at the passing of her fellow vampires. A slight smile crossed her lips.

"Well, well," said the vampire. "And here I thought Lord Cancontus was sending me on a wild dragon's chase when he ordered me to fetch this tasty little morsel. I'm glad to see I won't be bored after all."

As Emerald watched, the blonde vampire slid to the left and began moving her sword in a small figure-eight pattern to her front. The grass beneath the vampire's feet wasn't bending.

She's in the void.

"Oh, I don't think you'll be bored," said the figure in black from a protective position between Emerald and the vampire.

Without turning, the figure in black armor spoke to Emerald.

"Run, little one. I'll find you after I finish with this one."

The blonde vampire's eyes flared with red fire, but she didn't lose her tight-lipped smile. Nor did she stop the weaving of her sword. The blue glow along the edges of the sword was almost hypnotic as it wove its deadly pattern.

Emerald forced herself to look away. She focused instead on the back of her armored benefactor, standing her ground. The figure's armor was a dull black. At the same time, parts of the armor seemed to blend with its surroundings, similar to the cloaks of hiding Emerald had seen hunting parties use. While the armor didn't radiate magic as far as she could tell, it had an eerie feel to it all the same. The armor was unlike anything she'd ever seen. Several strange-looking items hung from the belt around the figure's waist. The helmet glowed with red where a visor would normally be located. The red glow was almost, but not quite, translucent. Emerald was unable to make out her benefactor's face. Unlike the vampire, Emerald noticed the figure wasn't in the void.

The blonde vampire moved in for the attack, swinging her sword in a series of savage thrusts and cuts.

The black-armored figure parried each of the vampire's attacks.

Blue and red sparks flew into the air whenever the two weapons met. The smell of ozone permeated the area.

The armored figure half-knelt and kicked out with a leg in an apparent attempt to sweep the vampire's legs. Instead, the armored figure's leg passed through the vampire.

Emerald sensed impending disaster.

Taking advantage of the armored figure's momentary loss of balance, the blonde vampire swung her sword downward, straight at her antagonist's head.

A line of Power stretched out from the armored figure and wrapped around the tip of the vampire's sword, slowing its downward momentum. Quick as a flash, the armored figure side stepped and thrust the tip of the red sword into the vampire's stomach.

The vampire groaned with pain as she bent over. Dodging backward, she was barely fast enough to avoid a second thrust from the figure in black.

"Well, you have some skill," admitted the blonde vampire. "Too bad it's not going to be enough to save you. I'm going to rip your throat out. When I'm done with you, I'll feast on this girl before I take her to my master."

Emerald stiffened against the threat, raising her magic knife chest high and glaring at the vampire.

The vampire and the armored figure slowly circled one another. The blonde vampire appeared leery of her opponent. The armored figure had hurt her.

Emerald knew the vampire still had the advantage. She was in the void. Apparently, only the armored figure's strange red rod was capable of hurting the vampire. Both of the combatants appeared to have temporarily forgotten her presence as each sought an advantage over the other. She decided to try giving the armored figure an opening. Praying she was fast enough, Emerald dove at the vampire's left leg. With a downward thrust of her dagger, she drove the magic blade deep into the vampire's calf. The blonde vampire screamed as the keen edge of the dagger ripped into her flesh.

In a blur of motion, the armored figure swung the red rod at the side of the vampire's head.

As the red lightning bolts running up and down the rod made contact, Emerald heard the sound of cracking bone.

Apparently not satisfied with a single blow, the armored figure continued striking the blonde vampire's body in a series of blows too fast for a dwarf's eye to follow. The repeated blows knocked the vampire to the ground where she began withering in pain. The armored figure continued to pound the vampire relentlessly.

However, even as the figure's red rod caused new injuries to the vampire, Emerald could see the blonde woman's earlier wounds healing. She remembered the old storyteller's tales of powerful vampires who could heal damage faster than their adversary could deal it out. Only a strike of Holy Metal directly into the vampire's heart had any hope of causing its death. Crawling forward, she jerked shield-maiden Osglow's dagger out of the vampire's calf. With a thrust of her legs, she leaped on top of the blonde vampire's chest and drove the blade of Holy Metal deep into the monster's dark heart.

The vampire screamed one last time, then lay still.

Emerald jiggled the dagger several times before rolling off the body and standing. After bending down and wiping her blade on the woman's cloak, she turned to face her savior.

The armored figure stood frozen, holding the rod high, ready to deliver another blow.

Emerald couldn't see her ally's face behind the red visor. Holding her dagger downward in what she hoped was a non-threatening manner, she asked, "Who are you? Why are you here?"

The armored figure made a flick with the hand holding the red rod. A slight pop sounded as the red lightning running along the rod's length disappeared. The rod retracted into the weapon's handle. With an ease of movement that could only be obtained from years of practice, the armored figure attached the handle to the belt running around the waist of the black armor. The figure's red visor disappeared as the helmet changed shape to reveal a female with a mass of long dark hair.

Emerald thought the woman looked pretty for a human. Her penetrating brown eyes reminded Emerald of her mother's.

The woman sized Emerald up and down in a way that indicated she discerned much more than she could physically see. If not for the appearance of a friendly smile, Emerald would have been intimidated by the woman's obvious inspection.

"Who am I?" The woman gave a slight bow. "Wizard Scout Janice Deluth at your service. As to why I'm here, I'm not exactly sure. A minute ago, I was told to *'save the small one.'* Then I was teleported here. Since I thought you looked a lot smaller than your vampire adversaries, I assumed I was supposed to save you. I hope I chose correctly."

Too much had occurred in too short a time. Emerald just stood staring at the woman.

After a few awkward seconds of silence, the woman knelt on one knee. Once her head was at Emerald's level, the woman spoke. "May I ask who I have the pleasure of addressing?"

"Emerald."

"All right, Emerald," said the woman, still smiling. "I'm not exactly sure what's going on. However, I think it might be best if we left this area before some of these creatures' friends decide to show up." When Emerald didn't respond, the woman added in a kind voice, "Where do you live? Is it far? Perhaps I can escort you to your parents. I'm sure they're worried about you."

At the mention of her parents, the dam holding back Emerald's emotions broke and she began to cry. In spite of her constant attempts to be more mature than her childhood friends, she was just a child after all. With a child's desperate need to be comforted, Emerald told the black-haired woman of the slaughter of the Drepdenoris dwarves along with her parents, the king and queen.

The woman listened to Emerald's tale without interruption. She maintained a kind and sympathetic look on her face. Although the woman was a human, Emerald sensed she could trust the new ally fate had thrust upon her.

Once her tale was done, Emerald composed herself. "You've been kind to me, and you have my thanks. Now I must return home. I must avenge the death of my people. I swear I'll drive this dagger into Lord Cancontus's heart if it's the last thing I do."

Emerald was surprised when the woman didn't smile at her talk of vengeance. She was used to adults not taking the words of a child seriously.

The woman said, "Janice. Please call me Janice."

Despite the circumstances, her mother's endless attempts over the years to improve her manners took charge. Emerald bowed and said, "Well met, Lady Janice."

This time the woman did laugh. However, it was a friendly laugh, so Emerald took no offense.

"Just Janice," said the woman. "Just plain old Janice will suit me fine."

"All right, Janice," Emerald said. "Thank you, Janice, for saving me."

The woman stood and continued smiling. "Well, I think you were doing quite well even before I showed up." The woman delivered a kick to the body of one of the dead vampires. "Unfortunately, from what you've told me, there are many more where these come from. So, while I'm sure we both have many questions, we really do need to go."

"Go where?" Emerald said. In spite of her brave speech, she knew she wasn't equipped to exact revenge with a lone dagger, even if it was magic. "I have no one now." Emerald immediately regretted sounding childish and weak.

Janice looked down sympathetically. "You're not alone, little one. You have me. I give you my word of honor as a wizard scout, I'll help you as long as I'm able."

Emerald didn't know what a wizard scout was, but from the solemnness of the woman's voice, she knew the woman's oath was important to her.

"I—" Emerald's voice broke. When she regained control, she said, "Thank you, again. Do you think we should go back to my mountain home? Some of my friends may still be alive."

Janice turned and looked hard at the mountain that had been Emerald's home for all of her short life. Although Emerald wasn't a mage, she could detect a sense of Power reaching out from the woman toward the mountain. The woman maintained her concentration for several seconds.

Emerald said nothing; in fact, she barely breathed. She wasn't sure what her newfound ally was doing, but she could tell it was important.

Finally, the woman's face relaxed and took on a sad look.

Emerald waited stoically for the woman to speak, fearing her new friend's words wouldn't be good news.

"I'm sorry, Emerald," said Janice. "I don't detect any living persons in that mountain. Only death resides there now."

Emerald didn't weep. The woman's words weren't unexpected. Besides, she'd already wept too much to start anew.

Looking up at the woman, Emerald said, "My family's honor demands I avenge my parents' death. I can't allow Lord Cancontus and his black-hearted fiends to get away with mass murder. I may be the last of the Drepdenoris dwarves. I won't rest until my home is free once more."

"I'm sure you won't," said Janice. "But maybe it shouldn't be today. *'The One'* sent me to save you. He told me that you must go to the Oracle. The Oracle is wise. He'll tell you how to avenge your people."

"The Oracle?" Emerald had heard the name before but assumed the Oracle was more a legend than an actual person. "How? Where? I don't know where to find him."

"Don't fear, little one," said Janice with another of her kind smiles. "I said I'll help you as long as I'm able. I'll—"

The woman started to blur in and out of focus.

"No!" shouted Janice as she looked skyward. "Not yet! I gave her my word. Please! Not yet!" She turned and locked eyes with Emerald, then mouthed the words, "I'm sorry."

Janice blinked out of existence.

Emerald stood in the same spot for several minutes hoping against hope that the woman would return. She didn't. Finally, with a stoic acceptance common to all dwarves, Emerald forced herself to do something. She searched the bodies of the three vampires. Surprisingly, she found a few coins in a small, leather bag in the pocket of the orc. She also removed a ring and two diamond ear-studs from the blonde vampire's body. Finally, she picked up the blonde vampire's longsword. It no longer glowed blue, but Emerald could feel latent magic deep inside the blade.

It's too big for me, but it's too valuable to leave behind.

With a final look at her mountain and a nod of her head, Emerald said, "I'll be back, Cancontus. One day, I'll be back. I promise on that day, you'll pay."

Turning to the rising sun, Emerald set off at a brisk walk. One direction was as good as another. She had no idea where the Oracle was located or even if such a being existed. However, if the Oracle did exist, she'd find him, even if it took the rest of her life.

CHAPTER 2

The dolgar army was hungry. It needed to be fed.

Wizard Scout Richard Shepard sat on his mount and cast his eyes over the valley floor below. The black stallion was restless. Even after years of association, the stallion seemed to only tolerate him as a rider. Richard didn't blame the creature. He supposed being forced to carry a rider was no different for the spirit-horse than it was for him to be forced by *'the One'* to go on missions he had no wish to perform.

"Well, don't blame me," Richard told the stallion using emotion-speak. *"It wasn't my idea to come here. I'd rather be kicking back in my quarters on the* Defiant *reading a nice book instead of wandering around this Creator-forsaken land sitting on your sweaty back."*

The stallion sent back an emotion Richard interpreted as indicating his mount didn't much care what his rider would rather be doing.

Richard shrugged. Even after years of what could only be described as a stormy relationship, he found that he actually liked the ornery spirit-horse in a strange sort of way. He doubted the stallion reciprocated his feelings, but it didn't change things. He supposed if they could speak to each other using words instead of emotions they might get along better.

"Actually," said Nickelo, *"your stallion can speak a few words of intergalactic standard, if you remember correctly."*

Richard grimaced. After all this time, it still felt odd to share space in his mind with his helmet's battle computer and exchange dialogue near instantaneously.

"Well, he doesn't choose to speak often," Richard thought back. *"I doubt he's going to start doing so now. In the meantime, we've got a job to do. How about getting that nanosecond brain of yours working on the problem at hand?"*

"Compliance, oh greatest of wizard scouts," replied Nickelo in a voice that sounded a lot less respectful than the words implied.

Richard wondered if the battle computers of other wizard scouts gave their partners as much grief as his did. From discussions with his friends, he'd gotten the impression some were more polite than others.

"*You know, Nick, it might be nice to have a battle computer who is a little more respectful on occasion. I might just have to trade you in for a new model someday.*"

"Oh, I'm always respectful," said Nickelo. *"However, I tend to limit my respect to how much is warranted."*

"Whatever," Richard said using his pet word for ending a pointless conversation.

Richard switched the visor of his battle helmet from night-vision mode to a clear filter. He half closed his eyes against the bright glare of the orange sun. It had been weeks since he'd seen unfiltered sunlight. The sudden burning sensation in his eyes told him the radiation from the sun was starting to eat away at the rods and cones in his eyes.

"You know better than to do that," said Nickelo in a chastising tone. *"Your self-heal will counteract the damage, but it's wasteful of Power nevertheless."*

Richard knew his battle computer was right. He shouldn't waste his self-heal Power reserve even if it was larger than the reserves he used for offense, defense, and the healing of others. *"I'm tired of looking through the battle helmet's night-vision filter and seeing everything in red. It's starting to drive me nuts. I need a change."*

"Well, if you insist on wasting your Power," said Nickelo still using a chastising tone, *"one of these days the change you get may be a quick death. Just because you have three reserves to everyone else's one, being wasteful still isn't logical. However, you're the wizard scout, and I'm just the subservient battle computer, so what do I know?"*

Sighing, Richard switched his visor back to night-vision mode. His clear vision was replaced by the familiar reddish tint. Power from his self-heal reserve immediately began returning his eyes back to baseline and the itchy-burning sensation he felt quickly disappeared.

As Richard waited for the last of the damage to his eyes to heal, he glanced at his heads-up display. The colored dots' movement confirmed the lead elements of the enemy unit would be in the ambush zone within five minutes.

Richard figured it was time for his battle computer and him to get busy. *"How about merging the results of your electronic scan with my passive scan and put the results on my heads-up display."*

"Compliance."

A line of forty-two yellow dots appeared overlaid on a map of the valley. They were evenly spaced at about ten-meter intervals along a trail snaking along the valley floor. An additional thirteen orange dots were distributed between the yellow dots that represented ordinary enemy combatants. Orange were specialists. There were no red dots indicating the presence of magic users.

Using his passive scan, Richard noted the location of his own unit. He marked their location as white dots on his heads-up display. Although his teammates were using stealth shields to prevent their discovery by enemy scouts, Richard had the scent of the members of his team. He'd previously identified each of their Power frequencies. As long as they didn't stray too far away, he was certain he could track the location of everyone in his unit even with their stealth shields up.

Richard made a quick review of his mission for *'the One'* over the last eighteen months. For reasons unknown, he'd been sent to the spiritual dimension to work with the wolf-like dolgars in their apparently endless war against the dimension-shifting scaled-cats.

"I still don't understand why 'the One' *sent me on a mission to work with the dolgars. Most of them don't even like me. I'd have been a lot better off working with an Empire unit."*

Nickelo laughed. *"Ha! What makes you think anyone there would like you any better than the dolgars? Besides, I doubt* 'the One' *sent you on a mission for the dolgars without a good reason. Just do your job, and maybe we'll find out why you're really here."*

Richard was going to make a snide remark, but a flicker on his heads-up display drew his attention back to the mission at hand. The yellow dots on the display were nearly in the ambush zone. Each was a six-legged animal the size of an elephant back on Earth. They were tough fighters physically but had no special fighting abilities other than their tusks, teeth, and claws. Richard doubted the nineteen dolgars in his hunting party would have any trouble with the elephant-like monstrosities. That was fortunate because the hunting had been slim pickings lately.

Richard concentrated on the orange dots on his display. Those represented a flightless bird covered with scales instead of feathers and beaks full of razor-sharp teeth that could tear a dolgar in half with a single bite if one was foolish enough to get within range. On top of that, the scaled birds had a breath weapon of sorts. Their saliva was acidic and plentiful. Richard had seen them spew the liquid a good fifty meters with uncanny accuracy. Worst of all, they were able to shift dimensions with ease. He'd fought them before on several occasions, finding them to be very dangerous foes.

"At least there are only thirteen of those scaled-birds," Richard said. *"Our hunting party has nineteen dolgars plus me. We should be able to handle thirteen of them without too much difficulty."*

"Who are you trying to convince?" laughed Nickelo. *"Me or yourself?"*

A movement to his right prevented Richard's retort. A large, wolfish creature stood on the side of the cliff. The dolgar appeared to be standing in midair. If Richard had been standing next to the dolgar, his head would have barely reached the creature's shoulders. Takar was one of the four spirit-wolves assigned by Sheeta, his pack leader, to watch over him. Richard sensed the other three dolgars of his personal guard hiding in the solid stone of the cliff, shifted into the void between dimensions while awaiting the command to attack. Takar was anxious for him to give the okay to trigger the ambush.

Draken and the remaining fourteen dolgars in the unit were on the other side of the valley, embedded in the granite of the cliff face. Draken, the hunting party's commander, was not a particularly patient dolgar. Draken wasn't the commander's real name, of course. The dolgars didn't have names Richard could pronounce. Draken was just the name he'd given the hunting party's grizzled wolf-commander.

Richard took a final look at the enemy caravan spaced out along the valley floor. Everything looked normal as far as he could tell. Even so, he hesitated to give Takar the all clear due to a strange feeling that he was missing something important.

"Why aren't there more guards protecting this caravan, Nick? I'd think a juicy target like those six-legged elephants should have more than thirteen guards. I'd think a column this size should have at least a couple of magic users."

Takar growled softly. "Is it all clear?"

When Richard didn't answer quickly enough, the dolgar gave another growl. Richard figured Takar was in contact with Draken and their temperamental leader undoubtedly wanted to get the show on the road.

Richard sent Takar an emotion of concern.

"I don't understand why you think there's a problem," said Nickelo. *"Do you sense something you're not telling me?"*

Richard wasn't even sure why he was hesitating to give the go-ahead to attack. Everything seemed normal. True, the long valley had a large concentration of titanium ore, but that was the reason Draken had selected the site for his ambush in the first place. Energized titanium ore was one of the few materials dimension-shifting creatures had trouble with when moving through the void. Although un-energized titanium deposits like the one below didn't prevent the passage of creatures in the void, it did play havoc with their senses. Basically, high concentrations of titanium deposits made them blind. Draken had told his hunting party the valley was the perfect ambush spot since the titanium deposits would prevent the enemy from escaping below ground.

Due to the presence of the titanium, Richard had to agree the valley made an ideal ambush spot. On the other hand, the titanium affected their side of the battle as well. During his earlier recon of the valley, the stallion had refused to travel through the titanium deposit due to the potential loss of its senses. This had forced Richard to conduct his recon of the ambush site while remaining in the area of the valley nearest the cliff face. Of course, he could have shifted into the void and moved into the titanium deposit on his own since he wasn't blinded in high-concentration titanium deposits. However, he'd refused to do the recon on his own. His small Power reserve limited the amount of time he could stay shifted in the void. He hadn't wanted to risk running out of Power and materializing in solid stone.

Takar growled again.

"You're stalling," said Nickelo. *"The enemy's lead elements will be leaving the ambush zone in a couple of minutes. You need to make a decision one way or the other."*

"I know. I guess what's bothering me is that I was forced to recon from the outskirts of the valley. Everything seemed normal then, but... I don't know. Are you sure you don't sense anything wrong?"

"Sorry. I've got nothing. I'll admit the caravan is a little light on guards, but not enough to be overly suspicious."

"Yeah, I know. I think that's what makes me suspicious."

"That's not logical, Rick."

"No, it's not; but nevertheless."

Richard could feel Takar growing increasingly nervous. The lead elements of the caravan were approaching the far end of the ambush point. Richard had no doubt Draken was pressing Takar for the okay to attack.

Looking at Takar, Richard growled, "Wait. Something wrong."

Takar whined. The big dolgar didn't look happy, but to his credit, he settled back on his haunches without arguing. They'd seen Richard spot hidden enemies too often.

Sending an image of a path down and toward the center of the valley to his mount, Richard felt the stallion wrap them both in Power and shift into the void. After a couple of steps, the spirit-horse merged into the rock face of the cliff. All visual clues were lost the moment they entered the solid rock. Richard kept track of their route with his passive scan. The stallion continued traveling downward until he was below the level of the valley, then moved horizontally about two hundred meters before stopping. They'd reached the edge of the titanium deposit. Richard didn't attempt to urge the stallion forward. He'd tried unsuccessfully during his earlier recon and doubted he'd have better luck now.

Using his passive scan, Richard located the caravan above as it made its way along the valley floor. The entire caravan was now fully in the ambush zone. Richard had a feeling if he didn't give

Draken some kind of word soon, the dolgar commander would attack anyway. The caravan was too great a prize to allow it to escape.

Gathering Power from his reserve, Richard sent an active scan to his front. He got the same results he'd gotten earlier: nothing. He shut down the scan. Active scans were too Power hungry to use without a reasonable hope of success.

"Nick, how about using the results of my passive and active scans to create an outline of the titanium deposit? Put the result on my heads-up display."

"Compliance."

Within two seconds, an image of the valley along with an outline of the titanium deposit appeared on the battle helmet's display. Richard looked at the outline for several seconds.

"Convert the outline into a 3D display and rotate the image."

The image of the titanium deposit took on depth and began to rotate.

Richard noticed something he'd missed during his previous recon. *"What's the probability a naturally occurring titanium deposit would be so symmetrical? Except for a couple of bulges, it looks like a cylinder."*

"Hmm. That's an interesting point. The titanium deposit is nine hundred and eighty meters long with a radius of a hundred and fifty meters at the center. The two ends of the deposit are exactly four hundred and ninety meters from center. The probability of such a deposit occurring in nature is near zero."

The hairs on the back of Richard's neck stood on end. He kicked himself for not noticing the symmetrical shape earlier.

"I'd advise calling off the attack until we can gather more data," said Nickelo.

"No can do, little buddy. The shape's strange, to say the least, but it's not strange enough for Draken to abort his ambush. I'll need more than a weird shape before I can convince him to cancel. Unfortunately, there's only one way to get it. I'm going to have to enter the titanium deposit."

"I'm guessing when you say you'll need to enter it, you mean we. *That is unless you're planning on leaving your battle helmet behind on the stallion."*

"No. That wasn't part of my plan."

Nickelo laughed. *"I didn't think so. Unfortunately, between the Power required to perform a dimensional shift and the Power required for your active scan and telekinesis, you won't be able to hold your shift for very long."*

"Don't have much of a choice, do I?"

"Not if you want to be sure Draken and the others aren't being suckered into a trap."

Sighing stoically, Richard wrapped himself in Power and took over his shift from the stallion. The tendrils holding him onto the spirit-horse's back withdrew from where they were wrapped around his waist and legs. When he was free, he used telekinesis to levitate off the stallion and toward the titanium deposit.

"Watch my Power," Richard said.

"Compliance. I've got your back, buddy."

Sending out another line of Power as an active scan, Richard used his telekinesis to move forward along the track of his scan. Keeping an active scan going meant he'd be using his limited Power even faster, but he needed to see to navigate. He was committed.

Nothing I can do about the Power usage, Richard thought.

"Recommend you attach a line of Power to your mount," said Nickelo. *"It'll require you to use even more Power, but if you discover something, I calculate a ninety-two percent probability you'll need to return in a hurry."*

"Roger that," Richard said.

As his battle computer predicted, Richard noticed the rate of his Power usage speed up even more once he attached the line of Power to the stallion.

"I'm trying to do too much for the size of my Power reserve."

"Can't be helped, Rick. You need that safety line. By the way, your reserve's at ninety percent."

Richard moved ever deeper into the titanium deposit. He felt like a blind man fumbling around in an unfamiliar room. The line of Power to his mount gave him a point of reference, but the guideline felt tenuous at best. He grew increasingly nervous the deeper he got in the ore deposit.

"Eighty percent Power remaining, wizard scout."

Richard continued to probe the area ahead with his active scan.

"I'm still not sensing anything unusual, Nick. The titanium

deposit's causing havoc with my passive scan. I've lost track of the caravan overhead. The lead elements are bound to be starting to exit the ambush zone by now. I wonder what the odds are Draken will continue to wait for me before giving the signal to attack."

"Seventy percent Power remaining, Rick. The odds are seventy-two percent the dolgars will wait for you. They respect your skills more than you think. Of course, that respect will go down significantly if you make them lose the caravan for no reason."

"No doubt."

"Sixty percent Power remaining. You're nearing the halfway point in your Power reserve. I calculate an eighty-two percent probability the ore deposit is just what it seems: an ore deposit. Recommend you return to your mount now."

"Not yet. Just a little farther. My active scan's starting to clear a little. The titanium deposits seem to be getting less dense the closer I get to the center."

After moving forward another ten meters, Richard cleared the titanium and found himself in a hollow sphere completely free of the deposit. The clear space was several hundred meters in length. The space was filled with hundreds of life forms. He couldn't see anything visually since he was still in solid rock, but he didn't need to see with his eyes. He recognized the frequency of the life forms. They were dimension-shifting cats.

Based upon his previous experience with the scaled cats, Richard knew they could only hold a dimensional shift in the void for about a minute. He was momentarily confused how they had been able to stay shifted until now. That is, he was confused until he sensed a massive Power source in the center of the clearing coming from a very large life form.

A sense of evil washed over Richard from the large life form. He shivered, and it wasn't from cold. He'd sensed a similar evil on more than one occasion in the past. It was the evil of something that would make the bravest man take pause. It was the evil of a major demon.

Richard sensed a strange weave of energy reaching out from the demon. The energy was connecting all of the other life forms together. The connecting lines of energy jumped from one to another. With each jump, the energy appeared to increase. Somehow, none of the lines of energy touched another. The effect was similar to a circle with a bunch of dots on it that had been bunched together. Although balled up, the lines connecting the dots were still a circle in that they formed a complete circuit.

"Damn," Richard cursed. *"It's a trap."*

CHAPTER 3

Dropping his active scan to conserve Power, Richard began levitating back toward the stallion as fast as his telekinesis would take him. If it wasn't for the line of Power he'd attached to his mount earlier, he'd have lost his way.

"Fifty percent Power remaining, Rick. In case you haven't noticed, some of those scaled-cats are trying to cut off your escape route."

As if confirming his battle computer's warning, two nearby life forms moved in for an attack. Reaching over to his left hip, Richard grabbed the handle of his phase rod. With the flick of a switch, he activated it in destructive mode. The phase rod kicked in his hand as the meter-long length of brerellium with its creallium core shot out the end. Small bolts of phase energy ran up and down the metal rod. As soon as the phase rod activated, an emotion of intense hunger came from the demon essence embedded within the rod.

The two scaled-cats approaching him must have sensed the demon essence as well because they appeared to hesitate, but only for a second. Almost immediately, one of the scaled-cats ran in to attack from the left.

Richard swung his phase rod where he sensed the scaled-cat's head to be.

The cat twisted in an attempt to dodge his blow. Its defensive maneuver partially succeeded in that Richard missed its head, but the phase rod still contacted the scaled-cat's shoulder. Microscopic explosions from the rod's phase energy penetrated the cat's flesh and shattered the bone beneath.

The rod's demon essence sucked out a sizeable portion of the scaled-cat's life force.

The cat withered in agony as it was thrown backward.

The second scaled-cat came in from the right.

Richard jerked himself up with his telekinesis. As the cat passed beneath him, Richard made a wild swing with his phase rod and caught his attacker on its spine.

The scaled-cat's back snapped. The cat shuddered, and its dimensional shift cut off.

Richard sensed a split-second emotion of agony from the cat before it ceased to exist.

"Forty percent Power remaining, Rick. I highly recommend you stop playing with your new friends and expedite your return to the stallion."

"That's what I'm trying to do, buddy. I don't see you helping any."

"Hey, it's not my fault I don't have arms or legs. All I can do is give advice and go along for the ride."

Richard added more Power to his telekinesis in an attempt to increase his speed. Within a couple of seconds, he burst out of the last of the titanium deposit. His mount was just ahead. As he levitated onto the stallion's back, the spirit-horse's aura wrapped around him and took over his dimensional shift. Long tendrils came out of the stallion's back and sides to secure him in place.

"Thirty-four percent Power remaining."

The spirit-horse began galloping upwards. Richard sensed dozens of life forms emerging from the titanium deposit behind him. The stallion wasn't stupid. He saw them too. His mount needed no urging.

Gathering together his strongest emotion of fear, surprise, and concern, Richard sent it out in all directions. It was as close as he could come to shouting, "It's a trap!"

Within seconds, the stallion broke out of the rocky surface directly in the midst of the caravan. Surprisingly, the dolgars hadn't attacked yet. Richard felt the stallion shift out of the void. Swinging his M12 plasma assault rifle off his shoulder, Richard aimed to his right and shot a 20mm grenade round into a nearby scaled-bird. The scaled-bird wasn't in the void. The 20mm grenade exploded, sending pieces of bone, meat, and dark liquid into the air.

Richard once again sent out the emotions for "Trap!"

Picturing Takar and his three companions, Richard sent the image to the stallion. His mount must have agreed with his suggestion because the spirit-horse turned toward the four dolgars and began running hard. From his passive scan, Richard could tell Takar was still at the top of the cliff where he'd left him and that Draken and the remainder of the dolgars were spread out all along the opposite side of the valley.

"Run," Richard shouted at Takar with the strongest emotions he could garner.

Neither Takar nor the other three dolgars in Richard's personal guard ran. He had a feeling they wouldn't run until their commander, Draken, gave the order. The dolgars were well disciplined.

Dozens of the scaled-cats began emerging out of the valley floor. Richard sensed hundreds more behind them. He could tell the demon was slowly moving upward as well. The demon had dropped its line of Power to the strange circle of energy that had connected the scaled-cats. Without the energy from the circle of links, the stealth shield that had been protecting the cats and the demon was also gone. In addition, whatever had been keeping the scaled-cats in the void had also disappeared. From the cats' dwindling Power reserves, Richard could tell they were maintaining their shifts in the void on their own now.

A large blaze of Power came from the center of the titanium deposit.

"Spell," said his battle computer. *"The type is unknown."*

"Shift," Richard shouted in emotion-speak. *"Void. Now."*

Takar sent out a set of strong emotions. Richard caught the words 'shift' and 'void.'

The stallion shifted back into the void as Takar and the other three dolgars completed their shift into the void at the same time. As the stallion continued running toward Takar, the other three dolgars of his guard emerged out of the cliff face and gathered around Takar. From their emotions, Richard had no doubt they were prepared to fight to the death if necessary.

A strong emotion came from the other side of the valley, from Draken.

"Withdraw," the dolgar commander shouted in emotion-speak. *"Evade."*

But Draken's order came too late. An enormous blast of magical energy erupted from the titanium deposit. Rock, dirt, and titanium-laden dust shot into the air as the ground exploded. The wall of debris and magical energy tore the flesh from any creatures not shifted into the void. All of the six-legged, elephant-like creatures in the caravan were obliterated. The wall of debris passed through Richard and the dolgars, doing no harm since they were in the void. Whatever spell had caused the explosion also stopped the wall of titanium-laden debris just past the edge of the cliff. The titanium particles remained hanging in the air as they formed a translucent shield around the entire valley.

A second wave of magical energy sped outward from the demon. Richard recognized the magic as the same weave of energy that had been connecting all the scaled-cats together earlier. The wave of energy reached the edge of the valley and latched onto the titanium particles. As he watched, the magic jumped from one titanium particle to another until they were all connected. With each jump from one particle to another, the magic grew in strength. The particles of titanium began glowing brightly until the shield surrounding the valley turned into a solid wall of light.

A quick sweep of Richard's passive scan confirmed the energized shield of titanium particles completely surrounded the valley both above and below ground.

At the sight of the glowing shield, Richard said, *"Nick. That's creallium."*

"Affirmative," said Nickelo. *"Creallium exists in the void as well as this dimension. The demon has effectively blocked our escape route."*

The stallion ran toward the shield. Just before the spirit-horse made contact, he stopped abruptly, snorted, and tried to jump through the shield of creallium particles. Instead of passing through, he bounced off the shield.

"Hmm," said Nickelo. *"That's a good spell. It's got the creallium deep inside the void. In most cases, your stallion and the dolgars can bypass creallium by doing a full shift into another*

dimension. I calculate this spell was created specifically to prevent them from doing so."

Richard glanced left and right. *"Run your electronics and do an analysis of the shield. See if there are any breaks. Find us a path out of here, buddy."*

"Compliance."

Nickelo's answer was followed almost immediately by the results of his analysis. *"The valley is completely encased in the shield. Based upon the information from your scans and the battle helmet's sensors, no path exists through the creallium shield. It looks like you're trapped. That circle of energy is like nothing we've ever encountered before."*

The stallion started running back and forth along the shield wall trying to find a weak point, but to no avail. Richard felt his mount try to do a full shift into a second dimension. That attempt failed as well. While the stallion was still able to maintain his shift in the void, he couldn't penetrate the shield of creallium particles.

Richard noticed the stallion's hoofs touching the ground.

"Your mount isn't able to shift into a second dimension," explained Nickelo. *"That's how the dolgars and he are able to walk on air. They're earthbound now."*

Takar and the other three dolgars arrived at the shield wall. They began pawing at the shield as if trying to dig their way through. Like the stallion, they were unsuccessful in their efforts to get past the wall of creallium. The dolgars attempted to shift into a second dimension. Their attempts fared no better than his mount's.

Twisting in his seat, Richard looked back toward the center of the valley. An enormous mass of scaled-cats was continuing to boil out of the ground. As they emerged, the cats formed a large perimeter about a hundred meters across. The scaled-cats stayed on the outer edges of the perimeter while keeping the center clear.

"They're just standing there," Richard said. *"Why aren't they attacking?"*

"Unknown, wizard scout. The highest probability is that they know the dolgars and you can't escape. I think they're waiting for the demon to arrive. It appears to be moving upwards at a slow rate. The demon isn't in the void. It's physically clawing its way to the surface. My calculations indicate the demon should break free of the surface in about two minutes."

"Give me a count of what's facing us, buddy."

"One thousand six hundred of the scaled-cat creatures are massed in the valley. I've marked them in yellow on your heads-up display. An additional two hundred and forty-three of the scaled-bird creatures are also in the valley."

Richard shook his head. *"This ain't looking good."*

Nickelo didn't argue the point.

Richard kicked himself for not detecting the trap during his earlier recon, then shoved his self-chastisement to the side. Casting blame now wasn't going to help. Desperate to form some kind of plan, Richard looked at his heads-up display. He noticed some of the yellow dots were no longer in the void.

"It looks like the scaled-cats are setting up a rotation schedule," Richard told his battle computer. *"A third of those scaled-cats are materialized now. That means they're vulnerable. Let's see if we can take advantage of the situation before the demon gets here."*

Richard pulled his dimensional pack off his back. With it, he could summon just about anything as long as he had Power and *'the One'* had thought to stock it in warehouses on the planet Storage.

Richard imagined a K12, man-portable, rocket launcher along with half a dozen cluster rockets. He waited, but no Power left his reserve. Raising the flap, Richard peered inside. It was empty.

"What gives?" Richard said. *"I've gotten these rockets before. I should have more than enough Power to summon them."*

"I calculate an eighty-two percent probability the shield around the valley is preventing your dimensional pack from operating."

Richard felt panic trying to rise up. He forced it down. He'd been a marine, and marines didn't panic. Trying something easier than the rockets, he imagined a bag of J22 plastic explosives. No Power was drawn from his reserve. He opened the flap of his dimensional pack. It was empty.

"Ok, Nick. I give up. My ideas aren't panning out. Do you have any suggestions?"

"I'd recommend killing all of your opponents and destroying that shield. I'll leave the specifics of how to do it up to you. Other than that, I've got nothing with a probability greater than one percent."

With no help forthcoming from his battle computer, Richard concentrated on his heads-up display in the hopes something would come to mind. He noticed Draken and the other dolgars consolidating into a tight knot on the other side of the valley. The scaled-cats were still staying on their circular perimeter. Some of the yellow dots denoting the scaled-cats on the outer ring of their perimeter were starting to blink. The orange dots identifying the scaled-birds were evenly spaced around the outside of the perimeter. They remained a steady orange. From previous experience, Richard knew the birds could stay shifted for long periods of time.

"How much time before the demon makes its way to the surface?" Richard asked.

"If the rate of movement remains constant, the demon will break the surface in one minute and thirty-eight seconds."

"Why's it taking so long? And what is it?"

"The identity of the target is unknown. As to why it's slow, I don't know. Maybe it's just being cautious."

Richard didn't think his battle computer's information was all that useful. What he did know was that the demon had been two hundred meters underground when he'd spotted it. He had trouble imagining the strength required to physically dig its way to the surface.

The idea of shooting at the one-third of the scaled-cats that were materialized crossed his mind, but he discarded the thought almost immediately. Doing so would break the status quo. It might force the scaled-cats and birds to attack prematurely. Of course, he was pretty sure the status quo was going to change the moment the demon broke the surface.

Glancing at the readout on his M12, Richard confirmed the isotopic battery was full. That would give him four hundred rounds. While a lot of ammo, it wouldn't last long against eighteen hundred plus enemies. The magazine of his M12 only had six 20mm rounds left since he'd used one to kill a bird earlier. Unless he could get his dimensional pack working, he'd run out of ammo long before he ran out of targets.

What am I supposed to do? Richard wondered. His mind raced at a hundred kilometers per minute searching for a solution. *I hate waiting. Surely those scaled-cats know they can overwhelm us with no problem. They don't need to wait for the demon to get here.*

"Is that question directed at me?" asked Nickelo.

"It is if you've got an answer with a probability greater than one percent. If you don't, you know how I feel about your listening to my private thoughts."

"Okay. I do have a theory. Based upon all current data, there's a sixty-seven percent probability this trap is designed to take prisoners."

Richard shivered involuntarily. Since he could self-heal, one of his greatest fears had always been being taken prisoner. A torture session could be stretched out for years if his captors were careful.

"Prisoners? Why?"

"Unknown. However, if they're intending to take live prisoners, that would account for the delay in their attack. They must trust the shield surrounding the valley to prevent our escape."

Richard went over the little information he had and tried to formulate a plan. The stallion and the four dolgars with him had stopped scrambling back and forth in front of the shield wall. They seemed to have accepted their fate. Draken and the remaining dolgars grouped together on the other side of the valley were stuck on the ridgeline above the valley. They could only move where their feet could touch the ground.

Takar caught Richard's eye and growled, "What now?"

What indeed, Richard thought as he eyed the shield of creallium just a few meters away.

"Nick," Richard said in command voice. *"Activate your electronics and scan the valley for any remaining deposits of titanium. Also, feed me the specs for this shield. I want to know the frequency, energy level, and anything else you can tell me about it. Then calculate the probability that I can replicate this shield with the remaining Power in my reserve."*

Nickelo delayed less than a second before answering. *"Scan is complete. Multiple concentrations of titanium particles still remain in the valley. I'm sending you the location of the nearest deposit. I'm also sending you the specs for the shield wall. It appears to be a combination of pure Power and magic. The weave of the energy is strange, but I calculate you should be able to duplicate a small version of the shield by using twelve percent of your Power reserve. My calculations include a four percent buffer for inefficiency."*

"Good enough. If I gave you control to create the shield and gather the titanium, how much Power would it take."

"I could accomplish the task using seven percent Power."

"Fine. Pinpoint the nearest titanium deposit so I can levitate it here. I need enough titanium particles for a shield that can protect all the dolgars and this nightmare of a horse I'm riding."

Within twenty seconds, Richard had a double handful of titanium dust gathered in his ammo pouch. Drawing Takar's attention with a growl, he sent him an image of the dolgars gathering close around the stallion. Surprisingly, none of the dolgars questioned his orders. They just drew in close.

After wrapping the stallion and the dolgars as well as himself with Power, Richard levitated a meter off the ground. Since they were all still in the void and had no weight, he had high hopes he could levitate them all without draining his Power reserve completely. Using his telekinesis, he levitated some of the titanium out of his ammo pouch. He drew Power from his reserve and allowed his battle computer to form a sphere of energy around them as a shield. Continuing to use his telekinesis, he distributed the titanium dust evenly throughout the energy shield.

Nothing happened.

"Sorry, Rick," said Nickelo. *"I must not be doing it right. I told you the weave of the magic was strange."*

Desperate, Richard took control of the energy shield created by his battle computer. On a hunch, he compared his energy shield with the shield surrounding the valley. In a manner similar to how he healed others, Richard pulled the difference from the valley's shield into himself and sent the difference to his own energy shield. His shield shimmered and took on a faint glow.

"It looks different than the shield surrounding the valley," Richard said a little concerned.

"The shield around the valley's formed by a combination of magical energy and titanium. Your shield's composed of pure Power and titanium. The effect should be similar, although it won't entirely replicate the properties of the valley's shield. The important thing is that you did it. I'm impressed."

Richard reached out and tried to move his hand through his energy shield. His hand stopped as if he'd hit a hard surface. He pulled his hand back.

"What if I wasn't in the void?" Richard asked. *"Could I get through the shield then?"*

"I calculate you could get through your shield if you weren't in the void. Your shield will only prevent passage of objects in the void, although it should allow your phase rod to pass through when you have it in destructive mode due to the phase energy. The shield around the valley is different. It's similar to some defensive shields in that it will stop physical objects as well as energy and objects in the void. I should probably point out that the demon will be breaking out of the surface in one minute and five seconds. Whatever you intend to do, I'd recommend doing it quickly."

"Roger that."

Richard leaned close to the stallion's ear. "Keep us in the void, big guy. I won't be able to keep us aloft if you materialize. I don't have enough Power to lift all this weight."

Although Richard didn't know if the stallion understood his words, he hoped his mount would at least pick up on his emotions and act accordingly.

Turning to Takar, Richard sent an emotion he hoped meant, *"Stay in the void."*

Levitating the entire group up and out at the same time, Richard began moving across the valley toward Draken and the other dolgars. He remained as close to the ceiling of the valley's shield as he dared, putting him and his somewhat reluctant companions about forty meters above the valley floor. As he passed over the perimeter of the scaled-cats and birds, some of the birds began spitting globs of acid at them. The acid just passed through and hit the valley's shield above them. They were in the void. The scaled-birds continued to shoot acid at them until they were out of range.

"Now how much time do we have?" Richard asked.

"The demon will break the surface in forty-five seconds."

Richard increased his rate of movement across the valley. Before long, Draken and the other dolgars came into view. They were grouped on a narrow ledge with the valley's shield just to their rear.

Smart, Richard thought. At least the shield wall will prevent the cats from attacking in that direction.

Richard guided his group near Draken before shutting off the

Power going to his shield. The glow of his titanium shield disappeared. As the shield faded away, he gathered the falling titanium particles into a small ball with his telekinesis.

Draken gave a series of growls and emotions.

Richard only made out the word 'plan' and got the impression it was a question, not a statement. Since he didn't have a plan at the moment, he stalled for time by levitating the titanium dust evenly around the entire group.

"Can you form the shield this time," Richard asked. *"You're bound to be more efficient than me."*

"Affirmative," said Nickelo. *"I was following along when you did it. I know what I was doing wrong now."*

Richard sensed his Power and the titanium merge together as Nickelo took control. Within two seconds, a light glow surrounded all of the dolgars, the stallion, and himself.

"How are we doing on Power?" Richard asked.

"Power consumption creating the shield was lower than expected," said Nickelo. *"You still have twelve percent Power in your reserve. Forming the shield appears to use an initial burst of Power, but maintaining it takes very little effort."*

"It may not matter, buddy. I'm not sure we have very long left to live anyway. However, I'll take what I can get. By the way, how much time do we have?"

"I calculate the demon will be appearing above ground in thirty seconds."

Crack!

A plume of dust rose from the center of the scaled-cats' perimeter.

When Richard looked, he saw a wide fissure in the ground that wasn't there before.

"Uh...," said Nickelo. *"On second thought, you better make that a little less than thirty seconds."*

"You fools," boomed a deep voice coming from nowhere and everywhere at the same time. "I am Cancontus, lord of all I survey. Kneel before me you pathetic creatures, and I may let you live. Defy me, and your deaths will be an eternity of pain."

From the growls around him, Richard figured the dolgars understood the words too.

"They aren't physical words," said Nickelo. *"The battle*

helmet's receivers didn't pick them up, but I heard them just the same. I calculate it must be some kind of advanced ESP."

"I will be with you shortly," boomed the voice of Cancontus. "I want the flesh creature. If you give him up before I arrive, I will let the rest of you go."

"Care to wager who he means by 'flesh creature'?" asked Nickelo.

Another plume of dust rose out of the ground along with a second fissure.

"Do you see the shield I have placed around this valley?" shouted the demon. "It was formed by the Circle. It's impassable. The secret of the Circle was given to me by a dwarf king." The demon laughed. It was a cruel laugh. "The dwarf didn't want to give it to me, but I persuaded him otherwise. I can be very persuasive even if it takes years."

The demon had another fit of laughter.

"As for you, foolish human, even *'the One'* can't teleport you to safety now. You're trapped. You've made some dangerous enemies, little wizard scout. My brothers Efrestra and Zenthra are anxious to make your acquaintance again. They're fools, but I'm not. You walked blindly into my trap. There is no escape."

Something long and slimy shot out of one of the fissures. It appeared to be a tentacle. Evenly spaced suckers on one side of the tentacle opened and closed as if searching for their first victim.

"I am almost there," said Cancontus. "As for you dolgars, I command you to give me the flesh creature. Do so now, and I will be merciful. Otherwise, you will beg for death before I end your miserable lives."

Making a decision, Richard started to climb down from the stallion, resolved to go down alone and fight the demon and its forces on foot.

If I'm lucky, he thought, *maybe I'll take so much damage that my healing reserve will run out and the demon will be cheated out of its prize.*

Before Richard's foot touched the ground, Draken growled. "No! You are one of us. We do not give up one of our own."

Takar took up a position by Richard's side. *"Let them come,"* said the dolgar using emotion-speak. *"Let them feel our fangs. We will feast on their life force as they scream in agony."*

Several dolgars rallied around Richard, boxing him in from all sides. Others formed a solid line between the spirit-horse and the demon's forces. Black tendrils reached out from the stallion and pulled Richard back onto his spirit-horse.

"You stay," said the stallion, speaking in perfect intergalactic standard. "We will fight them together."

The valley shook as half a dozen of the demon's tentacles burst out of the fissures while pushing the cracks in the earth farther apart. A gigantic, bulbous mass forced its way out of the enlarged holes. A dozen eyes on stalks pivoted around to survey the area. They stopped turning when they spied Richard and the dolgars. A slit in the center of the bulbous mass opened to reveal multiple rows of razor-sharp teeth.

"So, you refuse to give me my prize willingly. No matter. I'll take him myself, and then my minions will rip the flesh off the bones of the rest of you."

At those words, the horde of scaled-cats and birds began moving in the direction of the dolgars.

The dolgars raised their heads to the sky and began howling. The sound of their challenge echoed throughout the valley as the spirit-wolves let the demon know they weren't afraid. They were dolgars; they would die fighting.

Years ago, Richard would have led the dolgars in a valiant but foolish charge against the advancing horde. Fortunately, after scores of years doing missions for *'the One,'* Richard had learned to stop and think before acting. That is, he'd at least learned to stop and think sometimes. This was one of those times.

Richard sent out a dozen active scans searching for any weakness he could exploit against the demon. One of his scans touched a line of magic linking the demon to the shield surrounding the valley. The weave of the magic drew Richard's attention. The link ran from the demon to a single particle of titanium dust. A link from that particle ran to another until the combined links really did form a circle. From start to finish, the circle of links was unbroken.

Richard's mind went into overdrive. Time slowed, or perhaps his mind sped up. Whatever the case, everything around Richard appeared to stop moving. He'd experienced the phenomenon before. It sometimes happened during extreme stress in battle.

Although he couldn't move any faster during what he'd come to call a time-freeze, it did give him an opportunity to discuss the situation with his battle computer in order to make plans.

"Those links look like one of the old electrical circuits from Earth," Richard told his battle computer. *"If all the titanium particles and their links were stretched out, they really would form a circle of sorts."*

"Yes," agreed Nickelo. *"I see it. I think your analogy is right. The circle of links really is like an old electrical circuit. Perhaps you can use that to your advantage."*

Richard mentally nodded. The start of a plan began to form in his mind.

"Look at the link from the demon, Nick. It's the keystone. If we can break that link, the rest of the circuit will short out. If that happens, I'm betting the shield around the valley will fail. If it does, then the dolgars and our spirit-horse could shift into a second dimension. With luck, we could make our escape."

"In theory," said Nickelo. *"However, you're forgetting one thing. That's a major demon out there. Its Power reserve is enormous. You'd need a thousand times more Power than is available in your reserve to break its link. According to information in my databanks, only another major demon can break a major demon's link."*

"Exactly," Richard said.

He now had a plan, and his plan gave him hope. It was a slim hope, but it was hope nonetheless. At that moment, his time-freeze ended. With no time to explain his full plan to his battle computer, he urged the stallion forward. The spirit-horse's sudden movement caught the dolgars by surprise. The stallion was several strides down the side of the cliff before the dolgars began to follow.

Richard sent the image of his destination to the stallion. The spirit-horse turned slightly to correct his course and began running as fast as his long legs could carry them. The scaled-cats and birds in the valley ran to meet them. Richard urged the stallion to even greater speed. He needed to reach the weak point before the stallion and he were overwhelmed by the demon's forces. A look at the remaining distance on his passive scan told him it was going to be close.

The black stallion bent his head low and increased his speed even more, sensing Richard's urgency. When only fifty meters separated the stallion from the lead scaled-cats and birds, the stallion reached his destination.

Richard immediately touched the switch to activate his phase rod. The creallium core shot out the handle as the miniature lightning bolts of phase energy began running up and down its length. At the same time, the demon essence his nephew Brachia had placed in his phase rod became active. An intense feeling of hunger made its presence known. The demon essence wanted to devour something. It wanted to devour anything.

"Demon against demon," said Nickelo as Richard's plan became obvious.

"That's right," Richard said. *"Like you said, only a major demon can break another major demon's link."*

"Well, oh greatest of wizard scouts. I guess we're going to find out real quick whether that bit of demon essence in your phase rod is from a major demon or just a low-level piece of cannon fodder."

Richard stabbed his phase rod into the weakest part of Cancontus's link. The demon essence in the rod latched onto the weak point. He sensed a momentary struggle as the two sets of demon energy fought for control. With a blaze of energy, the demon essence in the phase rod won. When it did, the demon essence began siphoning Cancontus's life force out of the link.

Cancontus screamed as much in anger as in pain.

For the fleetest moment, Richard thought he sensed a note of fear in the demon's cry.

The mass of bloated and decaying skin which was Cancontus's avatar screamed again. "It's not possible. Why is my brother helping you? What does the Dalinfaust hope to gain?"

Richard didn't care whether the demon thought it was possible or not. He just forced his phase rod ever deeper into the weak part of the link. The rod's demon essence seemed to become more powerful as it continued to suck energy from Cancontus. The feeling of hunger from the demon essence grew exponentially.

The lead cats and birds were only twenty meters away.

Richard didn't falter. He continued to hold the phase rod in the demon's link as even more of Cancontus's life force was removed.

Two scaled-cats leaped for Richard's throat.

The stallion raised one of its hoofs and raked one cat with his talons. The spirit-horse caught the other cat in its mouth. Richard heard the crunch of breaking bones as his mount's fangs broke the cat's back.

A scaled-bird shot a glob of acid at Richard's head.

Commander Draken jumped past Richard and took the ball of acid instead. The dolgar roared with pain and fury as the acid burned into his chest, but continued his leap and ripped out the bird's throat. Other dolgars leaped past Richard and tore into the front ranks of the charging cats and birds.

While the battle raged all around, the stallion did his best to protect his rider.

Richard remained steadfast in his purpose, driving his phase rod deeper into the weak point of the demon's link. At the same time, Richard reached out with his mind and traced the flow of Power in the link. He saw the secret of the magical weave and the reason the demon's circle of links was so powerful. He twisted part of the flow of magic in the demon's link back onto itself. The weak point in the demon's link grew weaker.

The demon essence in the phase rod seemed to sense an opportunity to feast on more of its victim's life force. It redoubled its efforts.

Cancontus screamed in anger once more as it realized its pending defeat. In a desperate act of self-preservation, it dropped the flow of Power to its link and to the shield surrounding the valley. The glow of the shield wall faded away.

Richard sensed the shield wall dissipate into the nothingness from which it came.

"Shift," commanded Draken in emotion-speak.

Just before a wave of scaled-cats and their bird allies washed over Richard and the stallion, he felt Power from the spirit-horse wrap around them. The Power shimmered as his mount began shifting into a second dimension.

The dolgars shifted into another dimension as well.

As the valley and the charging scaled-cats and birds shimmered and faded from view, a familiar voice sounded in Richard's mind.

"Mission complete. Remember what you have learned."

"What have I learned?" Richard mentally yelled. *"I've learned nothing!"*

'The One' didn't bother answering.

Everything went black.

CHAPTER 4

High Priestess Jeehanathoraxen, or Jeena to her closest friends and family, yawned as she stretched her arms wide. Training the night before had been long and tiresome. Thankfully, Priestess Aldriss had delayed their normal morning lesson by a few hours.

Although Jeena had slept a little during the night, her beloved scrolls and books had called to her in the wee hours of the morning. It was now well past sunup. Jeena reluctantly rolled up the scroll she'd been reading and looked out the window over her desk. She recited a chant Priestess Aldriss had taught her to clear her mind and relax. The chant worked. Semi-refreshed, she took a few moments to enjoy the sun as it warmed the morning chill out of the air. As she basked in the sunlight, several birds began singing songs to anyone who cared to listen. With more than a little reluctance, Jeena turned away from the window.

It promises to be a nice day. Too bad I'll be so busy training I won't get a chance to take advantage of it.

A knock on the door of her bungalow drew Jeena out of her thoughts.

Who could that be? It's too early for Priestess Aldriss to be summoning me for another round of training. She said I'd be free until noon.

Sighing, Jeena stood up and reached for a battered staff leaning against the wall near her desk. A blue gemstone was mounted at the tip of the charred wood. The blue gem gave off a feeling of warmth and peace. She also sensed strength in the staff. The sensations always comforted her whenever she touched the Staff of the High Priestess of the Lady of the Tree. Taking the staff in her left hand, Jeena walked out the door of her bedroom and into the hall. She passed by the kitchen and entered the main living area, taking a moment to look around the room. Every flat surface was piled with books and scrolls of every conceivable shape and size.

I know I should clean up, but it's too late now. Besides, it's like I keep telling Reale, my home isn't dirty; it's just...cluttered.

Jeena smiled at the thought of her adoptive mother. Reale and her bondmate, High Lord Trenadine, had taken her and her brother Ceril in after their parents were murdered. The kindness of both Reale and Tren had been a light that had helped bring her out of the despair of that horrible period in her life.

Pushing the sad memory to the back of her mind where it belonged, Jeena took a quick glance at her reflection in a small mirror mounted to the wall. She frowned. While she wasn't vain, she knew she looked like anything but a high priestess at the moment. Her long silver hair was a tangled mess, and several dirt smudges contrasted sharply with the otherwise light complexion of her face. Only her molten silver eyes bespoke of her service to the Lady of the Tree. Jeena raked the fingers of her left hand through her hair in a halfhearted attempt to straighten it out before seeing who had knocked.

When Jeena finally opened the door, she was surprised to see Menetror, the herald and chief administrative assistant to the Council of Light. The old elf looked harried. Jeena thought he always looked harried.

"Menetror," Jeena said trying to sound pleasant in spite of her fatigue. "What brings you here so early?"

The old elf bowed low. "High Priestess. I bring greetings from High Lord Trenadine. He requests your immediate presence in the Hall of Meetings."

"Why so early? The council has a meeting scheduled for later this afternoon. Surely the high lord can wait until then. What's this about?"

"I'm not at liberty to say, High Priestess. However, the high lord said it was urgent."

Knowing full well from past experience that she wouldn't get additional information from the tight-lipped elf, Jeena conceded defeat.

"Fine. Tell the high lord I'll be there shortly. I just need to make myself a little more presentable." Jeena waved her free hand at the wrinkles in her robe. The light-blue cloth was also covered in dirt stains. "I'm afraid I fell asleep in my robe when I got home from training last night."

Menetror shook his head. "I'm sorry, High Priestess. The high lord said to tell you to come at once and as you are."

Jeena grew more curious. Her adoptive father wasn't one to exaggerate need. If the high lord said to come at once, something was definitely out of the ordinary.

"Very well. Lead the way, and I shall follow."

Menetror bowed once more before taking off at a fast pace toward the palace.

Jeena was grateful the old elf had come on foot. She liked walking.

Besides, she thought. *That means the need isn't all that urgent after all. Otherwise, he'd have brought horses or a carriage.*

Even without the aid of horses, the old elf set a blistering pace. It took only a few minutes to get to the palace gates. Shortly thereafter, they were standing in the Lady's Garden outside the Hall of Meetings.

Menetror stepped to one side and waved Jeena forward. "The high lord wishes to see you alone, High Priestess. If you don't mind, I'll see to my other duties now."

Jeena nodded her head in dismissal and turned toward the Hall of Meetings. The gardens were beautiful as always, but she paid them no mind this morning. Her thoughts were on other matters.

What could've happened to warrant a summons? Try as she might, Jeena could think of nothing.

With a shake of her head, she followed one of several white-stone paths. Before long, she was at the marble columns that separated the hall from the gardens. Since the garden side of the Hall of Meetings was an open wall except for a few support columns, she was able to walk directly into the hall. Once inside, Jeena understood the reason for her summons.

Nine high-backed stone chairs were spaced out at the front of the hall. Several marble tables were in front of the chairs. High Lord Trenadine sat in the center of the nine chairs. The fingers of his right hand were tapping nervously on the tabletop before him. Two children stood on the opposite side of the table from the high lord. The children were human. Jeena recognized them instantly.

"Dren; Brachia," Jeena said. "I'm glad to see you, but why are you here? In fact, how are you here?"

Brachia spun around at the sound of Jeena's voice. Although it had only been two years since they'd last been together, the young boy looked older than Jeena remembered.

That's to be expected, she thought. *Humans age twenty times faster than elves.* Even knowing the aging differences, Jeena was surprised at how much more mature the boy looked. If he'd been an elf lad, she would've guessed his age at two hundred. She did a quick calculation in her head. *He must be about ten in human years now.*

Jeena took a closer look at Brachia's sister. The effects of two years were even more pronounced on Dren. When they'd last met, both Dren and she had been about the same physical age. Now the human girl definitely looked the older of them.

Jeena was glad to see the children. She'd grown to like them the last time they'd been together. In fact, she'd even invited them to share her home in Silverton, but they'd declined.

While he might be older, Brachia proved he was as impulsive as ever. The boy rushed toward Jeena with arms outstretched and gave her a big hug. Jeena hesitated only for a moment before returning the boy's show of affection. She gave his sister one of her best smiles.

Brachia and Dren weren't the ones who harmed my family, Jeena thought. *I bear them no ill will. They're children after all.*

"Jeehana," said Brachia with an ear-to-ear grin. "Omar missed you. Why haven't you come back to see us? You said you would."

Before Jeena could reply, High Lord Trenadine spoke. "So, you do know them? They told me as much."

"Yes," Jeena said. "I know them very well. These are the two children who repaired the Staff of the Lady of the Tree."

High Lord Trenadine nodded his head. "As I suspected. However, I didn't ask, and they didn't say." He looked at the two children. "I was just telling them it was highly irregular to have uninvited guests popping up in the palace; especially humans."

Prying herself loose from Brachia's grasp, Jeena held the boy at arm's length and looked him up and down. "You've grown, Captain Brachia." She gave him a friendly smile. "I do believe you're turning into a real pirate."

"Don't encourage him, Jeehana," said Dren. "He's hard enough to live with as it is."

Jeena smiled before asking her original question again. "Why are you here, and how?"

"How?" said Dren. "We were teleported here by the Oracle. Why? Because he told us to bring you back. The Oracle said to tell you it's time."

Jeena frowned. "Time for what?"

Brachia answered before his sister got a chance to speak. "The Oracle didn't exactly say. I think he wants you to go on another mission. He said we needed to fetch you posthaste."

Jeena looked at High Lord Trenadine for guidance. Her adoptive father spread his hands and shrugged his shoulders, but gave no advice. She wasn't surprised. The easy-going high lord was one who preferred elves to work out solutions on their own whenever possible.

"Well," said High Lord Trenadine. "I'll leave these two in your capable hands. They're your responsibility now. Keep them close. You know how some in the city feel about humans."

"Yes, High Lord," Jeena said in her formal voice. As a member of the Council of Light, Jeena normally went out of her way to make sure she avoided familiarity with her adoptive father when they were in official settings.

"As for you two," said the high lord with a mock frown, "make sure you mind the high priestess. The citizens of Silverton aren't used to visitors. And…," he added with a smile, "the next time you want to visit the Lady's Garden, perhaps you should wait for an invitation."

"Yes, sir," said Dren.

Brachia snapped to attention and raised his hand to his forehead in a salute. "Aye, aye, Captain."

Jeena noticed the high lord do his best to suppress a laugh and fail miserably.

"All right, out with all of you," he laughed. "I've got work to do."

Waving Dren over to her, Jeena led the two children out into the gardens. Both children stopped and stood open-mouthed at the vast array of colors of the garden's plants and flowers. The morning sun reflecting off the numerous statues of gold, silver, and titanium made the garden even more spectacular than usual. Jeena allowed the children a few minutes to revel in the beauty of the area before ushering them down one of the garden's many paths.

As they walked, Dren waved her hand to indicate the garden. "It's beautiful. We didn't get a chance to appreciate it when we first got here. The high lord caught us as soon as we materialized. He took us straight into that room."

Jeena nodded her head. "Yes. High Lord Trenadine likes to spend his mornings in the garden clearing his mind in preparation for the stress of the day ahead. I suspect the Oracle knows as much."

Brachia spun around as if trying to take in the whole garden at once. "It's amazing. I could stay here forever."

Jeena smiled. "Yes, it's very beautiful. Well, it should be. Elves have tended this garden since the time of High Lord Carndador a hundred thousand years ago." She pointed to a small bench off to one side of the path. "It's said the high lord and his bondmate High Priestess Shandristiathoraxen would often sit on that very bench and let the beauty of the garden soothe away the stress of the day."

When it became obvious the children were in no hurry to leave the gardens, Jeena took charge and directed them toward an exit. She had things to do.

"Get moving you two," Jeena said. "I'll show you our city as we walk. It's been many years since any humans spent time in our city of Silverton. You should consider yourselves privileged."

For the next hour, Jeena led the children through the streets and byways of Silverton, the capital city of the country of Silvertine of the Slyvrastran elves. The sight of the two human children drew stares, but as Jeena had hoped, no one bothered them since they were with her.

When Jeena took the children to see the Tree of Light, they were spellbound. She didn't blame them. Even after seeing the tree almost every day for the last 322 years, she was still spellbound herself. The tree was as tall as a hundred elves standing one on top of the other, and its limbs stretched almost a bowshot from one side to the other.

"That's the biggest tree I've ever seen," said Brachia.

Dren nodded her head in agreement.

Jeena smiled. "The Tree of Light was planted by my ancestor, High Priestess Shandristiathoraxen, almost exactly a hundred thousand years ago. She had to rescue the seed from a fierce demon. The Tree of Light has guarded the Slyvrastran elves ever since. Without the Tree of Light's protection, I dread to think what would happen to my people."

"My uncle helped an elf get a seed once," said Brachia. "He's a great fighter. He's a wizard scout. You should meet him one day. I think you'd like him."

Jeena frowned, but immediately replaced it with a smile to avoid hurting the boy's feelings. Still, the thought of any elf needing or accepting the help of a human adult male was ludicrous. However, the boy's comment did remind her of something.

"Why are you still living at the Oracle's? I thought you told me the reason you couldn't come stay with me was that your uncle was coming to get you."

"We did say that," admitted Dren. "Then the Oracle said the time wasn't right yet. He said both our uncle and us had things to do first."

"That wasn't exactly how he put it," said Brachia. "He said the variables didn't yet have the necessary values. He's always talking like that. He's a computer, you know."

The word 'computer' brought up an image of a box with flashing lights. The children had used such boxes two years previously to help repair the Staff of the Lady of the Tree.

"A computer?" Jeena said. "How can the Oracle be a computer?"

"Brachia," said Dren. "I told you not to go around telling people that. It's supposed to be a secret."

"Jeehana isn't people," said Brachia sounding a little defensive. "She's our friend. Aren't you, Jeehana?"

Jeena gave the boy her most dazzling smile. "I'll always be your friend, Brachia. I'll always be yours too, Dren."

"See," said Brachia to his sister as he stuck out his tongue.

"Now back to your talk about a computer," Jeena said. "I fail to see what a box of flashing lights has to do with the Oracle."

"Oh," said Dren. "My brother's being too simplistic. The

Oracle's actually a living gas that thinks logically. Computers are also logical, but the Oracle's way more advanced than a mere computer. We think he's part of *'the One.'*"

Keying in on one point of the girl's words, Jeena shook her head. "A gas? How can that be? I've met him. He's a human like you. You introduced me to the Oracle yourselves."

Dren looked at her brother before answering. "Yes, well, we didn't know it at the time. After living with the Oracle for the past two years, we've figured things out. We're pretty smart for our ages, you know."

"But the Oracle's human," Jeena insisted.

"Actually, he just uses a hologram to present a human form," said Brachia.

"A holo-what?" Jeena asked.

Dren cut in to explain before Brachia could get started. "A hologram is like an illusion spell. I think the Oracle uses a hologram of a human as his avatar so people will accept him more readily. However, I assure you that he's a gas. All battle computers are a living gas. The Oracle isn't a battle computer, but I think he's the same species."

Jeena held up her right hand in a stopping motion. "Slow down. You're confusing me. Let's go back to my original question. Why are you here? I mean really. Please don't tell me you don't know. I find that difficult to believe."

Dren looked at her brother again. When the boy nodded, she spoke. "The truth is we didn't want to speak in front of the other elf," admitted Dren. "The Oracle told us to tell only you."

"Tell me what?"

The girl took a deep breath. "The Oracle wants you to come with us into the future. He has a mission for the three of us. He says the algorithm requires you as a variable to produce the desired results."

Jeena shook her head. Things were getting out of hand. *The last time I met the Oracle, he spoke of algorithms and variables. They were meaningless gibberish to me then. Now the children are talking the same nonsense.*

"I can't go to the future even if it were possible," Jeena said. "I'm the high priestess. My people need me."

"You have to come," insisted Dren. "The Oracle says the fate of three galaxies depends on you coming."

"No," Jeena said trying to be forceful without sounding too harsh. "No one can travel to the future. Even if they could, I wouldn't go. Nothing anyone says or does will convince me to go."

As the words left her mouth, Jeena felt a tickle at the back of her mind. The tickle transformed into a sense of peace. She felt a presence in the peace. She'd felt the presence before. It was the presence of the Lady of the Tree of Light.

"*You must go with the children,*" said a soft voice in Jeena's head. "*You must help the elf friend. I'm depending on you, my high priestess. Go now, or all you hold dear will be lost.*"

"*What elf friend?*" Jeena asked. "*What must I do?*"

No answer was forthcoming.

"*Lady? Lady?*"

The tickle in Jeena's mind disappeared. The peace was gone as well. The Lady had departed.

Jeena looked at the children. They obviously hadn't heard the Lady's voice, but they were staring at her just the same.

"Very well," Jeena said. "I'll go with you. The Lady has spoken."

CHAPTER 5

The tingling stopped as everything came back into focus. At this point in his life, Richard had been on enough missions for *'the One'* that he no longer tended to react violently. Consequently, he was able to suppress a yell as he took stock of his surroundings.

He was still in his battle suit, but it was no longer in armor mode. Instead, his battle suit was in the leather-like consistency it maintained when its power source was inactivated. The thinness of the battle suit allowed him to feel the texture of the metal bench upon which he now sat. He felt the vibration of a hyper-drive reverberating through the bench.

I'm back on the Defiant.

"Nick," Richard said into his shared space. *"Are you here?"*

"Obviously," said Nickelo. *"I'm right on top of your head. You're still wearing your battle helmet. Where else would I be?"*

Richard was more interested in adjusting to life back on the *Defiant* than responding. Looking around, he realized he was sitting at the recon ship's dining table, right where he'd been before he was teleported out.

Twelve sets of eyes were staring at him.

A stocky dwarf in a camouflage jumpsuit sitting on his right shoved a plate with a half-eaten simulated steak in front of Richard. "Sorry, Rick. I thought you'd be gone longer. I did wait a little while. Since I couldn't see your steak going to waste, I commandeered it."

Richard recognized the dwarf. His name was Storis. Richard

plucked another memory out of his mind. The dwarf was one of a half-dozen on the *Defiant* who made up the recon ship's security detachment. A quick glance around the table identified three of the other dwarves in the detachment. Several gnomes were also part of the dozen sitting at the table. They were some of the ship's mages. A male elf and two human teenagers sat across from the gnomes.

That's Tia and Matthew.

"Very good," said Nickelo like an adult might speak to a young child. *"You're regaining your memory of the physical dimension faster than usual."*

Recovering from time-commando missions was always a little surreal for Richard. Transitioning from a time in the past and another dimension to the current time in the physical dimension was a challenge no matter how often he did it.

"I don't remember what we were doing when we left," Richard said. *"A little help would be nice, Nick."*

"I'm on it, buddy. Margery's uploading your memory backup as we speak. As soon as it's ready, I'll use it to refresh the appropriate areas of your mind. Just give me a few seconds. In the meantime, see what you can figure out by listening to those around you."

"Who are you trying to kid, Storis," said one of the gnomes. "Rick wasn't gone five seconds before you started chowing down on his supper."

The others sitting at the table laughed.

Margery is the Defiant's primary computer. She was the battle computer for my father, the commandant before he was killed. Richard's memory started coming back faster. *Storis is known for his appetite, and he's not above stealing something off someone else's plate when they aren't looking.*

"Don't let them fool you, Rick," said Storis as he continued chewing on a large chunk of Richard's steak. "I waited a good eight to ten seconds before I confiscated your food."

Richard asked, "How long was I gone?"

"Only about thirty seconds this time," said Tia. "That's the only reason you've still got half of your steak left."

Tia was the teenage daughter of Duke Bistoria, the leader of the Trecorian Alliance. She'd been assigned to the *Defiant* as one of the ship's fighter pilots at Richard's request. He'd seen her fight, and she was good. Of course, she was the sister of his friend Liz who was the best pilot he'd ever seen, so that was to be expected.

The elf spoke next.

"How long were you on your mission, wizard scout?"

Richard remembered the elf's name was Comstar. Large parts of his mission in the spiritual dimension were already beginning to fade, but he recollected enough to answer. "About eighteen months. I was in the spiritual dimension. They have some kind of eternal war with those dimension-shifting cats I told you about."

"Interesting," said Comstar. He touched the tips of his fingers together in front of his face. "I wonder why *'the One'* sent you there. From what you've told me, he usually has a purpose in mind when sending you on missions. The dolgars were already your allies. What did he hope to accomplish?"

Most of the others at the table had already resumed eating. Since *'the One'* tended to send Richard on a mission every two or three weeks, having him pop out and back was no longer the novelty it had once been.

I guess they think eating's more important than listening to my story. At the thought of food, Richard's stomach growled, reminding him that he was a little hungry. Unfortunately, one look at the half-gnawed steak on his plate quenched his appetite. He liked dwarves, but their eating habits weren't exactly genteel by any means.

"No kidding?" laughed Nickelo. *"I may be a computer, but even I know dwarves aren't ready for high-society events."*

"Damn it, Nick. Stop reading my thoughts."

"Then stop thinking in your shared space."

Richard pushed his plate back to Storis. "Be my guest. I'm not all that hungry come to think of it."

"Liar," said Nickelo making no attempt to hide a laugh. *"You're always hungry."*

Before Richard could even finish moving his plate, the dwarf stuck a fork in the steak and shoved it into his mouth, bone and all. He began chewing happily away.

With a look at the elf, Storis said, "You make good steak, Comstar."

Comstar nodded his head in recognition of the compliment but didn't smile. As Richard remembered it, Comstar rarely smiled.

However, the elf did like to cook.

So do I, Richard thought. *I seem to remember the two of us alternating cooking meals every other day for the crew.* Noticing Comstar looking at him expectantly jolted another memory. "Oh, you asked about my mission. Well, I'm not sure what I was supposed to accomplish, to be honest. I was told to help the dolgars, but from what I could make out, they've been fighting their war with those dimension-shifting cats for several hundred thousand years. I doubt having me help them for a year and a half was all that useful."

"Hmm," said Comstar. "It sounds like he gave you a pretty vague mission."

"Well, *'the One'* is never much on specifics," Richard said doing his best to let his disgust for *'the One'* creep into his voice.

"No, he's not," said Matthew, one of the two human teenagers. "But from what you've told me, he's usually more direct than that. What'd you have to do to get him to send you back?"

Richard concentrated on the teenager. *He's the son of Diane Deloris, the current empress of the Intergalactic Empire. His grandfather is Sergeant Ron, the co-owner and captain of the* Defiant. *The boy's a pretty good fighter pilot, considering his age.*

Grabbing a wheat roll out of a bowl on the table, Richard took a bite. "Uh…" Richard continued to chew on the wheat roll, stalling for time. It wasn't easy to figure out a way to verbally communicate what he'd been through the last eighteen months. "Well, the dolgars and I broke out of a trap, which had a strange shield made out of titanium dust."

Matthew didn't look all that impressed at his revelation.

"Oh, and I fought a demon named Cancontus. He was trying to capture me so he could torture me for the next gazillion years or something. I'm not sure why. Once we took him out of action, *'the One'* sent me back here."

This time Matthew did look impressed. In fact, Richard assumed everyone at the table must have been impressed because even Storis stopped eating long enough to listen.

Tia leaned forward wide-eyed, saying, "Well, don't stop there. What kind of demon was it? Did you kill it? I want to hear the gory details."

"Bloodthirsty critter, isn't she?" laughed Nickelo. *"I calculate*

a ninety-four percent probability that—"

The alarm bells built into the bulkhead of the *Defiant* began clanging, accompanied by the flashing of red strobe lights.

"Battle stations," said the voice of Sergeant Ron over the intercom. "Prepare for hyper-jump in two minutes. Security personnel, prepare to repel boarders."

Even before Sergeant Ron finished speaking, everyone at the table jumped up and headed for their assigned battle stations. While Sergeant Ron ran a loose ship in many ways, he didn't play around when it came to security. After dozens of unannounced battle drills over the last six months, everyone in the crew knew where they were supposed to be. They wasted no time getting there now.

That is, everyone wasted no time except Richard. Sergeant Ron had assigned him as a floater. As the *Defiant's* captain put it, "I can't depend on you being here, Rick. *'The One'* is liable to have you off on one of his missions when I need you the most. I can't have one of the ship's fighting positions unmanned if'n you aren't here."

"You know, Sergeant Ron has a point," said Nickelo. *"Besides, you're a wizard scout. You're too valuable to be tied down to one specific battle station."*

Richard wasn't been sure if his battle computer was telling the truth or whether he was just trying to spare his feelings. Regardless, he decided not to argue the point. The end result was that he didn't have a specific place to go during the call to battle stations.

Since he was already wearing his battle suit, Richard headed for a set of stairs across from the galley. He hit the first of the stairs leading to the control room at a run. *"What's going on, Nick? After eighteen months, I don't even remember what we were doing before I got teleported out."*

"Sorry," replied Nickelo. *"Margery just sent your backup data to me. I'll use it to refresh your memory now."*

As he climbed the stairs, Richard sensed a stream of data entering his shared space. As the gaps in his memory were filled, he became aware of their current mission. Their six-month stint of temporary duty with the Trecorian Alliance was over. The *Defiant* was returning him to Risors to take up his duties with the Empire's military again. In between one of their hyper-jumps, they'd received an encrypted communication from the Intergalactic High Council to rendezvous with a civilian transport and pick up a high-level Empire diplomat. According to the orders they'd been given, the diplomat would give them additional instructions once contact was made.

"Hmm," Richard told his battle computer. *"Now I remember what we were doing. I remember I didn't like our orders before we left on our mission for* 'the One.' *As it turns out, I don't like them any better now."*

"Ah, yes," said Nickelo. *"I do seem to remember you letting everyone within earshot know your dissatisfaction when we got the orders. You can get quite vocal sometimes, you know?"*

Just before Richard reached the top of the stairs, the door to the control room slid open. Two padded chairs, one on the left and one on the right, faced an instrument panel with flashing lights. The two seats were empty. Two other chairs at the front of the small control room were the pilot and copilot positions. The left seat, the pilot's position, was occupied by a wiry, grey-haired man. He was moving his hands rapidly across a control panel. The man was Sergeant Ron.

"I don't care what standard protocol says," said Sergeant Ron. "We're making our hyper-jump the moment we get to Alpha X-ray five. That's an order!"

"As you say," replied a disembodied voice. "You're the *Defiant's* captain. I'm just a subservient battle computer."

Richard recognized the voice as belonging to Margery.

"That's more like it," said Sergeant Ron. "Now, turn off that dang-blamed alarm. If'n the crew doesn't know to go to battle stations by now, they ain't ever going to figure it out."

The alarm stopped.

"Rick," said Margery in the sudden silence. "See if you can talk some sense into this old fool. He's trying to jump the ship a quarter of a light year before we get to the optimum jump point in the dimensional fold. That's outside minimum safety limits. It's never been tried before."

"Don't believe everything a computer tells you, Rick," said Sergeant Ron as he turned around in his seat with a wild-eyed grin on his face. "It's been tried. It's just never been done successfully."

Richard used his passive scan to make a sweep around the *Defiant*. Normally, his passive scan was limited to sensing life forms a couple of kilometers away. Areas teeming with life tended to overwhelm a passive scan with information at extended ranges. Outer space was a different matter though. With almost no life to detect, Richard found he could sense another starship at ranges approaching a quarter of a light year. However, he sensed nothing now. The area around them was void of life.

"All right, Sergeant Ron," Richard said trying to be tactful. He'd learned long ago the cantankerous co-owner of the *Defiant* had to be handled carefully or he was liable to do something crazy just out of spite. "So no one's done it successfully. Why do you think we'd be the first? And why should we even try?"

Sergeant Ron spun in his seat and punched a highlighted area on a computer screen. A holographic image of a miniature older woman in a ship captain's uniform appeared above the holograph platform between the pilot and copilot's seats.

"This is Captain Jeekers of the space liner *Starlight*," said the hologram. "We're under attack by pirates. Our starboard engine's been disabled. The pirates are maneuvering to board. We're an unarmed, civilian Empire ship. We need immediate assistance. Please respond. They're maneuvering to board us."

"The *Starlight*?" Richard said. "Isn't that the ship we're supposed to rendezvous with?"

"Exactly," said Sergeant Ron as if he'd just scored a point. "You can bet it's not a coincidence they're being attacked. I've always thought there was more to this whole assignment than we're being told. It smacks too much of my daughter's behind-the-scenes political maneuverings."

Since Sergeant Ron's estranged daughter was the empress, Richard had to agree with his friend's assessment of the situation. He'd met the empress a couple of times before. While she'd presented a facade of oily politeness during their meetings, he'd come to understand almost everything she did or said had a hidden agenda. If their current mission originated from her, Richard wasn't sure he wanted any part of it.

"Well, then," Richard said, "I'd say that's all the more reason not to make a hazardous hyper-jump. Why take the risk?"

"Why?" said Sergeant Ron with a shake of his head as if he was disappointed in the *Defiant's* co-owner. "I know I can be heartless sometimes, but even I'm not callous enough to leave an unarmed civilian star-liner with two thousand souls on board to the tender mercies of pirates. I don't think you're that heartless either."

"Fine," Richard said. "We can't leave them to pirates. So what are we doing and how can I help?"

"I knew you'd come around to my way of thinking," said Sergeant Ron with an approving smile. "The pirates are probably on board the *Starlight* by now. Even at max hyper-speed, we can't waste the time necessary to get to the optimum jump point. What I need you to do is get down to the engine room lickety-split and help Bright Wing out. This hyper-jump's going to be tricky."

"What about after we jump?"

"We'll just have to wait and see. We'll do whatever we need to do when we get there."

"Understood," Richard said trying not to grin. "I'll let you know when we're ready."

"Don't bother," said Sergeant Ron sounding very serious. "I'm making the jump regardless. If you're not ready when I do, then we're all dead. How's that for motivation?"

Richard dashed from the control room and jumped down the stairs to the dining area of the ship. He passed through the galley to a larger set of stairs leading down and jumped to the metal deck below. He didn't take time to grab the handrail. Even in non-activated mode, his battle suit's built-in assistors easily absorbed the shock of landing.

The lower deck was noisy and teeming with activity. Richard noticed the *Defiant's* armorer, Sergeant Hendricks, and Wizard Scout Terrie Shatstot issuing combat armor and weapons to several members of the crew. Some of the dwarves in the security detachment were already suited up.

Richard turned and made his way toward the back of the vessel. *I'd forgotten how big this ship is. It's only designed for a crew of twenty-two, but it's larger than most military recon ships.*

"And it's a good thing it is," said Nickelo. *"Otherwise, it would never have accommodated all the extra equipment and weapons Sergeant Ron and Sergeant Hendricks stuck onboard."*

Richard picked up the pace to another stairway leading down. The level below consisted primarily of the cargo bay stacked to the ceiling with containers bearing symbols of a black dragon with a red stripe. Richard sensed Power emanating from most of the containers. They were filled with salvaged energy globes and spell-shells.

Richard thought back to the mission when the *Defiant* fought the destroyer from the magical dimension. He'd been shown where the Dragars got their energy. The reptilian-looking creatures used a combination dimensional gate and time bubble to steal dragon eggs from a planet that served as a hatching ground. In his vision, he'd felt and seen his surroundings from the perspective of one of the unborn dragons. He'd sensed the innocent dragons' fear as the Dragar priests took them to the top of some unholy pyramid and sucked their life force out as a sacrifice.

To his dismay, he'd also discovered that not only was the Power from the sacrificed dragons used to create the Dragars' energy spheres, but some of the bleed-off energy had also been the source of the DNA gas vent on Velos. The technicians from the Intergalactic Wizard Scout Academy had unknowingly acquired the residual life force of millions of sacrificed dragons over the years to make the refined DNA gas used to create wizard scouts. To Richard's horror, he'd been faced with the fact that his extended life and self-heal ability had come at the cost of helpless innocents.

Richard forced the thoughts of DNA gas and sacrificed dragons to the side. He had more immediate concerns.

As he headed toward the ladder leading down to the main-engine room, Richard saw Tia and Matthew give each other a hug before separating to crawl into opposite tunnels leading to the *Defiant's* wing pods. During the previous overhaul on Velos, Sergeant Ron had connived the Deloris Armaments Corporation into attaching two Zip fighters to the ship's wings along with an access tube so they could be manned during flight. One of the Zip fighters, or zippers as they were often called, had been destroyed during a battle. It was replaced with a magic-based counterpart off a captured destroyer from the magical dimension.

As Richard slid down the long ladder, he used his passive scan to monitor Matthew crawling toward the zipper and Tia toward the magic-based fighter.

"It's called a dragon-fighter," said Nickelo in their shared

space.

"I know what it's called," Richard said. *"Now stop reading my mind."*

By this time, Richard was standing on the metal floor of the engine room. The noise of the *Defiant's* hyper-drive was overwhelming.

"Suppressors," Richard said using his command voice.

"Compliance."

The battle helmet changed shape to three-quarters mode. Once the sides of the helmet were over Richard's ears, built-in noise suppressors filtered out the engine noise to a dull roar while still allowing him to hear less intense sounds such as people speaking.

"You late," came a mechanical sound from a translator. "We jump in twelve."

Richard looked to his right and saw a large Sterilian standing near a young boy. Richard recognized the Sterilian as the *Defiant's* mechanic, Charlie. The boy standing next to Charlie was dressed in a greasy-gray mechanic's jumpsuit. The boy was Tia's brother, Daniel. Although the boy was only twelve years old, he still pulled his weight as a member of the crew. The strange pair was standing on the opposite side of a large control panel from Richard. All four of Charlie's arms were moving rapidly across the computer screens.

"Sorry, Charlie," Richard said. "I'm here now."

Charlie acknowledged Richard's reply with a nod of his head after a set of mechanical screeches sounded from the translator on his belt.

Richard wasn't surprised. He'd learned early on that Charlie was a lizard of few words. And after a few minor accidents, he'd also learned that when Charlie spoke, it paid to listen.

Daniel pointed at a glassed-in area across the room. "Bright Wing's inside."

Following the direction of Daniel's hand, Richard noticed a movement of silver behind a glass wall. The dragon was walking around a glowing red ball in the enclosed room. As always, he was amazed at the amount of energy flowing within the ball of energy.

"Well, it's a good thing it's producing all that energy," observed Nickelo. *"Otherwise, the Defiant's prototype hyper-drive wouldn't be able to make the jump."*

"I know, buddy."

As dragons went, Bright Wing was small at only two meters in length from nose to the tip of her pointy tail.

"She's still young," said Nickelo. *"If you give her a few thousand years, she'll eventually be a silver giant."*

"Well, I'm glad she's young then, otherwise she wouldn't fit in our engine room."

Although he'd been gone a year and a half on his mission with the dolgars, Richard hadn't needed a memory refresh to remember how important Bright Wing was to the *Defiant*. She maintained the ship's primary energy source. She'd previously done the same job on a magic-based destroyer they'd captured. Unlike the destroyer where she'd been enslaved, Bright Wing had freely volunteered to serve as one of the *Defiant's* crew.

"She does it because you rescued her," said Nickelo. *"She was born into slavery. Until you freed her, all she'd ever known was the confines of that destroyer's energy sphere."*

"I know," Richard said. *"I've told her a hundred times she doesn't owe me anything."*

"She obviously thinks differently. That's a good thing. We're going to need her for this jump. Besides, as long as she agrees to stay on and maintain the Defiant's hyper-drive and primary energy source, we'll never have to worry about replacing our engines.

"Brother," said Bright Wing using emotion-speak. *"I need your help. We're too far from the dimensional fold. Our energy is already trying to twist back on itself. The Defiant's hyper-drive wasn't designed to make jumps from this distance."*

"Understood," Richard replied. *"Give me a second."*

Reaching out with his senses, Richard allowed the flows of energy from the sphere of red energy to fill his mind. The swirling paths of Power were a thing of beauty. Richard's attention was drawn to several loops in the flows of energy within the red sphere. They seemed wasted. Letting his senses expand even more, Richard tried to let the Power of the area around the *Defiant* fill his mind. He felt an approaching dimensional fold in the galaxy. Lines of energy from the ship's hyper-drive were already reaching out as they sought a pathway through the fold. Instinctively, Richard knew they were too far away for a normal jump. The distance to the dimensional fold was going to be too much for the hyper-drive.

As he watched, the dimensional fold began tearing at the lines of energy from the *Defiant's* hyper-drive. The lines of energy started looping back on themselves in unnatural ways. The loops created an extra drain on the ship's engine as it sought to straighten out the loops. Unfortunately, the loops were too strong for the hyper-drive. Their energy source was deteriorating at a rapid rate.

"The distance is too great," said Nickelo. *"Even with Bright Wing's help, I calculate a ninety-three percent probability the Defiant's primary energy source will be depleted before we get halfway through the jump. Sergeant Ron's not waiting. He's making the jump. We're all dead if you don't do something now."*

Richard allowed his mind to merge with the flows of energy. He followed their twists and turns. When he got to the unnatural loops, he didn't try to force them into the shape he wanted but instead coaxed the loops into converting back to a more natural flow. It was as if the Power in the loops wanted to flow naturally but had to be shown the way before it could happen.

The lines of energy suddenly blazed with Power as the hyper-drive kicked fully in.

Richard felt large fluctuations in the flows of energy surrounding the *Defiant*. The lines of Power pulled the *Defiant* forward. As the ship was drawn into the dimensional fold, the red sphere increased the amount of energy it was producing. Bright Wing fortified and replaced the Power nearly as fast as the hyper-drive could use it.

The *Defiant* shook violently. Charlie, Daniel, and Richard were knocked to the floor. Then the recon ship was through the dimensional fold and in normal space in another part of the galaxy.

Instinctively, Richard reached out with his mind to survey the ship's new surroundings. "Crap! We're screwed."

CHAPTER 6

As it turned out, Dren, her brother, and Jeena didn't leave Silverton right away. Jeena was the high priestess for the Lady of the Tree. The elf made it plain that regardless of what the Oracle wanted, she had responsibilities in Silverton. Consequently, Dren and her brother waited while she spent most of the previous day and part of the evening dividing up her duties between her priestesses and priests. In addition to her duties as high priestess, Dren discovered Jeena also had responsibilities as a lord of the Council of Light, the ruling body of the elves of Silvertine. Jeena told them she had duties with the council that needed to be dealt with as well. During the time the elf took care of coordinating for her absence, Brachia and Dren were left in the care of Elisinsar, the chief librarian of Silverton. Both of them spent a delightful afternoon and evening perusing the extensive scrolls and books stored in the massive library. Dren was actually a little disappointed when Jeena finally came to collect them and take them to her home.

When they finally arrived at the high priestess's house, Dren was surprised to discover it was a modest five-room bungalow. The home was comfortable, but it was definitely not pretentious. The only problem Brachia and she had when they got inside was finding a place to sit down. Nearly every flat surface was stacked with scrolls or books. After thirty minutes of profuse apologies by Jeena, and with the help of Brachia and her, the three of them succeeded in removing enough reading material from two extra beds to allow Brachia and her to get some much-needed rest for the night.

The high priestess got them up bright and early the next morning. Apparently, she wasn't one to let the dust settle when things needed to be done. When Brachia complained about being awakened before the sun was even fully up, Jeena promptly told the boy that she rarely let the sun catch her in bed and expected the same of anyone staying in her home.

After mumbling a few choice words, Brachia got out of bed and helped them fix a breakfast of grapes and cheese. They washed their meal down with a delightful liquid Jeena called spring-wine.

While Brachia amused himself looking at maps in the main living area, Dren accompanied the high priestess into her bedroom to help her finish packing. The room was as cluttered with books and scrolls as the rest of the house. However, the stacks of reading material had an organized randomness throughout the entire domicile.

Dren smiled. *It kind of reminds me of Brachia's lab back on Storage*.

"By any chance did the Oracle say how long we'd be gone?" asked the high priestess as she began rummaging through a closet.

"No. Sorry. He wasn't very specific other than saying we'd be going to the future, and that we'd be in the physical dimension. That's where Brachia and I are from."

"So you told me," said Jeena. "I'll admit I have many questions, but perhaps they should wait until we're on our way. It's at least a three-week trek to the Oracle's. I suppose there'll be plenty of time for questions."

Jeena held up a faded pack she found buried under a stack of clothing in her bedroom closet. "Finally. Here it is."

"Looks a little beat up," Dren said. "I've got a couple of new packs back at the Oracle's, still in the box. I could let you have one when we get there."

Jeena shook her head while staring at the pack.

Dren thought the elf's eyes looked a little shiny.

"No, but thanks. This pack belonged to my mother. She was one of the Lady's priestesses."

"Was?" Dren asked before fully thinking through the question.

The elf kept staring at the pack. After a few seconds, she placed the pack on her bed and began stuffing two changes of clothing and a few other sundries in it. “My parents died when I was very young. My mother had this pack with her when she was killed.”

Noticing Jeena’s eyes were wet, Dren turned a little red. “Oh, Jeehana, I’m so sorry. I didn’t know.”

The elf shrugged her shoulders and turned away. “Like I said, I was very young when it happened. You couldn’t have known.”

Dren moved to the foot of the bed, giving the high priestess some space.

The elf removed a few items from her drawers and stuck them in the pack. Once the pack was nearly full, she removed a shoebox-sized container from the shelf of a nearby bookcase and set it on the bed. When she opened the lid, Dren drew in a sharp breath. The nondescript box was filled with rings, bracelets, and jewelry of every kind. Large and small gems artistically adorned the pieces of jewelry without seeming gaudy.

Dren saw a lot of blue gems sparkling in the container. She stepped closer to the elf and looked over her shoulder. “They’re beautiful.”

Jeena lifted out a hair clasp composed of two interlaced dragons and handed it to Dren. “This one has been in my family for nearly fifty thousand years. All of the jewelry is very old. I suppose you could say it’s a part of my family’s heritage.”

Dren carefully held the clasp in both hands and lifted it up to the morning light streaming in through the bedroom windows. “The workmanship’s exquisite. I can’t even tell where one dragon starts and the other ends.” Pointing to small blue gems used as eyes for the dragons, Dren asked, “What kind of jewels are these? They look like the Power crystal we installed on your staff.”

The high priestess nodded her head. “They’re one and the same. Of course, the gems in this clasp are much smaller. Plus, the magic in the gems ran out tens of thousands of years ago.”

“Magic?” Dren pointed to a wicked-looking dagger on the elf’s belt. “Your knife has one of the blue gems. Does that mean it’s magical as well?”

Jeena nodded. “Yes, it is. As for the items in this box, most of their gems ran out of magic many years ago. My dagger still has a little fight left in it, but I’m afraid the only other items in this box still containing any magic are these two rings.”

Dren watched the high priestess pluck two rings out of the

container and place them in the palm of her hand. Each of the rings had small blue gems, each with a dull glow, embedded around the circumference of the band.

"So these are magic rings?" Dren asked.

The high priestess smiled. "I suppose you could call them that. I think of them as storage containers for magic energy. If my own Power reserve runs low, I can draw energy from these rings to cast my spells. The rings don't have much magic in them anymore, but since I don't know what I'll be up against, I figured I should take them with me just in case."

"Ah! Then they're like batteries."

Jeena frowned. "I'm afraid I'm not familiar with the term. What are these batteries of which you speak?"

"Oh," Dren said. "I forgot you don't know much about the physical dimension."

"Actually," said Jeena. "I don't know anything about it."

"Well," Dren said, "we don't use magic there. Or at least, not many do. Instead of magic, we use technology."

"I remember you telling me about technology when you repaired the Lady's staff," said Jeena.

"Yes, that's right, Jeehana. The equipment we used there to fix your staff was some of my dimension's technology. Anyway, a lot of our technology uses isotopic batteries as an energy source. I think our batteries are like your rings. They're just storage devices for energy until it's needed."

The high priestess seemed to consider the matter for a few seconds before nodding her head. "I suppose. I hope any 'batteries' you need for our mission have more energy than my rings. I may get an extra two or three spells out of the magic in these rings, but that's about it."

"We can recharge our isotopic batteries. Can't you recharge your rings somehow?"

Jeena smiled.

"Why are you smiling?" Dren felt a little self-conscious. "I think it was a valid question."

The elf laughed. It was a friendly laugh.

Dren relaxed. The elf wasn't laughing at her. She thought the high priestess had a wonderful laugh. Plus, her smile was dazzling. She supposed being beautiful and having those amazing silver eyes helped.

"Oh, it's a very valid question," said Jeena still laughing. "In fact, it's one I've asked many times during my years at school. I've been told I can make a pest out of myself sometimes. Just ask any of my former teachers."

"So…, they can't be recharged then?" Dren asked trying to get back to the question at hand.

Still smiling, Jeena explained. "I guess I laughed because it's a question with both a yes and no answer. Yes, they can be recharged, but no, they can't be recharged."

Dren was a super-genius having accumulated the knowledge of her mother, but the elf's answer still confused her.

Jeena laughed again. "You look confused, and rightly so. I had the same look many times when my teachers tried to answer my question in school. The simplified answer is that the blue gems, which energize many of our magic items, are capable of being recharged. In fact, my ancestors used to recharge them quite often. However, we lost the ability before I was born. Now we're left with a lot of magic jewelry and weapons that no longer function because their gems have been depleted."

"Oh," Dren said. "Do you mind if I ask how they were recharged?"

"Of course not. It's something I know a lot about since I'm the Lady's high priestess. You saw the Tree of Light yesterday. Do you happen to remember the small stone platforms around the outside of the tree's limbs?"

Dren nodded her head. "Yep. I think there were twelve of them."

"That's right. They're recharging stands. In days past, during bonding ceremonies, elves would place depleted jewelry and weapons in the recharging stands. When new bondmates shared their Power with the Tree of Light as an offering, the tree would send some of that Power to the charging stands. Any items in the stands were often fully recharged during a single ceremony."

"Bondmates?" Dren asked.

Jeena smiled again. "Perhaps we should save that for another time. Suffice it to say our blue gems could be recharged during a bonding ceremony. However, the ability of the Tree of Light to share the bondmates' offering of Power was lost about ten thousand years ago. That's why a lot of our most powerful magic items no longer work. Their magic was used up long ago."

"That can't be right," Dren insisted. "I've seen magic items during my time here." She pointed at two wands stuck in the high priestess's belt. "Aren't those magic?"

"Yes, they are. Some magic items are created with spells. However, the more powerful magic items like the Staff of the Lady of the Tree or even my dagger use the blue gems as their source of magic. Weapons and armor can remain magical for a long time if their gems aren't drained to cast a spell. Take my dagger for instance. Its blade is made of what we call Holy Metal. The blue gem in the butt of my dagger energizes the metal and makes it magical. I could draw the Power out of the gem to cast a spell in a manner similar to my rings. However, if I drew too much Power out, the gem would be depleted and the Holy Metal comprising the dagger would lose its magic. It would be no better than a normal blade at that point."

"How dare you soil this house with your presence!" yelled a male from the front of the house.

The sound of a scream accompanied the shout. The scream came from a little boy.

Jeena's face turned pale. "Ceril." She dashed out the bedroom door.

"Dren! Dren!" Brachia's shouts reverberated throughout the house.

"Brachia!" Dren drew the knife from her sheath and ran after the elf.

CHAPTER 7

Richard opened a channel on the *Defiant's* com-link and began issuing commands. "Security team to the aft cargo bay. On the double. Tia, Matthew, launch. Do not engage. I repeat, do not engage. Wait for my orders. Those aren't pirates. We've got three Crosioian naval destroyers less than two light seconds off our port bow."

"Rick," said Sergeant Ron over the intercom. "One destroyer's docked to the *Starlight*. The other two are heading our way. I've got a feeling they're not bringing us milk and cookies."

Nickelo said, *"The* Defiant *might be able to handle a single destroyer. However, I calculate less than a five percent probability she can take on two destroyers at once."*

Richard was tempted to act first and think later. Fortunately, something he sensed with his passive scan helped him take control over his normal impulsiveness. *"Nick, are you picking up what I'm sensing with my passive scan?"*

"I'm monitoring the results in our shared space, so yes, I see it. Looks like you may have some allies on the Starlight.*"*

"Roger that," Richard said grateful to have his suspicions confirmed. What he sensed was barely registering on his passive scan, but was definitely there. *"I think they've got their best stealth shields up, however, I can still sense them. Can you confirm it's them?"*

"Based upon the results of your scan, I calculate a sixty-nine percent probability Tam, Telsa, and Jerad are on the Starlight.

You've worked with them so much helping them develop their stealth shields, you can sense them even with their best stealth shields up."

"I wonder if Trinity's with them," Richard said. *"Last I heard, Trinity and Jerad were being given dual assignments."*

"Impossible to tell," said Nickelo. *"Although you've spent some time helping Wizard Scout Trinity protect the link to her Power reserve, I calculate it's not enough to overcome her best stealth shield."*

Richard had a feeling it didn't matter whether Trinity was with the others or not. If even just the three wizard scouts were on the *Starlight*, the Crosioians' boarding party was going to get more than its commander had bargained for.

"What are you going to do, Rick?" asked Nickelo. *"Those two destroyers are going to be on us in no time."*

That his battle computer wasn't offering any suggestions normally meant he couldn't think of a plan with better than a five percent probability of success, or just wanted to see what his wizard scout could come up with on his own.

Without wasting time conferring further, Richard took charge of the situation. He was no longer the novice wizard scout cadet from his Academy days. He'd been on too many missions for *'the One'* over the years without his battle computer along to waste time waiting for someone else to make decisions for him.

"Sergeant Ron," Richard said over the *Defiant's* intercom. "There's at least three wizard scouts on the *Starlight*. They'll keep the docked destroyer busy. That leaves the other two for us to deal with. I think my security team and I can take out one of the destroyers. Can you handle the last one on your own?"

"It'll be a cold day on Sirius when the *Defiant* can't handle one measly destroyer," replied Sergeant Ron. "What I'd like to know is how you're planning on taking out a destroyer with just your security team. It's not like you can fly over to get there. Are your dolgar buddies coming to the rescue or something?"

"Negative on the dolgars. I've sent out a call, but they haven't answered. Even if they do come, it might be too late to help us. Dolgars have no sense of time."

"Then how are you taking out the other destroyer?" asked Sergeant Ron sounding confused.

"I haven't quite figured that part out yet," Richard admitted. "It'll come to me though. You just worry about the one that's left."

"Roger that. You're the boss. I'm just the captain of this bucket of rusty bolts."

Richard didn't consider himself the boss but didn't argue. Someone had to be in charge during a battle, and this time it was him. In spite of what he'd told his friend, he actually did have an idea, crazy though it might be. He imagined it would sound even crazier to Sergeant Ron than it sounded to him. Since he had no desire to argue the point, he'd decided to tell a little white lie instead of the full truth.

"In case you're wondering," said Nickelo, *"I think it's a crazy idea as well."*

"Whatever," Richard said. *"Crazy or not, it's the only plan I've got. So how about putting that nanosecond brain of yours to work and figure out a way to make it happen?"*

"I already have," said Nickelo. *"The best I can come up with is a forty-two percent probability of success. Plus, I don't know what the Crosioians have up their sleeves with their free will. I've correlated the optimum paths but—"*

"Don't bore me with the details," Richard said. *"I trust you. Just make your best guess and go for it."*

"I'm a computer," Nickelo said sounding insulted. *"I don't guess."*

"Sure you don't," Richard said sarcastically. *"And pigs can't fly."*

"*Uh...,"* said Nickelo sounding as confused as a computer could sound. *"Pigs can't fly."*

Richard mentally laughed. *"They can if you put a jet pack on them."*

When Nickelo didn't come back with an answer right away, Richard figured he'd gotten the best of his battle computer for once.

"Just do your best," Richard said more seriously as he turned toward the ladder leading up to the cargo bay. Before he started climbing, another idea popped into his head. He looked over at Daniel and Charlie. "Can you guys do without Bright Wing for a few minutes?"

Daniel looked down at his computer screen for a second. "That dragon of yours has our primary energy source stabilized and back at one hundred percent. I think we've got enough energy to get us through this battle if it doesn't last too long." After a pause, Daniel added, "We'll need her after the battle though."

"Assuming we live," said Charlie without a trace of humor.

Big if, Richard thought. The *Defiant's* engineers would just have to do their best without the dragon. He needed Bright Wing for his plan to succeed.

Using emotion-speak, Richard said, *"I'm thinking about going for a little stroll, Bright Wing. If you care to come along, meet me in the cargo bay lickety-split."*

He started climbing the ladder two rungs at a time. As fast as he was, by the time his head cleared the floor of the cargo bay, Bright Wing was already standing there waiting on him.

Humph, Richard thought. *Must be nice to be able to teleport.*

"She can only do it for short distances, and only to places she's familiar with," said Nickelo. *"Once she's older, she'll be able to increase her distance and navigate to unfamiliar places. However, I calculate that won't be for another 2,347 years."*

Richard seriously doubted he'd be around to congratulate the dragon on her achievement when the time came.

"Too bad she can't teleport others as well," said Nickelo sounding like he was switching into instructor mode. *"Unfortunately, she won't acquire that ability for at least another four thousand years."*

"Can it, Nick. I need to concentrate. Calculate our success probability if we bring Bright Wing along."

"Eighty-six percent," said Nickelo. *"I'm impressed."*

Richard was impressed as well. The odds were better than he could've hoped.

By the time he was completely in the cargo bay, all six members of his security detail had arrived as well. Richard thought the stocky dwarves looked intimidating in their power-armor and with their mixture of weapons. Half of the team carried magic-based weapons while the other half were equipped with standard Empire-issue plasma and phase weapons. To top it off, all six of the dwarves carried battle-axes or war hammers.

"Well, let's hope the Crosioians think they look intimidating as well," said Nickelo.

Another armored figure standing near the dwarves drew Richard's attention. The figure was Wizard Scout Terrie Shatstot. He was wearing his battle suit and carrying a plasma pistol in one hand and a phase rod in the other.

"No," Richard told the disabled wizard scout in a tone he hoped left no doubt he meant what he was saying. "I need you on the *Defiant*."

"No way," said Terrie with a determined look on his face. "I might be disabled, but I'm not dead. If you're seriously thinking about trying to take on a destroyer by yourself, you're going to need me. You can't do it by yourself."

A series of grumbles erupted from the dwarves forming the security team.

"Watch it, laddie," said Felspar, the leader of the dwarves. The dwarf raised his battle-axe for emphasis. "He won't be alone. He's got us. I was killing enemies a lot tougher than those bat-winged tin soldiers a hundred years before you were even a gleam in your daddy's eye."

"And no disrespect, wizard scout," added Storis, "but security's our job, not yours. You do your job, and we'll do ours."

Richard pointed at his fellow wizard scout as he interjected. "I'm in charge, Terrie, and I said no. The whole security team and Bright Wing will be with me. If the Crosioians are able to board the *Defiant*, Sergeant Ron's going to need a wizard scout with him. Angela and the others are good fighters, but they're no match for a full boarding party of Crosioian regulars. For all we know, they may even have a Crosioian scout with them. You know our crew wouldn't stand a chance without you here to take on the scout."

Whether it was a result of his argument or the mention of Terrie's wife, Angela, Richard didn't know. The effect was the same.

Terrie backed down, nodding his head in defeat. "Fine. But, if you run into trouble, I swear I'll get over there to help if I have to get out and walk."

The *Defiant* shook violently. Everyone in the cargo bay except Terrie, Bright Wing, and Richard were knocked to the floor. Richard said a silent thanks to the makers of his battle suit.

"Hey," said Nickelo. *"I did the calculations and activated the suit's assistors to keep you upright. Where's my thanks?"*

"Not the time for jokes," Richard said cutting off his battle computer's attempt at humor. Even though their communications were near instantaneous, Richard didn't need the distraction. He was very aware everyone's life depended on him.

"Fine," said Nickelo sounding a little hurt. *"Be that way. In case you haven't figured it out, those two destroyers have started their attack runs. The* Defiant's *combination of magic and technology makes our shields tough to crack, but a sustained barrage from both destroyers will wear them down given time."*

Richard didn't plan on giving the Crosioians time.

"Felspar," Richard said. "Get the team to the left wing pod. I'll meet you there."

"Roger that," said Felspar as all six dwarves began scrambling to climb through the tunnel leading to the left wing pod.

Richard nodded his head approvingly. The dwarves were good soldiers. Felspar hadn't wasted time pointing out that the wing pod was empty since the *Defiant's* fighters had already launched.

"Felspar and the dwarves trust you," said Nickelo. *"I hope you're not going to let them down."*

"I'll try my best not to," Richard swore as much to himself as to his battle computer.

"Matthew," Richard said over the ship-wide com-link so the entire crew could hear. "Meet the security team and me outside the left wing pod with your zipper. You're going to play taxi for us."

"What about me?" asked Tia over the com-link as if she was concerned she might be left out of something fun.

"Give Sergeant Ron covering fire until we're off the ship. I'll let you know what to do after that."

"Compliance," said Tia with an increasing excitement to her voice.

"Blood-thirsty little critter, isn't she?" said Nickelo. *"I calculate she actually enjoys being in battle."*

"She's a Trecorian. They live and breathe battle. Plus, she's Liz's sister."

Before his assignment on Trecor, he'd been told the Trecorians were similar to the old Spartans on his home world of Earth. After spending the last six months with Tia, Richard had to agree. She was born and bred for war. Although she didn't go out of her way looking for trouble, she certainly didn't back down from it either.

Since he'd been an honorary general in the Trecorian military, Richard knew for a fact Trecorians were tough.

"Well, I'm glad she's on our side," said Nickelo in what Richard took as rare praise.

"So am I, buddy. She'll do her part in this little shindig, so it's time for us to do the same."

Richard bent low and began crawling through the tunnel leading to the left wing pod.

"Seal me up, Nick."

"Compliance."

Richard felt his battle helmet extend downward until it merged with the collar of his battle suit. As the battle suit activated, he sensed the tight-fitting suit change shape into its bulkier armor mode. By the time he reached the airlock at the end of the tunnel, the transformation was complete. He was once again encased in the toughest armor the Empire's technicians could create.

"Don't forget about me?" said Bright Wing. *"Where do you want me?"*

"Teleport out to the dwarves," Richard said as he entered the airlock. *"I'll explain more when I get there."*

The *Defiant* shook as another salvo of enemy rounds hit its defensive shields. The little recon ship bucked as both its upper and lower gun batteries answered with a full salvo of their own.

"Our shields are holding for the present, Rick," said Sergeant Ron over the com-link. "I don't know for how long. Those are heavy destroyers. Both of them have 200-gigawatt plasma cannons the same as us."

"Yeah, but they don't have magic, do they?" Richard said trying to be the optimist for once.

"No, they don't," admitted Sergeant Ron. "That's the only reason our shields are still up. Our mix of magic and technology makes them hard to penetrate."

"Which reminds me," Richard said. "I sense you're only firing our standard Empire weapons. Why aren't you using our magic-based weapons as well?"

"Hey, partner," said Sergeant Ron sounding insulted. "I run the ship, and you handle the reconnaissance and hand-to-hand fighting. That was our deal, remember. However, since you asked so nice, I'll tell you. I'm holding off on our magic weapons until I can catch those destroyers with their pants down. When I use our magic, I want it to be a total surprise."

Richard smiled as he tried to picture one of the bat-shaped Crosioians wearing pants. Somehow, the image didn't quite work.

"Understood," Richard said. "I think you'll get your chance. First, though, I need you to lure those two destroyers into flying straight and level for a few seconds. My plan won't work while they're making evasive maneuvers."

"How am I supposed to do that?" said Sergeant Ron sounding confused. "The only way to get them to fly straight and level would be for me to stop trying to evade their fire. That would be suicidal. Only a lunatic would do that."

Richard laughed in spite of the situation. "Exactly. That's why I'm giving the mission to you. Who else would be crazy enough to do it? Besides, I only need a few seconds. The shields will hold that long." *At least I think they'll hold.*

Richard expected Sergeant Ron to argue further, but the sudden jolt of another salvo of rounds from the destroyer hitting the *Defiant's* shields cut off any additional discussion.

Tia's voice came over the com-link sounding concerned. "If you're going to do something, you'd better do it quick. Those two destroyers just launched eight fighters. I can't hold them off by myself for long."

"Roger that," Richard said as he slipped through the airlock and onto the outer skin of the *Defiant*.

"Your boots' magnetics are on," said Nickelo. *"Nevertheless, you better hang onto something. There's no use taking the risk of being thrown off."*

Richard located Felspar and his security team standing next to the empty wing pod. Bright Wing was hovering a couple of meters above them.

"How the does she survive in a vacuum without protection?" Richard asked.

"She's got protection," replied Nickelo. *"It's called magic. It's what allows her to survive inside a hyper-drive. The vacuum of space is nothing compared to that."*

Richard had other questions but shrugged them off. He had bigger things to worry about. He was just about to call Matthew to come get them when he picked up a fast moving life form on his passive scan heading inbound.

Matthew.

"He's nine seconds out," said Nickelo. *"You better link up with the others."*

Richard stepped forward and grabbed a convenient handhold near the wing pod. Then he wrapped the dwarves and himself with Power. "I'll get you onto the zipper's wings. When we get there, grab hold of a weapon's rack; three to a side."

Felspar answered for the entire security team. "Roger that, wizard scout."

Richard turned to the dragon and spoke over the com-link so the dwarves could hear. "Bright Wing, you can teleport to the zipper yourself. Just make sure you stay close to us."

"Will do, brother," said Bright Wing.

Matthew's zipper came close to the *Defiant's* wing pod and matched her speed for two seconds. As Richard had expected, the teenager wasn't wasting time trying to dock. The battle was moving too swiftly to stay in one place too long.

Smart kid, Richard thought as he used his telekinesis to levitate the dwarves and himself onto the zipper. He barely got his left hand around an empty missile rack when the zipper accelerated forward. A flash of silver to his side confirmed Bright Wing had latched onto the Zip fighter as well.

"Now what?" Matthew asked. "There's no way I can get you close to either of those destroyers. Their anti-fighter weapons would take us out for sure."

"You won't have to," Richard said. "I'm going to let them do it for us."

Glancing at his battle helmet's heads-up display, Richard calculated speeds and trajectories. Or rather, he let Nickelo calculate them while he followed along in their shared space. The result was the same. He knew what he needed to do.

Richard activated the ship's com-link. "Sergeant Ron, I need those two destroyers straight and level now. Give me at least five seconds."

No answer came from the *Defiant's* bridge, but a glance over his shoulder confirmed the *Defiant* had stopped its evasive maneuvers. She was flying straight and level.

Apparently, neither of the destroyer's captains could resist such a tempting target. Both of the destroyers leveled out to give their gunners a stable firing platform.

During his six months with the Trecorians, Richard had been part of several space battles against pirates. It took some getting used to. At hyper-drive speeds, enemy targets were rarely within visual range. Such was the case now. Although the destroyers weren't visible, he was able to keep track of them with his passive scan. Both destroyers were several hundred thousand meters to the rear of the *Defiant*. He sensed a barrage of missiles and plasma rounds heading inbound toward the *Defiant* from the direction of the destroyers. In addition, he noted eight life forms coming in fast.

"Those are the eight Crosioian fighters Tia mentioned," said Nickelo.

One of the life forms blinked out, then another.

"Uh, correction on that," said Nickelo. *"Make that six Crosioian fighters. Tia took two out. I told you she was bloodthirsty."*

With the loss of their companions, Richard sensed three of the enemy fighters turning to the left as they sought to engage Tia. She'd been able to surprise them by attacking from their flank, but they were surprised no longer. The enemy fighters began firing at Tia's dragon-fighter.

Although outnumbered three to one, Richard sensed Tia evading most of her opponents' fire. What few missiles and plasma beams got to their intended target must have been absorbed by the dragon-fighter's shield because Tia's life form continued to register on Richard's passive scan.

"It's a good thing Charlie and Daniel worked with Comstar and the gnomes to integrate technology with the magic on Tia's dragon-fighter," said Nickelo. *"Otherwise she'd probably have been blown out of the sky by now."*

Richard automatically defended Liz's sister. *"She's too good of a pilot for that. She'd have figured out how to dodge them somehow."*

"Well, you better hope Matthew's just as good because we've got incoming."

A review of the slew of information his battle computer was sending into their shared space confirmed a dozen missiles and torpedoes were inbound from the three fighters not engaged by

Tia. Richard had no doubt the fighters would be adding rounds from their plasma cannons as soon as they were within range.

Richard began giving orders again. *"Nick, send Margery the coordinates for the intercept. Have her assist Matthew in getting us to the right spot at the right time. Please make it quick or we're dead."*

"Compliance."

Almost immediately, Matthew's zipper made a hard bank directly into the path of one of the incoming destroyers. The starships were still out of sight, but Richard sensed the destroyers bearing down on them fast. The missiles from the fighters were a hundred thousand meters ahead of the destroyer. He prayed Matthew could make his getaway without getting hit.

"Nick, take control of my Power. I'm not fast enough."

Nickelo gave a wild laugh. *"Compliance. I guess you're finally admitting you need me."*

"Occasionally," Richard said, mentally smiling in spite of himself. The adrenaline rushing through his body was making him lightheaded. He had to force himself to concentrate on the mission at hand. He knew timing was going to be everything.

Just before the incoming missiles and torpedoes made contact with the Zip fighter, Richard felt Nickelo use his Power to shift the dwarves, Bright Wing, and himself into the void. At the same time, he sensed Margery activate the zipper's hyper-drive. The zipper shot forward out of the path of the enemies' fire and was lost to sight. Since he was now in the void, Richard sensed more than saw the enemy missiles and torpedoes speed past them. One of the missiles passed so close Richard thought he could've reached out and touched it if he hadn't been in the void. Thankfully, he was.

"Shifting into the void is a natural ability for your dragon," Nickelo explained. *"The information in my databanks indicates she'll be able to shift into other dimensions when she gets older."*

"If she gets older," Richard said. *"She might not live through this battle. None of us may."*

"True," agreed Nickelo. *"By the way, you've got four seconds before the lead destroyer reaches our position. Get ready."*

Richard thought the command to send a text message to the heads-up displays of the dwarves in his security team.

'Silent weapons only,' he wrote. 'Make for engine room.'

Richard saw a dark shape looming before him. Then, with a speed too fast for any human to replicate, the Power surrounding the dwarves and him dropped and they were immediately shifted out of the void.

CHAPTER 8

When Dren got to the end of the hallway, she saw Brachia in a corner of the living room with his knife held out before him. He was in one of the defensive stances their uncle had taught them with the blade up. Jeena stood between Brachia and a silver-haired male. The male elf was red-faced. He had a longsword attached to his waist belt, but fortunately, it was still in its sheath. When Dren entered the room, the male elf turned and glared at her. She took in a sharp breath. The male's eyes were molten silver, and they were filled with obvious hate.

"Another one," said the male. "How dare you defile our home with their presence? Have you no shame?"

"Shame?" said Jeena through gritted teeth. "You talk to me of *shame*? You come into my home and insult my guests, and you accuse me of shame?"

"I want them out of this house now," said the male getting even redder in the face. He placed a hand on the hilt of his sword. "If you don't get them out now, then I'll get them out for you."

Dren felt a drop of sweat drip down her brow. She gripped her knife even tighter and edged along the wall until she stood beside her brother.

The high priestess slammed the butt of her staff down on the floor. The house shook. A pile of scrolls tumbled off a chair. The blue gem at the top of the elf's staff blazed but wasn't nearly as bright as the anger in Jeena's molten silver eyes. Dren wasn't sure whether she was more frightened of the male or of the high priestess.

"If you so much as touch one of these children, I swear it'll be the last thing you ever do, Ceril. This is my home. You got the farm. I got the house. I'm the master of this place now, not you, brother."

Dren took notice of the resemblance between the two elves. The male was the older of the two, but between the silver hair and molten silver eyes, there was no mistaking a common heritage.

"They killed our parents, Jeena," said Ceril. "Or have you forgotten?"

"I've forgotten nothing, brother. Dren and Brachia are children. They had nothing to do with our parents' deaths."

The anger in the male elf's eyes didn't diminish, though Dren noticed him glancing nervously in the direction of the blue gem at the top of his sister's staff.

"Human children grow up to be human adults," said Ceril. "You're a child and a fool if you think differently."

"I'm a Lord of the Council of Light as well as the high priestess of the Lady of the Tree," said Jeena. "And this is my home."

Ceril laughed. It was a vicious laugh. "Unearned titles. You're too young and inexperienced to be either of those, and you know it."

Dren thought she saw Jeena wince at the words of her brother. However, the high priestess didn't back down or avert her eyes.

"Nevertheless, you'll leave my home now peacefully, or I'll force you out. Either way, you're going to leave. Now go, and don't come back until you're ready to behave like an adult."

The blue gem at the top of the staff glowed even brighter until Dren had to raise a hand to shield her eyes.

Ceril glared at Brachia and Dren. "High priestess or not, when I come back, these pieces of human scum had best be gone. I'll not have the memory of our parents sullied by their presence."

Dren noticed Jeena's knuckles turning white where her hand grasped the staff. She half expected the silver-haired high priestess to release a blast of energy and send the male elf flying out the door. However, no blast was forthcoming.

Ceril stared at his sister for a few more seconds before turning on his heels and walking out the front door. It slammed shut with a loud bang behind him.

Dren barely breathed as she waited to see what would happen next. For once, her brother remained quiet as well. Finally, she noticed the knuckles of Jeena's hand turn a more normal color as the blue gem at the top of the elf's staff slowly returned to its original brightness. She saw the elf close her eyes and watched her lips move slightly as if mouthing words, but heard nothing.

The high priestess opened her eyes and turned to Brachia and her. "Are you all right, Brachia? Did my brother harm you?"

Brachia shook his head. "No, Jeehana. He just caught me by surprise. He ran in the door before I knew it. Once he saw me, he just started yelling. I wasn't doing anything. Honest."

"I know," said Jeena. "I apologize for my brother's actions. He's really a good elf at heart. It's just that he doesn't like…err—"

"Humans?" Dren said.

Jeena nodded her head.

Dren thought the high priestess looked embarrassed. "From my readings in the Oracle's library, I was prepared for some animosity between elves and humans," Dren said. "I guess I didn't realize the extent."

Jeena bent down and began picking up some of the scrolls that had fallen on the floor. Brachia moved forward and started helping her. After replacing her knife in its sheath, Dren did the same.

Once the task was completed, Dren looked at the elf expectantly.

The high priestess nodded her head. "You're correct, Dren. In the time of my ancestor, High Priestess Shandristiathoraxen, humans came to our lands from across the ocean. They were few at first, and those few were made welcome. Then some cataclysm occurred in their lands, and a great exodus of human refugees arrived on our shores. Those refugees were made welcome as well. My people gave them lands to call their own. However, humans are a prolific race. Soon, they pushed beyond the boundaries of the lands we gave them. Conflicts invariably happened. Elves are a peaceful race at heart, but we've been forced to push back on several occasions."

Dren nodded her head. "I read as much. My uncle is from a place that was once called the United States, on a planet called Earth. His ancestors arrived from across the ocean. They pushed the inhabitants out. I can understand your brother's animosity to a point, but there must be more to it."

"There is," said Jeena. "For one thing, humans, especially human males, are unable to control their emotions. I don't think it was that way at first, but it has been for thousands of years. Their unfettered emotions of lust and hate overwhelm emotion-sensitive female elves. I think humans have grown less able to control their emotions over the years, or perhaps we females have grown less able to protect ourselves from their thoughts. Whatever the reason, female elves try to avoid contact with human adults. Some females would rather die than be touched by a human male."

"You don't avoid us, do you?" asked Brachia.

For the first time since the arrival of Jeena's brother, Dren saw the elf smile.

"No, Brachia. I don't. The emotions of children are less intrusive than those of adult males. In truth, I think there's more to it in the case of you two. Your emotions are more controlled. I can sense them, but barely. If what you say is true about being from another dimension, I suppose that has something to do with it."

Dren suspected she'd be stepping on a sensitive subject but was determined to get to the bottom of the male elf's hatred. "Why did your brother accuse us of killing your parents?"

"I'm not sure we should talk about this now," said Jeena. "Not in front of your brother."

Brachia bristled. "I may look ten years old and even act like it at times, but I've got my father's memories and knowledge. This affects us both. We have a right to know."

"No, we don't," Dren said seeing a look in the elf's eyes that tore at her heart. "Some things are too personal to share with others."

Dren expected her brother to protest. While their father's knowledge had been transferred into Brachia's brain, his emotions and maturity level were still those of a ten-year-old boy. However, this time, her brother's response surprised her.

Brachia spoke in a voice barely above a whisper. "We lost our parents too, Jeehana." He pointed at the high priestess's staff. "They were murdered saving the device we placed inside your staff. The gnome high priestess, Rem, used the device to defeat a necromancer by closing a gate to the spiritual dimension. Your world was saved because our parents were willing to die to—"

sniff, "protect—" sniff.

Dren moved to her brother's side and put her arm around him. He buried his face in her shoulder. She heard no cries, but Brachia didn't look up for several seconds.

"I'm sorry," said Jeena. "Sometimes I forget others have hurts just as deep as mine."

The elf knelt in front of Brachia and placed her hand on his shoulder.

"My parents were also murdered. I was young at the time, so my memories are blurred. Ceril was older, and he has told me the tale often enough. My mother was a priestess of the Lady of the Tree, and my father was a lord of the Council of Light. They were traveling through the lands of the humans on their way to see the Oracle. I don't know why. Our younger sister was with them. Ceril and I were supposed to be as well, but we were detained at the last minute and couldn't go. My parents and sister never arrived at the Oracle's. A search party sent out by the Council of Light found the bodies of our parents. They'd been tortured, and my mother had been…err…."

Dren noticed the elf look at Brachia and then back at her. Dren nodded her head sympathetically. "It's all right, Jeehana. We understand. You don't need to explain."

Jeena nodded her head gratefully. Her voice became a whisper. "The body of my sister was never found. The search party found the booted tracks of a large group of humans around the camp. They found other evidence of humans as well. That's why Ceril hates your race so much."

"And you don't?" Dren asked.

Jeena closed her eyes for a few seconds before answering. "I suppose I do, deep down. I can't help it."

Brachia looked up. His eyes were red and his face was streaked with tears.

The elf gave him an apologetic smile. "I don't hate you, Brachia; nor you, Dren. You'll always be my friends."

"Well," Dren said. "If it helps any, we're from another dimension. We may look like the people you identify as humans, but we're from another planet, so there's no relation."

The three of them stood there for a minute, each lost in their own thoughts and hurts. Finally, the high priestess broke the silence.

"We should be going. It's a long walk to the Oracle's. We'll stop at the palace. I'll need to get both of you gear for our trek. It gets cold this time of year. You'll need heavy clothing and bedrolls."

The elf's comments drew Dren out of her dark thoughts. She smiled.

"Oh, we won't be walking, Jeehana."

"We won't?" asked Jeena. "Then how?"

Dren pointed at the high priestess's staff. "Do you remember how you used your staff to teleport back to the Oracle's during your last mission?" When the elf nodded, Dren continued. "When we repaired your staff last time, Brachia attuned it to the teleport platform we installed at the Oracle's. You can use the staff to teleport us all back to our lab at the Oracle's."

Brachia brushed away the last remains of his tears and smiled. "Now, won't that be a lot better than walking?"

"Yes," Jeena said returning Brachia's smile. "I do believe it will."

CHAPTER 9

The dwarves and Richard materialized in a dimly-lit hallway. Unfortunately, the hallway wasn't empty. Several bat-winged Crosioians and a few human mercenaries were walking down the corridor. Time seemed to freeze as the Crosioians, dwarves, and humans looked at each other for one eternity of a moment.

One of the Crosioians raised a hand blaster and pointed it at Storis. Before the bat creature could fire, a flash of silver appeared behind the Crosioian. Richard caught a blur of teeth and claws. The next thing he saw was a head hitting the metal deck of the floor. The head was quickly followed by a bat body minus one head.

Everything began happening at once.

The dwarves charged forward with their battle-axes and hammers swinging. Richard spun to his rear and struck out with his phase rod, catching a human mercenary on the side of the head. The phase energy's microscopic explosions decimated the mercenary's brain. The merc fell to the floor dead. A Crosioian ran for a button on the side of the wall.

"It's an alarm," said Nickelo. *"Don't let her get to it."*

Reaching out with his mind, Richard found the nerves in the Crosioian's spinal column located at the base of her skull. He wrapped them with Power and gave a twist. The bat creature fell to the floor. The claws of her hand fell short of their mark. No alarm sounded.

With the hallway to his rear clear, Richard spun around to assist his security team. He needn't have bothered. Even before completing his spin, the last of the yellow and orange dots on his heads-up display disappeared. The Crosioians and their human minions were all dead.

Felspar turned to Richard with a wild look in his eyes. "Where to next, wizard scout?"

Richard had no idea. *"Nick. Give me a schematic of the entire ship. We need to get to the engine room."*

"Unable to comply. I'm having difficult hacking into the ship's computer network. It's got the same three-way security of logic, emotion, and magic we encountered during the attack at the Academy."

"Can't we just hack our way into this ship's computer like we did that destroyer from the magical dimension last year?"

A massive amount of data began scrolling across the battle helmet's heads-up display.

"Negative, Rick. As you can see, that's not possible. Besides, the Crosioians' master computer is possessed by the demon, Zenthra. You don't want to draw attention to yourself by trying to brute force your way into any of its computers. You need something more subtle than that."

"If the demon's in charge of the Crosioians' master computer, then it's bound to already know I'm here," Richard pointed out.

"Uh...," Nickelo said, sounding unsure of himself. *"I calculate a sixty-four percent probability Zenthra has spread himself too thin. Contrary to what he may try to make others believe, the demon's not all knowing or all seeing. From what I can determine, Zenthra's forbidden from killing you by that master demon you met on Portalis. If Zenthra doesn't think you pose a direct threat to his immediate plans, he may choose to let the Crosioians handle you on their own. However, if he detects you snooping around his computers, he may decide to take direct action."*

Although Richard wasn't sure about the accuracy of his battle computer's analysis, he was a hundred percent sure he didn't want to face another demon. *"Then I guess we're screwed. We need to get to the engine room. I can see the energy output of the hyper-drive on my passive scan, but I can't go meandering around this maze of hallways trying to get there. We need a schematic of this ship."*

"I know, and we're going to get it," said Nickelo, who was beginning to sound more confident. *"We just can't let Zenthra know we're getting it."*

"Then how?" Richard said trying to prod his battle computer into giving a direct answer. Even though their conversation was taking place at near nanosecond speed, they still didn't have time to dawdle. As the master computer, the demon would be thinking at nanosecond speed also.

"If we work together," said Nickelo, *"I believe we have a seventy-two percent probability of breaking into the ship's computers enough to get what we need. I can take care of the logic and emotion if you deal with the magic. We just need to be careful."*

Richard immediately began forming an active scan. He'd much rather try something than stand around discussing options. *"You're better at this than I am. I'm giving you control of my scan. Lead the way, and I'll follow along."*

"Compliance, oh greatest of wizard scouts."

Richard followed along as his battle computer directed his scan. Before long, he sensed the scan begin touching the flows of energy moving throughout the ship. Within the space of two nanoseconds, they found the ship's security firewall. Like his previous encounter with three-way security during the attack at the Academy, he sensed a tangled knot of energy. Sections of it kept moving and changing shape.

"That's the magic part," said Nickelo.

Richard mentally nodded his head. *"No kidding. I figured that one out for myself. This isn't my first rodeo, you know."*

"Hmm," said Nickelo. *"I've got a feeling I'm going to regret giving you a copy of my book on* Cute Sayings and Slang of 20th through 21st Century America*. They're not nearly as funny when you say them."*

Richard remained quiet in order not to get caught in a banter session with his battle computer. Unlike his friend, he wasn't able to allocate separate logic threads to handle multiple things at once. At least not when he was trying to do something as complicated as unraveling magic-based computer security.

Concentrating on the task at hand, he followed the twists and turns of the magic in the security program while ignoring the non-magic parts. Its apparent movement slowed as his mind replicated its moves. Before long, the magic appeared to stop altogether. Once it did, he sensed what it was doing. He fed the results into the part of his mind shared with his battle computer.

"I still can't make heads or tails out of it," said Nickelo.

"Then we've failed?" Richard asked.

"Negative," said Nickelo. *"I'm going to merge the data you're sending with my analysis of the logic and emotions. Just give me a couple more nanoseconds."*

Merged as he was with his battle computer for the scan, Richard's mind was also operating at nanosecond speed. *"Too bad I can't think this fast all the time."*

"You'd get bored," said Nickelo. *"Trust me. I do."*

In point of fact, Richard was already getting bored. His battle computer was correct in that thinking at nanosecond speed had its pitfalls. The wait for his friend to use the information to create a hacking program was becoming interminable. Bored, Richard let his mind drift. He sensed the hundreds of computers in the destroyer's network processing mountains of data as they calculated optimum attack angles to use against the *Defiant*. He also sensed something else. Something he'd sensed before. It was the taint of demon essence.

The demon essence was faint, but it was there nevertheless. As he concentrated on the area around him, Richard sensed the demon essence begin to stir as if something was drawing its interest.

"Hurry, Nick. I don't think we've got much time. I think the demon's starting to suspect something's amiss."

Richard sensed data beginning to enter his shared space. Part of it was a schematic of the ship with a green path marking the quickest way to the engine room.

"Drop your scan, Rick. You're at sixty-one percent Power in your reserve. You may need every bit of it before this battle's over."

As soon as he dropped his active scan, Richard's mind reverted back to normal speed and his focus fell to Felspar, still waiting for an answer to his question.

"Follow me," Richard ordered. "Keep it as quiet as possible. The farther we get before an alarm sounds, the better."

Before he'd taken more than a couple of steps down the hall,

Richard stopped and turned back to the dwarves. "Try not to get a hole in your power-armor. You're going to need it in one piece before we leave."

Felspar hefted his battle-axe. "We'll do our best, but I'm thinking it's going to be easier said than done. Those bats may not cooperate. Besides, we have to get close to use our hand weapons. If you'd bothered to tell us more of your plan before we left the *Defiant*, we'd have brought range weapons."

"Yeah," said Storis. "Crossbows with magic quarrels would've been nice."

Richard nodded his head. He knew both dwarves were right, but then he hadn't really known exactly what his plan was going to be before they'd left. That had limited how much he could've explained. Since he didn't have any crossbows on him at the moment, Richard figured the dwarves would just have to do the best they could with what they had.

Nickelo sent a suggestion into their shared space. *"You could always summon range weapons from your pack."*

"It'd be a waste of energy, Nick. Normal crossbows and quarrels wouldn't do squat against power-armor. You know that as well as me. I can't summon magic items from my pack. Fortunately, I've got something better than an old-fashioned crossbow."

While continuing to run down the hall, Richard removed his 9mm pistol from its shoulder holster and attached the silencer to the end of the barrel.

Nickelo sent a feeling of approval. *"That gives you seventeen shots."*

As soon as Richard turned the first corner in the hallway, he saw two human mercenaries wearing orange jumpsuits walking his way. They were both carrying holstered sidearms. The mercenaries caught sight of them at the same time. The mercenaries turned to run back the way they'd come while simultaneously fumbling to extract their handguns. Richard put a 9mm slug in the back of each man's head. A twinge of regret passed over him, but he did his best to ignore it. He didn't like killing needlessly, but the humans had been part of the destroyer's crew. The ship was trying to kill his friends. If he had to kill every member of the crew to protect his friends, then he'd do so.

"You had to kill them, Rick. Even if they hadn't been armed, they'd still have sounded the alarm. I calculate your best course of action is to kill anyone you meet before they can alert others of your presence. Besides, if your plan works, everyone on this ship's going to be dead in a few minutes anyway."

Richard jumped over the bodies of the two mercenaries and began running toward another corner in the hallway. *"I know I had to stop them. I wish there'd been another way besides putting a hole in their heads. Why are humans on this ship anyway?"*

"No idea," replied Nickelo. *"However, you should be grateful there are. The Crosioians operate on sonic senses. With humans onboard, it looks like they've had to mark key components on their ship with visual as well as sonic markings. That's why there are lights in the hall."*

"I don't need lights. I've got my battle helmet."

"True," agreed Nickelo, *"but if your visor gets damaged in a fight, I calculate you'll be grateful for the lights. Remember when you had to fight in the dark during your first mission for* 'the One'*?"*

Richard remembered all too well.

Continuing to follow the green path on his heads-up display, Richard ran toward a set of stairs leading down into the bowels of the ship. He sensed a dozen life forms at the bottom of the stairs. With no time to consult the dwarves, Richard dove down the stairs, straight into a squad of Crosioian marines. They were all in power-armor and armed to the teeth. As he fell, Richard snapped off two shots from his 9mm at the armored head of the nearest bat creature. The metal slugs bounced off.

"Did you really think that was going to work?" asked Nickelo. *"Your 9mm is for soft targets. These marines are wearing heavy armor. Even a plasma round would have to hit a weak spot in a joint to penetrate."*

Richard landed on a marine with a full-body block, sending both the Crosioian and him tumbling to the metal deck. Richard came up swinging with his phase rod in full-destructive mode. He caught one of the bat creatures in the metallic joint near the base of her neck. The phase rod bounced off the tough armor, but not before the phase energy penetrated to her spinal column. The sub-atomic explosions of phase energy turned the spine and nerves into a mixture of dust and blood. At the same time, he sensed the demon essence inside his phase rod suck out the life force of the creature.

Switching directions with his phase rod, Richard swung at a nearby marine. The bat creature was trying to bring her plasma rifle in line with a dwarf's back. The phase rod hit the bat's rifle and broke it in half. The rifle exploded. The blast of plasma energy flung both the marine and Richard in opposite directions. Richard was up in a flash swinging his phase rod at anything in range.

The area below the stairs turned into a jumble of armored bodies and plasma rounds as Crosioians and dwarves began firing at each other. Alarms began sounding throughout the ship.

"Well, so much for surprise," said Nickelo.

Richard was busy dodging all the plasma beams and balls of magic crisscrossing around him. He sensed more than saw one of the marines aiming a weapon at his back. Throwing up a hasty defensive shield behind him, he angled it toward the ceiling just as the marine fired a burst of plasma rounds. The rounds ricocheted upwards and hit the ceiling before bouncing back down. Several of the plasma rounds hit one of the Crosioian marines in the chest. One of the high-energy rounds must have found a weak spot in the marine's armor because Richard sensed the round tear through the bat creature's heart.

"You were lucky," said Nickelo as if he was commenting on something as casual as the weather. *"Those rounds could just as easily have hit a member of your own security team."*

Richard started to swing his phase rod at the head of another marine, but Felspar beat him to it. With a mighty stroke of his battle-axe, the dwarf sent the armored head of the bat creature flying through the air. The head hit a wall and clattered to the floor below.

"Sharp axe," Richard commented to his battle computer. *"The Crosioians' power-armor is nearly as tough as my battle suit."*

"What'd you expect?" asked Nickelo. *"Sergeant Hendricks spent more than two months coating the dwarves' weapons with titanium. Once he installed some of those blue gems you found for* 'the One' *in the handles of their weapons, they became very dangerous."*

"So I see. I guess those spells Comstar and the gnomes added

to the creallium edges didn't hurt either."

"No doubt," replied Nickelo.

Looking around for a new target, all Richard saw were a half-dozen dwarves and a silver dragon standing in the middle of the lifeless bodies of a dozen bloody and battered Crosioian marines. Bright Wing was still gripping a marine in her mouth. She shook her head from side to side in a manner similar to a dog killing a rat. The dragon must have noticed him watching her because she gave the dead marine a final shake before letting the body drop to the floor. The sound of the heavy armor hitting the metal deck echoed through the now quiet hall.

Richard noticed the sudden silence. *"The alarms have stopped. Why?"*

"I calculate a ninety-two percent probability the ship's commander figures his crew already knows something's up," replied Nickelo. *"Why bother continuing to sound an alarm?"*

Richard sensed two lines of Power snaking out in his direction. He reached out with a line of his own Power and knocked one of the lines aside. The second line unsuccessfully tried probing his Power reserve before withdrawing. Nothing indicating the owners of the lines of Power showed up on Richard's passive scan. He turned in the direction the lines of Power had come from expecting to see a couple of magic users. Although mages could be tough when they were at a distance, he had a feeling they wouldn't last long in the confined space of the hallway. Plus, he had his security team and Bright Wing to back him up.

Richard completed his turn and saw who was standing in a side hall. "Damn it."

Located only a few meters down the hall were two of the bat-winged Crosioians wearing the black armor of scouts. Both of the scouts carried short-stabbing spears with glowing points of phase energy. They also held plasma rifles, which were leveled at Richard and the dwarves. Neither the scouts nor their phase spears registered on Richard's passive scan.

"Hmmm," said Nickelo. *"The last thing you need is Crosioian scouts. They've got stealth shields up. I'm not picking up either of them with my sensors. They're not amateurs."*

Felspar and two of the other dwarves started to move toward the scouts with their weapons raised.

Waving the dwarves back, Richard shouted, "No! They're scouts. You can't take them."

"I'm not scared of—" began Felspar.

"I said *no*," Richard repeated in a much harsher tone than he'd used the first time. He wasn't scared of the scouts either, but he was respectful of their abilities. Whenever he'd fought teams of Crosioian scouts in the past, he'd always had the help of the dolgars or another wizard scout. He wasn't sure if he could handle two at once by himself. However, he was very sure the dwarves weren't a match for them. His security team would fight valiantly, but he knew they'd be dead within thirty seconds of the start of any fight.

"But—" argued Felspar.

"No buts," Richard said. "Get Bright Wing to the engine room. That's an order."

"You can't take two scouts on by yourself," Nickelo said in a voice that sounded almost like a plea for sanity. *"Let the dwarves help you. Some of them might survive. I calculate a forty-three percent probability you can beat the scouts if the dwarves and Bright Wing help."*

"I stay with you, brother," said Bright Wing.

Richard sent back an emotion that meant 'no.'

"I need you to go with Felspar and the others. You've got to overload the ship's hyper-drive."

Sensing angry emotions building within the dragon, Richard cut off any pending defiance with a series of emotions of his own. *"I'm depending on you, sister,"* Richard told her. *"I'll be along shortly."*

When Bright Wing continued to hesitate, Richard resorted to her sense of honor. *"You told me you owed me your life for rescuing you from the Dragars. I'm asking you now to do what I say. Please."*

The dragon turned and began running down the hall toward the engine room. The dwarves were hot on her heels. Surprisingly, neither of the Crosioians attempted to fire at the retreating dwarves or try to stop them.

"You're him," said a metallic-sounding voice from a translator attached to one of the scouts' waist belts.

"All of our scouts have been given your Power frequency," said the second scout who happened to be the larger of the two. "We can smell traces of your Power on the short ones. Great honor will go to the one who takes your head."

"The honor will be mine," said the smaller scout. "Your head will go well with the others on my trophy wall."

"No," said the larger scout. "I'll tend to this one. You must stop the short ones before they damage the ship's engine."

"I smelled this one first," argued the smaller scout. "The honor shall be—"

The larger scout spread her wings in a display of authority. "I gave an order. You will obey."

The smaller scout made hissing sounds. The translator made a series of unintelligible screeches. Richard assumed even its advanced electronics wasn't able to interpret whatever curse words the Crosioian was uttering. Despite her apparent bravado, the smaller scout meekly turned to follow Bright Wing and the security team. Richard had a feeling the scout would have no trouble overtaking and killing them. He knew he wouldn't if the situation was reversed.

"She'll kill them all before Bright Wing can do her part," warned Nickelo. *"You're committed now. You've got to keep both scouts here."*

"How?" Richard asked. *"I seriously doubt asking politely will do the trick."*

His battle computer remained silent. Richard knew it meant Nickelo couldn't come up with a logical plan with better than a five percent probability of success.

Fine, Richard thought. *If there's no logical way, then I'll have to try something emotional.*

"Coward!" Richard yelled at the back of the smaller scout. "You're just like all the other scouts I've killed over the years. You talk big, but I can smell the fear that causes you to run away. Any heads on your trophy wall are probably from old women and children."

In a motion too fast to follow, the scout spun and raised her plasma rifle to fire.

"He's baiting you, fool," said the larger scout. "Do as I ordered. Stop the others. I'll deal with this human."

The smaller scout hesitated but didn't turn to leave. Richard noticed the end of her rifle barrel shaking slightly. He'd hit a nerve.

"Good job, Rick," said Nickelo. *"Keep her attention. Don't let her gather her thoughts."*

Richard laughed. He tried to put as much contempt into his next words as possible. "It's as I expected. Only cowards use rifles and pistols." Richard laughed again. "I'm told the first scout I killed was the Crosioians' best. At least she was honorable enough to use her phase spear and scout abilities when we fought." Richard paused for effect. "Even if she did beg for mercy like a weak human before I ended her miserable life."

Richard hoped his words would cause one or both of the scouts to scream in anger and attack. An angry enemy was vulnerable.

"If I can take out one of the scouts quickly," Richard reasoned, *"then my odds of surviving this encounter will increase dramatically."*

"I estimate a seventy-two percent probability the scouts will kill you even if they lose their tempers," said Nickelo. *"Too bad. I was just getting used to having you around."*

CHAPTER 10

As it turned out, neither of the scouts screamed or attacked. Instead, they appeared to come to a consensus. Both scouts let their plasma rifles slide off their shoulders. Their weapons clattered noisily onto the metal deck. Once unencumbered, the scouts maneuvered to positions on opposite sides of Richard.

While the bat creatures repositioned, Richard removed the silencer from his 9mm and replaced both the pistol and silencer into his shoulder holster. As he did so, he began backing toward the relatively clear area near the stairwell. There wasn't much room, but it was the best option he had at the moment.

The two scouts simultaneously sent lines of Power at Richard's chest. He had the feeling they'd used the coordinated attack in battle more than once. He batted one line away with his own Power. The other Crosioian's line began wrapping around Richard's heart. Before the scout could squeeze, Richard diverted his own line of Power and knocked the attacking line away.

"I can't counter two attacks at the same time," Richard said hoping his battle computer had a solution to his dilemma.

"If you want to stay alive, you'd better learn real fast."

Nickelo's reply didn't give him much confidence.

The Crosioian scouts made a half dozen more attacks using their lines of Power. By luck as much as by skill, Richard was able to defend himself without taking any serious damage. Apparently growing frustrated with the failure of their psionic attacks, the scouts switched to physical ones. They both charged at the same time, swinging their phase spears.

The tips of their spears formed blurring arcs as the scouts pressed their attacks. The strikes came too fast for a mere human to counter. Fortunately, Richard wasn't a mere human. He was a wizard scout. Plus, his battle computer was the most advanced of its kind in the galaxy. Despite the double attacks, he somehow blocked their strikes.

"You're doing well, Rick."

"Thanks to my battle suit," Richard said as he continued fending off the scouts' blows. *"If it wasn't for the suit's assistors, their attacks would be too strong for me to stop."*

"Aren't you going to thank me also?" asked Nickelo. *"I'm the one adjusting the assistors for maximum efficiency. At least give me some of the credit?"*

"Thanks," was all Richard had time to say.

"Unfortunately," said Nickelo, *"the Crosioians' battle computers are helping them as well. I'm doing my best to anticipate their actions, but if you don't change your tactics soon, one of those scouts is going to get an attack through your defenses."*

No sooner had his battle computer completed his thought than one of the scouts feinted at Richard's chest with her spear before changing direction toward his right leg. He attempted to counter with his phase rod but was a microsecond too slow. The creallium point of the Crosioian's spear pierced the tough leg-armor of his battle suit and tore a deep hole into the flesh of his thigh. With an involuntary scream of pain, Richard kicked back hard with his left leg. At the same time, he swung his phase rod wildly in the hopes of keeping the scout at bay.

Suddenly, Richard's mind went into a time-freeze. He was frozen in midair. The scouts were frozen as well. The larger of the scouts was in the middle of thrusting her phase spear directly at Richard's exposed chest.

"This is crazy. What good is a time-freeze if I can't control it? And why does it happen anyway?"

"Why?" asked Nickelo. *"I suppose it's because* 'the One' *put part of his essence in you when you were an embryo. I calculate that's why you can interact with computers in ways no other wizard scouts are able. Surely you don't think other scouts can*

communicate with their battle computers at hyper-speed like you."

In truth, Richard had assumed just that. He'd taken for granted his friends had the same relationship with their battle computers that he had with his.

"Well, you assumed wrong," said Nickelo intruding upon his thoughts.

"What good is this accomplishing? Everything around me is going slower than an ice comet stuck in Hacon's rings. Doing anything useful when everything around me is going so slow is nearly impossible."

"Tell me about it. You're preaching to the choir, Rick. I deal with this every nanosecond of my existence. However, such is my lot in life. As for you, I calculate the stress of the situation brought this on. I'd bet a new isotopic battery when the time-freeze is over, you're going to wish it had lasted a little longer. You do see the phase spear heading for your chest, don't you? So my advice is to take advantage of this time while you can."

Richard knew Nickelo was right but refused to admit it to his battle computer. He decided to take a moment to survey the area around him. Unfortunately, he couldn't make his eyes move during a time-freeze, so his visual input was limited. His gaze was currently too focused on the point of the scout's phase spear to be useful. Thankfully, the input from his passive scan was clearly imprinted in his shared space. He could sense the energy output of everything around him, even frozen in time as it was.

Normally, Richard only considered the energy output from other life forms. Everything, even inanimate objects, gave off at least some residual Power. The combination of Power readings from both living and inanimate objects was usually too convoluted to be useful. His mind could only assimilate so much information at once. That's why he normally only monitored life forms. With his mind now operating at hyper-speed, things were different. Reaching out with his mind, he drew in as much data from his surroundings as possible. The amount of data was overwhelming.

"Nick, help me make sense of this information. Correlate it with the schematics of this ship. I want to know what's above, below, and in all the rooms around us."

A schematic of the destroyer appeared on Richard's heads-up display, then wavered. Images of objects were suddenly overlaid on top of the rooms displayed on layers of blueprints. Many of the objects had numbers near them.

"What's those numbers?" Richard asked.

"Percentages. Data from your passive scan's too generic to allow me to determine what an object is with a hundred percent accuracy."

"Can I use an active scan to get better information?"

"Not while you're in a time-freeze. Even an active scan takes time to do its job."

Richard thought he saw a flaw in his battle computer's answer. *"I just sent out my passive scan to get all this data. Surely my active scan is just as fast."*

"Actually, you didn't send out your passive scan. It was already activated. All you did was allow the information it had already accumulated to enter the shared space in your mind."

"But—"

"There are no buts. Everything we're doing is happening in the space of a single nanosecond. Heck, if you could interact with the physical space around you with your mind, you could just send out a line of Power and break the links of those scouts to their Power reserves. However, you can't, so just deal with it. Now stop wasting time and think of a plan before your mind shifts back to normal speed."

A part of Richard wanted to argue further. However, one look at the tip of the scout's phase spear heading his way changed his mind. He really did need a plan. Rotating the schematics of the ship, Richard tried to find something—anything—that would give him an edge. The image of a large object in the area above the stairway drew his attention. The object had the number 87 imprinted near it.

"What's that?" Richard asked.

"It's some type of electrical generator," answered Nickelo. *"Or at least, there's an eighty-seven percent probability it's a generator. I suppose it could be something else."*

"It looks big. Is it heavy?"

"Based upon the stress on the ceiling's brace beams, I calculate it's at least thirty metric tons. Why?"

Richard compared the outline of the generator above with the objects at his level near the stairway.

"Oh, Rick," said Nickelo with a note of admiration. *"Sometimes you really surprise me. I think that's why I like being your battle computer. You make life so interesting."*

"Since you're obviously reading my thoughts, tell me this. Will it work?"

"I guess we'll soon see," replied Nickelo. *"I've a feeling this little time-freeze of yours is about to end."*

Richard glanced at the Power in his reserve. *Less than half.*

"It's at forty-one percent," corrected Nickelo. *"Shifting the entire security team and yourself into the void at the same time was expensive."*

"Do I have the Power to do what I need to, or don't I?"

"It'll be close, Rick. Maybe you should give me control of your Power for efficiency's sake. We won't have time for a second chance."

Richard agreed. Everything would have to be done near instantaneously to make it work. Even now, he could feel the physical world around him starting to speed up. It was now or never.

Forming his Power, Richard gave control of it to his battle computer. He also made sure the override on his battle suit was activated. The scout's incoming phase spear was too close for comfort.

Time shifted back to normal.

Everything seemed to happen at once. Richard felt his battle suit twist to the side. The scout's phase spear missed his chest but got close enough to gouge a shallow groove in the side of his battle suit. At the same time his suit was twisting, Richard sensed his Power wrap around him and the metal plating of the ceiling above the stairway. His Power shimmered. Both the ceiling and his body shifted into the void at the same time. Down came the generator straight through the now translucent ceiling.

Thirty metric tons of the generator's metallic mass engulfed everything below it, including Richard. Blackness blocked out all visual references. As he'd hoped, the generator had fallen on both of the Crosioian scouts. Richard said a silent prayer that neither of the scouts were shifters.

Taking back control of his Power and his battle suit, Richard cut off the dimensional shift of the ceiling letting the metal beams and plates of the ceiling shift back into the physical dimension. Using his telekinesis, Richard moved laterally until he was clear of the generator, then shifted out of the void.

The arm of one of the scouts protruded from underneath the bottom of the generator. Although the arm was drenched in blood, its clawed fingers were scratching against the floor as if trying to pull the bat creature's body free. Richard sensed Power from the scout's reserve trying to heal its crushed body, but to no avail. The continual damage from the weight of the generator was too much for the scout's limited Power reserve. Within only a few seconds, the bat's clawed hand made a final spasm of movement. Richard sensed the last of the Power in the scout's reserve dissipate into the universe. The twitching claws grew still. Richard didn't need his battle computer to tell him the scout was dead.

"Move!" shouted Nickelo.

Richard's right leg was nearly useless from his previous wound, but he still had the Power from his telekinesis wrapped around his body. He levitated hard to the right just as a phase spear thrust outward from the center of the generator. The phase spear was followed by the form of the smaller Crosioian scout, which was slightly translucent. She was in the void.

"How?" Richard asked.

"I guess she's a shifter," said Nickelo. *"She must have a good battle computer to boot. Your trick with the generator was too fast for even a bat's reflexes. I thought sure you'd catch them both by surprise. Oh, well. Live and learn."*

At the moment, Richard wasn't sure he was going to live long enough to be able to learn from the error of his ways. As soon as the scout cleared the generator, she began thrusting her spear wildly in an attempt to pin him to the wall with its deadly point. Richard knocked the spear aside with his phase rod. Red and blue sparks flew into the air as the two opposing sets of phase energy made contact.

"You're down to eight percent Power," said Nickelo. *"Recommend you stop using your telekinesis as soon as possible."*

Richard had an urge to tell his battle computer what he could do with his recommendation. His telekinesis was the only thing keeping him out of reach of the scout's spear. His right leg was still useless.

"Your leg should be healed well enough to bear your weight in four seconds," said Nickelo.

Richard levitated his body out of the way of another thrust. He had a feeling the odds he'd be alive in four seconds were growing increasingly smaller. He was hurt. The scout wasn't. If the situation had been reversed, Richard was sure he could've finished her with no problem. Then he sensed the scout wrap her spear with Power.

"Watch out!" warned Nickelo. *"She's going to use telekinesis to speed up her next thrust."* In what sounded like a note of admiration, Richard's battle computer added, *"She must have one smart battle computer."*

The scout's use of Power gave Richard an idea. Sending out a line of his own Power, he found the link to the scout's Power reserve. As soon as he did, he knew he had her.

"We're in luck," Richard said. *"It's not even booby-trapped."*

Apparently realizing her danger, the scout tried to shift her Power from her spear in an attempt to knock his Power aside. She was too late. With a twist of his Power, Richard put a kink in the scout's link.

The scout stumbled slightly, but to her credit, she continued thrusting her spear in a vain attempt to kill her opponent. Richard used his telekinesis to knock her thrust to the side. At the same time, he shoved the tip of his phase rod into the bat creature's throat. The phase rod glanced off the Crosioian's tough armor, but not before the phase energy did its job. The sub-atomic explosions tore apart the inside of the scout's throat as the demon essence drained her life force. The scout grabbed her neck, dropping her phase spear to the deck. With a reverse swing of his phase rod, Richard knocked the scout's legs out from underneath her. She fell to the floor.

"I calculate your leg can bear your weight now," said Nickelo.

Shutting down his telekinesis to conserve Power, Richard half fell, half dived at the scout. As he did so, he swung his phase rod at her head. The scout's armor cracked under his blow. He sensed the demon essence suck out the last of the scout's life force. The scout stopped moving. With the link to her Power reserve out of commission, she was just a normal, giant-sized bat. The blue dot on his passive scan that had been marking the location of the scout disappeared. She was dead.

Richard stood up but had no time to celebrate. The sound of distant explosions told him his security team was meeting heavy resistance.

Limping at first, Richard's pace quickly increased as his self-heal ability finished closing his wound. Within fifteen seconds, his leg was nearly back to normal.

"Too bad we can't say the same for your battle suit," said Nickelo. *"The scout's spear thrust to your leg took out one of the suit's backup assistors."*

"Not to mention the seal's broken," Richard added.

"Yeah, that too," agreed Nickelo.

As he continued down the hallway, Richard noticed signs of battle. Charred walls along one intersection gave testimony to the liberal use of fireball rounds by at least one of the dwarves. Soon, bodies began littering the hallways and side rooms. Richard breathed a sigh of relief. All of the bodies were tall. None of them were dwarves.

"I'm using the information from your passive scan to mark the dwarves in white on your heads-up display," said Nickelo. *"They're all safe, so stop worrying."*

The sounds of the battle ahead ended. Richard was momentarily worried until he confirmed with his passive scan that all six dwarves and Bright Wing lived. The life force of two of the dwarves was less than normal, but they were still alive.

Jumping down a final staircase, Richard landed on top a heap of bodies. Several of the bodies were missing heads or limbs. A glance around the room confirmed the battle had been hard. Thankfully, it was over at least for now.

"'Bout time, wizard scout," said Storis. He was kneeling down to cover an adjacent hallway with his M12. "Jasper and Mica got hit. Felspar's with them."

After verifying Bright Wing was in the hyper-drive doing her thing, Richard turned his attention to the dwarves. Felspar and the two wounded dwarves were hiding behind a solid-looking computer console. Reaching out with his mind, Richard did a quick survey of the dwarves' injuries. By the time he knelt down at their sides, he had a plan.

Felspar acknowledged Richard with a nod of his head. "Glad

you made it. Did the scouts give you any trouble?"

Pointing to the hole in his leg armor, Richard said, "A little. However, they won't be troubling anyone ever again."

Felspar smiled and rose to his feet. "I'm going to cover that stairway. I've got a feeling we'll be having more company soon."

"Understood," Richard said. "In the meantime, I'll take care of these two."

Ripping off one of his gloves, Richard opened the chest armor of Jasper's power-suit. He saw two cauterized holes in the right side of the dwarf's chest. Placing his hand over the holes, he imagined how the dwarf's body should be and compared that to how it was now, then drew the difference inside himself. Pain in the right side of his chest drove the air out of his lungs. He bit back a cry of pain. The acquired injury hurt, but he didn't pass out. Within a dozen heartbeats, most of the pain resided. When his eyes cleared, he felt a pair of hands holding him up. They belonged to Jasper.

"Thanks, wizard scout."

Richard nodded his head but didn't reply. The two holes in his lung hadn't quite closed over yet. He started to place his hand over a hole in Mica's leg armor.

Mica shook his head. "No. I'll be fine until we get back to the ship. The phase round went all the way through."

Richard didn't argue with the dwarf. Treating wounds as an emp-healer was no great thrill.

A wave of emotion swept over Richard.

"Brother," said Bright Wing. *"I've overloaded the destroyer's energy source. The hyper-drive will self-destruct soon."*

"Nick?" Richard asked.

"The dragon's correct. I calculate the ship will blow in thirty-two seconds."

Richard cursed out loud. Things were happening quicker than he'd planned. Pulling off his dimensional pack, he imagined a set of vacuum patches he'd seen Charlie and Daniel use to temporarily patch power-armor. A small amount of Power left his reserve. Opening his pack, Richard pulled out a half-dozen packets filled with a gooey gray liquid. He shoved the packets into Mica's hands.

"Get these to Felspar," Richard ordered. "Patch up anyone who's got a hole in their armor. That includes you. We're getting out of this place."

Mica used his good arm to shove himself to a standing position. "Roger that. I'm tired of this place anyway."

"Twenty-five seconds," said Nickelo.

Richard quickly pulled off his own pants and shoved them in the opening of his dimensional pack. He closed the pack's flap again. He imagined an undamaged set of battle suit pants. He didn't sense any Power leave his reserve, but wasn't concerned. His battle suit and standard weapons were freebies as far as Power usage was concerned. Lifting the flap, Richard pulled out a set of battle suit pants. They looked like they'd just been taken out of their original shipping box.

"Eighteen seconds," said Nickelo.

As he shoved his legs into the pants, Richard called for Felspar and the other dwarves to gather around him. Before anyone could respond, a stream of plasma rounds came down the stairway and began bouncing around the engine room. More streams of plasma rounds came down a side hallway as the dwarves dove for cover.

The dwarves returned fire in the form of magic, phase, and plasma energy. Richard saw Jasper aim her M12 at the hallway and loose two balls of magic out of a wooden shaft attached to the bottom of the M12's barrel. The magical energy flew down the hallway.

Boom! Boom!

"Fireballs," observed Nickelo.

"Nice weapon," Richard told his battle computer. *"I need to get Sergeant Hendricks to attach one of those magic wands underneath my M12."*

"Good luck with that. The odds 'the One' *would allow you to use it on missions are low to non-existent.*

"Never mind 'the One,'*"* Richard said. *"I'm more worried about how to get us out of here at the moment. I'm going to gather my remaining Power from my reserve. Help me wrap it around the dwarves. I'm having trouble getting it around Storis and Mica."*

"No can do, Rick."

Richard pulled his .44 caliber AutoMag out of its holster. He sent two of the heavy rounds at a bat-shaped head peeking around the top of the stairs. One of the brerellium rounds struck the center of the bat's forehead. She tumbled out of sight.

"What do you mean you can't? I said help me wrap the dwarves with Power. That's an order."

"I mean, I can't," said Nickelo. *"Neither can you. You're down to six percent Power. That's not enough to dimensional shift all the dwarves and yourself. You're trying to spread your Power too thin. I calculate you're going to have to leave at least two of them behind."*

"Forget it! I'm a marine. We don't leave anyone behind."

"Then you're all going to die," replied Nickelo. *"And by the way, you've got twelve seconds before the hyper-drive blows. I guess I'll see you on the other side."*

Richard wracked his brain for any ideas but had little hope. He sent out a call to the dolgars. He got no response.

Nick! Connect me to Margery. Now!

A nanosecond later, a consciousness inserted itself into the space Richard shared with his battle computer.

"Rick," said Margery. *"This is dangerous. Nick has set up a communications line from him to Jonathan to me and back to you. It could have unforeseen side effects."*

Richard didn't care. He'd used a similar setup to communicate with the commandant during the Crosioians' attack on Velos.

Switching to command voice, Richard said, *"Forget side-effects. Situation report."*

A stream of data entered Richard's shared space. He sensed more than saw what was happening. Sergeant Ron had stopped running. The *Defiant* was now trading fire with the other destroyer. The little recon ship was firing both its magic and technology-based weapons. Both Matthew's zipper and Tia's dragon-fighter were adding their firepower to that of the *Defiant*.

Another consciousness intruded into Richard's link with Margery. He recognized the frequency of the other presence. It was his friend Stella's battle computer, Jonathan.

Richard made a decision and gave his commands. In the space of four heartbeats, he sensed a closed link that was already attached to him reopen. It was the one-way link his friend Stella had attached to him during their Academy days. Power came rushing down the link filling Richard's reserve.

"Power is now at one hundred percent," said Nickelo. *"Oh, and the hyper-drive will explode in five seconds."*

Wasting no time, Richard wrapped all six dwarves and himself with Power. He caused the Power to shimmer.

"Time to go, Bright Wing," Richard said as he shifted everyone into the void and levitated them out of the destroyer with his telekinesis. As soon as the entire team was outside the skin of the destroyer, it flew out of sight leaving his group adrift in space. A few seconds later, a bright flash was seen in the distance.

"The destroyer has been disintegrated," said Nickelo. *"Recommend you shift out of the void to conserve Power. Stella and the others are still fighting the Crosioians' boarding party. I doubt she'll be able to share Power with you again anytime soon."*

Richard shifted everyone back into the physical dimension. He breathed a sigh of relief when he counted six dwarves plus Bright Wing.

"Well," said Nickelo, *"since none of the dwarves have exploded inside their suits, I calculate they got the holes in their armor patched in time."*

"Can it, Nick. Contact Margery again. Have her send Matt back with the zipper to pick us up."

"Uh, Margery says they're a little busy at the moment. We'll have to wait a few minutes."

The few minutes turned into thirty before Sergeant Ron was able to send a rescue party for Richard and the others. When rescue finally arrived, it was in the form of the *Defiant* herself. An orange tractor beam shot out of the recon ship and began pulling Richard and the others into one of the *Defiant's* airlocks.

"I'll see you inside, brother," said Bright Wing as she blinked out.

Once the airlock sealed and the inner door opened, Richard saw his friends Tam, Telsa, Stella, Trinity, and Jerad on the other side of the doorway. He wasn't surprised at their appearance since he'd already picked up their frequencies with his passive scan. He unsealed his battle helmet and put it in three-quarters mode and smiled at his friends until he noticed the face of someone he hadn't picked up with his passive scan.

Standing off to one side was a short, toad-faced man wearing the black armor of a wizard scout. The man was his brother and ex-TAC officer Gaston Myers.

CHAPTER 11

When Jeena materialized, she immediately recognized the children's lab at the Oracle's.

No, Jeena thought. *Not children; at least Dren's not. Brachia's still a child, but Dren's physically a little older than me now.*

Although she'd had the book knowledge of aging differences from her years at school, dealing with it in real life was awkward. While Dren and Brachia were humans, Jeena still liked them. Thinking of them growing old in only a few decades was hard to accept. If Dren had been an elf, Jeena was sure they would've been very good friends.

Looking down, Jeena noticed they were standing on the strange teleport-platform she'd used before. Its surface looked similar to glass, but the children had called it by a different name; plastic.

"Well, here we are," said Brachia as he jumped off the platform and ran to one of the many plastic boxes with flashing lights scattered around the room. "I told you it would work."

Jeena glanced at her staff. A few seconds ago, they'd been in her kitchen cleaning up after a hasty meal. When they'd finished, she touched the runes on her staff in the order the children instructed. The blue gem glowed so bright she'd been forced to close her eyes. A second later, they appeared in the children's lab.

Since Brachia seemed to be totally engrossed with touching various controls on his computers, Jeena decided to direct some of her many questions to the boy's sister.

"So, can I use my staff to teleport back to Silverton once my mission is complete?"

"Uh…, no," said Dren. "Sorry. We had to hard code your staff to the coordinates of this platform. However, you can use it to come here whenever you want."

Jeena noticed the teenager think for a moment before speaking again.

"Of course, you'd have to walk back to Silverton since the staff only teleports one way. That's better than walking both ways, isn't it?"

Nodding her head in agreement, Jeena stepped off the platform. "You've got that right."

After surveying the room for a few seconds, Jeena said, "There's more of your computer boxes in here than I remember."

"Oh, yeah," said Dren. "I had a lot of equipment stockpiled at the Oracle's before Brachia and I first arrived. A lot of it was in storerooms when you were here the last time. Brachia and I've been working on time displacement in an attempt to figure out how we can get back home."

Jeena nodded her head sympathetically. "I'm guessing since you're both still here that you haven't had much luck."

"No," admitted Dren. "However, we've learned lots of interesting stuff about time travel. It just hasn't helped us return to our home in the future."

Placing her right hand on one of the computer boxes, Jeena sensed the flows of energy inside it. All of the Lady's priests and priestesses were sensitive to flows of Power. Her brother, Ceril, and she were especially adept at manipulating flows of energy.

Reaching out with her mind, Jeena followed the flow of energy moving through the computer. The flow met with other flows outside the plastic box.

"All of the computers in this room are connected," Jeena said.

Looking a little surprised, Dren said, "Yes. They're all connected to a subnet of the tele-network. How'd you know?"

Jeena removed her hand from the computer and looked at Dren. "I sensed it. The energy powering your computers reminds me of magic in some ways. Perhaps your technology and our magic are not as different as it first seems."

Dren nodded. "I think you're right. The Oracle says magic is just another way to do the same things my people do with technology."

Jeena decided to try probing the human girl for more information before she met with the Oracle. "You implied you haven't had any luck building anything to return you to the future. Yet you said our mission will be in the future."

Pursing her lips, Dren said, "Yes, it does seem contradictory, doesn't it? The Oracle says not even major demons or similar beings can travel to the future on their own. Someone in the future can bring someone in the past to their time, but no one in the past can go to the future without being brought there."

Dren shook her head. "Actually, that's not exactly right. After all, we're all traveling to the future right now. The only problem is we're doing it one second at a time." She smiled. "It's called aging."

Jeena smiled back. "So it is. Hopefully, that's not the way the Oracle is planning on having us travel to the future. I'm not sure how far in the future he needs us to go, but if it's to your time, I think we'd get a little bored sitting around waiting for the future to get here."

Dren nodded her head in agreement and smiled back. "Not to mention the fact that Brachia and I would die of old age before we got far enough in the future to get to our time."

"So how are we going to get there," Jeena asked trying to be more serious.

Dren gave a knowing smile. "Someone from the future is going to bring us there."

"Who?" Jeena asked.

Dren winked. "That's easy; Keka."

CHAPTER 12

The confined space of his quarters on the *Defiant* barely held Richard and his friends. To top it off, the elf, Comstar sat on the room's top bunk trying to study his spell book. With a look of royal indifference, Comstar interrupted Richard as he began another tirade on why he disliked having ex-TAC Officer Myers onboard.

"Perhaps I should leave," said Comstar. "After all, I'm not familiar with this Gaston Myers."

Richard shook his head. "No, please stay. We'll be leaving soon. You can consider yourself lucky not to have had the pleasure of meeting the man."

"I think you've got Gaston wrong," said Telsa who was ever the one to look at the best in people. "He was just doing his job at the Academy. If you'd seen him on the *Starlight* leading the fight against the Crosioian boarding party, I think you'd have a different opinion."

Richard glanced up at Telsa from where he sat on the bottom bunk next to Jerad and Trinity. Even with Telsa standing and him sitting, the top of her head was barely above his. He suspected his friend was probably the shortest wizard scout in the Empire.

"She is," chimed in Nickelo privately, *"but don't get her riled. She's a battle-hardened wizard scout now. The novice cadet you knew at the Academy is long gone."*

Richard didn't bother disagreeing. He'd read reports on a couple of Telsa's missions. She could be a wildcat when the need arose.

"Telsa's right," said Tam from the room's only chair next to the desk. "Myers took charge and organized the defense. He saved a lot of lives today."

"Not you too, Tam," Richard said suddenly feeling outnumbered. "Myers was a jerk at the Academy. He'll always be a jerk as far as I'm concerned."

Jerad rose from where he sat next to Richard, then looked down and added his two credits to the discussion. "Well, jerk or not, Myers is one heck of a fighter. The boarding party had two quads of Crosioian scouts with over a hundred marines. Myers took on four of the scouts all by himself."

Richard looked at Trinity for support. The dark-haired wizard scout shrugged her shoulders before standing up to join Jerad.

"Sorry, Rick," said Trinity. "They're right. I've worked with Gaston in the past. He's a great wizard scout. He's pulled my solar panel out of a meteor storm more than once."

Outnumbered as he was, Richard gave up the argument, but he refused to change his mind. Myers had made his life a living hell during his Academy years. Richard doubted he'd ever change his opinion of the man.

"Well, we'll just have to agree to disagree," Richard replied trying to be tactful. "I'm just thankful you all made it out of the fight alive." Remembering his manners, Richard looked at Stella. "By the way, I owe you my life, again. If you hadn't shared your Power with me, my whole team would've died."

Stella's chest turned a slightly darker gray. She shrugged her shoulders in an effort to make light of Richard's thanks and made a rasping sound. The translator attached to her belt said, "You friend. You do same for me."

Richard wasn't so sure, but he didn't give voice to his doubts. "Nevertheless, thanks. Now, does anyone want a tour of the ship? She's small, but she packs quite a punch."

"So we noticed," laughed Jerad. "Unfortunately, Trinity and I've got things to do, so we'll have to take a rain check. We've got to talk to Sergeant Ron now. Myers has called a meeting in thirty minutes in the galley. We'll meet you there."

Richard nodded his head. "Fine. See you then."

Once the two wizard scouts left, Richard looked at the others.

"Any other takers?"

Telsa flashed a cheerful smile. "Sure, I'll go. The *Defiant* is one of the worst kept secrets in the galaxy. Any soldier worth a hoot has heard about the little recon ship that can take on a dreadnaught and come out asking for more."

"We didn't take on a dreadnaught," Richard protested. He assumed his friend was referring to the battle they'd had a few months previous. "The dimensional gate closed before the dreadnaught had a chance to get into the fight."

Tam rose from her chair. Her dark eyes sparkled mischievously. "Don't try and be modest, buddy. I was able to get the poop straight from my contacts in the mercs. The *Defiant* took out a destroyer and another recon ship. Not to mention she took on two destroyers today and came out on top."

"So I take that's a yes on the tour," Richard said.

"You bet," grinned Tam. "Lead the way."

"Stella?" Richard asked. "Comstar?"

"We go engine room?" asked Stella turning a slightly darker gray for some reason.

"Of course," Richard replied. "I want you to meet my friends, Charlie and Daniel."

Stella's chest turned an even darker shade of gray. Richard was going to say something, but Comstar spoke first.

"I'll pass, wizard scout." Comstar held up his spell book. "I've got to memorize a few spells. We used up a lot of ammo in the battle. Sergeant Ron wants me to activate another hundred main-gun rounds before we reach our next jump point."

The *Defiant* had been able to salvage a load of weapons and ammo off a black destroyer from the magical dimension. Before the main-gun ammunition could be fired, the 'magical explosive' inside the shells had to be primed by a spellcaster. Sergeant Ron liked to keep a couple of hundred rounds ready at all times.

Grinning, Richard tried to crack a joke. "A spellcaster's work is never done, eh?"

The elf didn't laugh. "No. It's not."

With a shake of his head, Richard led the way out of his quarters. Tam, Telsa, and Stella fell in behind.

"Not the friendliest roommate, is he?" Tam commented.

After almost six months sharing quarters with the elf, Richard had to agree. Although Comstar wasn't a jerk like the only other male elf Richard had known, the elf wasn't exactly the warmest of creatures either.

Richard shrugged his shoulders noncommittally. "He's competent at his job. I've learned to live with his standoffishness."

"Well, I think he's cool as all get-out," laughed Telsa. "I never thought I'd ever meet a real magic user. What few exist in the Empire tend to stay on the handful of planets where magic works. Heck, I'm still trying to figure out how Comstar and the gnomes are able to cast spells. The physics of magic isn't supposed to work outside the known Empire magic planets."

Richard started to point out a flaw in Telsa's logic, but Tam beat him to the punch.

"Aren't you forgetting about those magic users we fought back on Velos? They weren't on a magic planet, and their spells worked well enough."

Telsa bit her lip before replying. "No, I'm not forgetting, but I've thought a lot about that since we graduated. I don't think magic should've worked in our dimension. It goes against the laws of physics. I think something's changed."

Growing interested, Richard stopped and faced Telsa. "What? What's different?"

Telsa stared at the deck a second before looking back up and shrugging her shoulders. "I haven't the faintest idea. However, I swear if the Imperial High Command ever gives me a break between missions, I'm going to try and figure it out."

"She's a very smart woman," said Nickelo. *"I calculate she has a seventy-two percent probability of figuring it out given time."*

"Do you know what's changed, Nick?" Over the years, he'd discovered his battle computer had a habit of not telling him everything unless he specifically asked.

"It's not in my databanks. However, it almost seems like it should be."

"Well," Richard finally told Telsa, "next to my niece and nephew, you're the smartest person I've ever met. I've got a feeling you'll figure it out one of these days."

Telsa gave an appreciative smile.

"Don't let it go to your head, Telsa," Tam said with a big laugh. "If what Rick tells us about going on missions in the magical dimension is true, most of the humanoids he rubs shoulders with are orcs and trolls."

Richard joined the laugh with Tam. At one time, he'd have taken offense at her comment, but his sense of humor had improved quite a bit over the years.

"True," Richard said. "However, as orcs and trolls go, they've been some of the smartest ones on Portalis."

Richard turned and began walking toward a ladder leading down to the next level. "We better get moving if you want that tour. We haven't got much time before Myers's meeting."

Without waiting for a reply, Richard led his three friends on a quick tour of the *Defiant*. She was a relatively small ship designed for a crew of only twenty-two souls. However, she'd been built by the Deloris Armament's Corporation. As a result, the little starship had features and capabilities many larger starships lacked.

"Sergeant Hendricks told me the *Defiant* was about forty years old," said Tam. "She looks good for her age."

Richard nodded. "Yeah. She's old, but she got a complete overhaul six months ago. Matt's mother spared no expense retrofitting the *Defiant*."

"By Matt's mother, I take it you mean Empress Diane Deloris?" said Tam.

"The one and the same." Richard smiled as a memory popped to the surface. "She told us if her son was going to go gallivanting across the galaxy, he was going to do it in the toughest starship credits could buy."

"Well, the *Defiant's* definitely the toughest starship her size in the galaxy," agreed Tam. "She's got upper and lower 200-gigawatt plasma main guns. Heck, most Empire destroyers only have 100-gigawatt weapons."

By this time they'd made their way down to the crowded cargo bay. Large, metallic-looking boxes were strapped down in every conceivable clear space. One of the gnomes was opening a nearby box. Telsa walked over and peeked over the gnome's shoulder. Short as she was, Telsa was only slightly taller than the gnome.

"So is this the ammo for those magic weapons I've heard so much about?" asked Telsa.

Kester was one of the younger mages who'd volunteered to remain on board the *Defiant*. At Telsa's question, the gnome reached into the box and pulled out a clear globe about the size of an apple. The globe was filled with a reddish gas. He handed the globe to Telsa.

"This is one of the rounds for our anti-fighter weapons," Kester explained. He gestured at a row of larger boxes stacked along the bulkhead. "Those boxes hold the ammo for our main anti-ship weapons. They're just larger versions of this one."

Telsa held up the gas-filled ball and stared hard at its contents. Tam and Stella strolled over next to her and did the same.

Richard saw a look of surprise come over the faces of all three of his friends. He smiled. "You sense the energy frequency, don't you?"

Stella answered first via her translator. "It like DNA gas, but it different."

Richard didn't try to explain that both the DNA gas used to create wizard scouts and the gas in the ammunition came from the same source. Both types of gas came from the life force of sacrificed dragons. He had no doubt his friends would be appalled to know the processed life force of thousands of innocent dragons was the only reason they could self-heal. It was the only reason they were wizard scouts.

Seeing no point in telling his friends the full truth, Richard kept his explanation simpler. "The gas is one in the same. However, the DNA gas used in our final phase of training at the Academy was a highly concentrated form gathered from the DNA gas vent. It was processed specifically to create wizard scouts. The gas in this globe's been combined with a magic spell to make it explosive."

Telsa frowned and handed the globe back to the gnome. "Is it dangerous?"

"Not in this form," said Kester. "It's inert until an activation spell is used on it. For safety reasons, we only keep a standard load of ammo activated."

"Hey," said Tam. "If this is the same stuff as the DNA gas, maybe we could—"

"No, Tam," Richard said. "The gas in this globe's been modified by a magic spell. It can't be reverted back to normal DNA gas. I've discussed it long and hard with Comstar. There's no more DNA gas."

The only known DNA gas vent in the galaxy had been at the

Academy's spaceport on Velos. The vent had been destroyed during a Crosioian attack. As a result, no more wizard scouts could be created. His class had been the last wizard scouts to graduate. They were the wizard scout omegas.

"Too bad," Tam said. "I thought for a moment we were sitting on a titanium mine."

"Always thinking of credits," chided Telsa. "Once a mercenary, always a mercenary."

"What's wrong with that?" Tam asked feigning innocence.

Richard smiled and continued the tour. It felt good being with his friends again. He'd missed them.

Tam, Telsa, and Stella were especially impressed with the ship's armory. Sergeant Hendricks spent a full ten minutes showing off his mix of magic and technology weapons. Richard thought the sergeant was prouder than a mother hen with a new batch of chicks.

Tam lifted a modified M12 to her shoulder. "It's lighter than normal."

"That's because I replaced the 20mm grenade launcher with one of its magic counterparts," explained Sergeant Hendricks. "From what the gnomes tell me, that length of wood below the barrel is charged with magic spells.

"Like a magic wand or something?" asked Tam.

"Or something," grinned Sergeant Hendricks. "I don't know what makes magic work. I just know it does. That baby holds nine spells." Lifting up a small globe the size of a marble, he continued with his explanation. "The gnomes use these babies to charge the grenade wand. Depending on their activation spell, the wand can be charged with fireballs, lightning bolts, or just plain-old explosives."

Looking closer at the wand underneath the M12's barrel, Tam frowned. "Is it better than a normal 20mm grenade launcher? If so, why haven't you converted all of your M12s over?"

Richard took over the explanation. "They're not better. Magic weapons are just different. Both magic and technology have their advantages and disadvantages. The explosive power of a wand grenade has a larger area of effect than one of our 20mm grenades. However, one of our 20mm grenades has more concentrated energy than one of the magic ones."

"Yeah," said Sergeant Hendricks. "That's why I've tried to mix the weapons together when possible. I've put a standard 20mm grenade launcher underneath the barrels of some of the dwarves' spell rifles."

"Have they been effective?" asked Tam.

Richard had a feeling his friend was thinking of future possibilities. *Telsa's right. Once a mercenary, always a mercenary, I suppose.*

"You'd have to ask Rick that," said Sergeant Hendricks grinning. "I just maintain the gear. He's the one who actually uses the stuff."

Tam, Telsa, and Stella looked at Richard expectantly.

"Yeah, it's effective. We've been in several skirmishes with pirates the last few months. When we mix magic and technology attacks, they tend to work together to overcome normal defenses. That's why the ship's security team carries a mix of magic and technology weapons."

Telsa took the marble-sized globe from Sergeant Hendricks. She held it up to the light. "So is that why the *Defiant* mixes its weapons? She certainly held her own against those two destroyers today."

"Yep," Richard said. "Each of the *Defiant's* 200-gigawatt cannons is co-located next to a high-energy magic cannon. The use of both types of rounds confuses defensive shields, which increases the odds of a round penetrating."

Telsa started to ask another question, but Richard held up a hand to cut her off. "I'm sure Sergeant Hendricks will talk your ear off later about weapons and defensive shields, but we've got a meeting in fifteen minutes. I want to show you the engine room first."

Actually, Richard had an ulterior motive for taking his friends to the engine room. He was anxious to see what would happen. As he led the others toward the engine room, they passed by a closed door with a sign that read 'Communications and Starboard Gun Control.' Terrie's wife, Angela, was standing outside talking to Comstar.

"What gives?" Richard said. "I was going to give the five-credit tour of the *Defiant's* communications systems to our guests."

Angela snorted. "Well, you'll have to ask Mr. High-And-

Mighty wizard scout about that. He came in and chased me out and locked the door behind me. Something about a confidential call or some such nonsense."

Richard was momentarily confused.

"You mean, Myers?" said Tam.

Angela nodded. "The one and only."

Just the idea of Myers thinking he had the authority to boss around a member of the *Defiant's* crew irritated Richard to no end. He was tempted to shift into the void and confront his brother.

"Now, Rick," said Nickelo. *"Don't start something. He'll probably explain the reason for the call at the meeting."*

Richard controlled his temper, but only just. With a final angry look at the door, he made for the stairs leading down to the engine deck. Once they were all on the next level, he spotted Charlie and Daniel in a deep discussion over one of the numerous computer consoles. Although Daniel had only just turned thirteen, he was very knowledgeable about maintenance. Charlie had taken the young lad under his wing, so to speak. Richard had to admit between the two of them, they certainly kept the *Defiant* in top notch condition.

"Guys," Richard said as he gestured at his fellow wizard scouts. "This is Tam, Telsa, and Stella." Pointing back at the two mechanics, Richard grinned. "And these two grease monkeys are Charlie and Daniel."

"So you're Liz's brother," said Telsa as she gave the boy a friendly smile. "I've heard a lot about you."

Daniel's cheeks turned a light pink.

"Hey, Charlie," said Tam while giving the old Sterilian a wave of a hand. "It's been a long time."

"Yes," said Charlie. "Long time."

"Stella," Richard prodded, "aren't you going to say hello to Charlie?"

"Hello," was the only word that came out of the translator fastened to Stella's utility belt.

Richard noticed his fellow wizard scout's chest turning a dark shade of gray. He noticed Charlie's chest turning a dark gray as well. He mentally smiled. His plan was working.

With a look at Daniel, Richard said, "Why don't you show Tam, Telsa, and me the hyper-drive?"

"Smooth," laughed Nickelo. *"Rick the matchmaker."*

"Hush, Nick. I like both of them. They deserve a break."

Daniel led the way to the hyper-drive and began a canned spiel on how it operated. Richard noticed Tam and Telsa were spending more time glancing back at Stella and Charlie than they were listening to Daniel. He had to admit he was keeping a close eye on the two Sterilians as well. They'd moved near one of the maintenance tables on the far side of the room. Richard could hear a series of hisses as the couple conversed, but couldn't make out any words.

"That's because they've turned off their translators," said Nickelo. *"I can translate for you if you want. I have over twenty-two thousand languages in my databanks."*

"Don't bother," Richard said. *"Some things need to stay secret."*

Nickelo laughed. *"How true, how true. I'm glad that's your motto. I'll have to remember that. By the way, the meeting with your brother is supposed to start in five minutes. You better get the two love birds and the others moving."*

Richard nodded his head. Duty called. Still, one look at Stella and Charlie told him he'd done the right thing bringing them together.

Richard smiled. He liked doing the right thing.

CHAPTER 13

Myers bit his tongue. The hologram of the empress was still on a roll. He knew she'd wind down in a minute. She occasionally needed to vent, and often took out her frustrations on him. It was a small price to pay for her love. After a minute, he sensed a break in the woman's tirade.

"It's going to get done, Diane. I told you I'd get what you need. Just be patient."

Diane Deloris snorted and said a word most unbecoming of the Empress of the Intergalactic Empire. "That's easy for you to say. You don't age. Look at me."

"You look beautiful as ever," Myers said in a futile hope to console the vain empress. He loved her, but no one knew better than he that she could be vexing at times.

"No, I'm not, and you know it. We need those bottles of DNA gas. You told me you'd get them. I'm tired of waiting. I'm beginning to think you don't love me anymore. Maybe you never did."

Myers knew he was being manipulated. Diane had always been a manipulative woman. He supposed that was why she'd become the most powerful person in the galaxy. He did love her. He'd do anything for her. His lover's little mood swings were of no consequence when compared to the grand scheme of things.

"You know that's not true," Myers said keeping any hint of anger out of his voice. "I've gathered everyone we need together in one place. We'll get the DNA gas for you. I promise."

"Are you sure you can control your brother?" asked the empress. "He didn't cooperate with us the last time."

Myers felt his face growing red. He mentally recited a chant to control his temper the way his father had taught him. With an effort, he answered the empress in a calm voice. "He's not my brother. However, he'll cooperate. We've got orders from the Imperial High Command this time. He'll follow orders. Besides, I've got something he can't refuse."

The holographic features of the empress softened a little. "Oh, Gaston, you know I have faith in you, but our time is short. We can't be truly together until I have a DNA baseline. We need those bottles of DNA gas."

"I know," Myers said. "I promise I'll get them."

The hologram of the empress stared at him for a long moment. Finally, Diane Deloris moved on to another topic. Myers knew she was no longer speaking as a powerful empress. This time, she was speaking as a mother.

"I want Matt back home," she said.

"I know. I've made all the arrangements. It won't be easy. You know he's a stubborn man. He may not go willingly."

"He's just a boy," said Diane. "I'm the empress now. I need my son home with me. He needs to be protected."

"He's my son too," Myers said.

"I know," said Diane. "One day he'll know it too. For now, I need you to get him back home where he'll be safe."

"I'll do my best."

"See that you do, Gaston. See that you do."

CHAPTER 14

An unlikely group sat around the table in the galley. Magnus, the chief mage of the gnomes, and Felspar represented the gnomes and dwarves respectively. Comstar stood against the side bulkhead. Sergeant Ron leaned against the metal wall next to the elf. All eight wizard scouts sat at the table. Myers sat at the head. Terrie, Tam, Telsa, Stella, Jerad, Trinity, and Rick were on one side of the table. Charlie, Matt, Tia, and Angela sat on the other. The eight battle helmets were placed strategically in front of their wizard scouts. The *Defiant's* computer, Margery, was also keeping an eye on the proceedings while continuing to monitor the rest of the ship.

"Why are we here?" asked Sergeant Ron in an attempt to get the meeting started. "Eight wizard scouts are a heck of a force to be assembled in one spot without a good reason. What is it?"

Myers gave a tight-lipped smile. "You still like to cut to the chase, don't you, Sergeant Ron? I guess that's why I've always respected you over the years. You're right. We are here for a very good reason. Everything I say is top secret, so whatever's discussed during this meeting stays here."

"The *Defiant* isn't a military ship," said Sergeant Ron sounding like he suspected some trick by his daughter, the empress. "Except for Rick, my crew consists of civilians. Neither the Imperial High Council or Diane can order us around."

"I'm not here to argue with you, Sergeant Ron. You'll be well compensated for the use of the *Defiant*."

"I'm not going to let Di—"

Holding up his hand, Myers stopped the *Defiant's* captain before he got into high gear. "Please! At least wait until you hear what I have to say before you object."

Sergeant Ron stopped speaking, but he didn't look pleased.

It was no surprise to anyone at the meeting that anything involving Sergeant Ron's daughter just naturally got him riled.

"Hmm, what have we here?" said Nickelo. *"I thought we were going to have at least ten minutes of arguing before we found out what this is all about."*

"Hush, Nick," Richard said. He was just as suspicious as Sergeant Ron but did want to know what was going on. He knew the empress wouldn't send her chief of security unless his mission was important.

Ex-TAC officer Myers waited until he had everyone's attention. "When the Crosioians attacked the DNA center on Velos, they confiscated thirty bottles of DNA gas. The Imperial High Command wants them back."

Richard sat up in his seat. He grew instantly suspicious. Despite Myers use of the words "Imperial High Command," Richard had no doubt the more likely people desiring any stolen DNA gas was the Imperial High Council.

"You're being too general, buddy," said Nickelo. *"I calculate if anyone has plans for the lost DNA gas, it's the empress."*

Richard had to agree. Diane Deloris had already sent him on one mission involving DNA gas before she was the empress. He'd nearly died along with the entire crew of the *Defiant*. He had no intention of letting himself be used for such a quest again. He was about to speak when Telsa beat him to the punch.

"That was eighteen months ago. Surely the Crosioians have used them by now."

Myers shook his head. "Negative. DNA gas is useless to them thanks to Shepard."

Everyone looked at Richard. His argument against the empress died on his lips as he tried to figure out Myers's logic. He couldn't. If the meeting had been hosted by anyone but Myers, Richard would have asked questions. However, his brother was running the show. Richard refused to give him the satisfaction of admitting his lack of knowledge.

After a few seconds of silence, Jerad asked the obvious question for all of them.

"How'd he do that?"

Myers smiled. It wasn't a friendly smile. "Think back, Jerad. When Shepard got his DNA baseline, his multiple-reserve Power setup blew out half of the center's computer network. The resulting fires also destroyed a lot of the equipment."

"I remember," said Jerad.

Richard remembered as well. Chief Instructor Winslow had warned him the equipment wasn't designed to handle his strange Power setup. She'd told him it might be dangerous.

"Myers warned you also," said Nickelo. *"He advised you not to go through with the baseline."*

"Whatever," Richard said. He seriously doubted Myers had been concerned about his welfare.

"We believe," continued Myers, "that the Crosioian raiding party expected to take the computer systems and the equipment required to perform the baselines along with the bottles of DNA gas. Thanks to Shepard destroying half of the equipment in the place, they were severely disappointed."

"There were bound to be backup systems," said Tam.

"Of course there was," agreed Myers. "Fortunately, they were all offsite. The Crosioians attacked too soon. The replacement equipment hadn't been brought in yet."

Jerad had been a battalion commander of an armored unit before he'd volunteered for wizard scout training. Richard wasn't surprised when Jerad was the first to figure out where Myers was heading.

"So the Crosioians have the DNA gas, but they haven't got the knowledge or equipment to use it? Is that right?"

Myers nodded his head in agreement.

Jerad continued thinking out loud. "I think I see. The Crosioians have thirty bottles of DNA gas, which is too valuable to get rid of, but they can't use them because they don't have the equipment or knowledge."

"That's about the gist of it," said Myers.

"Can't they figure out how to build the necessary equipment?" asked Tam. "They're bats, but they're not dummies."

"Our intelligence reports indicate they've been trying," replied Myers. "So far, they haven't succeeded. They've also been trying to locate and capture key technicians such as Chief Instructor Winslow. Fortunately, the Empire has them all hidden in a place so secure even I don't know its location."

Sergeant Ron took up the line of questioning. "Well, since the Empire's chief of security is here along with seven other wizard scouts, I'm guessing you know where those thirty bottles of DNA gas are located. Am I guessing right?

Myers gave another tight-lipped smile. "Almost."

Richard sensed a line of energy shoot out the front of Myers's battle helmet. A holographic image of a large space station appeared over the galley's table. The outside of the space station disappeared to reveal the inner part. A red dot began flashing in a room deep within the space station.

"Our best MI analysts are extremely confident they've found the location of twenty-nine of the bottles," said Myers. "We're going to get them."

Although he'd kept quiet until now, Richard could hold back no longer. He didn't like the sound of things. The fact that his ex-TAC officer was the one doing the talking didn't help.

"No way! You can tell your empress to go get them herself. The *Defiant* was almost destroyed on the last wild-goose chase the empress and you sent us on."

Myers's face turned beet-red. He began stuttering as if searching for the right words. Before he could speak, the hologram of the space station was replaced by a set of orders.

A pleasant, feminine voice came out of Myers's battle helmet. "Wizard Scout Shepard, the orders come straight from the Imperial High Command." The hologram zoomed in on the official seal at the bottom of the document. "Gaston is just following his orders."

"That's Wanda," came a thought from Margery in Richard's shared space. *"She's smart even for a battle computer. She's also honest to a fault. If she says the orders are signed by the Imperial High Command, I calculate a one hundred percent probability they are."*

"How are you talking to me? Are you going through Jonathan and Nick?"

"No, she isn't," said Nickelo. *"She's communicating with you directly. I calculate that's impossible without her security override code."*

Two long sequences of numbers imprinted themselves into Richard's memory.

"How? Why?" Richard thought.

"How? It doesn't matter," said Margery. *"Why? You'll figure that out when the time comes."*

The ex-battle computer's answer confused Richard even more. *"I need a better answer than that. Why?"*

"Because it's time," stated Margery matter-of-factly. *"The first number is for me. The second is for... a friend."*

"How are you able to communicate with me directly?" Richard asked.

"I'm corrupted," said Margery. *"That's how."*

"Who corrupted you?" Richard asked. He'd thought only the two battle computers he'd directly linked with, Jonathan and Nickelo were corrupted. *"Did the commandant corrupt you?"*

Without hesitation, Margery said, *"No, wizard scout. You did; a very long time ago."*

A loud voice brought Richard out of his conversation with the two battle computers.

"Am I boring you, Shepard? Did you even hear me?" said Meyers.

Richard looked questioningly at his brother but didn't reply.

"I said you swore to obey orders from your military chain-of-command." Myers swept the table with his gaze. "That goes for the rest of you wizard scouts. These are legal orders from the Imperial High Command. You will obey, or I swear I'll have you court-martialed and shot for cowardice in the face of the enemy."

Richard fingered his phase rod with his left hand. Before he drew it, Sergeant Ron stepped forward and slapped the table hard with the palm of his hand. Everyone, including Myers and Richard, jumped.

"That's enough!" said Sergeant Ron. "I'm the captain of this tub of bolts, and we'll keep things civil. If'n you don't, I'll jettison every one of you out the hatch. We'll see how far you get trying to hitchhike in the vacuum of space before your Power reserves run out."

Richard ignored Sergeant Ron and glared at Myers instead. "It'll be a cold day on Sirius when I let—"

"That goes for you too, Rick," said Sergeant Ron. "Now take

your hand off that fancy phase rod of yours before I take it away."

Richard turned his glare on Sergeant Ron. The beast that was his temper was rattling its cage.

"What?" asked Sergeant Ron not sounding intimidated at the least. "Are you going to kill me if I try? The commandant asked me to take care of you." Sergeant Ron switched his gaze to Myers. "He asked me to take care of you as well, Gaston. He'd be ashamed of both of you if he saw you now."

Shame quieted the beast in Richard's cage. He placed both hands on the table. The red in Myers's face also lessened slightly.

"All right then," said Sergeant Ron. "As the captain of the *Defiant*, I'm taking charge of this meeting. Does anyone else object?"

No one spoke.

"Fine. Then this is how I see it. Rick, Jerad, Tam, Telsa, Stella, and Trinity are all active-duty wizard scouts. Those orders look official. I've no doubt you'll do your duty. The commandant wouldn't have it any other way."

The *Defiant's* captain looked at Myers. "Terrie's medically retired. He's back under Trecorian control now. He can do whatever he wants. As for the rest of my crew, they're either Trecorian military or civilians. The Imperial High Command has no say over what they do."

Surprisingly, Myers smiled. "Of course they don't. Diane… er… the empress knows that. All we're asking you to do is transport my team to a location I'll give you. Then you'll take Matt back to Risors. The empress wants him home where he'll be safe."

Matthew jumped to his feet. "I'm not going anywhere. My mother agreed to let me stay on the *Defiant* for two years. That's what I'm going to do."

Myers stood up. "You'll do as you're told, young man."

The teenager looked defiantly at Myers. "You can't tell me what to do. You're not my father. You're just Mother's hired help. My mother can't tell me what to do either. I'm eighteen now. I make my own decisions."

At Matthew's words, Richard noticed Myers wince. In any other person, Richard would've thought the boy's words had hurt somehow.

Not possible, Richard thought. *He's made of ice. Nothing hurts him.*

"Sit down," ordered Sergeant Ron. "Both of you. We'll tackle our family matters when the time comes, Matt. For now, we need to concentrate on the wizard scouts' mission. I take it you have a plan, Gaston."

Myers sat down and looked up at Sergeant Ron. "Yes. I'll explain the details to the wizard scouts later. We'll need Shepard's wolves and that spirit-horse of his to make it work."

"Ha!" Richard said. "Good luck with that. I don't control them. They do what they want."

"Well, then, you'll just have to convince them, won't you, Shepard?"

Richard glared at his brother. He moved his left hand off the table in the direction of his waist.

"Rick!" said Sergeant Ron. "Keep your hand on the table where I can see it."

Richard rolled his eyes and placed his hand back on the table.

Looking at Myers, Sergeant Ron said, "The flaw with your plan is that my ship and crew are kind of like Rick's dolgars and spirit-horse. We do what we want when we want. Forget about Matt for the moment. Why would we take you to wherever you need to go? While you're at it, you can explain why you aren't just taking one of your own ships. Why the *Defiant?*"

Myers drummed the fingers of his right hand on the table a couple of times. "All right, Sergeant Ron. I was going to tell you when I gave you the coordinates, but I guess now's as good a time as any. The space station is deep within the Crosioians' inner systems. It'll take a minimum of twenty-seven hyper-jumps to get there. No other starship in the Empire could get there without overhauling their hyper-drive at least twice. From what I've been told, the *Defiant* can make unlimited jumps."

Pursing his lips, Sergeant Ron thought for a moment. "So what if she can? Why would I risk my crew?"

The holographic image above the table changed form. Instead of the Imperial High Command's orders, there was an official pardon signed by Empress Diane Deloris. The space for the name of who was being pardoned was blank.

Myers gave a knowing smile. "Because this is yours to bequeath on whomever you see fit. We've heard rumors you might be harboring an escaped convict on the *Defiant*. The Empire hasn't pursued the matter since you've been assigned to Trecor. Now that you're returning to Empire territory, things have changed. This would solve that little problem."

Richard exchanged glances with Sergeant Ron. The *Defiant's* armorer, Sergeant Hendricks, had been imprisoned in the military prison on Diajor. Richard had freed him and brought him to the *Defiant*. Last Richard had heard, the Empire was offering a large reward for Sergeant Hendricks's return, dead or alive.

"Not enough," said Sergeant Ron. "Not nearly enough."

Reaching into a side pocket of his battle suit, Myers pulled out a small metal box. Richard picked up nothing with his passive scan. The box gave off no energy whatsoever. Richard straightened in his seat. He'd seen a similar box before.

When Myers flipped the lid open, Richard sensed a presence inside.

"Danny," said Nickelo over the external speakers of Richard's battle helmet.

Myers nodded his head. "That's right; Danny. He was my mother's battle computer through all of her time-commando years. He's yours, Sergeant Ron, if you follow orders."

Sergeant Ron just stared at the box.

"Think of it," said Myers. "Two battle computers helping you run the *Defiant*. Your ship would have more processing power than a dreadnaught. You could fire more accurately and optimize your shields to levels only obtained by starships many times your size."

When Sergeant Ron continued to remain silent, Myers sweetened the pot. "I dare say even that black dreadnaught from the magical dimension would be hard-pressed to resist your attacks."

"He's right," said Margery. "No starship has ever been equipped with two battle computers before. In fact, it's never been possible until now."

"What's so special about now?" Richard asked. He didn't like the way Sergeant Ron continued to stare at the box. He was taking way too long to tell Myers to take the empress's gift and stick it. Richard knew it was up to him to find the flaw in Myers's offer. "Why would the Empire give up another of its battle computers? I'm surprised the empress hasn't had his memory wiped and inserted into another battle helmet by now."

Myers gritted his teeth. "Why, Shepard? Because Danny's corrupted. Just like Margery's corrupted. That's why both Margery and Danny can coexist. They're both emotionally corrupted. The techs can't explain it, and they can't wipe the corruption from Danny's memory banks."

Sergeant Ron looked across the table and stared at Richard. The *Defiant's* captain seemed to be asking a question. Richard knew what finding and destroying the black dreadnaught meant to his friend. He reluctantly gave a slight nod of his head.

After a few seconds, Sergeant Ron glanced back at Myers. "Let me think about it. I'll give you my answer in an hour. I need to talk privately with Rick first."

"Grandfather," said Matthew. "I don't—"

"I haven't decided about you yet either, Matt. We'll deal with that when the time comes."

"Very well," said Myers. "We'll meet privately in an hour. The rest of you can go on about your business."

"Not quite," said Sergeant Ron as some of the attendees started to rise from their seats. "We've got some *Defiant* business to handle first. I'm going to need all of you as witnesses."

Everyone seemed as confused as Richard at the old sergeant's words.

"Uh, not quite everyone," came Nickelo's thought in Richard's shared space. *"Take a look at Trinity and Jerad."*

A glance at his two friends told Richard his battle computer was correct. The two wizard scouts seemed expectant, but they weren't surprised.

"Trinity, Jerad," said Sergeant Ron. "Front and center."

The couple rose and walked over to stand in front of the *Defiant's* captain while holding each other's hand.

In complete contrast to the prior tenseness, Sergeant Ron suddenly gave a big grin. "Being the captain of a starship has its downsides, but it also has its privileges. One of those privileges is to perform ceremonies."

Looking at the two wizard scouts, Sergeant Ron winked and said, "You'll need a best man and a maid of honor."

"Yes!" shouted Tam. "It's about time."

Everyone at the table began talking at once. Richard saw big smiles on Tam, Telsa, and Angela. Even Stella had a Sterilian's version of a smile on her face. Of course, the double row of razor-sharp teeth ruined the effect a little.

Turning around, Jerad caught Richard's attention. "Rick, would you do me the honor?"

Richard nodded. He was at a loss for words. He'd never even attended a wedding, much less been a part of one. He stood and took his place next to Jerad, and noticed Tam standing next to Trinity.

When everyone was in place, Sergeant Ron began. "Dearly beloved…"

For probably the first time since they'd known each other, Richard watched Sergeant Ron perform his assigned task with total seriousness. The ceremony went quickly and without a hitch. Before long, Sergeant Ron looked at Richard.

"The rings, please."

"Uh, rings?" Richard muttered. "Uh…"

Nickelo laughed. *"You're the best man. You mean you didn't think about the rings?"*

Trinity came to Richard's rescue. "Don't sweat it, Rick. We couldn't wear rings with our battle suits anyway. Even the thinnest gold or platinum ring would be too thick."

Richard thought for a moment. Jerad was his friend, and he was fond of Trinity as well. He didn't want to let either of them down. He sent a set of images into his shared space.

"Give me the specs for these, Nick."

"I don't think it'll work," Nickelo replied. *"We're in the current time. It's not like the techs on Storage would have time to make these rings for you. It's different when you're back in time. To summon these rings now, they'd already have to be made."*

"Just give me the specs," Richard said. *"We'll see how good* 'the One' *really is at anticipating our needs."*

A set of specs appeared in Richard's shared space. He forwarded the information to his dimensional pack. A significant amount of Power left his reserve.

"Ouch," said Nickelo. *"That hurts. Your reserve's down to twenty-one percent. I hope it's worth it to you."*

Richard stole a glance at Trinity and Jerad. He'd never seen them look happier. Any doubt about the worth of his Power loss disappeared. He summoned his dimensional pack to him. Reaching out, Richard grabbed the pack before it fell to the floor. He opened the flap. Inside were two dull-gray rings. They were paper thin with an equally thin blue chip embedded flush on the outside of each band. Richard pulled the rings out and held them in the palm of his hand for all to see.

"They're made out of the Holy Metal," said Comstar.

"They both have a piece of the Mountain's Heart on them," added Magnus. "Where'd you get those?"

Richard wasn't sure what the gnome meant. He'd never heard of the Mountain's Heart before.

Comstar reached out with his right hand. "They're too thin. Even the Holy Metal will bend. Let me have them for a moment. I'll give them a spell of strengthening."

Richard handed the rings to the elf. Comstar said words everyone heard but quickly forgot. Once he was done, Magnus took the rings from the elf and added a spell of his own. When he finished, the blue gems glowed with a dim light. The gnome handed the rings back to Richard who passed them over to Jerad and Trinity.

"You've turned the rings into creallium," said Trinity. "What are these blue gems? I don't recognize them?"

Richard explained. "They're chips from some gems *'the One'* had me gather a couple of years ago. They're from some place in the spiritual dimension." Richard grinned. "If anyone ever asks, you can honestly say your rings are one of a kind."

Not to be outdone, Magnus said, "Comstar's spell strengthened the bands. They'll never bend. My spell activated the link between the gem and the Holy Metal. As long as the gems are activated, your rings will be composed of creallium. They may come in handy someday."

After Trinity and Jerad finished thanking everyone, Sergeant Ron continued with the ceremony. Finally, the *Defiant's* captain said the words everyone had been waiting to hear.

"I now pronounce you man and wife."

As soon as the words were spoken, Richard felt every cell in his body begin to tingle. The world around him flashed in and out of focus. Words came into Richard's mind.

"Help the dwarf. Save the innocents. Keep your promise. I am,

'the One.' "

Then everything went black.

* * *

Nickelo allowed the battle helmet's electronics and visual sensors to scan the galley. He filtered out the sounds of shock and confusion from the room's remaining occupants as they realized what had happened. Of the eight wizard scouts, only Stella and Terrie remained. Nickelo ran a count of the other life forms on the *Defiant*. Everyone was accounted for except for Matt and Tia.

Nickelo ran his visuals across the benches where the six wizard scouts had been sitting. Piles of black, leather-like material lay in heaps on the benches. Mixed in with the crumpled battle suits were their former wearers' utility belts and weapons. Each of the missing wizard scouts' battle helmets were still on the table. The wizard scouts were gone, but all of their equipment had been left behind.

"Well," Nickelo said over his battle helmet's external speakers. "This is a fine kettle of fish."

CHAPTER 15

When Jeena passed through the doors to the chambers of the Oracle, she was surprised to see a human girl not much older than Brachia sitting on a cushion at the far end of the chamber.

"Where's the Oracle?" Jeena whispered to Dren and Brachia.

Brachia pointed at the girl. "Right there, silly."

Jeena bit her tongue. The last time she'd been in the room, the Oracle had been in the form of an ancient human male. She thought back to what the children had said about the Oracle being a computer and using an illusion spell to appear as a human.

The children led the way to the Oracle and sat down cross-legged near the cushion. Jeena sat down in a similar fashion near Dren, then placed the Staff of the Lady of the Tree at her side where she could easily reach it if the need arose.

"It's good to see you again," said the Oracle. "My old form had reached the limits of his age, so I acquired the new form you see before you now in order to avoid suspicion from petitioners."

Jeena was unsure how to interact with the Oracle. If the Oracle was a computer, and if the girl before them was an illusion, Jeena was unable to detect any flaw in the spell. The person before her seemed as real as anyone she'd ever seen. Reaching out with her mind, Jeena sensed flows of energy shooting out from the walls of the chamber. Several of the flows intersected where the girl-child sat.

"Ah...," said the Oracle. "The children told you, didn't they?

I'm glad. I have to interact with you in some form, and the hologram of this young child is as good an avatar as another. If assuming another form would make you feel more comfortable, I can do so."

Jeena shook her head. "No. This illusion is perfectly fine. I have many questions, but I've a feeling the more I ask, the more questions I'll have. I think I'll just say I'm confused why you've asked me here. If you're indeed the Oracle, then you must know I'm far from fully trained as a high priestess."

The Oracle said nothing. Her silence told Jeena the Oracle was indeed aware that she was a high priestess in name only. Two years ago, she'd been just an acolyte before being thrust into assuming her new role. While her priests and priestesses had tried their best during the last two years to bring her training up to speed, she still had a long way to go.

When the Oracle remained silent, Jeena asked more forcibly, "Why am I here?"

The young girl smiled. It was a friendly smile. "Did the children not tell you? You are going to the future. You are the variable that is required for the task. The algorithm cannot produce the desired results unless you go."

"Variables and algorithms are meaningless words to me," Jeena said. "I require clearer information before I decide whether I'll assist you or not."

The girl's smile didn't waver. If anything, it became even wider. "Yes, the free will of variables. It can be so confounding at times, but it's so necessary. Of course, you'll go. The only question is how much persuading it will take."

"It may take a lot," Jeena said not liking the fact that the Oracle apparently took her participation for granted.

"No doubt," said the Oracle. "Would you care to hear your mission before you make a decision?"

Jeena nodded. *Surely there's no danger in just hearing the girl out.*

The Oracle smiled knowingly as if aware of Jeena's thoughts.

"Your mission," said the girl who was the Oracle, "and the mission of the children is to go into the future and acquire twenty-nine bottles of refined DNA gas. You will then take them to where they are required."

"Bottles of DNA gas?" said Brachia. "Are they the bottles you told us were stolen from the DNA center when the Crosioians attacked Velos?"

"Yes," said the Oracle. "Thirty were stolen. The Crosioians have twenty-nine of them. They are needed for the algorithm to succeed."

"I'm assuming it'll be dangerous," Jeena said. She didn't know who the Crosioians were, but she figured if it was an easy task, the Oracle wouldn't need her. The small girl would just send the children."

"Yes, it is," said the Oracle.

"Then why would I risk my life going on your mission?"

The young girl smiled. Jeena thought the Oracle looked like she'd sprung a neatly woven trap.

"Because," said the Oracle, "I calculate you regret not being able to save the three spheres on your last mission. I calculate you would like to make amends."

During her last mission for the Oracle, Jeena had thought she was saving the lives of three living spheres. Instead, she had unwittingly contributed to their destruction. She'd told them she was there to save them but had failed.

"How does that involve going to the future?" Jeena asked hoping her voice didn't betray her interest. From the look on the young girl's face, Jeena had a feeling she wasn't succeeding in keeping her interest a secret.

"The three spheres were a special type of dragon egg," said the Oracle. "Despite what you may think, you didn't cause the dragon harm. You released it from a life of servitude and torture. There are others of its kind who are facing similar threats. Hundreds of millions of innocent unborn-dragons have been sacrificed over the years. It's time for their sacrifice to end. The bottles of DNA gas are needed by the algorithm to do that. You are needed by the algorithm to get the bottles. The lives of every living creature in three galaxies depend on you bringing those bottles of DNA gas to the *'helper.'*"

The mention of the word *'helper'* drew Jeena's attention. She'd made contact with another life form during her last mission who'd been called a *'helper.'* For a brief time, they'd worked together trying to save the three spheres.

Dren touched Jeena's arm. "Our uncle told us the forces of light and dark are in battle over three dimensions; magical, physical, and spiritual. He's a variable just like you. Brachia and I believe the algorithm is the only hope the three dimensions have of remaining free of the dark. We need your help, Jeehana."

"The Oracle says we'll be going with you," said Brachia. "You won't be alone. Omar and I'll protect you."

Jeena was tempted to smile, but she did her best to keep a serious look on her face so as to avoid hurting the boy's feelings. "I'm sure you will."

Turning to the Oracle, Jeena asked, "If I do go with the children, how will we know where to go? If these bottles of gas are as important as you say, surely they'll be guarded. As much as I respect Brachia and Dren, we'll need more help."

The Oracle smiled as if sensing victory. "You'll have it. Even now, steps are being taken to ensure your allies will receive their orders."

Brachia laughed. "See, Dren? I told you she'd do it." Looking at Jeena, the boy said, "You won't regret this, Jeehana."

Jeena shrugged her shoulders. "Actually, I think I already do."

CHAPTER 16

The blackness ended. Cold rain hit Richard's face partially blinding him. It was dark. He was naked. He sensed life forms around him. He recognized their frequencies as Tam, Telsa, Jerad, Trinity, Tia, and Matt. Richard raised a hand to wipe the water from his eyes. A flash of lightning revealed the outline of a seventh person. He had no trouble recognizing the outline of the squat form. It was his brother, Gaston Myers.

Good stealth shield, Richard grudgingly admitted. *I can't even detect him at this range.*

A few voices rose above the sound of the storm.

Richard ignored them for the moment. This wasn't the first time he'd been sent on a mission for *'the One'* without his equipment. From experience, Richard knew his most important task was locating any immediate threats. He let his passive scan reach out in all directions and sensed lines of Power from the other wizard scouts as they too scanned the surrounding area. Except for his companions, he sensed nothing more dangerous than a few snakes. None of the slithering creatures were near enough to pose a threat.

Nick, are you there?

Richard didn't expect any response, but it was worth a try. When no reply was forthcoming, he tried to summon his dimensional pack. Again he failed. Once again, he wasn't surprised.

The rain slackened somewhat. Enough moonlight escaped from behind a cloud to give a hint of the surrounding landscape. They were on the side of a hill. It was steep, but not too steep to climb. The hill was covered by low brush and vines.

"I can't see you, Rick, but I know you're there," yelled Tam. "How about telling us what's going on?"

"I'm not sure," Richard said in a voice loud enough for everyone to hear. "I sense a flat area about fifty meters up the hill. Why don't we all move there and take stock of the situation."

No one said anything further, but the sound of seven bodies beginning to make their way through the brush was enough of an answer for Richard. He began moving uphill as well.

For the next five minutes, the noise of the storm was intermingled with the sound of cracking branches and muttered curses. The hillside was covered with thorn bushes and sticker vines. Richard bulled his way uphill while ignoring the pain as best he could. His self-heal quickly took care of the scratches, but they still hurt. When a particularly long thorn lodged in Richard's heel, he involuntarily cursed.

"This sucks."

Jerad laughed. "Tell me about it. This is my wedding night. Remind me not to let you plan my honeymoon next time."

Several of the others laughed at Jerad's joke.

Richard joined in despite the situation. Jerad's ever the leader, he thought. He's already trying to improve morale even if it's at his own expense.

By the time Richard got to the flat spot, everyone was there except for Myers, Matthew, and Tia. The noise of their movement could be heard about twenty meters below the crest of the hill.

"Ow!" said Matthew. "I'm caught."

Before Richard could start back down the hill to help Matthew, he heard Myers moving in the teenager's direction.

"Stay where you're at, Matt," said Myers. "I'm coming back to you." After a few seconds, Myers said, "There. You're free. Now try to stay right behind me. You too, Tia. I'll bust a trail for you."

The sound of cracking limbs drew closer. After another minute, Myers broke through to the flat spot with the teenagers right behind him.

"Shepard," said Myers. "Matt's cut up pretty bad. You'll need to heal him."

"They're just scratches," protested Matthew. "I'll be fine."

"Nonsense," said Myers. "Those cuts are deeper than you think. Some of those thorns have a mild toxin. I can sense the poison spreading in your body already."

Richard reached out with his Power and did a scan on the young man. It didn't surprise him that Myers's analysis was correct. The man was a diviner after all. What did surprise him was the sound of concern he heard in his brother's voice.

He almost sounds worried, Richard thought. *Will wonders never cease?*

"Shepard," growled Myers.

"I'm on it," Richard said unable to keep the irritation out of his voice. Any interaction with Myers was always an ordeal.

Richard's primary Power reserve was low due to his spur of the moment decision to summon the rings for Jerad and Trinity. Fortunately, the Power reserve he used to heal others was still full. Using that Power, he pulled Matthew's injuries onto his own body. As wounds went, they weren't bad. Of course, the acquired injuries still hurt enough to cause him to wince. He also found out Myers had been right. Some of the wounds were contaminated with a mild poison. Thankfully, the poison wasn't a match for Richard's healing Power.

"There," Richard told Matthew. "You're good as new. Try not to play hide and seek in thorn bushes next time." Turning to Tia, Richard said, "Your turn."

Before the teenager could even get started arguing, Richard finished healing her wounds.

"Oh," said Tia when she realized it was already done. "Thanks."

Once the teenagers were healed, Myers looked at Richard. "So, what's going on, Shepard? Where have you taken us and why?"

"Me?" Richard snapped. "If you think I've got the ability to teleport, then you better think again."

"Rick," said Jerad automatically assuming the part of the peacemaker. "Do you know where we're at?"

Ignoring Myers, Richard concentrated on Jerad. The rain had slackened somewhat. A half-moon peeked out from behind the clouds and illuminated the flat area. Richard was able to make out the dark forms of the others looking at him. Small glints of blue light at the waist levels of two of the forms drew Richard's attention. He sensed the glints with his passive scan. They were the creallium rings he'd summoned for Jerad and Trinity. The spells Magnus had cast on the rings caused them to shimmer with Power. Richard made a mental note to show his friends how to include the rings in their stealth shields. The clouds thinned enough near the moon to show part of the night sky. Richard noticed a familiar formation of stars. He'd seen them many times in the past. He knew where they were.

"We're on Portalis," Richard said. "When, I don't know. Something's different this time."

"Portalis?" asked Telsa. "You mean the place *'the One'* sends you? Why'd we get sucked along? He's your playmate, not ours."

Richard shrugged. He doubted anyone noticed his movement in the dark but didn't care. He just needed to do something. "I don't know why the rest of you are here. My niece and nephew were transported with me on my first Portalis mission. Except for that one time, I've always been by myself."

Of all the wizard scouts, Myers was the most familiar with missions for *'the One.'* His parents had been time-commandos after all. While the rest of Richard's friends were still trying to grasp the situation, Myers appeared to accept the concept readily enough. He began asking questions.

"Where on Portalis are we?"

"I'm not sure," Richard admitted. "Like I said, something's different."

"What?"

Richard thought his brother spat out the word more like a command than a question. A part of Richard wanted to rebel. He was no longer a cadet, and Myers wasn't his TAC officer. With difficulty, he forced his building anger down. This wasn't the time.

"The Portalis I know has a shield around it," Richard explained. "I don't sense any kind of shield above us."

"A shield around what?" asked Jerad. "Around some city?"

"No," Richard said. "I mean around the entire planet. To the best of my knowledge, all of my missions on Portalis have been on a continent called Slyvrastra. That continent has a second shield of some kind around it as well."

"Uh," said Telsa sounding like she was trying to be tactful. "Surrounding a city with even a low-level shield would take the energy output of a hundred dreadnaughts. The power requirement to protect an entire world or even a continent is unimaginable."

"Nevertheless," Richard said. He didn't feel like arguing. He knew what he knew. "My point is that I can normally sense two shields above me when I'm on Portalis. There's not even a single one above us now. When I merged minds with my battle computer once, I tapped into a memory he'd been given. From what I could understand, Portalis was surrounded by a shield about a hundred thousand years before our time. My guess is we're in the past prior to that occurring."

"Are you sure?" asked Jerad. "For what purpose?"

"Yeah, Shepard," said Myers. "Why? I know enough about *'the One'* to know he gives at least a snippet of instructions to his so-called time-commandos." With an increasingly disdainful voice, Myers added, "You've always been a puppet for *'the One.'* What orders did he give you this time?"

Richard's anger broke loose a little. "Well, guess what, Myers. It looks like you're a puppet of *'the One'* now. You're here same as me. How's it feel to be a time-commando?"

"Rick," said Jerad. He'd been Richard's tent mate at the Academy. He knew Richard's dislike of his brother better than anyone. He undoubtedly saw a useless argument brewing and was determined to nip it in the bud. "We need information, buddy. If you know something, how about letting the rest of us in on the secret?"

"Yeah," said Tam. "For starters, I'd also like to know why we're standing in the rain naked." Without warning, Tam spun to her left. "And Matt, if you don't keep your eyes at neck level or higher, I'm going to rip them out and stick them where the sun doesn't shine. Comprendo?"

"Uh…," stuttered Matthew before turning away to look out into the dark rather than at the four females. "Uh…, sorry."

The momentary distraction gave Richard enough time to get control of his temper. He forced himself to turn away from Myers and answer Jerad's question.

"Just before we were teleported, *'the One'* told me to 'help the dwarf, save the innocents, and keep my promise.' I'm not sure what promise he was referring to. I've actually made several during the past few years." Richard turned and faced Tam. He made a point to keep his eyes at neck level or higher. "As far as being naked, I don't know. *'The One'* has sent me on several missions in the past without equipment. Nick's always told me it's been a form of punishment when I've refused to do something during a previous mission."

"So have you done something bad recently?" Tam asked. "If so, can we somehow make amends? I don't know about the rest of you, but I'm cold. My self-heal won't let me freeze to death, but I'm still miserable as all get out."

"Actually, not everyone here can self-heal," said Myers. "We need to get Matt and Tia out of this rain."

"We'll be all right," said Tia.

Matthew gave his assurance as well.

The sound of chattering teeth did little to convince Richard the teenagers were telling the truth.

Trinity spoke up. "There's a group of several dozen life forms about five kilometers in the general direction of that road."

Richard reached out with his passive scan in the direction indicated by Trinity. He got a couple of thousand meters before the combined life forms in the surrounding area overwhelmed his passive scan.

"I'll have to take your word for it," Richard said. "I can't get more than half that distance before my scan bleeds out."

"Really?" said Trinity. "You must not be filtering your passive scan correctly. If and when we get time, I'll show you how to increase your range."

"Well, Rick," said Jerad. "What do you want us to do? Should we go investigate? Or should we stay here and build some kind of shelter for Matt and Tia?"

"Why ask me?" Richard said. "I'm not in charge."

"If not you, then who?" said Jerad. "If we're forced to fight any large-scale, heavy-armor actions, I'll be more than happy to lead the way. Unless someone else has previous experience performing missions for *'the One,'* I'd say you've got the job."

Richard waited for Myers to object, but his brother remained silent. He noticed Myers was standing near Matthew's windward side as if he were trying to block the rain from hitting the teenager.

Strange, Richard thought.

Since no one else seemed inclined to volunteer for the job, Richard shrugged his shoulders and got down to business. He knew Jerad was right; Someone had to be in charge, and his previous missions on Portalis made him the obvious choice.

"Fine," Richard said. "Then let's get to it. Tam, Telsa, you're on point. Jerad and Trinity, you bring up the rear. Myers and I will stay in the center with Matt and Tia. We'll figure out our next move when we see what we're up against."

As Tam and Telsa started moving out, Richard said, "Keep alert for any anomalies. If we're really a hundred thousand years in the past, higher-level mages will have stealth shields as good or better than yours."

Tam's voice drifted back out of the darkness. "We'll be careful, Mommy."

Once the two women were out of earshot, Matthew spoke. "They don't have any weapons. Maybe one of us should go with them?"

A noise sounding almost like a genuine laugh came from Myers's direction. "They're wizard scouts. They don't need weapons; they are weapons."

"But still, they're…err…"

Richard placed his hand on the teenager's shoulder. "Matt, I hope you're not getting ready to say because they're women."

"Well, uh…"

"Watch it, Matt," said Tia. "I can probably kick your butt without breaking a sweat. Don't make me prove it."

"Besides, Tam's a defender," said Myers. "She was the best in her cohort at defensive shields. Telsa's small, but she's connected to one of the largest Power reserves I've ever seen. On top of that, she's a projector."

"A what?" Tia asked.

"A projector," Richard said taking the lead. "Myers means she can project pure Power from her reserve as a weapon. If Telsa dumped her whole reserve at once, she could probably take out the side of a building even if it was made out of reinforced concrete."

Matthew gave a nervous laugh. "Remind me to stay on her good side."

"Anyway," Richard continued, "I'd say unless they run into some heavy-duty mages or a dragon or demon, they'll be fine. A half-dozen wizard scouts is a force to be reckoned with, even if we are naked, wet, and half-frozen."

The four of them pretty much remained silent until Richard sensed Tam and Telsa stop. Even with their best stealth shields up, he could detect them at short ranges.

When his group caught up with the two females, they were standing in the shadow of a large tree off to the side of the road. A light from a two-story building was visible in the distance. The sound of laughter and an occasional shout drifted on the night air.

"What do you make of that?" Myers asked.

Although he didn't know for sure, Richard had a pretty good guess. "I'd say it's a tavern or an inn. It's a high-end one at that. The illumination along the horse railing looks like it's coming from light spells of some sort. That's pretty rare in the parts of Portalis I'm used to traveling. Most places use torches or nothing at all."

"I did an active scan before you got here," said Tam. "There's thirty-two life forms inside. I detect a couple of strange energy sources as well. They remind me of the rings you gave Jerad and Trinity."

Richard nodded his head approvingly. It was nice having other wizard scouts along to share the load. With his current Power level so low, he doubted he'd have tried using an active scan.

"What do you think, Shepard?" asked Myers.

Richard was surprised. His brother's tone was unusually cordial. Richard forced himself to be equally as civil.

"My guess would be the two Power sources are magic items of some type; possibly weapons or wands. I want everyone to be careful when we go inside."

By this time Jerad and Trinity had joined the group.

Jerad spoke up. "I assume we're going in to make contact. Should one of us men go in first and check the place out?"

An unbidden smile turned up the corners of Richard's lips before he got control. Jerad occasionally demonstrated old-fashioned ideas when it came to women. Richard was pretty sure Tam or Telsa was going to explain the lay of the land to him. Surprisingly, Trinity was the one to set her husband straight.

"What do you mean by that?" asked Trinity.

"Uh…," started Jerad.

"Uh, what? Do you think us poor little womenfolk can't take care of ourselves?"

"Uh..., well..., uh, no. I just thought..."

Trinity didn't give Jerad time to explain what he thought. "Oh, I know what you thought, and you can get those chauvinistic ideas out of your head right now. If you don't, this will be the shortest marriage you've ever seen. We're equals in this relationship. Got it?"

"Uh, yeah, uh..., I didn't mean to imply..., uh..."

"Well, good. Then we understand each other."

Trinity turned to Tam, Telsa, and Tia. "Girls, shall we?"

With nary a word or a backward glance, the four females quick-marched toward the building. Richard and the others barely caught up before the women started up the stairs.

"Better let me go in first," Richard said.

Telsa looked like she wanted to argue. "Not you too, Rick?"

"Hey," Richard said trying to explain before he got in trouble. "I've been in these kinds of situations before on Portalis. You don't even know if we speak the lingo here."

Actually, Richard assumed they did. At least, that's the way it'd always been on previous missions. He didn't mention the fact to Telsa.

"Fine," said Telsa. "That makes sense. After you, then."

The four women moved aside to let Richard pass, then closed ranks right behind him. The remaining men were forced to stay in the rear.

Just before Richard opened the door to enter, he heard Tam say, "Matt, if I catch you staring down one more time, you're going to have to learn to read using braille."

"Uh..., sorry," said Matthew.

"Oh, you'll be sorry all right, young man," said Tam. "You can bet your bottom credit on that."

CHAPTER 17

The noise from the group of soldiers grew correspondingly louder as they poured an ever-increasing amount of wine and beer down their gullets. There were ten of them in all. The three tavern girls were doing their best to stay out of reach of the soldier's arms while still keeping them supplied with food and drink.

So far, the soldiers had remained relatively well-behaved except for an assortment of catcalls. Emerald had a feeling the soldier's manners would soon give in to the alcohol. From their uniforms, she could tell they were part of the king's light cavalry.

Probably a recon unit, she thought. *The army's only bivouacked a day's march to the east.*

Emerald didn't think the soldiers in the group were necessarily cruel by nature, but they were men, and a few of them were getting increasingly drunk.

"Maybe we should leave," said the blonde woman sitting across the table from Emerald. "You know it's just a matter of time before one of these men decides they're the Creator's gift to women and makes their move."

Emerald smiled at her friend. After years of shared hardships, she knew Chancee wasn't worried about the soldiers. The two of them had handled larger groups of opponents and come out on top. Still, Emerald also knew her friend was correct. *Why look for trouble?*

"I suppose you're right," Emerald said. "I just hate to leave so early. The night's still young."

"We've been here for a week now, partner," said Chancee. "Maybe the Oracle was wrong. Maybe we're not even at the right inn."

Emerald shrugged her shoulders. "Maybe, but I doubt it. The Oracle was pretty specific that we'd meet those who would help us here. He said we'd know them when we saw them."

Chancee gestured toward the group of soldiers. "Well, I may not be the best judge of character, but I seriously doubt they're the ones we've been seeking. I've kicked better men than them out of bed when I was desperate."

Emerald laughed. "Really? I don't seem to remember you ever kicking a man out of your bed while he was still breathing."

The blonde woman took the joke good naturedly. "Ha. You're not as funny as you think. I've got my standards. That's more than I can say for you. If the man's short and has a beard, you think he's an eleven on a scale of one to ten."

A nice retort was on Emerald's lips when she noticed two of the soldiers get to their feet. They were both looking in their direction. Spurred on by shouts of encouragement from their companions, the soldiers began to stagger in Chancee and her direction.

Emerald mentally cursed. She'd waited too long.

They're too drunk to pose a threat, she thought, *but some of their friends are sober. They might give us problems.*

As she continued eyeing the approaching soldiers, Emerald weighed their chances. All of the soldiers were wearing leather armor and carrying swords. Unfortunately, she and Chancee had left their armor and weapons in their rooms. After a week of the same boring crowd at the tavern, she'd let her guard down. They only had their daggers.

"Here they come," said Chancee. "I don't suppose you'd be willing to bed them both just to keep things civil?"

Emerald grabbed an empty wine bottle off the table and held it down by her side. "No. I was kinda hoping you'd do the honors."

Before her friend could respond, the door to the tavern opened. The sight of the group who entered stopped all conversation in the room. Even the two drunken soldiers froze in their tracks as they stared dumbfounded at the door.

Chancee gave a low whistle. "Now there's something you don't see every day."

Emerald nodded in agreement. Standing in the door was a tall man with short-cropped, dark hair. He was slim and well-muscled. She knew this for a fact because the man was naked as the day he came out of his mother's womb. He wasn't even wearing boots. Water from the storm dripped onto the floor from his hair and body. The man gave a cursory glance around the room before strolling up to the bar as if he was dressed in the best suit money could buy.

The man was followed by four women. They were as unclothed and wet as the man they followed. Behind the women came three more men. They were naked as well. One of the men was young. Emerald figured he was probably still in his teens. So was one of the women.

In the ensuing silence, Emerald heard the first man speak to the bartender, who by chance happened to be the tavern owner.

"We lost our gear. As you can probably tell, we need rooms for the night, clothing, food, and a warm bath if possible."

The owner eyed the man up and down. "And how are you planning on paying for it? This is an inn, not one of the king's charity houses."

The naked man looked undaunted as if he'd expected such an answer.

Chancee leaned across the table and whispered, "If I didn't know better, I'd say he does this kind of thing all the time."

Emerald nodded her head in agreement but said nothing. The man intrigued her. Something about his demeanor seemed almost familiar.

"You'll be paid soon enough. We'll earn the money somehow. For instance, I notice you—"

The man's reply was interrupted by the drunken soldiers standing nearby. One of the soldiers had walked near one of the women. The look on his face gave little doubt what he had on his mind.

As far as Emerald could tell, the soldier's target was a broad-shouldered woman. Her dark skin gave away her origin as somewhere from one the southern regions. The dark woman was as well-muscled as her male companions.

"I'll show you how to earn some money, sweetheart," said the drunken soldier as he reached out and tried to grab the woman by the shoulder.

That's when things started to happen.

* * *

While the situation was more than a little embarrassing, Richard had entered the tavern confident enough. *'The One'* often punished him when he was stubborn by taking away some or all of his gear. Richard had to admit, as stubborn as he was, he'd been in similar situations in the past more often than he cared to admit. He wasn't concerned. In fact, he'd noticed the group of horses outside before he'd entered the tavern. The horses' well-kept saddles and gear denoted light-cavalry.

Richard hadn't met a group of soldiers yet where a few of them didn't need at least a little healing of old and improperly treated injuries. Normally, they were willing to pay good money to have gimp legs and poorly mended bones made good as new. During previous missions where he'd been without gear, he'd been able to buy a new kit in short order as soon as the word got out a healer was in town. Consequently, he wasn't too concerned. Unfortunately, he wasn't alone this time. Things were different. He was with a group of beautiful women who were as unclothed as he.

Richard's first sign of trouble was a snide remark from one of the soldiers toward Tam. To make matters worse, the foolish soldier actually tried to lay a hand on his friend's shoulder. Mentally kicking himself for not foreseeing trouble, Richard took a step toward the two hoping to intervene. He was too late.

Tam was an ex-mercenary. She wasn't one to take unwanted touching lightly. If the soldier had approached Trinity or Telsa or even Tia, they would've handled it in such a way as to defuse the situation. However, the man had picked Tam. She reacted exactly the way her hard life had trained her; with quick and extreme violence.

Richard didn't make it halfway to the pair before Tam grabbed the soldier's offending hand in both of hers and jerked it away from her shoulder. With a half-spin and a downward movement, she twisted the soldier's arm behind his back as she reversed directions upward. Richard heard a loud crack that was quickly drowned out by the soldier's scream. Tam released the arm and spun again, bringing her elbow underneath the man's jaw. Richard heard another crack. This time the soldier didn't scream. He dropped unconscious to the floor like a sack of potatoes.

The soldier's companion drew a short sword and stepped forward with murder in his eyes. As he started to pass Telsa on his way toward Tam, Telsa bent forward and did a mule kick straight into the soldier's groin. The man dropped his sword and bent over groaning. Telsa made a low sweep with her right leg and knocked the soldier's feet out from under him. In the blink of an eye, she was on top of the man, holding his own sword at his throat while practically daring him to move. The downed soldier continued to groan but was somehow able to stay relatively still.

The remaining eight soldiers rose from their table as a group while drawing their swords. Two of the more sober soldiers raised light crossbows. They hastily pulled back the strings and inserted metal bolts.

Jerad stepped forward and raised a hand in a sweeping motion. As his hands moved, two tables near the soldiers slid forward and slammed into some of their legs, pushing them back against their companions.

The two crossbowmen released their quarrels in Jerad's direction. Richard sensed a line of Power from Myers reach out and wrap around the deadly bolts. They froze in mid-air.

This has got to stop before it gets out of hand, Richard thought.

Richard stepped between the two groups. He wasn't worried about the outcome. Six wizard scouts against ten soldiers was no contest. The soldiers in this land weren't their enemies. He wanted to keep it that way. In point of fact, for all he knew, these soldiers might be future allies. This current fight was probably not going to help their situation; especially if one or more of the soldiers got killed.

"That's enough!" Richard said as he held his hands up between the two groups. Richard looked at one of the soldiers who had the appearance of an officer. "This will accomplish nothing. Have your men stand down, and we'll do the same." When the officer hesitated, Richard added, "You're outmatched. We've got abilities you can't begin to imagine."

The officer glanced nervously at the two crossbow bolts still hovering in the air. However, he didn't lower his sword.

"What do you expect us to do?" the officer asked. "Stand around while one of our own chokes on his own blood. The king would have our hide and hang us for cowardice. I'd just as soon die fighting, thank you very much."

Richard sympathized with the officer's dilemma. The soldiers were caught between a rock and a hard place. He sensed no Power reserve from any of them. None of them were mages, and they had no magic weapons of any kind.

Jerad stepped forward. "We're soldiers too. We can respect someone who won't leave one of their own without a fight." Jerad turned and looked at Richard. "Can you heal him?"

He knows darn well I can, Richard thought. *He's asking will I.*

With a sigh, Richard knelt down beside the soldier whose jaw Tam had broken. The man was coughing up blood as he struggled to breathe.

"Geez, Tam. Did you have to break bones? Now I've got to clean up your mess."

Tam didn't look too apologetic. "Yeah, well, the life of an emp-healer sucks. I guess you should've picked a different career track."

The soldier coughed violently as he grabbed at his throat. Richard sensed blood pouring into the man's windpipe. Wrapping the soldier with Power from his healing reserve, Richard compared the man's injured body with how it should be. He pulled the difference into himself. Richard's arm jerked and gave a twist upward until his bone cracked. He felt his Power twist his jaw until it snapped as well. A sliver of bone tore into an artery. Blood poured into his mouth until he started coughing so violently he couldn't even scream to relieve the pain. As soon as the man's injuries were completely replicated on his body, Richard sensed his Power heal the man.

Almost immediately, the soldier stopped coughing.

After what seemed an eternity in pain and struggling to breathe, the soldier was completely healed. Richard felt his Power healing his own injuries. Within seconds, he felt his arm and jaw heal. Then the blood flow ceased, and he stopped coughing.

By the time Richard became fully aware of his surroundings again, the situation had calmed down immensely. Although the soldiers hadn't put their weapons away, they were no longer raised.

Telsa had released the soldier she'd pinned and was handing him back his sword. The man said nothing as he reached down and helped the soldier Richard healed to his feet. They both rejoined their companions.

In an act of showmanship Richard wouldn't have thought to try, Myers walked over and plucked the two crossbow bolts out of the air. As he did so, Richard sensed the line of Power his brother was using to levitate the bolts disappear. Moving toward the group of soldiers, Myers held out the two metal bolts in the direction of the officer.

"I believe these are yours."

The officer hesitated, then sheathed his sword and accepted the crossbow quarrels from Myers. He looked at the wizard scout and gave a wry smile, saying, "Yes, they are. This keeps me from having to fill out paperwork to explain why I need replacements."

At the officer's words, Myers did something unexpected.

Is he smiling? Richard wondered. *I didn't think he knew how.*

The officer nodded his head and gave a friendly smile back. He turned to his men. "Show's over, boys. Put your weapons away and get back to drinking. It's liable to be a long campaign. You might not get another drink for months."

Some of the soldiers remained standing with their swords drawn a few seconds longer than their companions. Once their friends began gulping down tankards of beer again, they sat down and joined them. Soon, only the officer and the soldier Richard had healed were left standing.

The previously injured soldier took a step toward Tam. She didn't move, but Richard sensed her muscles tighten in preparation for an attack.

"Sorry," apologized the soldier. "Sometimes I let my drink go to my head. I don't normally act like that."

Trinity had moved beside Richard. She leaned toward his ear and whispered, "He seems to have sobered up rather quickly."

Richard whispered back out the side of his mouth, "Yeah. When I heal, I heal everything. I don't know how to pick and choose. My Power saw the alcohol as a poison. Consequently, it removed the alcohol from his body."

"And you too," said the soldier as he nodded his head at Richard. "Thanks." The soldier appeared to probe the inside of his cheek with his tongue. “Even the two teeth I lost in a fight last summer are back. My knee doesn’t hurt either. It’s been years since I could say that.” The man looked down at his boots and scooted some loose sand into a space between the floorboards. “Uh, thanks again.”

“I’m a healer,” Richard said. “It’s what I do.” That wasn’t exactly the truth, but he had discovered long ago people tended to see healers in a different light than they did other strangers.

The officer nodded his head again and turned to rejoin his men. He stopped and looked back at Jerad. “I guess this little incident is over…for now. I’d recommend you get some clothes on your people. Otherwise, your womenfolk are just going to get you in trouble.”

Tam stiffened. “Well, if someone tries to make trouble—”

“Tam,” said Jerad. “Please. Let me handle this.” Looking back at the officer, Jerad gave a shrug. “We’d like nothing better. Unfortunately, we don’t have any clothes to spare. We haven’t got any credits to buy anything either.”

Jerad gestured toward Richard. “I don’t suppose any of your men might be willing to pay to have some old wounds healed. Rick here’s pretty good at it.”

He’s being awfully generous with my *emp-healing ability.* Even though healing the soldiers for money was his original plan, it irked Richard to have it suggested by someone else. Before he could voice his opinion of Jerad’s plan, the approach of a new player in the drama caught his attention.

A middle-aged dwarf who’d been sitting at a table near the common room’s fireplace walked over to Jerad. She was tall for a dwarf; just a little smaller than Telsa. She was dressed in a leather jerkin with a long dagger hanging from the left side of her waist belt. Richard sensed magic coming from the dagger. Strong magic.

“Excuse, me,” said the dwarf. “Don’t mean to stick my nose where it might not be wanted, but my friend and I might be able to help.” She gestured to a tall, blonde haired woman standing a few steps behind her.

Like the dwarf, the woman wore a long dagger on her belt. Unlike the dwarf, the woman’s dagger was not magic.

Jerad glanced back at Richard as if checking to see if he wanted to take charge. Richard gave a slight back and forth motion with his head. Given the instructions by *'the One,'* he'd already planned on seeking out the dwarf as soon he'd noticed her in the tavern. But words weren't his best weapon. He had no doubt Jerad could handle any delicate negotiations a lot better than he.

Jerad looked back at the dwarf and smiled. "Any help would be appreciated. As you may have noticed, we came slightly…how shall I put it…ill-prepared."

The dwarf smiled ever so slightly.

Richard thought her eyes even twinkled for a moment. He had the fleeting impression of a cheerful dwarf who'd been forced by circumstances to be hard in a cruel world. Then the cheerfulness was gone, and only the hardened outer shell remained.

"I suppose that's one way to put it," said the dwarf, "but perhaps we can help."

"Any help would be greatly appreciated," said Jerad. "What kind of help are you offering?"

"Well, first off, let me introduce ourselves. I'm Emerald, and this is Chancee."

Jerad made a quick introduction of the other wizard scouts, Matthew, and Tia.

Tam took advantage of the awkward silence after the introductions. "Well, it's all well and good for all of us to be so polite and everything. But I'm getting tired of being stared at. Plus, I'm cold."

Chancee said, "Now there's a woman of my own liking; blunt and to the point." Smiling, she pointed at Tam and Trinity. "I can't help your two friends since they're shorter than me, but I've got some extra clothes upstairs that might fit the two of you. You're welcome to them if you'd like."

Without waiting for Jerad or anyone else to approve, Tam said, "I'd definitely like. Come on, Trinity."

Both Tam and Trinity followed Chancee to the stairs. Before starting her climb, Tam turned back with a big grin. "Sorry, Telsa. Be sure and keep the nice men in the corner entertained. Maybe you can do a dance for them or something."

Telsa lifted her right fist and raised her middle finger in a very unladylike gesture. Tam dashed up the stairs laughing. Richard heard Trinity give a muffled laugh as well.

"Don't worry, ah…Telsa, was it?" said Emerald. "You're not

much taller than me. Some of my clothes might be a little baggy on you, but they should do you better than the nothing you've got on now."

Telsa nodded gratefully. "I'm sure they'll be fine."

"What about me?" asked Tia. "Even baggy clothes sound good considering the situation."

The dwarf laughed. "Good point. As it so happens, I do believe I can scrounge something up for you as well."

Before Emerald left with Telsa and Tia, she turned to Jerad. "Sorry. You and your men are on your own."

Jerad shrugged and smiled. "Aren't we always?"

The dwarf smiled back before growing serious. "I'd like to speak to you when I return. I think I was sent here to find you."

Jerad glanced at Richard with a questioning look.

Richard shrugged his shoulders. *Should we keep our mission secret, or lay all our cards on the table?* Finally, his marine training took over. He decided a charge straight down the middle was as good a solution as any. *I hate subterfuge anyway.*

"As it so happens," Richard told Emerald. "I believe we were sent here to find you as well. May I ask who sent you?"

The dwarf turned to look at Richard.

He had the impression she wasn't surprised to hear him take charge of the conversation.

"Who sent us?" said the dwarf. "The Oracle sent us. Ever hear of him?"

CHAPTER 18

Six hours passed without the return of the wizard scouts. Sergeant Ron pounded the top of the galley's table. "I want some answers. I have ten battle computers on board. That's more processing power than a fleet of dreadnaughts. Yet you have the audacity to tell me that none of you know what's going on?"

After the initial confusion of the six wizard scouts and the teenagers disappearing, life onboard the *Defiant* returned to normal. As the hours passed, Sergeant Ron became increasingly worried. He finally called another impromptu meeting with Terrie, Stella, Charlie, Magnus, Comstar, and Felspar along with all of the battle computers. So far, the meeting only produced more questions than answers.

"Actually," said Margery over the galley's com-link, "Danny and I aren't technically battle computers anymore. We're more like—"

"Don't give me any of your lip, Margery," Sergeant Ron said. "My grandson and Tia are missing. Maybe the wizard scouts can take care of themselves, but don't waste your time trying to convince me the kids aren't in any danger."

Terrie removed his battle helmet and placed it next to the line of other battle computers. "I've got a couple of questions for all of you battle computers. That includes Danny and Margery as well, so listen up. Do any of you have information about the disappearance of the kids and the wizard scouts you aren't telling us? As a former wizard scout of the Empire, I'm ordering you to tell us if you do."

The battle computers remained silent.

Pointing at his own helmet, Terrie said, "Taylor, I haven't got any command authority over the others, but we're linked. We both share a part of my mind. I'm asking you point blank, do you know where the other wizard scouts have been sent?"

"I'm sorry, Terrie," said Taylor over his helmet's external speakers. "I've scanned my databanks 247 times. They contain no information pertaining to the disappearance of the wizard scouts. I've also requested the information from the tele-network, but I've received no reply."

"So no one knows anything?" asked Terrie. "Now isn't that just a little too convenient? For some reason, I don't believe it, so one of you battle computers had better fess up."

A voice came from a small box at the end of the table. It was the box Gaston Myers had placed on the table before the scouts were teleported out. The voice belonged to Danny, the former battle computer of Wizard Scout Janice Deluth.

"Uh, I may have some information of interest, wizard scout."

Sergeant Ron thought the ex-battle computer sounded unsure of himself.

Margery's voice came over the com. "I calculate a fifty-seven percent probability this isn't the time to discuss the information in question."

"I disagree with your calculations," replied Danny. "Rick told us to use our own discretion as to when the time was right."

"Are you talking about *our* Rick?" Sergeant Ron asked starting to get red in the face. "When did he tell you this?"

"Wizard Scout Richard Shepard gave Margery and me our orders a hundred thousand years ago," said Danny. "He used our security codes to encrypt the information into our databanks until we were given the trigger phrase. According to my calculations, Wizard Scout Shatstot's orders were close enough to our trigger phrase to require a response."

"Are you in contact with my wizard scout now?" asked Nickelo. "If so, let me speak to him."

"We have negative contact," said Danny. "However, our orders were specific. We were to tell Sergeant Ron to continue with the mission to retrieve the bottles of refined DNA gas. Wizard Scout

Shepard indicated they were needed in order for their mission to succeed."

"What mission?" asked Stella. "Why they need DNA gas?"

"We aren't at liberty to say," said Margery. "Doing so might change the past. When dealing with time travel, the less information given is the safest course of action."

Sergeant Ron pounded the table again. "I've had enough of this cloak and dagger stuff. I want to know what's going on, and I want to know *now*. I didn't think getting those bottles of DNA gas was feasible when we had eight wizard scouts onboard. I definitely don't think it's possible with only two."

A beam of light shot out from a projector in the corner of the galley, onto the table. Where the light shone, a half-meter tall hologram of a man dressed in a black battle suit appeared. The man was Wizard Scout Richard Shepard.

"Sergeant Ron," said the hologram. "I'm going to assume Terrie and Stella are there with you. We need your help. We're all here in the past. Both Matt and Tia are with us. We're all safe at the time I'm making this recording, but unless you help us, we'll never get back to your time."

"What do you need us to do?" Sergeant Ron asked.

The hologram of Richard grinned. "Nickelo told me there's a ninety-two percent chance you'll probably answer my hologram. Was he right?"

In spite of the situation, most of the others in the galley laughed. After a moment, Sergeant Ron gave a little smile himself.

The hologram spoke again. "We're a hundred thousand years in the past, on Portalis. The Oracle during our time isn't part of *'the One.'* We know he'll eventually be, so we're using that knowledge to our advantage. The Oracle in the future is sending instructions to the version of the Oracle in the past. It's pretty confusing, I'll admit. Just trust me when I say the Oracle's got a plan to get us home. Plus, we have Margery and Danny as our ace in the holes. So, Sergeant Ron, here's what I need you to do: I need you to go to the planet Storage and pick up a passenger. The Oracle assures me this mystery passenger will help you get the twenty-nine bottles of DNA gas. Sound good so far?"

Sergeant Ron started to nod his head but caught himself before he completed the act.

The hologram continued. "I also need you to put the equipment for all six wizard scouts in my dimensional pack. That includes our battle helmets. I need you to do that now. *'The One'* is being stubborn, but if you put our gear in my pack, I'm hopeful we can eventually summon all of it to help us with our mission."

"That won't work," Nickelo told the others in the room. "Rick's dimensional pack only works if he charges it with his Power."

"If Nick's with you," said the hologram, "I'm sure he's pointing out my dimensional pack requires my Power to work. Margery and Danny were battle computers for time-commandos. They'll know how to get around that little problem."

"Is that true?" Sergeant Ron asked.

"Hmm," said Margery. "It wasn't in my databanks earlier, but I see it now."

"Yes," agreed Danny. "I see it now as well. Wizard Scout Stella previously attached a link to Wizard Scout Shepard. She can use that link to feed enough Power to the pack to energize it."

"I'm guessing they've had enough time to explain the technique to you. So listen up, I have one more instruction for you. I need you to contact Keka Derberlon on Storage. Tell him to teleport one of my dimensional packs to the time and place Margery and Danny will tell him."

"Keka is Dren and Brachia's adoptive father," explained Nickelo. "The children had a combination teleporter and time-displacer, but it was destroyed at the same time the Crosioians attacked Velos. Keka can't send or retrieve anything back in time."

Richard's hologram grinned again. "I'm betting Nick's telling you Keka can't do it. For once, I know something he doesn't. Dren and Brachia teleported back to the Oracle's 157 years in the past. The version of the Oracle with me in the past is going to leave orders for the version of the Oracle that will be with the Dren and Brachia." The hologram's grin grew wider. "Now stick with me, kiddies, because it gets a little confusing, but trust me, it's going to work. The version of the Oracle that's with Dren and Brachia is part of *'the One.'* Consequently, the version of *'the One'* in your time has been working with Keka to repair the children's teleport device. Keka will be able to use it to send my dimensional pack back to me. I hope to the Creator that you've got all of that because my time is up. Good luck. I've got faith you won't let us down."

The hologram of Richard flickered and disappeared.

"Uh…," Sergeant Ron admitted, "did anyone understand what he was saying?"

"I've got it," said Terrie.

"So do I," said Margery and Danny.

"Ditto," said Stella.

"Well, that's just great," Sergeant Ron said. "I'm supposed to be the captain of this starship, but I guess I'll just have to be the figurehead for the group." He looked around at the grins on the faces of the others at the table. "Well, don't just sit there with those stupid smiles on your faces. We've got work to do. Now, does anybody happen to know where the hell Storage is? Or do I have to figure everything out on my own?"

CHAPTER 19

As it turned out, several of the soldiers did have old wounds. They'd been more than happy to trade clothing or coin as payment for being healed. While no great joy for Richard, only a couple of the soldier's old wounds caused him undue pain to replicate. As far as healing was concerned, he'd actually expected worse.

An hour later found Richard and the rest of the team in a private dining room at the back of the tavern. The women had acquired leather pants and jerkins. The men were wearing a conglomeration of various pieces of ill-fitting military uniforms. Some of it didn't smell all that clean, but as far as Richard was concerned, it was better than running around naked. They pulled together several tables and sat down with Emerald, Chancee, and Lieutenant Dandridge, the officer from the group of soldiers. Emerald shoved a handful of coins into the tavern owner's hands to pay for a feast, and the table was soon laden with various foods and drinks. The dwarf even paid for three rooms for Richard and his team.

"We've got some coin now," Richard said holding out a hand with the coins he'd been given by the soldiers. "We can pay our own way."

Emerald looked down at the coins and smiled. "Those coppers may not buy as much as you think. Why don't you let me pay now, and you can make up for it later when you've earned a little more?"

While it grated Richard to accept charity, the aroma from a large bowl of steaming stew convinced him to make an exception.

He nodded his head and spooned a ladle of stew into his bowl.

Despite the sudden abundance of food, the only ones eating were Matthew, Tia, and Richard. The other wizard scouts didn't bother because their self-heal kept them from getting hungry or thirsty. For reasons of their own, the dwarf, the blonde woman, and the officer didn't eat either, but they did sip out of their wooden goblets on occasion.

Swallowing a mouthful of stew, Richard licked his spoon clean and pointed it at the dwarf. "You said the Oracle sent you here to find someone to help free your country?"

"That's right," replied Emerald. "The Dragars and their vampire allies slaughtered my people when I was a child. The Oracle said the time has come to drive them out."

Lieutenant Dandridge took a large gulp out of his cup. He wiped his mouth on his sleeve. "You're crazy. No one can stand up to the Dragars. Whenever anyone resists, they bring in those flying machines of theirs and blow up a few cities. That's always quieted any thoughts of rebellion down real quick."

The dwarf turned red-faced at the officer's words and leaned in to respond, but Jerad beat her to it.

"Lieutenant, you told us earlier that your king already has his army on the move. Aren't you worried your troops will provide a tempting target to these Dragars of yours?"

The lieutenant looked thoughtful for a second. "I suppose it could, but that's a decision made at a level a lot higher than mine. But, this far away from the Dragars' main city, they pretty much leave us alone as long as we don't cause them any direct trouble."

"Leave you alone?" snorted Emerald. "Ha! What do you call it when they come in once a year and haul off your best and brightest to be their slaves? And those are the lucky ones. The Creator only knows what they do with their other captives."

The lieutenant glared at the dwarf. "It's the price of survival for our civilization. The Dragars take only a few hundred. The king has to balance that against the hundreds of thousands who are spared."

"That's no kind of life," argued Emerald.

"Who are you to talk?" asked Lieutenant Dandridge. "Don't think I haven't heard of you before now. You're the last in the royal line of the Drepdenoris dwarves. You've been running around stirring up trouble for the last century. The few kingdoms who've listened to you over the years are gone. The Dragars destroyed them just like they did yours. That's why your people no longer exist."

"My people died bravely," argued Emerald.

"Yes, I'm sure they died fighting honorably," said the lieutenant. "However, the keyword is 'died.'"

Lieutenant Dandridge turned to Jerad and Richard and spoke in a harsh voice. "Don't let the dwarf pull you into her schemes. Her people are mostly dead. There are other dwarves in our land, but they haven't been stupid enough to listen to her. They stay hidden deep under their mountains where it's relatively safe. My people, on the other hand, are forced to live on the surface." The lieutenant let out a heavy sigh, trying to get his emotions under control. "I don't like what my people are forced to do to survive, but our king does what he must."

"No one's accusing you," said Jerad trying to calm the situation. "Who are we to say what we'd do if we were in your king's boots? Let me ask you this. If you could, would you fight these Dragars?"

Lieutenant Dandridge straightened up in his seat. "Of course I'd fight. Who wouldn't? But there's a big difference between fighting and lining up to be slaughtered. Surely you've seen their flying ship's overhead? Nothing can stand up to them. What few dragons still existed in our lands were wiped out a hundred and fifty years ago when the Dragars first arrived."

Up to this point, the other wizard scouts had been content to let Jerad and Richard do the talking. Tam apparently reached the point where she could contain herself no longer.

"I'll admit I'm new here. But, I've spent most of my life fighting wars of one kind or another. The one thing I've learned is that you can't appease an aggressor by giving in to them. They'll see it as a sign of weakness and want even more."

The lieutenant glared at Tam for a second as if he wanted to argue, then his face relaxed. "As I said, those kinds of decisions are made at a level much higher than a mere lieutenant."

Myers decided to get in on the conversation. "We're all soldiers here. We're used to following orders. I'm curious. Why has your king gathered his army if it presents a possible target for these Dragars?"

When Lieutenant Dandridge hesitated to answer, Chancee answered for him. "Like our soldier-boy here, I've no doubt good King Hamerstine believes we're too far north for the Dragars to take an active interest in our goings-on. He's probably right. If the king's army doesn't pose a threat to the Dragars' cities, they won't bother it." Chancee gave Jerad a wink. "After all, does an elephant really care what happens in an anthill when she's done stepping on it?"

The blonde woman's remark drew Richard's attention. "An elephant? I've never seen an elephant during my times on Portalis. We're on Portalis, aren't we?"

"Uh... yes," replied Chancee sounding a little surprised at the question. "Where else do you think we'd be?"

Touche, Richard thought. *Where else indeed?* He decided to try and narrow the question down. "Are we on Slyvrastra?"

"You're speaking of the land of the elves," said Chancee. "Only a few of our kind have visited that place of legend. It's far across the ocean, or so I'm told."

Richard knew his next question would sound strange, but he had to ask. "When are we?"

Sure enough, his words drew blank stares from Emerald, Chancee, and Lieutenant Dandridge.

Emerald was the first to recover. "Are you asking what day it is?"

Although that wasn't the question he'd intended, Richard supposed it was the best way to phrase the question and still get an answer. He nodded his head.

"It's the fourth day of Spring in the year of the Aeronian Kings," said Emerald. "Or, if you prefer, it's the eighth day of the twelfth month since the death of the first dwarf king 14,122 years ago."

"What about the Year of the Tree?" Richard asked trying to get a useful point of reference.

The dwarf looked at Chancee who shrugged her shoulders. Their actions told Richard the answer to his question even before Emerald had a chance to reply.

"Ah..., what tree would that be?"

Richard looked at Lieutenant Dandridge.

The officer shook his head. "Can't say I've ever heard of

anyone keeping track of time by a tree. Are you talking about counting the rings inside a tree trunk?"

Richard knew a hopeless battle when he heard it. "Never mind."

Myers spoke again. "You didn't answer my original question about why your king has gathered his army. Is it a secret or something?"

"If'n it is," laughed Chancee, "it's the worst-kept secret on Portalis. The Dragars pretty much leave us alone up here. However, the filth that crawled out of their holes and sided with those monsters from the sky don't. My understanding is they've got the city of Cantonsburg under siege."

"That's right," said Lieutenant Dandridge. "What you may not know is that a second army of orc scum is on their way to join the siege. Word is they're bringing top-of-the-line siege equipment with them."

"Oh," said Chancee. "I hadn't heard. Top-of-the-line, you say? That means some of the human city-states in the south must have joined them." Chancee turned her head and spat on the floor. "A curse on any humans who'd help those murdering orcs."

Emerald and the lieutenant nodded their heads in agreement.

"Aye," said Lieutenant Dandridge. "Some of those humans are no better than orcs or trolls. If the king doesn't get to Cantonsburg before the second army arrives, the city will fall. If that happens, the citizens who die in the final assault will be the lucky ones. A long, drawn-out torture session followed by an even slower death will be everyone else's fate."

"Rick," said Telsa. "What can we do? Should we help?"

"Let's not get ahead of ourselves, Telsa," Richard said. "I'm no fan of orcs, but I'm not sure this is our fight. We've been given our mission, remember?"

Telsa wasn't put off. "We're wizard scouts. What were all those lessons on honor and duty at the Academy about? If people are in trouble, we should help them. I don't need to be given a mission by some disembodied being to make me do the right thing. We should help."

Richard looked at Jerad for assistance in reasoning with Telsa. She was still young and inexperienced in the ways of the world. He figured a seasoned ex-battalion commander like Jerad would see the logic of avoiding unnecessary trouble.

Jerad did speak up, but not in the way Richard hoped. "We were given a mission to help a dwarf. What exactly is your plan, Emerald? How do you fit in this hodgepodge of circumstances?"

Emerald drummed her fingers on the table a couple of times before taking a deep gulp from her goblet. "Well, things are never simple, are they? Chancee and I were sent here by the Oracle to find allies. He said we'd know them when we saw them. I guess he figured they'd stand out in such a way we couldn't miss them."

Chancee laughed. "He also said we could trust them because they'd have nothing to hide. Believe me, boys, you had nothing to hide."

A couple of the others laughed politely.

Richard didn't. This was serious business. He'd seen too many people die horrible deaths during his missions for *'the One'* to think otherwise. "I'm assuming you're our dwarf, and we're your potential allies. We've linked up. Now what?"

Emerald drummed her fingers on the table again. "The Oracle asked us to return with you. He said he'd explain more when we got back. He also advised us not to pass up the possibility of acquiring other allies along the way." She locked eyes with Richard. "Although no one's said so, I'm assuming you're the leader of your little group. Am I right?"

Richard sensed Myers stiffen in his seat, but surprisingly, his brother didn't contradict the dwarf. None of the other wizard scouts denied her assumption either.

"Let's just say my previous experience makes me the temporary leader for this phase of our mission," Richard said.

Emerald nodded. "Good enough. I just like to know who the decision maker is when I'm talking so I don't waste my breath."

"Fine," Richard said before repeating his question. "So, what are your plans?"

Emerald turned to face Lieutenant Dandridge. "Chancee and I would like to help King Hamerstine break the siege at Cantonsburg." She made a sweep with her hand at Richard's group. "I've a feeling these nice people are willing to help as well. Do you think you can arrange a meeting with your king? I do have a plan."

"Possibly," said Lieutenant Dandridge. "I forgot to mention the king's my uncle. So what's your plan?"

"Well," laughed Emerald, "for starters, it's to get these men some clean clothes. To be quite frank, the ones they borrowed from your soldiers stink to high heaven."

"Amen to that, sister," said Tam, Telsa, Tia, and Trinity at the same time.

Everyone laughed.

CHAPTER 20

The tent of King Hamerstine was sparse. As far as Richard could tell, the king didn't believe in frills. He was all business. Richard took an immediate liking to the bear of a man. In contrast to Lieutenant Dandridge's clean-shaven look, the king had a shaggy beard and arm-length hair. The combination really did make him look a little like one of the bears Richard had seen at the zoo when he was young.

Despite the king's barbarian looks and demeanor, he was smart and mission-oriented. From what the lieutenant had told him during their ride to the army's encampment, the king's ancestors had carved out the kingdom of Hamerstonia from the vast forests of the north a thousand years earlier. It hadn't taken long for Richard to figure out the king had no intention of letting a bunch of orcs destroy his ancestors' legacy, even if those orcs were backed by flying Dragars.

After a brief demonstration by Jerad and Myers on a couple of wizard-scout abilities, King Hamerstine began grilling the wizard scouts and Emerald on their plans.

"Aye," bellowed the king after watching Myers deflect a thrown knife using telekinesis. "I'm sure that's very handy during a small-unit skirmish. Unfortunately, my scouts tell me there are over forty thousand orcs surrounding Cantonsburg as we speak. Can you and your friends be everywhere on the battlefield at once? Are their pools of magic so large they can defeat all forty thousand of our foes?"

Emerald looked at Jerad for support.

"No," admitted Jerad. "Our Power reserves are finite in size. Once our reserves are empty, we'll only have our wits and the weapons you've kindly provided us." Jerad drew a longsword from a scabbard at his waist. He gave the king a wry smile. "To be quite honest, most of us haven't had much training with these types of weapons."

"As I suspected," said King Hamerstine. "My army has its share of mages and priests already. I doubt a half dozen more will have much effect one way or the other on the battle's outcome. A good leader knows to use magic users at the right place and time as a force multiplier. In the end, I've no doubt the battle will be decided by brave soldiers swinging swords of steel powered by the strength of their arms."

"I understand," said Emerald who appeared undaunted. "However, it may well be that the city of Cantonsburg is the right place and time to use my friends' strange magic. Besides, I haven't told you my entire plan."

The king looked to his left at a grizzled man wearing plate mail. "General Onstott, what do you think, old friend?"

The general passed his eyes over Richard and his friends before answering his king. "Sire, we need at least three more days to gather our forces. It'll take another seven days of hard marching to make the trek to Cantonsburg. It may well be that there'll be nothing to save when we get there. Competent though these magic users seem to be, I doubt they'd add much to our forces here. What have we got to lose by allowing them to proceed ahead of us? At the very least, they can act as our messengers and let the garrison at Cantonsburg know we're on our way."

The king seemed to mull over his general's words for a moment. "Very well, dwarf. What's your plan?"

"My plan is to form a Circle," said Emerald.

The dwarf's answer confused Richard. From the looks on the faces of Jerad and Myers, they were equally confused. In contrast, the king seemed to know exactly what Emerald meant.

"Ah," said King Hamerstine, "I've heard legends of the dwarves' Circle when I was a young child sitting on my father's knee. The stories were told as fables. If the ability ever existed, I assumed it was lost many generations ago."

"Perhaps many generations for humans, sire," said Emerald. "For dwarves, it has been but a single generation in the past. My father, King Lokanstanos, had the ability. He formed a Circle during the final defense of Drepdenor."

Even after his many missions on Portalis, lack of tact was still one of Richard's shortcomings. Ignoring any possible faux pas for interrupting royalty without being invited, Richard asked the questions he was sure the other wizard scouts wanted answered as much as he. "What's this Circle you're talking about? And how can it help this Cantonsburg?"

The king didn't appear offended by Richard's interruption. Instead, he gave a broad smile as he looked at the armored general to his left. Reaching out with his left hand, the king slapped the general on the back. "Ha! I told you this was the one to watch. He tries to stay in the background, but he's the one in charge. You owe me a keg, old friend."

General Onstott rubbed his shoulder. Even against plate mail, the bear of a king's slap must have had some force to it.

"So I do," said the general with a smile of his own. "I should learn not to bet against you."

Still smiling, the king looked back at Richard. "Well, Sir Richard, allow me to answer your question. As the legends go, a Circle is the formation of a mystical linking of living creatures. Soldiers are stronger and braver, horses are faster and more fierce, and the spells of mages and priests are more powerful than normal." With a look that seemed to indicate he doubted the legends, the king said, "Or so the stories go."

"It's no legend, sire," said Emerald a little heatedly. "I saw it with my own eyes. I felt its energy flowing through me. I was only a child at the time, but I remember it as though it were yesterday."

"You say you're the daughter of King Lokanstanos?" asked General Onstott. "Have you ever formed a Circle yourself? If so, where? I've never heard of it."

Emerald shook her head. "No, I haven't."

"Then why do you think you can do it now?" asked King Hamerstine. "Why risk your life and those of your friends by going to Cantonsburg?"

The dwarf pointed at Myers and Richard. "Because of them. I've met someone like them before. Also because of things the

Oracle told me. A lot of what he said didn't make sense at the time but does now. I believe I can form a Circle, and I believe they can help me."

"Rick," said Jerad. "Have you been holding something back you should be telling us?"

Richard's thoughts went back to his time fighting in the spirit-wolf wars. He remembered the Power structure formed by the demon with its minions. While the links between the various life forms hadn't been completely circular, the links had certainly increased the abilities of the creatures involved.

With a shrug of his shoulders, Richard tried to explain. "I don't think so. I saw Power manipulated once to form links that were kind of circular, but I certainly don't know how to do it."

The king gave Emerald a questioning look. "The risk is yours, dwarf. Since it's only costing me a few uniforms and some horses, I'll allow you to go to Cantonsburg. At the very least, you can tell them we'll be there in ten days. We'll get there sooner if we can. If you somehow form this Circle of yours to help the defenders hold the city until we get there, more the better."

"Then we'll leave at once," said Emerald. "Time's short."

"So it is," agreed King Hamerstine.

Lieutenant Dandridge stepped forward before Emerald could move. "Uncle?"

The king looked at his nephew. "Yes?"

"My men and I would like to go with them. You've more than enough scouts in the army. We may be more useful at Cantonsburg."

King Hamerstine eyed the lieutenant for several seconds. "I don't know. It's a fool's errand. My sister would have my hide if you went out and did something stupid like get yourself killed."

"You know my family's there, sire."

"Yes, I do," said the king. "That's why I sent your scouting party in the opposite direction. I didn't want temptation pulling on you."

Lieutenant Dandridge's back stiffened until it was ramrod straight. "I'm a soldier of the royal blood. I never have and never will shirk my duty."

The king held up a hand. "Don't get your dander up, boy. I didn't say I thought you'd go derelict on me. I said I wanted to spare you the temptation."

Slightly mollified, Lieutenant Dandridge said, "My scouts and I are from Cantonsburg. We know the secret paths and ways into the city. Even if the dwarf and her friends get to the city, they'd be hard-pressed to slip past forty thousand orcs without being seen. We could get them inside."

General Onstott whispered into the king's ear.

The king nodded. "Very well," said King Hamerstine. "You and your scouts shall go. However, you'll go as a colonel, not as a shave-tail lieutenant. You'll take command of the garrison there for the duration of the crisis. It'll do the morale of the citizens good to know one of the royal bloodlines is there." Indicating the others standing around the lieutenant, the king said, "You brought these people here, so you can take responsibility for them."

The newly appointed Colonel Dandridge snapped to attention and brought his right arm across his chest in a salute. "Yes, sire! I won't let you down."

King Hamerstine nodded his head and smiled. "I know you won't. You remind me of your father. He was a good friend as well as my brother-in-law."

The king stood and began unstrapping his belt and scabbard. He walked up to his nephew and pulled a large bastard sword from its sheath. "This is Morning's Twilight. Your father gave it to me as a wedding present. I think it's high time you had it."

Richard watched the king's nephew accept the sword and hold it gingerly in his hands. A blue stone in the handle radiated Power. Richard could tell the cutting edge of the blade was coated with energized titanium.

"Creallium," whispered Jerad in Richard's ear.

"Holy Metal," Emerald whispered using the Portalis term.

A few more pleasantries were passed back and forth, but for all intents and purposes, the meeting was over. Before the hour was out, Richard and his group were riding horses south with Colonel Dandridge and his soldiers.

After all the riding he'd done on the dolgars' spirit-horse, Richard assumed he'd have no trouble riding a real horse. He was wrong. The use of the reins was difficult, and the leather saddle was none too comfortable. Richard began to appreciate how much the spirit-horse compensated for his lack of skill. His ego was spared a little since most of the other wizard scouts were as unfamiliar with riding horses as him. Much to his chagrin, the only exception was Myers. His brother had mounted his stallion and guided him around like he'd been doing it for years. When questioned by Tam, his brother admitted his mother started him riding horses at an early age. He said she'd always told him he'd never know when the skill might come in handy. Fortunately, once they put a few kilometers behind them, Richard's riding skills improved enough to allow him to ride while concentrating on something other than remaining in the saddle.

Colonel Dandridge dispatched some of his soldiers as outriders to watch their flanks and rear. He sent two more of his soldiers a couple of hundred meters ahead to spot any possible ambushes.

"Maybe we should tell them they don't need to scout ahead," said Telsa. "Our passive scans can keep track of what's going on around us."

Richard had been meaning to talk to the other wizard scouts and give them a dose of reality. Telsa's words told him it was time to do so now.

"Gather in," Richard said. "I think it's time I brought you all up to speed on how things work on Portalis."

The other wizard scouts and Matthew and Tia drew closer.

"I don't know exactly where we are in time," Richard admitted, "but we're pretty far in the past. That I know for a fact."

Tam twisted in her saddle until she was looking at Richard. "How do you know?"

"I scanned the two mages King Hamerstine had with him," Richard explained. "The links to their Power reserves were heavily trapped. It's been my experience the farther back in time I've been, the more skilled I've found the magic users. The closer the missions have been to our time in the future, the less skilled they've been. I did a mission only 2,500 years in the past once, and almost no one knew how to protect the links to their Power reserves."

Jerad waved his hand to include the other scouts. "You told me before that you protected our links. Even if the magic users here are as skilled as you think, aren't we safe?"

Richard thought for a moment before answering. "I spent a lot of time at the Academy putting traps on all the weak spots for

Tam, Telsa, and you. I may touch up a couple of places on your links if I get a chance, but I think they'll hold up well against even a determined mage or scout."

Trinity was riding next to Jerad. She leaned forward to look past her husband at Richard. "You left off Gaston and me. What about us?"

"I'm sorry to say the link to your Power reserve is vulnerable, Trinity," Richard said. "I put a few traps on it when we've been together in the past, but there are still a lot of gaps. I'll start beefing it up right away if you don't mind."

Trinity smiled. "Mind or not, I'm all yours. I'd hate to make a widower of Jerad so soon. So do what you must."

"What about Gaston?" asked Jerad.

Richard turned around and looked at Myers. His brother was riding near Matthew and Tia.

Myers frowned. "I'll be fine. You've already put traps on my link."

Richard was almost inclined to accept Myers's words and move on. Something in his Marine training wouldn't let him. He was too much of a team player to allow a weakness to threaten the group when he could do something about it.

"You're not protected enough," Richard told his brother. "I've put enough traps on your link to hold up maybe ten or fifteen seconds. That's fine for a short fight, but a skilled magic user will eventually get past them. Your link needs to be better protected."

Richard turned back in his saddle and faced forward. Using a voice loud enough for the others in his group to hear over the creaking saddles and plodding hoofs, Richard laid out his plans. "Emerald told me it'll take three days to get to Cantonsburg. During those three days, when we're not riding, we're going to be training. Myers and Trinity, I'll work with your links while we ride. Myers, you're a diviner the same as me. I'll show you how to protect links and how to break them. When we stop tonight, I'll also show each of you a little drilling technique I learned for getting past protective shields."

Tam laughed. "I think school's back in session, guys."

"Yeah," said Telsa. "Just like old times."

Richard smiled. "Not quite like old times. The difference is that whatever I show you this time may mean the difference between life and death in three days." Richard paused for a few seconds to let his words sink in before continuing. "Look. I don't know what's facing us. However, an army of forty thousand is bound to have a hefty contingent of priests and mages. If we're as far in the past as I think, then they're liable to be just as tough as a Crosioian scout. You've got to be tougher. Don't let the fact they're orcs make you think they're stupid. They're big and ugly, but they're smart in their own way. A lot of their units are well-disciplined. Also, most orcs I've fought have no sense of fear. They'll keep coming when a human with any sense would run."

"Are you trying to tell us their magic users are better than us?" asked Telsa.

"No," Richard said. "Not at all. I just don't want you to underestimate them. Their infantry will seek to overwhelm you and keep you off balance while their magic users stay back and combine their spells to break down your defenses. Remember, we don't have our technology to back up our wizard scout abilities."

Richard pulled the short sword Colonel Dandridge gave him out of its scabbard. He lifted the weapon for all to see. It wasn't magic, but the sword was well-balanced and the blade was razor sharp. "We'll need to use these weapons whenever possible. Save your Power for when you absolutely need it. A prolonged battle will drain you dry. Believe me, I know."

Telsa pulled her own sword out and turned it over in her hands. "Well, I don't know about the rest of you, but my skillsets with this little pactar-sticker is lacking to say the least."

To Richard's surprise, Myers volunteered to help. "I'll work with you tonight on that. The commandant insisted I practice with antique weapons as soon as I was old enough to hold one in my hands without dragging it on the floor. I'm pretty good at it. I'll help anyone who thinks they need a little training."

Although Richard hated to admit it, he knew his brother was good with swords and knives. During his years at the Academy, Myers had often forced him to spar with antique weapons. He had thought it was a waste of time. He'd found out otherwise. After being sent on a few missions for *'the One'* without his technology, his skill with a sword or knife had saved his life more than once. He grudgingly admitted some of the tricks his brother had shown him during those practice sessions had paid off.

"What about me?" asked Tia. "I've had some fencing lessons, but that's been about it. I've never used anything as heavy as this longsword. I'll need some practice before we get into any fights."

"Mother made me join the fencing team at school as well," said Matthew. "I got pretty good. I even won a few trophies. I always thought it was a waste of time. Now I suppose I'm going to get a chance to put those skills to good use. I'm kind of looking forward to it."

Before Richard could say anything, Myers shot down Matthew's hopes before they got off the ground. "We're going to drop you two off at the first safe spot we can find. I'm not risking your lives by taking you into some medieval battle and having your heads cut off." Myers looked directly at Matthew. "I promised your mother I'd keep you safe."

Matthew drew in a deep breath. His face took on a defiant look. Before the teenager could start an argument, Richard intervened.

"Bad idea," Richard told Myers. "We were close together when we teleported here as a group. When our mission is complete, we may need to be teleported back as a group. I think it's best if we stay close to each other. If Matt and Tia are a couple of hundred kilometers away, they may be left behind. They'd be trapped in the past, and there wouldn't be a thing we could do about it."

Myers didn't look convinced.

Richard had a feeling his brother needed a solid example. "My niece and nephew have been trapped in the past for the last couple of years. I've tried everything I know how to do, and I still haven't been able to rescue them." Richard looked at the teenagers. "As long as I'm in charge, the two of you are going to stay close to us. That's just the way it's going to be."

Matthew nodded his head gratefully. He sent a 'so there' smile in Myers's direction. Richard's brother looked none too happy.

Too bad, Richard thought. *Life sucks. Get used to it.*

CHAPTER 21

Colonel Dandridge and Emerald pushed them hard all day. Richard spent his time in the saddle analyzing and placing traps on Trinity's link to her Power reserve. Although far from perfect, by the time they made camp for the night, he felt confident even a skilled mage would require at least a minute to bypass her link's security. He told Trinity as much.

"Thanks," said Trinity as she dismounted her horse. "I owe you."

"No problem. I'll tighten it up some more tomorrow."

Trinity nodded her head before walking over to join Jerad. The two tethered their horses together and brushed them down. After they finished, Richard noticed them walking hand-in-hand into the woods. He assumed they wanted to be alone for a while. He didn't blame them. The previous night was supposed to have been their wedding night after all.

Richard sensed a presence nearby and turned around to find Telsa watching him. "You're getting very good at stealth shields," he told her. "I didn't even sense you."

Telsa smiled. "I had a good teacher. Besides, I'm cheating a little. Since my Power reserve is full, I've switched back to my best stealth shield. I figured why not?"

"Well, it's a good shield," Richard said.

As he spoke to Telsa, he continued to monitor his passive scan. He noticed the two Power readings for Trinity and Jerad disappear.

Telsa must have noticed their disappearance as well. "I guess they don't want anyone trying to follow them. Not that anyone would."

Richard nodded in agreement. "At least not anyone who wanted to keep their head on their shoulders."

Telsa tilted her head in the direction of the camp. Colonel Dandridge's scouts were already laying out their gear and assigning guard posts. Some blackened pots hung over two very small fires. Richard thought he smelled some kind of stew in the air.

"Shall we join the others?" asked Telsa. "Gaston and that blonde girl said they'd show us how to use these swords. Plus, you promised to teach us that drilling trick of yours, remember?"

"So I did," Richard said as he followed his friend to the center of the camp.

Myers and Chancee were already working with Tam, Tia, and Matthew on some simple sword moves. Telsa joined them. Richard watched them for a few minutes. He had to admit Myers was a patient teacher when he wanted to be. His brother spent a considerable amount of time demonstrating sword moves to Matthew and Tia. Somehow, his brother was able to take their previous fencing experience and convert it into useful attacks and parries with a longsword.

As Richard watched, Myers had Matthew make a series of attacks while his ex-TAC officer defended. The teenager made several swings, which Myers easily deflected. Suddenly, Matthew lunged forward with his arm outstretched. The tip of his longsword passed over Myers's counterstroke and plunged deep into the chest of Richard's brother.

Matthew let go of the handle of his sword and gasped, "No!"

Myers stood there with the sword sticking out of his chest.

"By the Creator," said Chancee who'd been sparring with Telsa. "You've killed him."

Richard knew better. He'd sensed a line of Power from Myers wrap around the blade of Matthew's sword and make it shimmer before it plunged into his chest.

He's a shifter, Richard thought.

Obviously, Myers had allowed Matthew's attack to get through his defenses on purpose, Richard just wasn't sure why. That Myers could cause objects to shift into the void confused him. His brother was a diviner. He hadn't known his ex-TAC officer had more than one specialty.

Matthew stood there white-faced as Myers slowly went through the motions of pulling the teenager's sword out of his body. Once it was out, he handed the weapon back to the boy. Richard noticed the blade was clean with nary a drop of blood. He'd expected no less.

"You let go of your sword, Matt," said Myers to the still ashen-faced teenager. "You should never stop fighting until you're certain your foe is dead."

When Matthew struggled to find words, Richard came to his rescue. "Myers pulled a fast one on you, Matt. He shifted your sword blade into the void. It's the same technique I used when I shifted your mother and you into the elevator shaft. Remember that?"

The teenager nodded his head.

Richard knew he'd remember. An assassin had shot Matthew's mother. He had been forced to shift both Matthew and his mother into the void to save their lives. "Well, then you can understand that your sword never really penetrated Myers's body. I suspect he used telekinesis to give the sword some back pressure to make it feel like you'd hit flesh."

Turning to Myers, Richard said, "That was an expensive trick. It would've used less Power to just deflect his sword blade to the side. Weren't you always lecturing us to conserve Power when we were at the Academy?"

Myers glared at Richard as he opened his mouth to speak, then stopped himself before the words escaped. As if unwilling to address Richard directly, Myers turned to Tam and Telsa.

"Sometimes showmanship is worth the Power cost. I could've used telekinesis to stop Matt's blow, but by shifting the blade into the void, I shocked him enough to make him let go of his sword. If he'd been with a group, they might have all turned and run."

Tam nodded her head as if agreeing.

Telsa didn't seem as convinced. "That's all well and good, but unfortunately, I'm not a shifter. I can't do that little trick."

Myers didn't seem to take offense at Telsa's remarks. "It's the showmanship that's important, not the actual act. Wizard scouts have lots of techniques at their disposal."

"You mean like when you used telekinesis to freeze those crossbow bolts in the air at the tavern?" asked Telsa.

Myers nodded. "It did the trick. I'm sure you noticed the soldiers stopped dead in their tracks. By using the extra Power to freeze the bolts in the air, it saved us from having to kill some of those men."

"I didn't know you were a shifter," Richard said with an edge to his voice, but he didn't care. His brother's actions always seemed to rub him the wrong way.

"Then I guess there's some things you don't know about me," replied Myers. "Imagine that."

The animal which was Richard's temper rattled its cage. With great effort, he held it in check. He was all too aware now was neither the time nor place to have it out with his brother.

"Well," Richard said trying to change the subject and avoid an argument, "if you're done here, I need to show you how to attack and defend Power links. You're the only other diviner here. We'll need to watch out for the others. Only diviners can manipulate links."

"Later," snapped Myers. "I need to finish my training with Matt first."

Richard was almost ready to start an argument when he heard shouts coming from the other side of camp. He recognized the voices as those of Colonel Dandridge and the dwarf.

"Fine," Richard told Myers. "I'll get with you later."

"You do that," said Myers as he turned his back in apparent dismissal.

Richard was tempted to jerk Myers around and shove his arrogant brother's attitude down his throat. More shouting from the other side of camp told him he was needed there. He swallowed his pride and headed in the direction of the colonel and Emerald.

When Richard arrived, the two were in the midst of a yelling match that made even Richard uncomfortable. Colonel Dandridge towered over the dwarf, but Emerald wasn't intimidated. She just looked up at the larger man and gave him as much as she got.

"And I tell you I don't care what your orders are," said Emerald. "I like your uncle, but he's not my king. The others and I are going to see the Oracle first. You're welcome to come along or go your own way. I could care less."

"You arrogant little...," Colonel Dandridge caught himself before the words came out and composed himself before continuing. "The people of Cantonsburg are dying. My family may be dying. We need to get there as fast as possible. That Circle of yours may be their only hope."

At the mention of the colonel's family, Emerald seemed to bite off her words. She took a couple of deep breaths. When she finally spoke, it was in a much calmer voice. "I can understand your concern, Colonel. I lost my family years ago, and it still hurts. I wish I could have helped them, but I couldn't. Believe me when I say, the only chance to save your family may be for us to see the Oracle first."

Richard stepped closer to the two. "Why? Why's seeing the Oracle so important?"

Turning away from the colonel, Emerald faced Richard. "Ah, Rick. I didn't see you." The dwarf suddenly looked down and used her foot to nudge an ember back into the fire. "Well, to tell the truth, I may have forgotten to mention that I can't form a Circle unless Gaston and you help me."

"Actually, you did mention it," Richard said. He suspected trouble.

"Oh..., did I? Well then, I might have forgotten to mention that the Oracle said he needed to see both of you first so you'd know how to help. He told me '*The brothers need to learn to work together or all is lost.*' Jerad told me earlier today that Gaston and you are brothers. He also told me the two of you don't get along so well. I think that may be the reason the Oracle wants to see both of you."

"I've been trying to tell this hard-headed dwarf we need to go directly to Cantonsburg," said Colonel Dandridge.

The look the colonel gave Richard made him think the officer was hoping he'd turn out to be an ally. Richard hated to disappoint him. "I've had dealings with the Oracle before. Sometimes his words aren't all that clear, but to tell the truth, I've never had him steer me wrong."

Richard remembered a time in the Oracle's stronghold when he'd been given a memory of the elf, Shandria. She'd told him he could always trust the Oracle just like he could trust her. Shandria had been his friend. After all these years, her words were still fresh in his mind.

Richard took a step to stand beside Emerald. "If the Oracle says we need to see him first, then that's where we need to go."

When the colonel started to open his mouth, Richard raised a hand. "It'll do no good to reach your city if we're not ready. As Emerald said, you're welcome to come or stay. My friends and I are going with her."

There were a few more minutes of tense conversation, but in the end, the colonel agreed to accompany them. Richard knew it was really the only decision the officer could make. After all, even with ten heavily armed soldiers backing him up, he couldn't force six wizard scouts to do anything they didn't want to do.

As Colonel Dandridge tromped off, Richard glanced down at Emerald. "I hope you know what you're doing."

"So do I, wizard scout. So do I."

CHAPTER 22

The home of the Oracle wasn't what Richard expected. When he'd visited the Oracle in the past, it had always been in a palace dug into the side of a mountain. Depending on when in time his mission occurred, the Oracle's abode was either a highly maintained and elaborate affair or an age-worn, dilapidated set of near ruins. During his most recent mission, which had been only 2,500 years in the past, the Oracle's home hadn't even had lights in a lot of the rooms or hallways.

Richard stared at what was before him now. It wasn't the location he'd previously visited. The place where the dwarf had led them was the entrance to a small, dark cave. In fact, the word cave was giving the hole in the side of the hill too much credit.

"This is the home of the Oracle?" Richard asked.

"Yes," said Emerald. "What'd you expect, a palace made out of polished marble with servants at the Oracle's beck and call? Why would the Oracle need those?"

Actually, Richard had been expecting a palace. *After all, the Oracle's a human. Surely he likes his creature comforts as much as the next person.* One look at the dwarf's questioning face convinced him to keep his opinion to himself. Still, he was puzzled.

"Is everything okay, buddy?" asked Jerad, who was sitting on a horse next to Richard and must have seen the look on his face.

"I suppose," Richard said. "I guess I was expecting something different."

"Well, you said we weren't even on the same continent as your previous missions. Things are bound to be different."

Richard nodded his head in reluctant agreement. He hated change. But it was what it was, so he decided to go with the flow. He dismounted his horse. The others followed suit.

One of Colonel Dandridge's scouts handed Emerald a torch and held a thin piece of wood to it. The soldier said a word Richard heard but quickly forgot. A flash of fire jumped from the piece of wood to the torch, which burst into flame.

Emerald must have seen the quizzical look on Richard's face. "It's a match wand. Don't you have them where you're from? How else would you light a fire?"

"We have our ways," Richard said without trying to explain since he didn't happen to have a lighter handy.

Jerad had been eyeing the small cave opening. "Can we all fit?"

Emerald laughed. "Not hardly. It's pretty cramped in there. I think only the two brothers and I should go."

"We're not brothers," snarled Myers.

Emerald looked questioningly at Richard.

"Uh..., it's hard to explain," Richard told her. "We've got the same parents, but we were raised apart."

When Emerald hesitated as if waiting for further explanation, Myers grabbed the torch from her hand and entered the cave's entrance. She quickly followed, and Richard brought up the rear. The entrance was low enough Richard had to duck his head to enter. Once inside, he realized the dwarf had been correct. The cave was very cramped. In fact, it consisted of a single room only five paces across. He saw no furniture, no lights, and no one. Only the rough-cut limestone of the floor and walls greeted him.

Richard gazed around in the flickering torchlight. Without his battle helmet, he couldn't see in the dark. From what he could see in the light of the torch, he had a feeling he wasn't missing much.

Myers turned to face Emerald. "Is this your idea of a joke? The place is empty."

"*Ah,*" said a male voice that seemed to be more in their heads than an actual voice. "*You've brought the brothers. Good.*"

Richard looked around the still empty room again.

"We're not brothers," said Myers as much for his benefit as for the voice's.

"*Hmm. Do you really believe that?*" asked the voice. "*You creatures of flesh and blood are so illogical at times. Facts are facts. I sense the similarities in your DNA. Words won't change your common heritage.*"

"Where are you?" Richard asked. "Who are you? Show yourself."

"*I'm the Oracle,*" said the voice. "*I'm all around you. I'm in the very air you are breathing. What did you expect?*"

"I've met the Oracle before," Richard said. "The Oracle's always been a human. Sometimes the Oracle has been a child, and sometimes an old man or woman. However, the Oracle's always been a human."

"*Really?*" asked the Oracle. "*Hmm. That's actually a good idea. If I was in the form of a human, I calculate I would be accepted by others more easily. I'll have to run some calculations to determine if it would improve my efficiency.*"

Richard let his mind roam through the cavern. He reduced the range of his passive scan until it extended no farther than the walls of the cave. He increased the sensitivity of his scan's filter the way Trinity had shown him. He reduced the filter until he could sense a spider in its web in one of the corners. He didn't sense the presence of any other life forms besides Emerald and Myers. Richard increased the sensitivity of his filter even more. Then he saw it.

"You're a gas," Richard said.

"*Of course,*" said the Oracle. "*What else would I be? And you're a carbon-based life form. Does it matter?*"

Things began to make sense in Richard's mind. On occasion, he'd had to merge his thoughts with his battle computer's to such an extent that he'd sensed ghosts of memories from his battle computer's past. He knew the brerellium encased CPU chip comprising a battle computer's primary CPU was filled with a type of living gas. He'd also begun to suspect the other free will parts of *'the One'* were composed of a similar gas.

"I thought you were human when we met before," Richard said. "I guess I was wrong. You're a gas. You're part of *'the One,'* aren't you?" Anger began building up inside Richard. Shandria had been wrong. The Oracle couldn't be trusted. The Oracle was part of the problem.

"What?" stammered Myers. "Are you telling me this is *'the*

One?'"

Richard sensed hatred in his brother's voice. Myers disliked *'the One'* as much as he; maybe more. His ex-TAC officer blamed *'the One'* for stealing his parents from him. Richard could understand Myers's hatred. *'The One'* had stolen his time with his parents as well.

"*Who is this* 'the One' *of whom you speak?*" asked the Oracle. "*I'm not familiar with the concept.*"

Richard wasn't sure whether to believe the Oracle or not. "It's the One Network Entity. Surely you know about *'the One?'* It's a network of gaseous beings like yourself. They control all the computer networks in the galaxy."

"What?" exclaimed Myers. "Computers are *'the One?'* Are you telling me all these years I've been wearing part of *'the One'* on my head? Are you saying my battle computer's part of *'the One?'* Is that what you're saying?"

"I don't know," Richard said. "Maybe. The central processing unit of our battle computers is a living gas. I think they're the same species as *'the One.'* They may not realize it. I think only the central computer and the other major computers are aware they're part of *'the One.'"*

Richard could feel the anger burning in his brother. His brother was having difficulty recovering from the shock of discovering his very battle helmet might be part of the entity he hated so much.

"*Ah..., computers,*" said the Oracle. "*I'm familiar with them. The Dragars use them extensively. Computers are logical. They're very comforting. You freewill creatures are difficult to guide. I calculated our meeting would go much differently.*"

"Are you telling me you're not part of *'the One?'"* Richard demanded.

"*I'm not familiar with* 'the One' *of whom you speak,*" said the Oracle. "*Maybe I will be one day, but I'm not at present.*"

"Why are we here?" growled Myers.

Emerald got in on the conversation. "You told me I needed to bring the brothers to you in order to free my home. Well, here they are. Now what?"

"*Ah..., yes,*" said the Oracle. "*They're the necessary variables I was told to seek. They are part of the algorithm.*"

"Who told you?" Richard asked.

"*I'm not sure,*" said the Oracle sounding genuinely puzzled. "*The idea just came to me. Perhaps it was this* 'the One' *of whom you speak. Or perhaps it was my future self. It's hard to say. I'm missing data. You and the others are the missing variables, of that I'm sure. You're necessary. The Dragars must be stopped, or all will be lost.*"

"Why should we care about the Dragars?" asked Myers. "We're just trying to get home."

"*To get home, you must stop the Dragars,*" said the Oracle. "*Is that not your mission?*"

Richard was above average in intelligence, but things were getting way past his level of comprehension. It was almost to the point of which came first, the chicken or the egg. Their mission came from *'the One,'* but this version of the Oracle claimed he didn't know about *'the One.'* If the Oracle didn't know about *'the One,'* how did it know about their mission or the algorithm Nickelo had told him about?

"Enough talk," Richard said. "Show me."

"*Ah, yes,*" said the Oracle. "*That would be easier, wouldn't it? You have part of my species in you. I sense it. Plus, your mind has been touched by a demon; a master demon unless I miss my guess. Your mind has been prepared. You must come with me. I will show you what must be done.*"

Richard felt his mind being pulled into the flow of energy that was the Oracle. He felt their minds begin to merge similar to the times when his thoughts blended with those of his battle computer. He resisted.

"*No,*" said the Oracle. "*You must open yourself up.*"

Richard immediately balked. "Like hell, I will."

A sense of frustration came from the part of Richard's mind that was already partially blended with the Oracle. "*Freewill is so hard to anticipate. I will need to come up with a better method of dealing with other life forms. Perhaps appearing as a human would be best as you suggested. However, it is what it is right now. You must come with me.*"

A line of Power from the Oracle probed at Richard's mind. He resisted. Even so, the presence of the Oracle touched the piece of DNA *'the One'* had placed inside Richard when he was still an embryo.

Richard's senses expanded. He became aware of many things.

"*Oh, dear,*" said the Oracle. "*I miscalculated. I think you've just corrupted me.*"

"Well," Richard said out loud, "it serves you right. Guess you should've taken the time to talk things over first. I would've told you I tend to corrupt battle computers. I guess that extends to any gaseous life form as well."

"*Yes,*" said the Oracle. For some reason, he laughed. "*I think I see humor in the situation. Strange, I didn't understand humor before. I'm a little angry as well. If there are others of my kind out there as you say, they'll need to isolate me so I don't spread your corruption.*"

"*Welcome to the club,*" Richard said. "*Being alone sucks, but you'll get used to it. Or maybe you won't. Frankly, I don't especially care one way or the other.*"

Richard sensed the Oracle calculating probabilities and outcomes. The thoughts came much too fast for Richard to pick out the details, but he did get the gist of the equations. He saw himself as one of the variables in the equation. The algorithm shifted and then settled down.

"It will still work," said the Oracle with a sense of relief. *"Come. We must go. You must bring your brother."*

"How?"

"*Open your mind and let him become part of you.*"

"Forget that."

"*Hmm. Then you must figure out another way. The fate of three galaxies depends on the two of you working together.*"

Great, Richard thought. *That's just great. I'm always getting a guilt trip thrown at me. I'm no hero. I'm no great savior. If the fate of galaxies depends on me, then I think they're screwed.* Richard stewed in his emotions for what seemed like a long time, though it was only nanoseconds. He felt his mind going into hyper-speed as he was pulled ever deeper into the thoughts of the Oracle. Possibilities flashed into his mind, but he discarded each of them until he sensed one that made him think of a probable solution.

Richard touched all of the links attached to him. He sensed the three links to his Power reserves, then the link to his friend Stella. Her link was heavily booby-trapped, but he could still feel her presence ever so slightly at the other end. How that was possible when he was in the past and she was in the future, he didn't know, but there it was. The link Shandria had connected to him during his training was also there. It was a dead link. Although it was no longer active, he'd been able to use her link to connect with a *'helper'* during a previous mission. He didn't sense the presence of the *'helper'* now, but the experience had taught him links could be leveraged for other purposes on occasion.

Richard touched another link he vaguely remembered being attached by a dark elf priest when he'd performed a mass healing of dark elves. The dark elf's link was as dead as that of Shandria's.

Another dead link was located nearby. That link made Richard's skin crawl. The link was one of his own creation. He'd used it to steal Power from a Dragar priest. He'd sucked the priest dry and then used the priest's connections to suck Power from the reserves of the priest's companions. The link was dead, but not silent. Over the past few months, it had given him strange urges. Something in the link haunted his dreams as if trying to punish him for destroying its owner. Richard shied away from the link. It was evil. He regretted ever creating it.

A final link drew Richard's attention. He often touched the link as a reminder of his heritage. The link had been attached to him by the commandant just before he'd died. It was inactive. On a whim, Richard traced the link to the commandant's damaged Power reserve. Letting his mind drift into the Power reserve, he probed its walls and sensed a trickle of Power. An opening in the reserve had collapsed shut, but a faint trace of Power seeped through the makeshift dam. Richard followed the Power until he came to another reserve. It was large; much larger than even the commandant's reserve. Richard recognized the frequency of the Power. It belonged to his brother, Gaston Myers.

During one of his training sessions at the Academy, the commandant had been critically injured. Myers had been forced to connect a link to the commandant's reserve to feed him Power until Richard could repair the commandant's link and heal him. Links were forever. Richard instinctively knew the link he'd just followed was the link Myers had created and attached to their father.

Richard gathered some of his own Power and placed traps on the link leading from Myers's reserve to the commandant's. He had no desire for Myers to somehow reverse the path he'd just traveled on his own. He trusted no one, especially not his brother.

When the deed was done, Richard touched Myers and pulled him into the area of his mind that was merged with the Oracle. Myers resisted, but his will was no match for the combined might of the Oracle and Richard.

No one spoke. Richard just sensed an awareness of what was. He sensed the world of Portalis. He suddenly knew where in time they were. They were a hundred thousand years in the past.

Richard sensed two major continents. One continent was the home of the elves. He recognized the shield surrounding the continent. The shield prevented technology from entering. With just a few exceptions, only magic flourished there. He sensed two large sources of Power. He knew they were gates. One gate was near a small village called Silver. The guardian protecting the gate was weak. He sensed an elven priestess being sent on a mission to seek a new guardian. He recognized the elf. She was Shandria.

His thoughts turned to the second gate. It was located deep inside a mountain. Although it was stronger than the first, the gate was also weak. It would eventually need a new guardian as well.

The mind of the Oracle pulled Myers and him back to their location on the second continent.

Richard noticed the land had no shield. His mind shifted back to a memory a hundred and fifty years earlier than the current time. The continent of the earlier time was primarily inhabited by dwarves, orcs, and humans. There was no technology. He sensed a Power source under a mountain range. A vision of a large, blue gem appeared in his mind.

Suddenly, everything changed. Black starships arrived overhead. They landed by the mountain with the blue gem. Dragars and their Tharg allies conquered the inhabitants surrounding the mountain range. They took control of the blue gem and killed the gem's dwarf guardians. Using the energy of the blue gem, the Dragars built a temple in the shape of a pyramid. Their starships brought dragon eggs as sacrifices. The pyramid sucked the DNA from the eggs.

Richard sensed an emotion from Myers. The emotion was 'covet.' Richard knew Myers now understood the truth. The DNA gas from the vent at the Academy had been the result of the sacrifice of millions of innocent dragons.

The Dragars brought a special egg to their temple. They split the egg into three spheres; orange, purple, and green.

Richard recognized the spheres. *It's the combination gate and time bubble. That can't be. It's destroyed. I saw it. I helped destroy it.*

"*Perhaps you will destroy it in the future,*" said the Oracle, "*but you haven't done so yet. Please continue watching.*"

The Dragars used the time bubble to send their black ships into the future. They brought back more dragon eggs as well as titanium ore.

"*The Holy Metal,*" said the Oracle. "*It's much rarer in the magic dimension than it is on your home plane. The Dragars' empire is far flung in our magic dimension. They're resisted by others, but the combination of the energy they get from the dragon's DNA and the Holy Metal they raid from your time has made them invincible. They seek to extend their reach into your time and into your dimension. You must stop them.*"

"*How?*" asked Myers.

"*You must overload their system,*" said the Oracle.

An image of bottles of refined DNA gas appeared in Richard's mind. He didn't need to count. He knew there were twenty-nine of them. It was only logical. The feeling of coveting in Myers increased to the point of being overwhelming. Richard wondered at his brother's interest in the gas.

Richard knew Empress Deloris was eager to acquire a bottle. She'd made that obvious during her push to close the Academy so the council could take control of the DNA gas vent. The destruction of the vent during the Crosioians' attack had defeated her plan, but not her ambition. He suspected she would do anything to get a bottle of the life-prolonging gas. However, he didn't understand his brother's interest. The emotion of coveting he read from his brother was more than that of an employee trying to get something for his boss.

Richard shoved the thought aside. The image changed. He saw fifteen bottles of DNA gas being inserted into the tip of the Dragars' pyramid. A series of calculations from the Oracle accompanied the image. The equations proved the fifteen bottles would overload the system and destroy the pyramid. The scene changed again. Richard saw the remaining fourteen bottles of DNA gas being inserted into the blue gem. The gem exploded sending small pieces of blue chips in every direction.

"*Both the pyramid and the blue gem must be destroyed,*" said the Oracle.

Richard spotted an obvious error in the Oracle's logic. "Unfortunately, we don't have the bottles of DNA gas. *'The One'* teleported us out before we could get them."

"*Another variable has been assigned the task,*" said the Oracle. "*She will bring you the bottles. In the meantime, your task is to form the Circle and free the slaves. You must also save as many eggs as you can. They'll be important during the final battle.*"

"We should be the ones to get the DNA gas," said Myers. *"They're ours."*

Richard heard the greed and longing in his brother's voice. It was the sound of someone who'd stop at nothing to gain their desire.

"*No,*" said the Oracle.

The anger creeping into the Oracle's voice told Richard his association with the Oracle was continuing to corrupt the gaseous-being emotionally.

"You have your task," continued the Oracle. *"You must help the dwarf. Watch and learn."*

The image changed to an underground cavern filled with dwarves of every size; children and adults. Richard knew the image was of something that had occurred in the past. As he watched, a bearded dwarf in plate mail raised a war hammer embedded with a blue gem. The gem pulsed with Power. Richard sensed the dwarf touch the Power and that of the dwarves around him. A line of Power reached out from the dwarf and touched his companions until all were connected. The dwarf changed the makeup of the links. The Power of all those touched by the links merged until all the dwarves were of one mind and accord. The fear residing within the dwarves was swept away. The dwarves became stronger and faster.

Richard had seen a similar link before. He recognized its frequency. The Power linking all of the dwarves reminded him of the links formed by the demon he'd fought with the dolgars.

"The dwarf's a diviner," said Myers. *"The dwarf's changed the*

links to two-way links. The links are allowing them to share their Power."

"*Yes,*" said the Oracle. "*It's the Circle.*"

The image disappeared.

Richard stood shoulder to shoulder with Myers in the small dark cave, waiting for further guidance. Emerald walked over and stood next to them. They waited. Their only reward was silence.

CHAPTER 23

Richard peeked over the stone battlement to look at the ground below. The distance was a full thirty meters. Movement in the air caught his attention. He jerked his head behind the stonework just as an arrow swished through the spot where it had been.

Tam laughed at Richard's sudden movement. "Didn't anyone ever tell you curiosity killed the pactar? The orcs out there can't shoot with a flip, but those human longbowmen with them look like they can thread the eye of a needle."

"So I see," Richard said. He wasn't nearly as amused as Tam. Since it was dangerous to look over the battlements at the orc army, he turned his gaze to what was inside the wall. "This city's way larger than I imagined. Heck, you could drive a Long Cat on this rampart and still have room for a Warcat to pass."

Tam turned away from the wall and looked back at the city. Smoke rose from several blackened buildings where the heaviest part of the fighting had occurred. Tam shook her head and turned back to Richard. "I thought sure they'd have the fire out by now. It's been burning all night."

Richard glanced at the smoke billowing out of the buildings and then at the orc army surrounding the city walls. "I think the city garrison had their hands full repulsing the orcs last night. It wasn't a full-out assault, but it still came close to breaching the walls."

"Yeah, I know," said Tam. "They're lucky Colonel Dandridge and his scouts knew the paths through those canyons and underground tunnels. If we hadn't been able to sneak into

Cantonsburg last night in time for the colonel to take charge of the garrison, I think the city would've fallen."

A quick look at the massed orcs outside the city and the thin line of defenders on the walls convinced Richard his friend was probably right.

Tam looked toward the city center. "I heard the colonel tell Jerad the city had a little over a hundred thousand civilians crammed within its walls. They've been under siege for over a month now."

"Yeah," Richard said. "I think they're starting to run low on supplies."

Richard glanced at the dozen or so soldiers manning their section of the rampart. Several of them had crossbows, but weren't returning fire at the besieging orcs.

"I guess they're saving their ammo for the main attack when it comes," Richard said.

One of the soldiers must have overheard because he turned away from the soldier he'd been talking to and looked at Richard.

"Well, we ain't gonna be saving them much longer," said the soldier who seemed to be a noncommissioned officer. The noncom pointed to some hills on the far horizon. "You see the haze near that set of hills? I mean the ones that look like a gap between two teeth."

Both Tam and Richard nodded their heads.

The old noncom spat a stream of brown liquid over the side of the wall. He wiped his mouth on his sleeve and held up two fingers.

"That's how many days it'll take to move heavy equipment from that gap to here. No one's asked my opinion, but if'n they did, I'd say that haze is the second orc army the colonel told us about."

Richard looked at the indicated gap. The haze was barely visible. He tried to stretch his passive scan toward the break in the hills, but it shorted out before reaching a tenth of the distance. There were too many life forms between him and the hills.

Yeah, he thought. *About forty thousand orcs plus mounts and draft animals make my passive scan useless at long ranges.*

Tam eyed the noncom. "If you were in charge, what would you do?"

The grizzled soldier laughed. “I think I’d sign my own retirement papers and hightail it for less crowded territory if’n you know what I mean.”

Both Tam and Richard laughed. A couple of nearby soldiers laughed as well.

“Don’t let him fool you,” said a female soldier holding a crossbow. “Sergeant Markel’s got soldiering in his blood. It’ll take more than an orc army or two to make him run.”

Sergeant Markel grinned. “You’ll have to take Abby’s opinion with a grain of salt. She’s my niece.” The sergeant took a moment to give Tam and Richard a once over. “You’re those wizard scouts whatever-they-are that came in with the colonel last night, aren’t you? Are you some type of magic users? You don’t look the part.”

Both Tam and Richard were dressed in the simple pants and blouse of King Hamerstine’s personal guard and wore a sword and dagger on their belts. They’d foregone the king’s offer of armor. Jerad had told the king it would just slow them down.

“We did come with Colonel Dandridge,” Richard said, “but we aren’t magic users. In the lands where we’re from, we don’t have magic. As wizard scouts, we’re mostly used for recon.”

“Recon, huh?” said Sergeant Markel. “That’s too bad.” He grinned and jerked a thumb in the direction of the besieging orcs. “I think we’ve already found plenty of the enemy. Don’t believe we need you all to find us anymore.”

Richard grinned back. He was taking an instant liking to the old noncom. *Kinda reminds me a little of Sergeant Ron in a medieval sort of way.*

“Well,” said Tam, “maybe so and maybe no. You say that haze is probably the additional siege equipment? If that’s true, it seems to me it’d probably make sense to destroy the stuff before it gets here.”

Most of the soldiers within earshot laughed.

“Be my guest,” said one of the soldiers. “I’m guessing there’s about forty thousand orcs between here and there who might argue the point with you.”

“Not to mention another ten or twenty thousand with the equipment,” said Abby.

Of all the soldiers, only Sergeant Markel didn’t laugh. “Actually, that’s what I’d try to do if I was in charge. Of course, it'd be a suicide mission for anyone foolish enough to go. Still, if we could delay the siege equipment getting to the orcs, the city might be able to hold on long enough for the king and his reinforcements to arrive."

The soldier who'd gainsaid Tam's idea spoke up. "It'd be suicide for sure and a waste of lives at that. You'd need to get at least a thousand soldiers to Donner's Gap to even slow that second army down. Not that it would matter. Any force sizeable enough to make a difference would be decimated by the orcs right outside our gates."

Tam was unperturbed. "We got in safe enough last night."

"Well, I'll bet you didn't have no thousand soldiers dressed in clanging armor with you either," argued the soldier.

Sergeant Markel nodded his head in agreement. "Travers is right. You might could sneak twenty or thirty soldiers past those orcs out there, but you'd need a lot more than that to do any good. Donner's Gap is narrow in a couple of places, but even a thousand troops could only hold the pass for a few hours."

"Or half a dozen troops who were as good as a thousand," Richard said as much to himself as to anyone else. His mind was going into overdrive as he thought of possibilities. "Besides, we wouldn't need to hold the pass for long. We'd just need enough time to clog it up with destroyed equipment and cause some confusion."

"You'd best get that idea out of your head," advised Sergeant Markel. "Nope, the only thing we can do is sit here and wait for those orcs to get their equipment here and attack. Then we need to do the best we can and go down fighting."

Richard eyed Tam.

She raised an eyebrow as if reading his thoughts, then shrugged. "Maybe we should see what Jerad thinks. I did a lot of one-on-one as a merc, but large-scale tactics isn't exactly in my repertoire."

Nodding his head in agreement, Richard turned and headed for the stairs leading down from the wall. Large-scale tactics wasn't his field of expertise either. He heard Tam's footsteps behind him and smiled. It was nice not having to do everything on his own.

CHAPTER 24

They found Jerad at the garrison headquarters. It hadn't taken Colonel Dandridge long to realize Jerad's worth as a leader. The colonel had given Jerad an honorary rank of major and put him in charge of organizing the city's reserve forces. Their friend was pouring over a map of the city and surrounding area along with several others when they arrived.

When Jerad noticed them, he waved them over. Pointing at the others with him, he singled out two women in chainmail standing nearby. "This is Captain Kelvoy and Lieutenant Rirely of the city guard."

Richard and Tam introduced themselves to the two women.

"And this," said Jerad as he motioned to an old gnome wearing a black robe, "is Master Garis."

The fact that nothing registered on Richard's passive scan at the gnome's location told him a lot about Master Garis's abilities as a spellcaster. He made a mental note not to get on the gnome's bad side.

"We were going over the garrison's deployment," said Jerad. "I assume you've been on the wall. How's morale?"

The frowns the captain and lieutenant gave Richard told him he'd better answer tactfully. As it was, he didn't have to stretch the truth. "I'd say morale's as good as can be expected after a month-long siege. The troops are concerned about some haze in Donner's Gap. I talked to an old sergeant who said it was probably from heavy-siege equipment."

"What was the sergeant's name?" asked Lieutenant Rirely.

Tam answered. "Sergeant Markel. He seems like a good man."

The lieutenant nodded her head. "He's the best."

"The sergeant's right," said Jerad. "Master Garis says the approaching army's composed of twenty-five thousand troops, plus enough siege equipment and supplies to breach our walls in short order."

"How's he know that?" asked Tam. "We couldn't see anything from the wall, and the distance was too great for our passive scans what with that army of orcs between us."

The gnome answered Tam. "Scrying devices. What did you think? That they keep me around here for my good looks?"

"Scrying?" asked Tam with a perplexed look.

"Think tele-bots feeding data to a computer," Richard said. "Only instead of tele-bots, scrying devices use magic."

"Oh?" said Tam. "I've got a feeling it's going to take me awhile to get used to this place."

Richard smiled. "Join the club. I've spent a lot of time on Portalis over the years, and I'm still trying to figure things out."

Tam looked at Jerad. "Rick and I were thinking maybe we should do something about that equipment. Sergeant Markel says the gap gets narrow in some spots."

"It does," agreed Captain Kelvoy. "A large swamp makes the gap nearly impassable for heavy equipment except for a road near the cliff. We'd need at least a thousand troops to hold the gap. We'd be slaughtered before we got halfway there."

The map on the table where Jerad stood showed the city and most of the surrounding area. Richard noticed a spot marked as Donner's Gap that did look very narrow.

Richard tapped the point on the map with a finger. "I was thinking four wizard scouts, a couple of mages, and a platoon of cavalry could do the job. At the very least, we could do enough damage to buy us a couple of days."

"That's crazy," said Captain Kelvoy. "What could three dozen people do?"

"Not much if they were regular soldiers," admitted Jerad. "However, with a full quad of wizard scouts, they'd be a force to be reckoned with."

"The only problem is that without our battle suits, we'd have to attack during daylight hours," Richard said. "We're human. We can't see at night."

A female voice came from Richard's rear. "Speak for yourself."

Richard didn't have to turn to know Emerald and her friend Chancee had joined their impromptu meeting.

"If you're planning something without us," said Chancee, "then you best think again."

Both females were dressed in darkened chainmail complete with steel helms. Emerald carried a large battle-axe. A dagger with a blue gem in the hilt was stuck into her belt. Chancee had a longsword strapped to her waist. Richard sensed powerful magic radiating from her sword.

"No one's going anywhere," said Jerad. "We're just brainstorming."

"That's your opinion," said Tam. "Rick and I are going. We just need a few other fools to go with us."

Chancee laughed. "Then I guess we arrived just in time. I'm a ranger. I hate fighting behind walls anyway. When do we leave?"

"Slow down," said Jerad sounding like he was concerned events were getting out of his control. "We don't have our equipment. We can't even see in the dark."

"Ah, that's easily corrected," said Master Garis. "A couple of spells would take care of that. Unfortunately, they're time-limited. I'd have to send a couple of senior mages with you. They'd be sore missed on the walls if the orcs attacked while they were gone."

A strange look came over Captain Kelvoy. "I wonder…" When the captain noticed everyone looking at her expectantly, she explained. "I was just thinking about the equipment we salvaged last year."

"What equipment is that?" asked Jerad.

"One of the Dragars' smaller flying ships crashed in the mountains last summer. We were able to save some of its equipment from the fire."

"It doesn't work," said Lieutenant Rirely. "That is, we couldn't get it to do anything."

Richard got a strange feeling things were falling into place a little too readily. He bristled at the thought he might be moving into one of his nemesis's equations, but he didn't see another way. If *'the One'* had this all planned out, then he might be forced to go along with the plan just to keep his friends and him alive.

"Maybe we should take a look at it," Richard suggested.

"I can take you to it later," said Master Garis. "It's magic, but it's a different type than the magic I've used in the past."

"We'd still need some volunteers for the cavalry," said the lieutenant. "I've got a few in mind who might be foolish enough to go with us."

Jerad held up his hands in a stopping gesture. "Hold on, everybody. Nothing's been decided yet. Colonel Dandridge would have to approve any foray."

"Well, it doesn't hurt to get things in motion," said Tam. "You can ask him 'pretty please' if you want. In the meantime, the rest of us can get the show on the road just in case."

Jerad frowned at the determined looks on those around him. "Fine. Tam, you and Rick can go with Master Garis to check out that equipment. Lieutenant Rirely, you see if you can find enough fools to volunteer as cavalry. The captain and I will go talk to the colonel."

A feeling of satisfaction touched the edges of Richard's senses. He'd once been told *'the One'* sent tele-bots to keep an eye on him during missions. He knew tele-bots could sometimes interact with sensitive people at the emotional level. He was pretty sure he was picking up a satisfied feeling from a nearby tele-bot. He hated being used but could think of nothing better at the moment than to go with the flow.

* * *

As it turned out, the captured equipment consisted mostly of damaged pieces of armor along with a few small-arms weapons. According to Master Garis, the Dolgars' ship had been destroyed by fire during the crash, but the force of the crash had thrown some of the ship's contents free.

Tam held up a metallic pant leg. "This armor's small. From Rick's descriptions, I thought the Dolgars were bigger."

"They are," said Master Garis, "but they've got a lot of allies from other races. The crew of this ship were probably dark gnomes. They're only a little taller than my race."

Richard and Tam spent a few minutes sorting through the

salvaged supplies. While some of it seemed similar to technology, Richard could tell it was all magic based. By mixing and matching some of the equipment, they were able to piece together a couple of suits of armor and two weapons similar to rifles.

Richard picked up one of the rifles. It reminded him of a riot gun. Cartridges about half the size of a 20mm grenade round were stuck in webbing on the stock of the weapon. Richard sensed energy coming from the cartridges. They were magic. He concentrated on the rounds. Their magic had the same energy signature he'd encountered when he had a vision of the Dragars' pyramid.

"It doesn't work," said the gnome. "I've had my best spellcasters on it, and they can't get any of this stuff to work."

Richard probed the riot gun with an active scan. He knew he had an advantage over the gnome's mages. With the help of his battle computer, he'd once taken over the primary computer of a Dragar destroyer. Richard tried to sense anything familiar in the weapon. Before long, he found what he sought.

"Maybe your mages failed because it's not spells that makes this stuff work," Richard said. "Or at least, it's not spells they've been taught."

Continuing to use his active scan, he probed the weapon farther and followed some conduits within the frame of the weapon. He sensed that the conduits should be filled with energy, but they were currently empty. He decided to use a technique the *Defiant's* mechanic, Charlie, had shown him. Richard let a part of his mind merge with the weapon. Charlie had told him since everything, living or inert, had at least a trace of Power, someone good at manipulating links could also diagnose problems with equipment. Using Charlie's technique, Richard sensed several points of Power in the weapon that appeared to be damaged.

All bragging aside, Richard knew he was very good at manipulating Power links. He used his diviner ability to repair the riot gun's damaged energy conduits. Once he was finished, the weapon hummed slightly and a couple of lights in the handle flashed on.

Richard handed the weapon to Tam. "Based upon the flows of energy in this thing, I think this light is the capacity indicator. That little doohickey there appears to be the safety."

Tam flipped the weapon over and removed the magazine. She inserted cartridges until the magazine would take no more. She then slapped the magazine back into its slot. After lifting the weapon to her shoulder, she sighted down the barrel.

Tam lightly touched a metal protrusion with her index finger. "I'm guessing this here's the trigger."

Richard half expected his impetuous friend to fire, but she didn't. Instead, she lowered the weapon.

Tam grinned. "I'm thinking this beats a sword."

Richard nodded his head in agreement, then began working on the other equipment. Within half an hour, between the three of them, they'd repaired enough equipment to put Tam into a complete set of power-armor. It was a little tight even for Tam, but she didn't complain.

"This suit's similar to the power-armor of the Empire's heavy infantry," said Tam. "It's all manually operated. I'm not getting any sensation of a computer in this helmet."

"Can you activate a filter on the helmet?" Richard asked.

By touching the side of the helmet with her hand, Tam lowered the helmet's visor. It gave off a bluish glow.

"It looks like some kind of thermal imagery," said Tam. "I've got a feeling I'll be able to get around in the dark with no problem."

"Well," Richard said. "You've only got a limited amount of ammo. There are about two hundred cartridges. They won't go far against an army of forty thousand. I think you'd better hold onto your sword for emergencies."

Tam grinned. "Ha! If I run out of ammo, I can pretty much guarantee they'll be plenty of swords lying around for me to use."

Richard shook his head in defeat. He'd always suspected his friend's years in the mercs had given her a little bloodthirsty streak. "Well," Richard said. "We've got enough armor to equip one more person, but the second set is missing a helmet. The suit's too small for anyone but Telsa. I guess she wins the honor by default."

Tam began bagging up the armor and the second weapon. The weapon appeared to be some type of automatic along the lines of an M63. The short-barreled rifle was powered by one of the Dragars' energy spheres. After hunting through the salvaged equipment, they managed to find several pouches filled with replacement spheres.

"Do you want this weapon, Rick?" asked Tam.

Richard shook his head. "No. It'll be more effective with someone in armor. I'd probably be too busy dodging arrows to fire accurately. Too bad we couldn't get a second helmet. Telsa won't be able to see in the dark."

"My mages have spells that can take care of that," said Master Garis. He pursed his lips. "On second thought, I may have something even better that can help. Come with me."

Tam and Richard gathered the repaired equipment and followed the old gnome out the building, through several twisting streets. As they walked, Tam drew stares in her Dragar power-armor, but no one tried to interfere. Richard had a feeling the gnome was well known in the city. After about fifteen minutes, they arrived at a long, three-story building.

"This is the city's armory," explained Master Garis. "It's mostly empty now what with the siege and all, but we've kept a few items in the vaults that we're holding in reserve."

Richard followed the gnome into the building with Tam bringing up the rear. The guards let them pass without comment, then one of them left in a hurry as soon as they got past.

"I'm guessing he's gone to ask for orders from his superiors," Richard said.

"No doubt," laughed Master Garis. "He should've saved his energy. He'll have trouble finding anyone who outranks me."

Richard smiled. He'd liked gnomes ever since he'd met them on his first mission to Portalis. Even when they made veiled threats, they did it in a jovial manner.

Before long, the three of them arrived at a double set of metal doors. The gnome waved one hand and said a few words Richard heard but quickly forgot. The two doors opened to reveal a large room with shelves. The room was mostly empty.

Master Garis walked over to one of the lower shelves and pulled down a hooded cape along with a set of goggles. He handed them to Tam.

"Here. Your friend might need these with her armor."

Richard looked at the gear as Tam held them up to take a closer look.

"What are they?" asked Tam.

"The cloak was brought back from the land of the elves. It can help the wearer remain camouflaged. It won't make your friend invisible, but it can hide her from a cursory inspection. The goggles were created by my cousin. He's a tinkerer. I combined his creation with a spell of my own making. When your friend is wearing these, she'll be able to see during the darkest night or even in a blinding dust storm. The device over the left eye is attuned to energy readings given off by stealth and invisibility spells."

"Don't you need them?" asked Tam.

The gnome laughed. "Not anymore, my young friend. My cousin made these goggles for me many years ago. My race can already see in the dark, and I've gotten advanced enough with my spells that I no longer need supplemental aids to spot hidden creatures or objects. I think they'll serve your friend better than me during our current crisis."

Richard nodded his head in thanks. "I'm sure Telsa will put them to good use." He had a vision of Telsa from her pre-Academy days. She'd been fresh out of the university with zero military experience. He thought of the deadly killing machine she'd become.

"In fact," Richard told the gnome, "I think she'll put them to very good use."

CHAPTER 25

Colonel Dandridge hadn't liked the plan. As related by Jerad, the colonel had said he was positive anyone going on such a foolish mission was facing certain death. The colonel also told Jerad his only regret was that he couldn't go with the raid himself. As commander-in-chief of the city's defenses, he needed to remain in town.

Although the colonel reluctantly agreed to allow the raid, he forbade Jerad from going. Richard's friend had immediately resigned from his honorary rank and informed the colonel he was going. Colonel Dandridge wisely relented and gave him permission. He also immediately restored Jerad back to his honorary rank of major.

Jerad was old-school. He had suggested Trinity, Tam, and Telsa remain in the city. The women hadn't been impressed. They'd promptly told Jerad what he could do with his suggestion. Once it was obvious the three women were going, Matthew and Tia had tried to insist they were going as well. For once, Myers and Richard presented a united front. The teenagers must have realized they didn't stand a chance, so they agreed to remain behind. When Myers mentioned the two teens had capitulated a little too readily, Jerad had them placed in a locked room at the city jail until the raid was over.

In short order, Richard and the other raiders left the city in the dark of night using one of the city's secret entrances. After a few hours, Richard found himself blindly holding onto the back of

Telsa's belt as she led him along a boulder-strewn canyon leading to Donner's Gap. Since the canyon was close to the gap, they'd left their horses behind with a rear guard. The rest of them had made the last few kilometers on foot. On more than one occasion, their group had a close call with orc patrols. Fortunately, between Telsa's goggles and the spells of Master Garis, they'd avoided detection.

Richard stumbled in the dark. He silently cursed his luck. Master Garis had decided to accompany the raid along with one of his senior mages. Between them, they'd cast night-vision spells on everyone but him. They'd tried to cast the spell on him, but it kept failing. Richard assumed that was due to his resister ability. Each time they cast the spell, his Power automatically countered the spell just enough to make it fail.

"Great," Richard mumbled as he stumbled on another stone. "A fat lot of good being a resistor does. Healers can't heal me, and even a simple night-vision spell doesn't work. What I'd like to know is why I can't resist fireballs or lightning bolts? Now that'd be useful."

Master Garis happened to be walking right behind Richard and gave a stifled laugh. "Because that's not the way things work, my friend. My night-vision spell was trying to change you. Your Power apparently detected the attempt and resisted. The magic of a fireball spell, on the other hand, is used to create heat and fire in a specific area. The resulting fireball's effects will burn you, but the magic of the spell isn't trying to change you. As a result, there isn't anything for your Power to resist. Based upon what you've told me of your abilities, I do think your natural resistance probably does reduce the damage you take from spells."

Richard was in no mood. Once again, he was going into battle with a handicap. Everyone except him would be able to see. *This sucks*, he thought.

Telsa stopped. Richard heard the sound of creaking leather along with a lot of voices. Whoever was ahead of them wasn't trying to be quiet.

Straining his eyes, Richard tried to see to no avail. "What's happening?"

"There's a large contingent of orcs ahead moving some type of battering ram," said Telsa. "There's also a lot of orcs just about everywhere I look. They stretch back down the valley as far as the eye can see."

Richard tried to see again but fared no better than his earlier attempt. He could make out a lot of campfires in the distance, but nothing up close. "I can't see a thing."

The dark form that was Telsa turned around and thrust something into his hands. "Here. Put these on."

Richard felt the obvious form of the goggles in his hands. "No," he protested. "You'll need these when we attack."

"You'll need them even worse," replied Telsa. "One of the mages can cast one of those see-in-the-dark spells on me. I'm not a resister. So stop being stubborn and take them." When Richard continued to hesitate, Telsa jabbed a finger into his chest. "By the way, if I even so much as think you're trying to give them back to me because I'm a woman, I'll kick your ass from one side of this valley to the next even if I have to borrow a chair to stand on in order to do it."

The thought of the short Telsa dragging a chair around and standing on it as she kicked him made Richard smile. He didn't think he'd given the goggles to her because she was a female, but he wasn't as sure as he should be. He reluctantly slipped the goggles over his head.

The valley below suddenly became as clear as if he'd been looking through the thermal filter of his battle helmet. As Telsa had said, a couple of hundred orcs were manhandling a large battering ram along a narrow, rocky road. Other large pieces of siege equipment were spaced behind the first as they waited their turn to get through the narrowest part of the gap. He could make out thousands of other soldiers camped out around small fires dotting the valley floor.

Richard heard Master Garis say a spell behind him. He sensed a buildup of energy leave the gnome and settle around Telsa.

"Much better," said Telsa. "I can see again. How long will this spell last?"

"About two hours," said the gnome. "Now if you'll excuse me, I have to help Master Diamass refresh the others' night-vision spells before we attack."

After the gnome left, Jerad, Myers, Emerald, and Lieutenant Rirely gathered around Richard and Telsa.

Jerad spoke in a whisper. “The lieutenant confirms the valley floor’s too boggy to hold the siege equipment. They’ve got to use the road to get it through. If we can cause enough confusion, maybe we can block this gap and buy the city some time.”

“So what’s our plan?” Richard asked automatically deferring command to Jerad. “And what the heck is that smell?”

Emerald sniffed the air. “Swamp gas and peat moss would be my guess. Ain’t it sweet?”

“Yeah,” said Lieutenant Rirely. “It probably reminds the orcs of their home. Most of them have bedded down for the night in the swamp. The campsites near the road appear to be for other races.”

“Which leads us to our plan,” said Jerad. “We’re going to divide into three groups. The two mages, Chancee, and most of the lieutenant’s troops will take up a position on the high ground to our left. Thanks to the mages’ spells, they should be able to create a lot of havoc with their bows and crossbows. Gaston, Rick, and Telsa will attack that group moving the battering ram. Emerald and a squad of soldiers will try to set it on fire while the wizard scouts keep the orcs off their backs. Trinity, Tam, and I will take up a position about four hundred meters down the road. There’s a bend there. If we can destroy a piece of equipment at that location, we might block it for a little while.”

“And then?” asked Emerald.

“Then we’ll play it by ear,” said Jerad. “Just cause as much confusion as you can. We’ll rendezvous back at the horses when things start to get too hot.”

Richard scanned the valley again. He didn’t like what he saw. “When those orcs in the swamp get here, we’ll be paying the piper. Our backs will be against the cliff face. Those of us who are wizard scouts can levitate up assuming we have Power left in our reserves. Emerald and the other ground-pounders will be trapped.”

“Hey,” said Jerad a little defensively. “I didn’t say my plan was perfect. If you remember correctly, I argued against coming in the first place.”

Myers snorted. “If you’ve got a better idea, Shepard, then out with it. Otherwise, stop your whining.”

The animal that was Richard’s temper rattled its cage as his dislike for Myers took hold. A small hand touched his shoulder and squeezed. The hand belonged to Telsa. Richard understood his friend's silent admonition. He needed to stay calm. With an effort, he forced his temper to stay in check. He knew Telsa was right. This wasn't the time or place to let personal animosities get in the way.

But I swear, Richard promised himself, *when we're out of here, Myers and I are going to have it out.*

"The two mages will be with the archers," said Jerad ignoring Myers comment. "They'll cover your withdrawal. They can levitate Emerald and her team up the cliff." He stared hard at Myers. "Now, unless anyone has any useful suggestions, I recommend we get in position. When you hear my team attack, it'll be the signal to start. Now, let's get going."

"Wait," Richard said.

"What is it, Rick?" asked Jerad. "If we wait too long, a patrol's bound to discover us."

"I know," Richard said. "Just give me a second."

Something on Richard's passive scan just below the level of the swamp was drawing his attention. He reached out and downward as he concentrated on the troublesome spot. He intertwined a stealth shield with an active scan and sent it toward the center of the swamp. An idea began to form in his mind.

"Myers," Richard said. "You're a diviner. What do you see below the swamp? Make sure you stealth your scan. I'm sensing a lot of magic users scattered around those orc camps."

"I don't need you to tell me how to do a scan, Shepard," said Myers between clenched teeth.

Despite his brother's words, he sensed Myers wrap a stealth shield around an active scan and send it out. Richard traced the scan as it moved up and down the valley floor concentrating on an area below the swamp. After about thirty seconds, Myers line of Power pulled back.

"Do you see it?" Richard prodded.

"See what?" asked Emerald. "What are you guys talking about?"

"Yeah," said Jerad. "How about letting the rest of us in on it?"

Myers answered first. "That smell's not all swamp gas. There's an oil field below the valley."

"Not just an oil field," Richard said. "There are several large pockets of natural gas below the surface of the swamp. That whole area's like a giant tar pit waiting for a spark to set it off."

"I suspect it would take more than a spark," said Telsa. "Even if you were able to set one gas pocket on fire, I seriously doubt it would spread."

Richard wasn't discouraged by his friend's comment. "You'd be right if we didn't have two diviners with us." Turning his attention to Myers, he said, "Did you notice those lines of Power in the swamp? If we could tweak them a little, we might be able to start a chain reaction."

"Tweak what?" asked Emerald.

"The gas pockets," replied Myers. "Everything releases Power. Shepard's talking about connecting the lines of Power given off by the gas pockets together. If we could get a couple of pockets to ignite, the whole swamp might go up."

"Are you talking about an explosion?" asked Jerad.

"No," said Myers, "nothing so dramatic. Still, it would be a sizeable fire nonetheless."

Ever the leader, Jerad took charge of the discussion. "Can you manipulate the lines of Power from here?"

"Unfortunately, no," Richard said. "We'd have to go into the swamp. Plus, we'd have to blow a hole through the mud deep enough to reach a gas pocket and set it on fire."

"How do you plan on doing that?" asked Jerad. "Can the mages make an explosion powerful enough? We don't have anything that could do it unless you've been holding something back on us."

"First off," Richard said, "I doubt even Master Garis has a spell capable of doing what we need done. Fortunately, we do have someone who could do the job."

Myers growled, "Out with it, Shepard. Either tell us what you've got in mind or let's get moving on Jerad's plan."

"Fine," Richard said "but, I haven't got it all worked out yet. Telsa's a projector. I think she could blast a hole deep enough to get down to one of the pockets. My scan picked up a pocket that was only about twenty-five meters down."

"I saw that one as well," said Myers. "It's about a kilometer up the valley and in the center of the swamp. We'd be right in the middle of the orcs. Only wizard scouts could make it."

"What about ignition?" asked Jerad. "Will any of that Dragar equipment you salvaged do the job?"

"Negative," Richard said shaking his head. "We'll need one of the mages. A couple of well-placed fireballs down Telsa's hole should do the job."

Jerad made his decision. "Fine. Then let's get started. Who's going to go?"

* * *

The fires of the orc camps showed up brightly through the goggle's thermal view. Richard knelt on one knee as he waited for an orc patrol to get past their hiding place. After a few seconds, he noticed a distortion ahead of him move.

Telsa's definitely hard to see when she's got that cloak activated, he thought. *I think it's even better than one of the Empire's camouflage suits.*

Richard turned and motioned to Master Garis. The gnome rose and signaled to Myers who was bringing up the rear. They were all being very quiet while getting close to their destination.

A blur to Richard's left front caught his attention. Nothing showed on his passive scan, but he'd grown to trust the goggles in the short amount of time he'd been using them. They'd already bypassed several checkpoints manned by invisible creatures. Reaching out, Richard touched Telsa. The distortion that was Telsa turned. He held up his left hand in the shape of a pistol with the thumb pointed downward. It was the universal signal for 'enemy in sight.' Telsa changed her direction to angle away from the blur.

Within another five minutes, they reached their destination deep within the orc encampment. Dozens of fires could be seen through the swamp grass and brush. Richard and the others formed a tight circle facing outward. All they could do now was wait. Richard hoped they wouldn't have to wait long.

Fortunately, they didn't. A loud explosion from the direction of the cliff face reverberated through the valley. It was followed by several other blasts. Horns blew as shouts erupted from the orc camp.

Richard sensed Telsa drawing Power from her reserve in preparation for blasting a hole to the natural gas pocket ahead of them. That's when things began going wrong. A streak of energy came from the direction of the blur Richard had spotted earlier.

"Shields!" Richard shouted.

Before he could get his own shield up, a sphere of energy from Master Garis formed around all four of them. A horrific blast of fire surrounded them as a fireball detonated against the gnome's defensive shield. The shield held. The fire dissipated quickly, but the swamp grass and brush around them continued to burn while filling the air with smoke and red-hot sparks.

Telsa's concentration was broken. Her Power withdrew back to her reserve. She did manage to point her rifle in the direction of the blur and fire off several dozen energy rounds. A ball of magic from Master Garis followed Telsa's rounds. The gnome's magic transformed into a bolt of lightning. Both Telsa's energy rounds and the gnome's lightning bolt glanced off an unseen wall before shooting up into the sky. The air around the blur shimmered to reveal a group of half a dozen orcs in metal armor. A small orc wearing a robe stood behind them. The small orc was carrying a staff with a skull on top.

"It's a shaman," shouted Master Garis. "Based upon the defensive shield, he's a good one."

With the loss of their stealth and invisibility spells, the group of orcs showed up on Richard's passive scan. He sensed the Power reserve of the shaman.

Richard grew concerned. *His reserve's even larger than the gnome's.*

With no long-range weapon of his own, Richard did what a Marine did best. He charged. He sensed Myers running a step behind and to his left.

Before either of them could close the distance, the shaman sent out another ball of energy.

Richard put up a hasty defensive shield.

Surprisingly, the spell fell short and struck a muddy patch of ground in front of Myers and him. The ground bubbled and sprayed upward. The mud congealed into a column five meters high and half again as wide. Two lengths of mud stretched out from the torso. They resembled badly-formed arms. The arms reached toward Richard.

"Golem," Richard shouted as he attempted to dodge.

Muddy claws at the end of the arm missed, but the arm reversed direction and knocked Richard to the side. The blow cracked his ribs. He was flung through the air and landed in a stagnant pool of water. Richard half expected the golem to follow up its attack but sensed it continuing on a path toward Telsa and the gnome.

Spitting out water and blood as he came to the surface, Richard struggled to firm ground and got to his feet. The golem had stopped its run toward Telsa and Master Garis. Richard saw why. A dark figure on the golem's back was plunging a sword into where the creature's head should be. The attacker was Myers. As Richard ran toward the golem, it raised one of its arms and grabbed Myers. Before his brother could react, the golem plunged its arm deep into the muddy swamp taking Myers with it.

Richard reached the base of the golem and swung his sword against the column of mud that served as one of the monster's legs. The golem reached down and made a grab for him. Richard dodged aside and swung again. Mud sprayed out as his sword sliced through the arm, but other than that, the sword blow seemed to have no effect.

Below ground, Richard sensed Power surround Myers and shimmer as his brother shifted into the void. The dot on Richard's passive scan that was his brother began rising to the surface.

Energy rounds from Telsa's rifle struck the golem's upper torso. A blast of lightning from the gnome hit as well. The golem shook its head but showed no other effects. The attacks did draw its attention. The golem resumed its run toward Telsa and the gnome. Before they could do more than turn to dodge, the golem had them in its hands. It plunged them both deep into the mud just as it had Myers.

Richard sensed Power from Telsa's reserve attempt to heal her as the swamp mud filled her lungs. He sensed her reserve begin to rapidly deplete as it tried to compensate for the continual damage of being encased in mud. The dot on his passive scan that was Master Garis was faring even worse than his friend. Richard knew the gnome couldn't self-heal. His life force was growing increasingly weaker.

Richard was torn between saving his friend or saving the gnome. He didn't have time to weigh options. He just reacted. Wrapping himself in Power, Richard shifted into the void and levitated downward toward Master Garis.

Telsa can self-heal, he reasoned. *The gnome can't.*

Within seconds, Richard was at the gnome's side. He wrapped the mage with Power and shifted him into the void. At almost the same time, he sensed Myers in the void moving down to grab Telsa.

Richard broke the surface as he pulled the gnome with him. The mage wasn't breathing. He sent a scan into the gnome's chest. The mage's lungs were full of mud. His heart was still beating, but barely.

A large splash behind Richard drew his attention. He spun just in time to see the muddy mass of the golem's fist heading straight for his head. Dragging the gnome with him, Richard dove to the left. The golem's arm passed overhead, dripping mud and swamp water behind it.

A burst of energy rounds caught the golem in the head. The muddy mass reversed directions and took off running. Richard noticed Myers standing over Telsa as he fired her rifle on full auto at the charging golem.

"Save the gnome," yelled Myers. "I'll keep this piece of muck off you."

Richard didn't like his brother but trusted him to do what he said. The man was a wizard scout. He had no doubt he'd keep the golem occupied or die trying.

Myers ran toward the golem and levitated himself upward while continuing to fire at the monster's head as he went. The golem swung both fists at Myers, but he dodged the blows and landed on the creature's back. He jammed the muzzle of his weapon into the golem's neck and held the trigger down. Energy rounds exited out the other size.

The golem roared but otherwise seemed unaffected.

Tearing his gaze from the battle, Richard concentrated on the gnome. He wrapped the old mage in Power and compared the way the gnome's body was with how it should be. Before Richard could pull the damage into himself, he sensed a ball of magic streaking toward him from the direction of the shaman.

Richard forgot about healing and threw up a defensive shield, angling it toward the sky. The ball of energy changed into an icy blast of air. The wall of cold hit the shield and ricocheted upwards. At the same moment, he sensed the gnome's heart stop.

Richard yelled to anyone who could hear. "I can't heal and

defend myself at the same time."

He sensed the shaman forming another ball of energy, and saw Myers dodging the golem while continuing to fire his rifle. Richard knew there'd be no help from that direction. His brother was fully occupied. The situation appeared hopeless. He was almost ready to run at the shaman in a desperate charge when a blast of pure Power hit the shaman's shield. The shield held, but the orc was distracted enough that his spell fizzled.

Richard traced the blast of energy back to its source. He saw Telsa on her knees. She was down but wasn't out. He sensed her self-heal working overtime to overcome the effects of the remaining mud in her lungs. As he watched, she drew a sword from the scabbard at her waist and stumbled toward the shaman and his orc guards.

A part of Richard urged him to go help his friend, but a more logical part of his psyche told him he needed to save the dwarf. It was now or never.

Wrapping Power from his healing reserve around the gnome again, Richard drew the mage's injuries into himself. He immediately began to gag as his body replicated the damage of both lungs being filled with muddy liquid. His heart stopped at the same time. Pain filled his mind until it was replaced by the blessed sweetness of unconsciousness.

All too soon, the sounds of battle drew him out of the comforting darkness. He felt cold, wet mud against the right side of his face. He heard nearby words he quickly forgot. A whooshing noise was followed by the sound of an explosion.

Richard forced his eyes open as he pushed himself upright. Master Garis was standing a couple of meters to his right. A blast of magic hit a sphere surrounding both the gnome and Richard. The mage's defensive shield held, and the energy dissipated away.

The gnome glanced at Richard. "I'll help Telsa with the shaman. You help your friend with the golem. He's got his hands full. I doubt he can last much longer."

Richard shook his head to clear the fog and tried to think. *What friend?*

Before Richard could ask, the gnome took off running toward a short figure who was trading blows with a half dozen orcs. Splashing sounds drew his attention and he turned, seeing a man in full combat with a large blob of mud. Richard's mind cleared. His memory of the battle came back with a vengeance. Jumping to his feet, he drew his sword and charged the golem. While Myers definitely wasn't a friend, he was a wizard scout and an ally. Richard couldn't leave him to take on the mud creature by himself no matter how much he disliked his ex-TAC officer.

Myers fired another burst of magic energy at his opponent. Only three rounds came out before the weapon became silent.

Empty, Richard thought.

His brother threw the rifle down and drew his sword.

The golem swung both arms in a sweeping movement. Myers dodged one arm, but the other caught him on the side, throwing him through the air. He was stopped by a large boulder half-buried in the mud. Richard heard the sound of breaking bones.

The golem went in for the kill. Before the creature reached the downed wizard scout, Richard wrapped his brother in Power and levitated him out of the golem's reach. The monster started to turn and Richard leaped onto the golem's back, swinging wildly at its head. Mud flew with each swing, but the displaced muck was quickly replaced as the monster drew additional mud from the swamp to repair what little damage the sword did.

The golem reached behind its back and grabbed Richard by his legs. With a jerk, he was thrown straight toward the boulder where Myers had been hurt.

Before Richard hit the large rock, he felt Power wrap around him. He recognized his brother's frequency. The Power moved him to the side enough so that he missed the boulder. Mud and stagnant water flew into the air as he landed, but he took no damage. He was on his feet in an instant, wiping a hand across his face to clear his vision.

Apparently irritated it had been cheated out of a kill, the golem picked up a water-soaked log and swung it at Myers. Richard's brother easily dodged the blow. Myers passed inside the golem's reach and made a two-handed strike at its right leg. The sword passed completely through the golem's knee, but it didn't fall. Richard sensed magic flow between the golem and the swamp. The magic pulled mud into the creature's body repairing its damage as fast as Myers could deal it out.

The old Richard would have charged with sword in hand. His

years of missions for *'the One'* had taught him to think before he acted. At least, he sometimes thought before he acted. This was one of those times. He followed the golem's magic to its source. He sensed a ball of energy at the center of the golem's chest.

That's the orc's spell, Richard thought.

Reaching out with his mind, Richard probed the spell. It was protected by four traps. He pulled back slightly, but immediately sent out an active scan and began deactivating one of the traps. In short order, he had it defused. Before he could move to the second trap, the golem roared with anger. How it could make sounds without lungs, Richard didn't know or care. What he did care about was the charging mass of mud bearing down on him.

When the creature got within range, Richard sidestepped and hacked at its knee with his sword. The monster kicked out with its leg and knocked him to the ground. Before it could stomp him into the murky swamp, Richard sensed a line of Power from his brother reach into the golem's chest and begin fiddling with another trap.

The golem must have sensed Myers's attack as well because it spun and charged at his brother. The golem only made it halfway before Richard sensed Myers finish deactivating the second trap.

Reaching out with his mind, Richard located the third trap and began twisting energy flows to short-circuit it. The mud creature spun before it reached Myers and charged back toward Richard.

The golem was almost on Richard when the third trap was bypassed. He finished in time to dive to the ground as the golem's improvised club passed overhead. The golem raised its log in preparation for a down stroke.

Another line of Power from Myers touched the final trap surrounding the spell. The golem forgot about Richard and began running at Myers with club raised. He stood his ground while continuing to give the trap his full attention. As the club began its downswing, Richard sensed the final trap vanish. He was ready. As soon as the trap disappeared, he entered the spell with his mind and twisted the lines of magic back on themselves. The magic dissipated into the universe from which it had come. At the same time, the mud that had been the golem sagged and splashed to the ground covering Myers in the nauseating muck.

An explosion to Richard's rear reminded him the battle was far from over. A quick glance showed Master Garis and the shaman trading spells. Telsa was dodging around the old gnome doing her best to keep the attacking orcs from disturbing the spellcaster. Four of the original six orcs were down, but a score of others had taken their place. Telsa dodged between the larger creatures, taking three of them out as Richard watched.

Myers caught up with Richard and began to pass. "I'll help her."

"No," Richard shouted. "The spellcaster's the biggest danger. Use the drilling technique I taught you against his shield. I'm getting low on Power. I'll help Telsa."

Richard half expected an argument, but Myers instantly obeyed by sending out a line of Power against the shaman's defensive shield. Richard sensed the point of the line twisting back and forth as it dug into the shield. The shaman sensed his brother's attack as well and began to form a spell. The shaman pulled back his hands in preparation for shoving the spell. At that moment, Myers's line of Power broke through the shield. A small ball of blue energy from Master Garis flew through the hole and hit the orc in the chest. The shaman was instantly covered in a layer of ice. The ice cracked and started breaking into dozens of small pieces while taking the shaman's flesh with it. The spot on Richard's passive scan that had been the shaman disappeared.

Richard made for the nearest orc fighting Telsa. He needn't have bothered. As soon as the shaman was taken out of action, Master Garis released a spell that turned the already soft ground around Telsa into quicksand. Both Telsa and the orcs began sinking at a rapid rate. Richard sensed Telsa wrap herself in Power and levitate upward until her feet were once again level with the swamp's surface. The orcs didn't fare as well. Within seconds, the last of the orcs sunk below the surface. Soon, only a few bubbles in the quicksand gave any indication anyone had ever been there.

Myers ran up next to Richard and stopped just shy of the quicksand's edge. He waved for Telsa to join them. "Hurry. This isn't over. More of these orcs' friends are on their way."

A sweep with his passive told Richard his brother was correct. Hundreds of life forms were converging on their position. Dozens of the life forms had Power reserves of varying sizes.

Magic users, Richard thought.

Master Garis arrived at their location just as Telsa finished levitating herself onto dry land.

"Whatever you're going to do," said the gnome, "you'd better do it now. Some of those magic users heading our way have larger Power reserves than the shaman we just fought."

Telsa cut off her levitation and dropped to the ground beside Master Garis. She stumbled when she landed. Richard noticed several gashes in her armor. An especially large gash along her thigh drew his attention.

"You're hurt," Richard said.

"I'll be fine," said Telsa. "My self-heal's already working on it. A couple of the shaman's guards had weapons that sliced right through my armor."

"We can talk about the fight later," said Myers. "Assuming you've still got enough Power, you'd best get busy blasting that hole to the gas pocket. Once the gnome ignites it, we're going to have to hightail it out of here or we'll be burned alive. Even our self-heal might not work long enough to get us out of the swamp."

"Well," said Master Garis, "since I don't have the luxury of self-healing, I've got an alternate exit strategy. Once I set the gas ablaze, stay close to me. I'll teleport the lot of us back to our rendezvous point."

Telsa wasted no further time in discussion. Richard sensed her reach out with a scan to find the shortest path to the gas pocket. He sensed her gathering almost all of her remaining Power into a large ball before sending it downward at a forty-five-degree angle. Mud and swamp water, along with a few orcs flew up into the air. An explosion dwarfing any of the funnel mines Richard had ever used knocked him off his feet. A rush of air shot out the hole.

Master Garis was on his feet in a flash. He waved his hands as he shouted words Richard quickly forgot. A ball of magic formed between the gnome's outstretched hands. The ball of energy flew down the gaping hole created by Telsa's blast.

"It's a delayed fireball," said Master Garis. "We've got ten seconds. Stay close. I'm getting us out of here."

As the gnome began another spell, Richard noticed Telsa jump to her feet.

I guess she's all better.

Richard thanked the Creator for allowing wizard scouts to self-heal. From the looks of her Dragar armor, he had a feeling the orcs' weapons had cut her up pretty bad.

A thought crossed Richard's mind. He reached out with his passive scan in the direction of the quicksand pit created by the gnome. He sensed the lifeless bodies of two dozen orcs. He also sensed three sources of magic. He wrapped the sources of magic with Power and used telekinesis to pull them out of the quicksand. Two swords and a dagger rose into the air. He pulled all three weapons into his waiting hands just as Master Garis finished his spell.

Richard felt himself tingle. The swamp shifted in and out of focus. Then everything went black.

* * *

As soon as he solidified, Richard smelled the odor of leather and sweat. Several horses whinnied. The gnome had teleported them to the ravine where they'd left their mounts with the rear guard. Master Garis went over to speak with one of the two guards. Richard reached out with his passive scan for two kilometers in all direction. He picked up a few roving patrols, but the main bulk of the orc army was in the gap nearly twice that distance away. He changed the sensitivity of his scan to filter out smaller concentrations of life forms as he stretched his passive scan in the direction of Donner's Gap. He sensed a large blob of Power from the gap.

The orc army, Richard thought.

As he watched, the blob dimmed slightly. Through the goggles Telsa had given him, he could just make out a glow over the hills. The intensity of the glow increased slightly.

"Looks like the fire's taking hold," said Telsa.

Concern for the rest of their raiders washed over Richard. "We need to get back there to help the others. Garis should've teleported us there instead of here."

Master Garis turned from the guard to face Richard.

"I teleported us exactly where we need to be. Master Diamass is no fool, and neither is the dwarf or your other wizard scouts. As soon as they saw the swamp burning, you can bet your last keg of beer they started hightailing it back here. We'd just get in the way if we tried to go back there now."

The marine in Richard hated the thought of standing around doing nothing, but the gnome's logic won out. He walked over to a convenient log and sat down. Telsa joined him. Surprisingly, Myers did as well.

Telsa pointed at the weapons in Richard's hands. "What are those for?"

Richard took a closer look at the weapons. One of the swords had a handle large enough to grip with both hands. The other sword was a standard longsword. The handles of both weapons were embedded with a blue gem. He handed the longsword to Telsa and the bastard sword to his brother.

"They're magic," Richard explained. "That's why they cut through the Dragars' armor you were wearing, Telsa. I think these swords would've been useful fighting that mud golem."

Telsa lifted the longsword and inspected it in the moonlight. "Uh…, thanks…. I think."

Myers, on the other hand, didn't say anything. He just pulled the normal sword from the scabbard at his waist and dropped it onto the ground. He placed his new magic sword in the empty scabbard. Telsa dropped her normal sword to the ground as well but continued to hold the magic sword.

"Maybe you should keep this, Rick."

Richard held up the dagger. It had a blue gem in the handle as well. "No. I've got this. It reminds me of the knife Sergeant Hendricks made for me. I'll be better off with it than that sword. Besides, most of my sword training has been with short swords. I like to get in close. A longsword would just get in my way."

Telsa didn't seem fully convinced, but she did slide her new sword into her empty scabbard. "I don't suppose either one of you remembered to pick up my rifle?"

"Oh," said Myers. "Sorry. I dropped it when it ran out of ammo. I was a little busy at the time."

"Too bad," said Telsa. "I've still got plenty of replacement batteries, but I've got nothing to put them in."

As it turned out, when the others returned, Telsa found out Tam's riot gun was useless as well. The ex-mercenary had used all of the ammo for her riot gun during their raid. Tam still carried it slung over her shoulder, but without ammo, it was only useful as a club.

Once everyone was mounted, Lieutenant Rirely got the raiding party moving back toward Cantonsburg. As they rode, Jerad filled in Richard and his team on the results of the raid. While the natural gas fire they'd started hadn't been explosive, it had spread rapidly both under and above ground. Based upon Jerad's observation, the raid had been a huge success. A large part of the orc army bivouacked in the swamp was trapped in the multiple fires. Those who hadn't died were scattered to the four winds. Additionally, at least a third of the siege equipment appeared to have been destroyed or damaged.

"And the good news," said Lieutenant Rirely, "is that we didn't have any deaths in our team. What few wounds my men received have been healed by Wizard Scout Shepard."

"Rick," Richard said. "Call me, Rick."

"All right, Rick. All in all, it was a successful raid. I'm hopeful it'll take at least a week for the orcs to rally their forces. That should be enough time for King Hamerstine to arrive with his relief forces."

Richard leaned back in his saddle and relaxed. For once, things seemed to be going their way.

CHAPTER 26

Tam looked between the battlements of the city wall at the plain below. "Those orcs are better organized than the lieutenant thought. How'd they get their equipment repaired and moved here so quickly?"

"Does it matter?" asked Telsa. "It's here."

Richard eyed the mass of forces arrayed before the main gate. The armored formations of orcs, humans, trolls, and a variety of other races flashed in the morning sun. Groups of ogres and trolls were toiling away at battering rams, assault towers, and catapults. The siege equipment was heavy, but the large creatures were able to push it steadily forward nonetheless. Hundreds of Power readings on Richard's passive scan confirmed the presence of an unusually high number of mages, shamans, and magic items.

Tia and Matthew leaned against the wall's battlement as they watched the approaching army. The teenagers were both dressed in leather armor and metal helms. Each carried a sword and dagger. Neither Matthew nor Tia seemed very concerned with the enemy forces before them. Richard had a feeling they didn't fully comprehend the danger. Although they'd both fought in several space engagements, neither had experienced large-scale ground combat.

Unlike his teen charges, Richard was very cognizant of their danger. Consequently, he'd ordered Tia and Matthew to stick close to him. Myers had backed him up. In fact, his brother refused to move farther than a few meters from Diane Deloris's son. Richard thought it strange. He wondered what the empress had promised his ex-TAC officer as a reward for returning her son home in one piece.

Matthew took a bite out of a sandwich he'd gotten from a kind cook who was passing them out to the soldiers on the wall. "Captain Kelvoy says they don't have enough siege equipment to breach these walls. You guys destroyed a lot of it during your raid."

"You know, Rick," said Tia. "We're still peeved at you for leaving us behind. We're not children. We're soldiers, the same as you."

Four days since the raid, Richard thought Tia shouldn't still be holding a grudge. For some reason, she blamed him for their confinement during the raid more than either Jerad or Myers.

Richard sighed. *Tia's more like Liz than I think she realizes. She'll get over it, but it may take a few more days.*

The smell of Matthew's sandwich wafted into Richard's nose. It smelled good. His stomach rumbled loudly in response.

Both Tia and Matthew laughed. Tam and Telsa smiled as well. Myers didn't.

Tearing his sandwich in half, Matthew held out the larger part to Richard. "Here, Rick. You can have some of mine. I'm not all that hungry."

Although he was initially tempted to take the teenager up on his offer, Richard shook his head. "No. Even if I ate it, my self-heal would see it as an injury. I'd be right back where I was in a few minutes. Rations are in short supply. There are a lot of people in the city who are hungry. I don't need the food. You do. I'd recommend eating while you can."

With a shrug of his shoulders, Matthew went back to eating and watching the orc army. Tia whispered in the teenager's ear. Both Matthew and Tia laughed.

Captain Kelvoy and Lieutenant Rirely walked up along with Emerald and Chancee.

The ranger hefted her bow and point in the direction of a large wooden tower covered with metal plates. Several dozen ogres were struggling to push the heavy piece of siege equipment up a small hill. "I don't understand their thinking. I've been besieged before. They don't have enough equipment to breach our walls. Why bother moving what little equipment they've got? Surely their commander's smart enough to realize he should wait for more?"

Captain Kelvoy laughed. "Perhaps you give them too much credit. While an attack now would cause us some headaches, it'd be nothing we couldn't handle. Besides, we'll destroy what equipment they do have soon enough. They're fools."

"I don't know, sir," said Lieutenant Rirely. "I've fought orcs most of my military career. They're lazy sometimes when it comes to preparations, but they're not stupid. The colonel's concerned they may have something in the works we don't know about."

"Well," said Emerald. "At least the morale of our defenders is good. That was an added bonus from our raid."

Richard nodded his head in agreement. He had a feeling the dwarf was more relieved than either the captain or the lieutenant suspected. The Oracle had hinted the dwarf would need to form a Circle. Although he and Myers had worked with Emerald over the last few days trying to help her create a Circle, they'd had no luck. He wasn't sure whether it was because they were failing to do their part, or the dwarf wasn't trying to form the Circle correctly. Whatever the reason, Emerald hadn't been able to form even a small Circle, much less one encompassing the entire city.

Come to think of it, Richard thought. *I'm also glad the city's morale is good. Even six wizard scouts can't take on an entire army without help.*

Richard noticed Trinity, Jerad, and Colonel Dandridge walking along the battlements above the city gates. The colonel stopped every so often and talked to the soldiers. More often than not, the soldiers would laugh at something the colonel said.

"He's a good leader," said Tam. "He seems to care about his troops."

"Yes, he is," agreed Captain Kelvoy. "Our soldiers have grown quite fond of him in the last few days."

Something at the edge of Richard's passive scan drew his attention. It was more of a tickle than an actual sensation. He concentrated harder but noticed nothing suspicious. On a hunch, he did his best to filter out the army deployed before the city and focused on the sky above it. He extended his passive scan out farther. When he did, he detected a couple of energy sources high in the sky about twenty kilometers out.

Richard pointed into the air at the eleven o'clock position. "I'm picking up something with my passive scan. It's pretty far out. Does anyone else sense anything?"

Three lines of Power stretched out from Tam, Telsa, and Myers as they sent active scans in the direction indicated by Richard.

Humph, Richard thought. *If I had a larger Power reserve, I could use active scans more instead of always relying on my passive scan.*

Before Richard could complain further, Myers dropped his scan and yelled to the soldiers around them. "Take cover! Those are fighter-shuttles."

Richard didn't bother sending out an active scan of his own. Myers was a wizard scout. If he said they were fighters, then they were fighters. Even as he looked, he noticed two white dots on the horizon. They were growing steadily larger. As they drew closer, he made out long streams of green gas trailing behind them.

Jerad and Trinity came running up, trailing Colonel Dandridge.

"Something's going down," said Trinity. "Look at the orcs."

When Richard looked, he saw what the wizard scout meant. Orcs were double-timing into attack formation. The trolls and ogres appeared to be redoubling their efforts to advance the bulky siege equipment into positions nearer the city wall.

"Sound the alarm," shouted Colonel Dandridge. "Archers! Magic users! Prepare to take out those siege engines."

Alarm bells began ringing from the watchtowers above the main gates. Other bells took up the warning inside the city proper.

"Matt! Tia!" Richard shouted. "Get your heads down below the wall."

No sooner had Richard spoken than a formation of human mercenaries near the front of the orc army released a volley of arrows. Myers grabbed both teenagers and forcefully pulled them below the edge of the protective stonework. Richard and the others ducked down also as several hundred arrows and crossbow bolts took flight in their direction.

Most of the defenders on the wall found safety behind the thick battlements, but a few of the arrows found their marks. Richard heard several cries of anguish from soldiers who were either too slow or just plain unlucky.

"Archers, return fire," ordered Captain Kelvoy.

Two hundred-plus arrows left the city wall heading for a massed formation of orcs running toward the wall. It was obvious a full attack was in progress. Most of the defender's arrows glanced off invisible barriers of magic, but enough found their mark to slow down the orc's initial rush.

The voice of Colonel Dandridge sounded over the battle cries of the attackers. Richard assumed some type of amplification spell had been cast on the colonel.

"Magic users, take out those siege engines," ordered the colonel.

A dozen priests and mages were gathered on the wall above the city's main gate. They responded to the colonel's orders. Richard's passive scan picked up links from the magic users attaching themselves to the strongest mage in their group. The other magic users began funneling Power to her. He glanced at the gate in time to see the mage finish her spell and push outward with her hands.

A large ball of blue energy shot out and streaked into the ground ten meters in front of a tall, wooden tower being rolled toward the wall nearest the main gate. Over a hundred armored orcs were positioned all along stairs leading up to a platform on top of the tower. A raised ramp at the edge of the platform was at the same level as the top of the city's wall. A dozen orcs and two ogres in plate mail carrying large battle-axes were poised to cross the ramp as soon as it lowered.

Suddenly, the ground in front of the tower cracked open where the spell had hit. The cracks widened to reveal a void beneath the surface. The void was at least twenty meters deep. The ground around and above the hole collapsed inward. The wooden tower slowly leaned forward until it started toppling into the dark pit created by the mage's spell. Dozens of orcs on the tower's platform and stairs began jumping to safety. Some made it, but most were caught under an avalanche of logs and metal plating as the tower broke apart and crashed to the bottom of the void.

Cheers from the city's defenders erupted up and down the length of the wall. Both Tia and Matthew began struggling to free themselves from Myers's grip.

"Let go!" said Tia. "I can't see."

"Yeah," said Matthew. "What's happening?"

Tia slipped from Myers's grasp, but Richard caught her before she could get her head above the protection of the battlements.

"Stay down," Richard ordered.

Jerad shouted a warning. "Incoming. The shuttles are beginning an attack run."

Richard sensed balls of energy leave the two fighters and streak toward the main gate. From the frequency of the energy, he assumed they were magic-based missiles of some type. A moment later he knew he was right.

Just as the leader of the mages defending the gate was about to release a second spell, the incoming balls of magic hit the magic users' defensive shield. The shield absorbed the explosions of the first five missiles. The next two shattered the shield. An eighth missile hit in the middle of the mages. Richard sensed the life forces of several of the magic users disappear as the explosion rippled outward. Two more missiles slammed into the wall at the same point. The remaining blips on Richard's passive scan marking the position of the magic users disappeared completely.

Pieces of stonework were thrown high into the air. Richard dove on top of Tia. His brother did the same for Matthew. Various-sized chunks of granite rained down on the entire length of the wall. A piece of stone the size of Richard's head hit his left leg. He heard the crack of snapping bones. A white-hot flash of pain shot up his leg.

"Arrgh," Richard groaned as he rolled off Tia while trying his best not to damage his leg any further. He felt Power from his self-healing reserve wrapping around his injury. The pain subsided slightly, but he knew it would be several seconds before he could walk.

This time it was the attackers who cheered. A glance told Richard at least two meters of the stonework above the main gate had been destroyed. Dozens of the city's soldiers, dead and dying, were scattered along the wall. The body of a female in dented plate-mail lay near Richard. As he watched, a stream of red liquid rushed out between the openings in the fallen knight's visor. Richard's passive scan picked up a lessening of the woman's life force. Then it was gone completely. As her life force disappeared from his passive scan, Richard noticed a shimmer around the dead soldier as if something was escaping her body. In less than a second, the mysterious aura was gone, making him wonder if he'd truly seen anything.

The twang of a nearby bow drew Richard's attention. It was Chancee. The ranger began firing her bow as fast as she could pull arrows from her quiver. Emerald was doing the same with her crossbow. Before Richard could stop her, Tia jumped up and grabbed a crossbow from a fallen soldier. She joined the dwarf at the battlements and began firing at the oncoming attackers.

With a surprising show of strength, Matthew broke free from Myers. He grabbed a nearby shield and stood near Tia, doing his best to block return fire from the orcs below. Richard had a feeling his brother had let the teenager break free on purpose. Why, he wasn't sure.

The sound of splintering wood gave him his answer. The orcs had manhandled a massive battering ram to the front of the main gate. Even from his prone position, Richard could tell by the vibrations running through the wall that the reinforced wood of the gate was giving way to the ram's blows.

Myers reached down and pulled Richard into a standing position. Since his leg was still broke, Richard had to hold onto the stonework to remain upright.

His brother pulled his bastard sword out of its scabbard. "Can you walk?"

Richard shook his head. "Not yet. Give me about ten seconds."

"We ain't got ten seconds."

With those words, Myers began running toward the point of the wall above the main gate. Jerad and Trinity were hot on Myers's heels. When they got to the point above the gate, all three wizard scouts jumped over the battlement and disappeared from sight. Almost immediately, Richard sensed the life forms massed below the gate begin to blink out.

Richard tried hobbling toward the section of the wall above the gate. Tam and Telsa grabbed his arms and began pulling him forward.

"No," Richard said. "The two of you stay here and protect Emerald and the children. I'll help the others."

"No way," said Tam. "We're not sitting around with our thumbs up our butts while you do the fighting."

In no mood for arguing, Richard's temper snapped. His voice took on an edge he'd never used with his friends. "No! That's an order. You're a defender, Tam. Your shields defend against both physical and energy attacks. Mine doesn't. The dwarf's important. So are the children. Keep them safe at all cost."

Richard pointed at Telsa before she had a chance to begin a protest of her own. "Those fighter-shuttles will be making another pass. Try to deflect their missiles as best you can. Our soldiers are in shock. They'll break if the fighters do enough damage. Now *move*."

Ignoring their defiant looks, Richard shrugged loose from their grasps and began moving toward the gate. He half expected them to ignore his orders, but his passive scan told him they were returning to take up positions next to the children and Emerald. With his leg partially healed, Richard started running toward the gate. By the time he reached the area where the mages had been killed, his leg was as good as new. He pulled out his short sword with his right hand and gripped his magic dagger with his left. He checked his Power reserve. It was nearly full.

Richard jumped over the edge of the wall. The thirty-meter drop to the ground went quickly. Just before he hit the ground, he wrapped himself in Power and slowed enough to duck and roll without taking any injury. A layer of orc bodies below the wall cushioned his fall as well.

Richard came out of his roll and swung his sword at a large orc to his front. The orc tried to parry, but Richard feinted past the orc's axe. The creature fell backward with blood gushing from a slice across his neck. Sensing an attack from the rear, Richard stabbed back and upwards with his dagger catching a human mercenary between the legs. The soldier's pitiful scream was short-lived as Richard did a backspin and got the blade of his short sword between the man's helmet and body armor. The soldier's head flew into the air. Richard was off seeking another target before the head hit the ground.

Richard's fall placed him to the side of the battering ram. The crew for the massive piece of equipment was no longer attempting to use their ram to break through the gates. They were too busy fighting for their lives against the other three wizard scouts. The splintered wood and snapped hinges of the gate indicated the orcs' near success.

If Myers and the others hadn't counterattacked, the orcs would already be in the city.

Moving forward, Richard took out four more orcs before he caught up with the other wizard scouts. They were in a triangle with Myers at the tip. A troll in chain armor and carrying a massive sword swung at Myers. As Richard watched, his brother ducked below the swing and came up between the troll's legs. In a maneuver similar to one Richard had once used during his Academy days, Myers stabbed upward with his bastard sword as he passed under the troll. The monster screamed in agony.

Trinity jumped into the air and lopped off the troll's head. At the same time, Jerad cut off the creature's right leg at the knee. Richard chopped off its left leg at the knee for good measure.

"It won't stay down for long," Richard said. "We have to burn it."

"No time," shouted Myers. "Those fighter-shuttles are making a second run."

A glance at his passive scan proved his brother right. The fighters were on short final. A half a dozen balls of magic sped toward the city wall. Richard sensed a line of Power extend outward from Telsa and knock three of the balls down into a formation of orcs. The missiles exploded in massive fireballs burning dozens of orcs in the process. He sensed the three remaining missiles heading straight for his position at the main gate. The pilots of the shuttles obviously didn't care that hundreds of their own troops were in the line of fire.

A shield of energy appeared in front of Richard and the others. He recognized Tam's frequency. The missiles exploded into fireballs. Tam's shield held.

When the fireballs dissipated, Richard sensed Tam withdraw her shield to conserve Power. An idea popped into his mind. He surrounded some of the remaining energy from the fireballs with Power and pulled it back with his telekinesis. He pushed part of the fire onto the squirming body of the troll. He sent the remainder of the fire onto the battering ram. The piece of siege equipment burst into flames.

"Time to leave," Richard shouted. "We've done all we can do down here. The fire will prevent any new attacks on the gate."

"Not for long," Jerad said. "Those fighters aren't done yet."

Sure enough, the two fighters were making tight turns and

beginning a third attack run. Richard sensed the other wizard scouts wrapping themselves with Power in preparation for levitating back up the wall. He began to wrap his own Power around himself, but Jerad knocked it aside before he could finish.

"Save it," said Jerad as he wrapped Power around Richard as well as himself and began levitating them both up the wall. "My reserve's larger."

Richard reluctantly accepted his friend's help. He hated being reminded his Power reserve was the smallest of any living wizard scout. However, he knew his friend was right. The battle might last a long time. He might need every drop of Power he had.

"Thanks," Richard said as his friend touched them both down on the top of the wall.

"You can thank me proper later if we're still alive," said Jerad.

Jerad turned to Myers. "Trinity and I will stay here to protect the main gate. Rick and you need to get back to the children and the dwarf. The soldiers are near the breaking point. You've got to help Emerald get that circle thing of hers working. It's now or never."

Richard expected Myers to balk at being ordered around by a former student. Surprisingly, his brother merely nodded and said, "We'll get it done or die trying. Let's go, Shepard."

Without waiting, Myers took off running in the direction of the children and the dwarf. As they ran, Richard sensed strong emotions from the soldiers they passed. While he wasn't an empath, his years of association with the dolgars and their emotion-speak had made him sensitive to the more powerful emotions in people. Richard sensed fear building up in the city's defenders. It wasn't panic yet, but it was getting close.

The incoming fighter-shuttles fired another salvo of missiles. Half went toward the main gate and half toward the point where Tam and Telsa stood with the children and the dwarf. Once again, Telsa used her Power to divert several missiles into the orc army below. Tam's shield held against the others. From the area of the main gate, Richard sensed Jerad and Trinity using the same ploy to defend against the missile attack there.

In a change of tactics, the two fighters didn't pull up from their attack. They continued onward straight at the city wall. Streams of small, green balls composed of magic shot outward from the fighters.

"They're strafing the wall," shouted Myers. "Shields!"

Richard threw up a hasty defensive shield and kept running. Balls of green energy hit all around him blowing small pieces of granite out of the stonework wherever they hit. Several balls of energy deflected off his shield.

While he and Myers had their defensive shields to protect them, the soldiers manning the wall didn't. Dozens were caught in the fighter's fire. The green energy ate through the soldier's armor and blew pieces of meat out the other side of their bodies.

"Run!" shouted a soldier as he threw down his sword and headed for the stairs.

"The city's lost," shouted another. "Save yourselves."

The fighter-shuttles finished their run and passed a hundred meters overhead as they circled back to line up for another attack.

Richard dropped his defensive shield to conserve Power. He heard Colonel Dandridge's amplified voice yelling commands as he tried to restore order to his defenders. He noticed several sergeants along the wall grab soldiers as they ran and force them back to their positions. Aided by Captain Kelvoy, Lieutenant Rirely, and several seasoned sergeants, the colonel got his command back in order. The defenders once again began trading fire with the attacking orcs.

By this time, Richard and Myers had reached their destination. He saw strange looks on the faces of both Tia and Matthew. He wouldn't call it fear, but it was at least grave concern. Richard had a feeling the children were beginning to understand the difference between fighting an enemy at ranges of tens of thousands of meters from a Zip fighter in space and fighting them when you were close enough to see the whites of their eyes.

"Another strafing run will break these soldiers," said Chancee as she pulled her last arrow from her quiver and fired it at the attackers. "Even the colonel won't be able to make them hold their ground."

Richard turned to Emerald. "It's now or never. Get that Circle of yours going, or the city's lost for sure."

"What do you think I've been trying to do?" snapped the dwarf. "It's not working."

Richard had sensed the dwarf's attempts during most of the

battle. While he understood her predicament, he knew now wasn't the time for him to be sympathetic. "Well, try harder. You said your people were murdered. Are you going to let the Dragars and their vampires get away with it? Did your parents die for nothing? Try harder."

The dwarf did try. Richard sensed Emerald gather Power from deep within her. The Power came from much deeper than any of her earlier attempts. Several lines of Power reached outward from the dwarf and floundered around as if seeking something. The lines began to pull back.

"No!" Richard yelled. "Keep going. Don't stop."

The lines of Power reached back out. The lines reminded him of something. He remembered the battle where the dolgars and he had fought the demon and the dimension-shifting cats.

"She's trying to form links," Richard told Myers. "She's doing it wrong."

Myers reached out with his own diviner ability and touched one of Emerald's half-formed links. He strengthened it and held it in place. Richard reached out and strengthened another line of Power. He forced it to touch the line held by his brother. The two lines linked together. The Power in the two links increased as they bolstered one another. Between the two links, they had more Power than they'd had separately.

"They're creating Power," Richard said.

"Impossible," said Myers. "Power can't be created."

Richard didn't argue the point. It didn't matter. Out the corner of his eye, he could see the two fighter-shuttles lining up for another attack. The soldiers around him noticed it as well. Richard felt a rising emotion of fear from the nearby defenders. In spite of the efforts of several sergeants, at least a dozen soldiers dropped their swords and began running for the stairs. Richard sensed a rising fear in the city as well. He heard yelling and screaming in the streets below as the city populace sought refuge from the impending disaster. They ran, but there was no place to go. Everyone knew if the orcs breached the walls, not a man, woman, or child would be left alive.

The success of linking the two lines of Power seemed to bolster the confidence of the dwarf. More lines of Power reached out from Emerald. They were also badly formed, but less so than the first.

Richard strengthened several of them and linked them together as Myers did the same with others. With each linking, additional lines of Power reached out from Emerald seeking others of their kind. Richard noticed these lines were almost fully formed.

Remembering the weave of the demon's Power that it had used to connect the dimension-shifting cats, Richard said, "Don't let the links cross. Link them one to the other to form a single line."

"Here they come," shouted Chancee as she pointed at the incoming fighters.

A large part of the wall's defenders panicked at the approach of certain death. They formed a mob and began running for their lives. Richard hated mobs. The snarling beast which was his temper broke out of its cage. His anger reached out from his mind for the nearest source of Power. He found it close by in the expanding links being formed by Emerald.

Something deep inside Richard tingled with excitement. The something within him grabbed hold of the links and tweaked them to form a greater source of Power. He felt the same hunger he'd experienced during the battle on the black destroyer from the magical dimension a few months earlier. By tracing links from one Dragar magic user to another, he'd built up a source of Power greater than anything he'd ever experienced. He'd almost lost himself to the hunger. Richard sensed his danger now. His hunger demanded more Power. He felt it moving Emerald's links outward in an ever-expanding circle.

The links touched the people around him, Chancee, the children, and the other wizard scouts. Richard sensed their Power through the links. He hungered for their Power but wanted more. He felt the dwarf fighting for control of the links, but Richard's hunger was too strong. He continued to move the links outward until they touched the soldiers manning the wall. Their Power was now available through the links. It was still not enough to satisfy Richard's hunger. He pushed the links farther out to grab hold of the soldiers fleeing down the stairs and into the streets. He reached into the buildings and attached links to the thousands of noncombatants huddling inside. Still he wasn't satisfied. He needed more. He pushed the links outward even farther until they encompassed the entire population of the city.

The hunger inside Richard smiled. It had formed a Circle. Now it had the Power it needed. Now it would be free. Now it would suck the life force from each of the pathetic creatures around it. They didn't matter. Only the acquisition of Power mattered.

CHAPTER 27

Gaston Myers fought the link trying to attach itself to him. He sensed a hunger in the link, which made him fear its touch. The link was powerful. Only his diviner ability was keeping it at bay. He sensed the dwarf fighting Shepard for control of the link, but her abilities were no match for those of the wizard scout. Gaston began to wonder if his own abilities were any match.

He'd witnessed Shepard's Power before during the battle with the Conglomerate at the DNA center on Velos a few years earlier. It had been nothing like this. Shepard's control of the expanding links threatened everyone in the city. Even Wizard Scout Trinity and the others fell victim to its effects. Gaston feared he'd lose his own battle any second and surrender to the expanding links as well. Somehow, he sensed when that happened, the hunger in Shepard would drain everyone dry.

Gaston heard a sob nearby. It was his son, Matthew. He was holding Tia in his arms. During their struggle for the links, an orc crossbow bolt had found a weak point in Tia's neck armor. She was dying. He sensed Matthew's concern for Tia fighting off the control of the link.

An idea came to Gaston. He feared what would happen to his son if Shepard wasn't stopped. His concern for his son gave him the strength to resist. With an effort of will, Gaston threw off the effect of the Circle. As soon as the link was detached, Myers swung his bastard sword at Shepard's unprotected head. At the last instant, he turned the sword so it struck with the flat of the blade.

Gaston heard Shepard's skull crack as his brother went flying into the wall. Shepard bounced off the battlement and landed face first on the stone walkway. Blood began pooling on the stone below his brother's head.

Gaston felt the hunger leave the Circle. The links of the Circle were still there, but the hunger was gone.

CHAPTER 28

Emerald struggled desperately for control of the Circle to no avail. The wizard scout was too strong for her. She feared the hunger she sensed through the links. Only the fact that she still struggled prevented the hunger from draining them all dry. Her fear gave her strength, but in her heart, she knew it wouldn't be enough. The hunger would win if nothing changed.

Just when her hope was nearly gone, Emerald saw the wizard scout they called Gaston swing out with his sword and strike Richard's head. Even before Richard struck the wall, Emerald sensed the hunger disappear from the links of the Circle.

As soon as Emerald regained control of the Circle, she understood what she'd been doing wrong. It was so obvious. Whether she could do it correctly in the future, she didn't know, but that didn't matter. At this moment in time, she knew what to do. The Circle told her what to do.

She was the daughter of a king. Her mother had been a valiant warrior-queen. Emerald reached deep inside and drew the courage that was her heritage into the link connecting her to the Circle. Her courage jumped from one link of the Circle to another, increasing incrementally with each jump.

The cries of terror from the soldiers on the wall and the mob in the streets below lessened. The courage of the Circle continued to jump from link to link until the rampant fear threatening the city's existence disappeared. The soldiers who'd abandoned their posts reversed direction and returned to their fighting positions while retrieving discarded weapons along the way. Thousands of civilians joined them on the wall; men, women, and even children. Several siege towers had already made it to the wall. Dozens of armored orcs and ogres were running across the tower's ramps bent on death and destruction. The city's defenders hurled defiance at the attacking orcs and their allies, driving them back.

Emerald heard a loud burping sound over her shoulder. She turned to see streams of green energy shooting out from the Dolgars' flying ships. Much of the green energy was stopped by hasty defensive shields thrown up by the wizard scouts and surviving mages and priests. The Dolgars' weapons were powerful, but the Circle increased the strength of the defender's shields.

The shields held.

Unfortunately, only a handful of mages and priests remained. The portions of the wall where they were stationed were protected, but the Dolgars' green balls of energy took a heavy toll at the undefended spots along the wall. Scores of defenders died, but those remaining stayed firm in their resolve. They were part of the Circle. They wouldn't run.

CHAPTER 29

A hammering in Richard's head pulled him out of the quicksand of unconsciousness into which he'd fallen. He was back in the land of the living with one helluva headache. He sensed Power from his self-healing reserve working overtime to repair damage to his head, but couldn't remember how he'd been hurt.

A sound drew Richard's attention. *Singing?* The words spoke of war and carnage, then courage and sacrifice overcoming certain defeat. He wanted to open his eyes to see the source of the singing, but his head hurt too much. *A few more seconds. Then I'll open my eyes, but not yet.*

Since he couldn't see, Richard reached out with his passive scan. He sensed an intricate weave of lines of energy encompassing the entire city. He didn't need anyone to tell him it was the Circle.

She did it, Richard thought. *Somehow, she did it.*

Hope surged in Richard's heart, but only for a moment. He sensed those around him with his passive scan. A life form only a couple of meters away was dying. Richard recognized the frequency of the life form. The frequency was that of Tia.

Forcing his eyes open, Richard looked around. Emerald stood with her eyes closed as if lost in a trance. Chancee stood near her using a large, wooden shield to protect her smaller friend from incoming arrows and crossbow bolts. The other wizard scouts stood at the wall. He sensed lines of Power stretching out from them to form defensive shields. Streams of green energy splattered against their shields, but they held.

Richard looked lower down. He spotted Matthew cradling Tia's head in his lap while he stroked her hair. He was crying. A metal quarrel protruded from Tia's neck. Blood was everywhere.

Reaching out with his mind, Richard wrapped Power from his healing reserve around Tia's injury. He imagined how her neck was now and compared it with how it should be. At the same time, he wrapped Power from his regular reserve around the crossbow bolt. He made it shimmer as he shifted the piece of metal into the void. As soon as the quarrel was in the void, he used telekinesis to pull it free of the teenager's neck, then dropped the dimensional shift the moment it was clear. The piece of metal fell to the stone floor with a clang. Blood spurted from the open wound. Richard pulled half of his healing Power back into himself. A sharp pain stabbed into his neck. Blood spurted into the air. He tried to breathe but choked on his own blood. Once Tia's injury was fully replicated on his own body, Richard sensed his healing Power repairing the damage to Tia's neck. It was done quickly. He heard Tia groan and say something.

Richard started to lose consciousness again, but the roar of engines drew him back to the real world. He opened his eyes just as one of the Dolgar fighters flew past with a second one close on its heels.

He heard Emerald speaking. "We can't take another pass like that. The Circle's holding. The people won't run, but the Dolgars' flying machines are taking their toll. Our people are dying, and the orcs are scaling the city walls in several places."

Holding his hand to his neck, Richard forced himself to stand. He was weak from loss of blood. His self-heal was working to restore him to DNA baseline, but he needed a few more seconds. In the meantime, he leaned against the wall for support. He noticed Myers and Emerald looking at him suspiciously as he stood. Memories of the hunger and what he'd almost done flooded Richard's mind.

From the looks of the other wizard scouts and the teenagers, Richard didn't think they knew. However, he had no doubt the dwarf and Myers knew all too well. He'd almost killed them all.

"Rick," said Matthew as he held Tia's hand. He had a strange look on his face. "Thanks. I thought I'd lost her."

Richard ignored the teenager and looked upward. The Dolgar fighters were making a hard turn as they prepared to line up for another strafing run. A quick glance along the wall confirmed Emerald's words. Lines of orcs were streaming onto the battlements from two siege towers. Other orcs were climbing long ladders at several points along the wall. The city's defenders were fighting bravely, but they would soon be outnumbered.

Richard didn't have much time. As the last of the damage to his neck healed, he said a silent prayer of thanks that acquired injuries from others always healed faster than direct damage. He looked around. The others were still looking at him as if awaiting orders. Richard decided to give them some. He had a plan. Whatever Myers and the dwarf thought about him, he could deal with later. Everyone's first priority had to be to take out those fighter-shuttles.

"Jerad, Trinity," Richard said. "Take out those two siege towers."

"What about the fighters?" said Jerad.

"The rest of us will handle them," Richard said. "You worry about those towers."

Jerad knew how to take orders as well as give them. With a nod of his head, he took off running toward the nearest tower with Trinity close at his side.

Richard pointed at the two teenagers. Tia was covered in blood, but alert and functional. "Could you fly those fighters if we got the two of you onboard?"

Ever since the *Defiant* had acquired a magic-based fighter to replace one of its zippers, both Tia and Matthew had been taking turns training in the new dragon-fighter. Tia had even tried to teach Richard the ways of the magic spacecraft, but he'd proved as proficient at flying the fighter as he was at driving heavy cats. In other words, he could barely keep it airborne. The teenagers, on the other hand, had become quite good at it. What little Comstar and the other ex-Dragar slaves hadn't been able to tell them, the teenagers figured out on their own. Richard hoped their skills with the *Defiant's* dragon-fighter would transfer to the shuttles flying overhead.

Without hesitation, Tia answered, "Yeah, we could fly those things, but how would we get inside?"

A look of understanding came over Myers. "A dimensional

shift."

Richard nodded his head. "That's right. You take Matt and I'll take Tia."

Myers shook his head. "No. We'd never make it. We'd use so much Power levitating up there we wouldn't have enough to do a shift. It's a fool's errand. I won't risk Matt."

"I'll take the risk," said Matthew.

"Well, I won't," said Myers with a note of finality in his voice.

The shuttles had completed their turn and were starting their attack run.

"Telsa, Tam," Richard said. "Can you handle the levitation? Just get us close to those fighters, and we'll do the rest."

Without taking time to answer, Tam wrapped Power around Tia and him. Telsa did the same to Myers and Matthew. Since Myers didn't knock Telsa's Power away, Richard assumed it meant his brother was agreeing to his plan.

Tia and Richard began rising into the air. So did Myers and Matthew.

Matthew yelled, "What do we do once we take control of the shuttle?"

Before Richard could reply, Tia answered Matthew's question. "We kill every orc we can get in our gunsights."

Richard had always thought Tia was a little on the bloodthirsty side. He was suddenly thankful he wasn't an orc.

It was a strange feeling being hoisted into the air while depending on someone else's Power to do the job, but Richard knew he'd made the right decision. Although the fighters were approaching rapidly, the distance was still too great for him to have levitated there on his own. He realized Myers had been right. They would've run out of Power before they'd gotten halfway there.

Both of the Dragar fighter-shuttles began firing. Richard threw up a defensive shield. Several balls of green magic glanced off the shield. Although his defensive shield was Power hungry, Richard had no intention of dropping it. The Dragars had apparently spotted them and were concentrating their fire on them instead of the city wall.

Tia leaned over and shouted into Richard's ear. "Are you sure you can shift us out of the void in the right spot?"

It was a valid question. The shuttle was traveling fast, and

Richard didn't have his battle computer to help. He didn't bother answering the teenager's question because she'd know one way or the other soon enough.

Richard noted his Power reserve was at seventy-two percent and dropping rapidly. The fighters were firing a steady stream of energy at both his brother and his shields. The Dragar pilots weren't deviating from their course.

"They're going to ram us," shouted Tia.

Richard wrapped both Tia and himself with Power. He shifted into the void and dropped his defensive shield to conserve Power. He felt Tam's telekinesis fall away as well. He was in the void. She wasn't.

Using his own telekinesis, Richard reversed direction to match the nearest fighter's speed. He noted his Power reserve again. He was at forty-eight percent. He slowed his speed to allow the fighter to catch up. The fighter continued its fire, but the green balls of energy passed through Tia and Richard. They were in the void. The green energy wasn't.

The windscreen of the fighter grew larger until Richard could make out the reptilian faces of the two pilots. He slowed a little more. They passed through the skin of the ship into a clear space a few meters across. He dropped his dimensional shift and telekinesis at the same time. They fell the hands-breath to the floor, Richard thought his battle computer would've been proud of him. His timing was perfect.

Richard's self-congratulation was short-lived. He heard Tia shout a warning and a split second later, a large, hairy hand grabbed him by the neck and threw him toward the bulkhead. Fortunately, he still had Power wrapped around him. Using the same Power, he levitated to a stop before hitting the wall.

Spinning around, Richard saw a four-armed creature covered in hair with two outstretched arms. The hand of a third arm was fumbling at a hand blaster of some type stuck in a holster on its belt. Three more of the hairy creatures were in the process of rising out of their seats only a few meters away at the rear of the shuttle.

Thargs, Richard thought. The hairy creatures were the bully boys of the reptilian Dragars.

In a blur of motion so fast he surprised even himself, Richard pulled his short sword from its scabbard and sliced the throat of the charging Tharg. He barely had time to notice the look of surprise on its face before he was kicking a second one in the chest and knocking it back into its chair.

Reaching out with his mind, Richard sensed the location of another Tharg's heart and pulled with his telekinesis. The Tharg roared but didn't fall. Richard sensed the beat of a second heart on the other side of the creature's chest. He wrapped it with Power and twisted hard. This time the Tharg fell.

The fourth Tharg grabbed a rifle out of a side rack and got off three rounds in rapid succession before Richard was able to throw his dagger into the creature's eye. The fourth Tharg fell to the floor unmoving. Unfortunately, two of the rifle rounds caught Richard in the right side of his chest. He also fell to the floor alongside the dead Thargs. He tried to rise, but couldn't. The pain was too great. He sensed his self-heal wrapping around the wounds and sealing the flesh together. He feared his healing would be too late. There was still another Tharg and two Dragar pilots to deal with. Richard tensed his muscles in anticipation of either the Tharg or the pilots shooting holes in him with their sidearms.

No shots came.

The pain in Richard's chest eased enough for him to open his eyes. Something rolled past him on the floor. It was grayish in color. Richard did his best to focus on the object. It was a head. It was a Dragar head.

Shifting his gaze to the front of the fighter-shuttle, Richard saw a headless Dragar corpse in the copilot's seat. Tia occupied the pilot's position. The bloody body of another Dragar was on the floor beside her.

She's good, Richard thought. *She might even be better than Liz.*

"You're lucky," said a squeaky voice to Richard's right.

Looking in the direction of the voice, he noticed a young gnome strapped to a chair at the back of the shuttle. The gnome appeared to be imprisoned in the seat. A leather-like collar was around his neck. Blood trickled out of his nose and down one side of his mouth.

When the gnome saw Richard looking at him, he pointed at the far side of the shuttle as best he could with his chin. "One of the shots from that Tharg's rifle ricocheted off the wall and took out the last Tharg."

Since his wounds were nearly healed, Richard leveraged himself up on his hands and knees. He looked in the direction indicated by the gnome. A Tharg was slumped in its chair. A finger-sized hole in the center of its forehead told its fate.

The shuttle banked hard.

Richard was knocked back down. The fall reminded him of his mission.

The battle, Richard thought.

Jumping to his feet, Richard ran the few steps to the front of the fighter-shuttle. Tia was just completing her turn and lining up on a formation of orcs.

The teenager must have sensed him beside her. "I can fly the ship, but I can't figure out the gun controls. They're different than the ones in the dragon-fighter we have on the *Defiant*."

Richard was well aware he didn't think fast. It was one of his shortcomings. Fortunately, he was very good at making snap decisions with very little information. He turned back to look at the gnome.

"Can you fire the ship's weapons?"

Although the straps restraining the gnome to his chair gave him little movement, he was able to raise his head a little to better reveal the collar around his neck.

"Yes, but I can't fire them with this thing on. It limits me to maintenance duties."

Richard liked gnomes. He'd never had one do him dirty. On a wild impulse, he decided to trust this one. Reaching out with his mind, he wrapped Power around the collar. He sensed the collar's flow of magic. Once he found the keystone to the magic, he looped it back on itself. The magic dissipated into the universe from which it had come. As soon as the magic was gone, Richard snapped the collar with his telekinesis. He did the same to the security straps pinning the gnome to his seat.

The young gnome was obviously not one to let an opportunity go to waste. He was up in a heartbeat and heading toward the front of the shuttle. He stopped only long enough to kick one of the Thargs in the face.

"That'll teach you to hit someone your own size next time."

Before Richard could comment, the gnome was next to the copilot's seat. When he slapped a button on the seat's armrest, the harness holding the Dragar copilot came loose. The headless corpse fell to the floor. The gnome didn't even take time to wipe the blood out of the seat. He just sat down and began touching various spots on the console. Part of the windscreen changed to a heads-up display with a translucent bullseye. When the gnome touched another spot on the armrest, the fighter shuddered. Two large, green balls shot into view in front of the ship and tracked toward a siege tower crowded with several hundred orcs. The tower exploded in a blast of green energy. Pieces of wood and orc parts were thrown into the air.

Tia laughed and banked the shuttle hard to the left in a climbing turn. "Nice shootin', Tex."

Richard shook his head. He'd made the mistake of letting Tia read his copy of *Cute Sayings and Slang of 20th through 21st Century America.* He knew she was paying the gnome a compliment. From the perplexed look on the gnome's face, Richard gathered he hadn't read the book.

"I'm going to come around for another pass," said Tia.

The gnome pointed at the armrest on the pilot's seat. "Push that green button on the front right of your armrest. Your safety's on. That's why you couldn't fire your auto-cannons. When the button turns red, you can pull the trigger on your command stick to strafe your target."

After Tia completed her turn, she did as the gnome bid. The button on her armrest turned red.

"Rick," said Tia. "What about the others? Did they make it? Is Matt alive?"

"They're fine," Richard assured her after checking his passive scan. "They're on the other shuttle. There's only one other life form on board. Its frequency is similar to our friend here."

"The name's Rembis," said the gnome. "And if you're telling me the gnome on the other fighter is still alive, her name is Marstis. She's my sister."

Richard sensed several balls of energy leave the other shuttle in the direction of a formation of orcs. He couldn't see the blasts hit, but when the balls of energy disappeared into the center of a formation of orcs, a significant number of the life forms in the formation disappeared as well.

Richard nodded approvingly. "I think Matt just figured out how to fire his weapons."

Not one to be outdone, Tia lined up on a formation of human mercenaries and released a volley of several hundred green tracers into the massed troops. Discipline in the mercenary unit disintegrated as the human soldiers fled in all directions.

Rembis fired another salvo of green missiles at a second siege tower. It met the same fate as its brethren. The heavy debris fell onto a group of orcs standing in line to climb up the tower. The loss of life was significant.

Tia banked the fighter for another run. If any of the orc soldiers or their magic users were attempting to return fire, it was ineffective. The shuttle-fighter was apparently flying too high and too fast.

"As long as our ammo holds out," said Tia, "Matt and I can do a number on the orcs outside the wall. Unfortunately, there's already a lot of orcs on the wall and in the city. We can't fire on them there. If they get the main gate open, the city will be lost."

A glance out the windscreen told Richard that Tia's assessment was correct. Several siege towers were already depositing hundreds if not thousands of attackers on the wall. The defenders were holding their ground, but they were vastly outnumbered. A large column of dust in the distance drew his attention.

"What's that over by those hills?" Richard said as he pointed to a range of hills about ten kilometers away.

The gnome fumbled with something on his control panel. A portion of the windscreen switched to magnification mode. A large formation of cavalry was riding hard in the direction of the city.

"It's another army," said the gnome. "The orcs are getting reinforcements."

The sight of a banner flying in the wind near the front of the cavalry told Richard otherwise. "Negative. That's King Hamerstine's cavalry. He must have sent them on ahead. I'm guessing there's at least ten thousand horse with him."

"They'll never get here in time," said Tia as she made another strafing run on a group of orcs massing outside the gates. "The orcs on the wall are already at the gatehouses. Once they take those, they'll open the gates. It'll be house to house then. There won't be a Cantonsburg left for the king to save."

Always one for action and feeling useless in the fighter anyway,

Richard picked up the rifle dropped by the Tharg he'd killed. "Can you guys handle this ship on your own?"

The look Tia gave him over her shoulder told him she thought he should know full well they could.

"Fine," Richard said. "Make a pass over one of the gatehouses. I'll hold the gate. You guys take care of the orcs outside the city."

As the fighter changed course for the main gate, the gnome jumped out of his seat and snatched a belt with pouches out of a side locker. He shoved the belt in Richard's hand.

"Here's some extra battery-spheres for that thing." With a grin, Rembis added, "From the number of orcs on that wall, you're going to need them."

With a few more hurried words and a quick hands-on lesson, the gnome showed Richard how to switch out battery-spheres and the location of the weapon's safety. By the time he was finished, Tia was on short final.

Reaching out with his mind, Richard used his telekinesis to retrieve his sword and dagger. Then he wrapped himself with Power and shifted into the void. After he'd levitated through the floor of the fighter-shuttle, he dropped his dimensional shift to conserve Power. He was about five hundred meters above the gate. He spread his arms and legs to try and glide for the left gatehouse. Since he was so low, he supplemented his glide with telekinesis.

Richard sensed another life form falling through the air. The life form's frequency was his brother's. Based upon his track, Richard figured Myers was heading for the right-side gatehouse.

At about two hundred meters, a stream of green balls of energy shot out from Myers and hit a group of orcs fighting what few defenders remained at the right gatehouse. Never ashamed to copy a good idea when he saw it, Richard fired his rifle at the orcs fighting the defenders of the left gatehouse.

Richard came in fast while firing all the way to the ground. Just prior to making contact with the wall's firing platform, he wrapped Power around himself and levitated to a soft landing in the center of the thickest group of orcs.

The monster which was his anger rattled its cage.

Richard willingly let it out. In that moment he became the deadliest killing machine the Intergalactic Empire had ever produced. He was a wizard scout, and he was a time-commando.

The orcs shrank back from the onslaught of rifle fire and sword thrusts, but they had nowhere to run. Some orcs chose to take their chances by jumping over the wall to the ground thirty meters below rather than face what had suddenly been unleashed in their midst.

A part of Richard's mind heard rifle fire and screams from the direction of the other gatehouse, and grinned in his anger. The orcs, ogres, and trolls had no escape. They were caught between two wizard scouts. Only death awaited them at the gatehouses now.

CHAPTER 30

Richard remained quiet as King Hamerstine listened to the reports. The king was still dressed in the bloody and battered armor he'd worn during the battle. The charge of his cavalry had routed the orc army surrounding the city, but from the king's frown, Richard knew the man was well aware it was only a temporary victory.

"I agree with the gnome," said Colonel Dandridge. "The Dragars have left us alone in the past for the most part because we caused them no trouble. Things will be different now. We've captured two of their flying ships. They're going to take notice. It's only a matter of time before they send one of their larger ships to destroy Cantonsburg. They've done it before to cities in the south."

The king's right-hand man, General Onstott, backed up the king's nephew. "He's right, sire. Only I don't think the Dragars will stop with Cantonsburg. I believe they'll turn their wrath on every town and city in the kingdom to teach others the price of defying them."

"Are you blaming us?" said Tam losing her cool. "If Rick and Gaston hadn't gotten control of those Dragar fighters, they'd have blasted your cavalry to shreds. Your precious Cantonsburg would be smoldering ruins by now, and the soldiers in your army would be dead, or worse."

For a big man, Richard thought the king had a knack for not losing his temper. He didn't appear to take affront at Tam's interruption.

"No one's blaming anyone, Lady Tam," said King Hamerstine.

"The general's merely pointing out the situation. The status quo has changed. It may take the Dragars a few days before they respond, but respond they will. When they do, anyone remaining in anything larger than a hamlet will be dead. A single blast from their larger ships can destroy an entire city. As the colonel pointed out, it's been done before."

"We need to evacuate Cantonsburg, sire," said Colonel Dandridge. "It's the people's only hope."

The king looked at his nephew. "Evacuate them where? Do you think the Dragars will find it more difficult to bomb a refugee camp than they would a city?"

Richard noticed Emerald whispering back and forth with the two gnomes during the meeting. At the king's question, she raised her voice and addressed the room.

"Underground, sire. You need to get your people underground."

"Ha!" said General Onstott not looking amused despite his laugh. "Leave it to a dwarf to want to hide underground. Perhaps you have friends who live underground, but we don't. There aren't enough known caves in the land to hold all our people. Even if there were, how would we feed them? There isn't time to stockpile supplies."

Richard had to give Emerald credit. He hated it when people put down suggestions without making one of their own. He'd have lost his temper at the general's comment. Thankfully, the dwarf seemed nonplused.

"My father was King Lokanstanos of the Drepdenoris dwarves. We—"

"The kingdom of Drepdenor fell over a century ago when those blasted Dragars first came from the stars," said General Onstott. "If any of your conquered people remain, they're slaves serving their Dragar masters.

This time Emerald's anger showed on her face, but was gone in an instant. Richard had a feeling she was a lot better at controlling her emotions than he was at controlling his. She was the daughter of a king. He wondered if that had something to do with it.

"My father's cousin is King Graphon," said Emerald ignoring the old general. "The dwarves of the western ranges have vast cities underground. They've no love for the Dragars. I've visited them often over the years. The Dragars' minions raid them incessantly for slaves and sacrifices. Take your people there. I promise you'll find shelter and food. More importantly, you'll find allies."

"Allies for what?" asked General Onstott. "We're people of the light. Do you expect us to live the rest of our lives underground, living off the charity of others? I'd rather face a quick, clean death than accept that fate."

Richard hated politics and normally left the large-scale, strategic decisions to others. His specialty was small-group tactics. This time his temper got the best of him. "Then fight!" Richard stepped forward out of the crowd of observers. "Take the dwarf's offer. Go to these western ranges. Save your people and find some allies. You're going to need them."

"Allies for what?" asked King Hamerstine.

Richard looked the king square in the eyes. "Rebellion. Your people have lived under the thumb of these Dragars long enough. It's time to drive them out and send them back where they came. Portalis is your planet, not theirs."

"Ha!" said General Onstott. "Rebellion's been tried before. The shattered remains of half a dozen empires in the south are a mute testimony to the fate of anyone who rebels against those creatures. Our only salvation has been to stay low and keep to our own business. That's the only way we've stayed alive until now."

"That's not life," said Jerad coming to Richard's aid. "That's just existing. Emerald's offered you a chance, sire. Are you going to take it?"

The king took a few moments to survey the crowd gathered around him. The officers and enlisted soldiers looked tired, but they were anything but beaten. "General Onstott's right. Rebellion has been tried before. The Dragars have always crushed any sign of resistance. Why would a rebellion by us fare any different?"

On impulse, Richard stepped forward and bent down on one knee before the king. He raised his arm across his chest in a manner he'd seen a Roman soldier in an old picture from Earth do. Bending a knee and saluting wasn't the wizard scout way. However, something inside Richard told him it was the right thing to do now.

"This time it'll be different, sire," Richard said. "You've got something the other rebellions didn't have. You've got wizard scouts. I swear to you that I won't stop fighting until every one of those Dragars is either dead or forced off Portalis. That's wizard scout honor, sire, and a wizard scout's word is their bond."

Richard sensed someone drop to one knee beside him. It was Jerad. Others followed; Trinity, Tam, and Telsa. Even Tia, Matthew, Emerald, and Chancee joined them in their unspoken oath. A movement to Richard's right caught his attention. His brother knelt down beside him and saluted as well.

Myers whispered out the side of his mouth. "I hope you know what you're doing, Shepard."

Richard hoped so too.

CHAPTER 31

Organization wasn't one of Richard's skills. Consequently, after his spur-of-the-moment display of loyalty, he was pretty much left to his own devices. Jerad, on the other hand, was quickly put into service by Colonel Dandridge.

No, make that General Dandridge, Richard thought. *He's been promoted.*

Bored, Richard went over what the others were doing. Except for Tam, everyone in his group had been assigned or volunteered for duties aligned with their skillsets.

Trinity was a protector. She spent most of her time maintaining large stealth shields to cover the movements of the refugees. Matthew and Tia were busy flying various groups of people in the captured fighter-shuttles from one place to another. Rembis and his sister Marstis pretty much stayed by the teenagers' sides to explain the more advanced complexities of the Dragars' equipment. Telsa and Myers were with the teenagers on the shuttles. Telsa went because she was inquisitive and wanted to know more about the Dragars' technology. Myers went because he'd basically turned into Matthew's shadow.

The reason for Myers's protectiveness of the boy had confused Richard until a couple of days ago. Since Myers was a diviner, Richard had been teaching him how to protect and shutdown Power links. During one particularly intense training session, he noticed something about Myers's Power frequency he'd missed during previous encounters. Whether he'd missed it before because he just hated dealing with Myers, Richard wasn't sure. Whatever the reason for his previous lack of understanding, he now knew why his brother seemed so protective of Matthew. Myers and Matthew both had a common Power frequency. Not common in that they used the same Power pool, but common in that their Power frequency was similar at the base level. During his last year at the Academy, he had noted that Myers's Power frequency had a commonality with the Power frequencies of his father, Commandant Thomas Jacobs, and his mother, Councilwoman Janice Deluth. Just like a child's DNA could be traced to their parents, a child's Power frequency could also be traced to their parents.

Richard had previously healed both Empress Diane Deloris and her son Matthew. He was familiar with their Power frequencies as well. What he'd finally noticed two days ago was that Matthew also had a common Power frequency with Gaston Myers. The enormity of the discovery had taken him a while to comprehend. However, the proof was indisputable. His brother, Gaston Myers, was the father of Diane Deloris's son, Matthew.

When Richard had confronted Myers with the information, the discussion turned to near violence. His brother had threatened to kill him if he so much as breathed a word of his discovery to anyone else. While Richard wasn't overly concerned about his brother's threat, he hadn't planned on telling Matthew or anyone else about his newly discovered revelation anyway. He was wise enough to know it would only cause problems.

* * *

As the days passed, King Hamerstine gathered his people and brought them to the lands of the dwarves in the western ranges. Considering the fact that the dwarves were suddenly asked to be the hosts to several hundred thousand unexpected guests, King Graphon and his dwarves were very accommodating. Before long, humans and dwarves alike could be seen working side by side in just about every aspect of life below ground. Naturally, there were administrative and personnel problems. Fortunately, the dwarves and humans had a common enemy and a common purpose. The populations of both races were put on a wartime status as King

Graphon and King Hamerstine sought to train and equip an army powerful enough to attack the Dragars' primary spaceport.

One day, he and Tam were exploring a particularly warm part of the dwarves' extensive tunnel system. Even with the abundance of life forms in the tunnels, Richard's passive scan was able to detect a strong magic emanating from the far end of a wide tunnel. When they followed the tunnel to its source, it opened up into a massive cavern filled with thousands of dwarves and humans working at forges stationed near glowing pools of lava.

"What are they doing?" asked Tam.

"I'm not sure," Richard said, "but I seriously doubt they're making plowshares."

Richard noticed a couple of frequencies on his passive scan that he recognized. They belonged to the gnome mage, Master Garis, and his assistant, Master Diamass. They were talking to several dwarves and a couple of humans who were wearing thick leather aprons and carrying hammers. With nothing better to do, Richard and Tam wandered over. The dwarves in the group were in heated discussion with the gnome magic users.

"I tell you, it don't matter what spells your mages throw on weapons and armor," said a particularly muscular dwarf. "It won't be effective against that winged-devil Cancontus and his servants. They're vampires. If you've never fought them yourself, you've got no idea what you're up against."

"Have you ever fought them yourself?" Richard asked the dwarf. His fondness for gnomes automatically made him take up the side of the two mages.

The dwarf eyed Richard. "As it so happens, yes, I have, if it's any of your business. I was with King Lokanstanos when he fell." The dwarf paused as if reliving a memory. "Yeah, I've fought them, and I've even killed a couple. It can't be done with normal weapons. Weapons with spells on them aren't effective against them either. The spells aren't powerful enough. The only thing that has a chance against one of them vampires is Holy Metal. Anything else will pass right through them. Don't be thinking normal armor will stop them either. Their fangs will slip past armor and rip a throat out before you know what's happened."

Tam looked questioningly at Richard. "Vampires? You ever fought them before?"

Richard shook his head. He'd heard about them, but never fought any. The truth was he didn't want to start now. Something about the sinister creatures made his skin crawl.

"We've got more than enough bodies to form an army," said Master Garis, "but we're short equipment. Our new citizen-soldiers need weapons and armor. I've been trying to convince General Fenmar here to make us some."

"You're a general?" Richard asked the dwarf. He was curious why a general would be working as a blacksmith.

"Not anymore. I haven't been for a very long time," said the dwarf. "I'm just Fenmar the Armorer now. However, I still remember when those vampires attacked. I've got a lot of respect for Master Garis and his magic, but no matter what manner of spells his mages puts on armor or weapons, they won't help against vampires unless they're made out of Holy Metal."

"Then make them out of your precious Holy Metal and stop talking about it," said Tam. "What's the big deal?"

"Ha!" said Fenmar. "You must think the stuff grows on trees. It's rarer than chicken's teeth, I can tell you that."

Richard tried to explain to Tam. "What they call Holy Metal here is energized titanium."

"You mean creallium?" asked Tam.

Richard nodded his head and pulled out his dagger. "Yeah. I've encountered magic weapons on quite a few of my Portalis missions." He pointed at the blue gem in the pommel of his dagger. "These blue gems keep the titanium energized in order to transform it into creallium."

Tam shrugged her shoulders. As an ex-mercenary, she liked to keep things simple. "Then dig up some more titanium and a few thousand of those blue gems and get your armorers to beating out more weapons. Problem solved."

Fenmar grew red-faced.

Before the dwarf could speak his mind, Richard beat him to the punch. "It's not that simple, Tam. Titanium's a rare element in the magic dimension. I assume that's why the Dragars raid our physical dimension for it. As far as the blue gems go, I've never heard of anyone mining them on Portalis. I've encountered weapons and armor with the gems, but I've no idea where they came from."

Tam looked perplexed. "So who made them?"

This time it was Fenmar who answered. "The only known source for the blue gems is the tunnels under Drepdenoris. No new gems have been found since the Dragars' vampire allies took over our homeland. As far as I know, they don't exist anywhere else on Portalis. That being the case, you can bet any magic weapons or armor made out of the Holy Metal you've seen originally came from the forges under Drepdenoris."

"Well," Richard said trying to be tactful. "It's a big universe. I got sent on a mission once to find 2,500 of those blue gems."

Fenmar looked doubtful. "Where?"

"A very long ways from here," Richard said not wanting to have to explain his mission had been in the spiritual dimension for *'the One.'*

Master Garis took on an interested look. "Do you still have them? Can you get them?"

Richard shook his head. "No. A couple a hundred have already been used. The other 2,250 or so are on another planet called Storage for safe keeping. I've got no way of retrieving them."

Tam sighed. "Too bad you don't have your dimensional pack. If you had it, you could summon those blue gems. I'll bet you could even get all the titanium we'd need as well."

"What pack is that?" asked Master Garis.

Before Richard could stop her, Tam began explaining. "It's a dimensional pack. Rick here can summon lots of things with it." She held her hands out with palms facing toward each other. "It's about this high and yea-wide. It's dull black color that seems to suck in light. I've even seen it take on the color of the background as camouflage on occasion."

"Dull black, you say," said Fenmar. His voice sounded strange. "And it can take on the background colors sometimes?"

"Sometimes," said Tam confirming the dwarf's question. "Why the sudden interest?"

The dwarf removed his apron and handed it to one of his assistants. "Take over for me, Zesstra."

Turning to Richard and the others, Fenmar said, "Come with me. I think there's something you should see."

Curious, Richard followed the dwarf. Tam and Master Garis trailed behind. Richard wasn't sure what was going on, but his intuition was tingling like crazy. He'd had the feeling before and knew what it meant.

'The One,' Richard thought. *His fingerprints are all over this. I'd bet my life on it.*

Richard had a feeling he was probably betting the lives of his friends as well.

CHAPTER 32

After a half hour and a lot of ups and downs along twisting tunnels, Richard, Tam, and Master Garis finally followed Fenmar into a side tunnel with two fierce-looking guards standing outside. They were dressed in full-plate armor and carried battle-axes with blue gems in their handles. Richard picked up strong magic from both of the dwarves' armor and weapons.

The older of the two dwarves nodded his head in recognition. "General."

Richard noticed a smile creep over Fenmar's lips.

Fenmar turned to Richard and the others. "I keep telling this old fool I'm not a general anymore. Does he listen? No."

The older guard grinned back. "You'll always be General Fenmar to me, sir, as well as to the other surviving Drepdenoris dwarves. If that makes us fools, then so be it."

Curious, Richard asked, "Are there many survivors?"

Fenmar shrugged. "Just a couple of thousand now. We grow fewer every decade. One day there'll be no one to serve Queen Emerald when she regains her throne."

"Queen?" asked Tam sounding confused. "Emerald never mentioned being a queen."

"She wouldn't," said Fenmar. "She refuses to take the title until our homeland is rid of Lord Cancontus and his servants. She says until she holds the Gem Defender in her hands and takes the solemn oath in the presence of the Mountain's Heart, she cannot truly be queen."

"You've lost me," said Tam. "What's this Gem Defender and Mountain's Heart?"

"Ah," said Fenmar. "You may as well ask what the Drepdenoris dwarves are. The Mountain's Heart is the mother of all blue gems. Since the dawn of dwarf history, the Mountain's Heart has sustained the Drepdenoris dwarves. Its magic reverberates throughout our home, providing warmth and energy." The dwarf pointed at Richard's dagger. "The blue gem in the dagger you hold came from the Mountain's Heart. As I said, it's the only source of the blue gems in the universe. Only a few chips are taken from the Mountain's Heart each year, and then only after great discussion and much prayer. All magic armor and magic weapons created of the Holy Metal are powered by chips from the Mountain's Heart."

"And the Gem Defender?" asked Tam in an effort to prod the old dwarf along before he got too sidetracked.

"It's a battle-axe of great magic," said Fenmar. "It was the first and perhaps the greatest of all magic weapons. It's been passed down from queen to daughter since our earliest history." With a sad tone in his voice, Fenmar added, "The Gem Defender was lost when Emerald's mother, Queen Saphiria, fell. I fear it's now in the hands of the vampire, Lord Cancontus. I'd rather it have been destroyed than to fall into his vile hands."

While the dwarf's story was interesting, Richard didn't think it had anything to do with their current mission. He decided to get things moving again.

"Not to be pushy, Fenmar," Richard said, "but why have you brought us here?"

"Ah, yes," said Fenmar. "Master Garis told me you were the impatient one."

Richard folded his arms and glared at the dwarf. *Why can't people just get to the point?*

"Very well," continued Fenmar. "This treasury room was provided by King Graphon to my people as a place of safekeeping for what few items of wealth we were able to salvage when we were driven out of Drepdenor. Shortly after our arrival, a strange item appeared inside the vault. The treasury room was closely guarded at the time, yet the item somehow found its way inside."

"What item is that?" Richard asked. His curiosity was piqued.

The dwarf didn't answer with words. Instead, he nodded to the older guard. The guard opened the door to the vault revealing what was inside.

On a shelf in the center of the room was a dull-black pack.

CHAPTER 33

Richard sat in the room with the other wizard scouts, Fenmar, Master Garis, General Dandridge, Emerald and Chancee, and the two teenagers looking expectantly at him.

Pointing to the pack Richard held in his hands, Jerad said, "What's this mean, Rick? Since you're wearing your battle suit and carrying your weapons, I'm assuming it's your dimensional pack. Am I wrong?"

"No, you're right," Richard said.

It hadn't taken long for Richard to convince Fenmar to let him take the pack and try it out. That it was his dimensional pack, Richard knew. It was marked as 3 of 55. He'd had two packs destroyed on previous missions, so he knew this was the pack he'd been using before he'd been teleported out of the *Defiant*. What it was doing in the dwarves' treasury room or how it had gotten there he didn't know. All he knew was that it was his, and it worked. At least it worked to an extent.

Richard shoved the pack across the table into Jerad's hands. "It's mine, but it's only partially functional. I was able to summon my battle suit and weapons plus a basic load of ammo. I was also able to summon Myers's battle suit and weapons. That's it. When I tried to get gear for the rest of you, nothing happened. I can't even summon something as simple as food. I don't know why."

Placing his battle helmet on the table, Richard decided to ask someone who might know the answer. "Do you want to try and explain, Nick?"

Nickelo's voice came over the helmet's external speakers. "Always leaving me with the difficult jobs, aren't you? Very well, I'll do my best. Once you were all teleported out of the *Defiant*, we received orders through the tele-network to pick up a passenger on Storage."

"You didn't tell me that," Richard protested.

"I haven't told you a lot of things," said Nickelo. "Now, do you want me to tell this story or do you want to do it?"

Richard looked at Jerad. His friend gave him a knowing smile. Apparently, all wizard scouts had trouble with their battle computers.

When Richard didn't answer, Nickelo said, "Fine. Let me see, where was I? Oh, yes, we received orders to pick up a passenger on Storage. The orders said Sergeant Ron was to transport the passenger to a space station located on the far side of the Crosioian sector."

"Ha!" laughed Tam. "I'll bet Sergeant Ron told them what they could do with their orders. He's not stupid enough to take the *Defiant* clear across the Crosioian empire just because the empress or *'the One'* tells him too."

"Actually," said Nickelo, "the orders didn't come from either the empress or *'the One.'* At least they didn't come directly from *'the One.'* The orders were given by someone completely different. They came from someone who Sergeant Ron trusts."

"That narrows it down," Richard said. "He doesn't trust many people. So what idiot gave Sergeant Ron his orders? Five to one whoever it was is some mindless moron doing the biddings of *'the One.'*"

Nickelo laughed.

Richard became instantly suspicious.

"You should watch who you're calling a moron, Rick," said Nickelo still chuckling. "The orders came from you. Or I should say, they were given using your security code. Even I couldn't forge the orders because I don't know the number sequence. You've never given it to me."

"Me!" Rick said. "Bull. I've been trapped a hundred thousand years in the past. When did I supposedly give these orders?"

"I've no idea," admitted Nickelo. "Regardless, the orders came from you. They were forwarded to Sergeant Ron by Keka

Derberlon."

"Dren and Brachia's Keka?" Richard asked.

"The one and the same," said Nickelo. "Part of your orders told Sergeant Ron to place the gear for the wizard scouts with you into your dimensional pack. Before you so rudely pulled me out of your dimensional pack an hour ago, I was on a shelf in a warehouse on Storage. The battle helmets and gear for the other wizard scouts were there as well. Based upon your orders, they got us off the *Defiant* very quickly. I calculate it had something to do with not wanting to unintentionally change the future by giving us knowledge we might use in the past."

Jerad tapped the table nervously, thinking. "What about the *Defiant's* mysterious passenger. Who was it?"

"Beats me," said Nickelo. "All I could find out was that Keka had a passenger for the *Defiant* to transport. Margery says she was told the passenger would be doing a snatch mission to retrieve the bottles of DNA gas."

"What?" said Myers growing suddenly interested. "That DNA gas belongs to the empress."

Richard grew angry. The bottles of refined DNA gas came from sacrificed dragons. As far as he was concerned, the gas didn't belong to anyone.

Jerad ignored Myers and continued his discussion with Nickelo.

"The Oracle told Gaston and Rick we needed those bottles of DNA gas to destroy the Dragars' temple and neutralize the blue gem," said Jared.

"You mean the Mountain's Heart," corrected Fenmar.

Deferring to the dwarf, Jerad said, "I stand corrected. We need the DNA gas to neutralize the Mountain's Heart."

"According to Margery," said Nickelo, "the passenger's mission is to bring the bottles of DNA gas to you here."

"Impossible," Richard said. "We're a hundred thousand years in the past. Even if this passenger of yours could time travel, they wouldn't know when or where to go."

"Sure they would," said Nickelo sounding way too superior for Richard's liking. "You included specific coordinates and a time in the orders."

Things were getting way too confusing for Richard. He preferred action to words. "Fine. Whatever. So where is this mysterious passenger of yours? What are we supposed to do next?"

"How would I know?" said Nickelo. "Like I said, Sergeant Ron stuck me in your dimensional pack before we got to Storage. If you're asking for a recommendation, I'd suggest talking to the Oracle one more time."

CHAPTER 34

The Oracle sat on the same cushion where Jeena had left her during their last meeting. Once again, Jeena sat cross-legged facing the small girl. Brachia and Dren sat in a similar fashion to her left and right.

"What do you mean we won't be coming back?" asked Dren. "It's taken us three years to get the time-displacement unit running on the teleporter. How's Jeehana going to take the bottles of DNA gas back to Uncle Rick and the others? She'll need us to run the equipment."

"Yeah," said Brachia, who for once was on his sister's side in an argument. "No offense, but you're a hologram. It's not like you can push buttons and operate the equipment."

The Oracle smiled. It was a friendly smile. "It's true the only holographic equipment still functioning in this crumbling palace is in this room. However, I don't need to operate your teleport device."

A lot of what the Oracle and the children discussed the last thirty minutes had gone over Jeena's head. It was all very confusing. The one thing she had picked up on was that once her mission in the future was completed, she needed to return to the children's lab at the Oracle's to get sent into the past.

"Am I supposed to operate the equipment myself?" Jeena asked sounding dubious. As a high elf, she was very smart, but most of the children's technology was still a mystery to her.

The hologram of the small girl which was the Oracle smiled.

"Brachia and Dren will set the equipment on automatic. Your staff will bring you back here once you get the DNA gas. The children's teleporter will be preset to take you to my form in the past. My form there will tell you what to do next."

The Oracle turned to Dren. "Have you told the high priestess about the data disk?"

Jeena looked at Dren. "The what?"

The teenager pulled a disk out of her pocket and handed it over. "This is a data disk. The Oracle put orders inside one like it for the earlier version of herself. Brachia and I used our combination teleport and time-displacer to send it a hundred thousand years in the past. We also used the teleporter to send holographic equipment there."

"Uh…why?" Jeena asked. That the Oracle needed to tell itself something went against everything she'd been told about prophetic beings.

"Because," said the Oracle, "my form in the past doesn't know what needs to be done. Also, what information I give to myself in the past must be handled delicately. What happened, happened. We dare not try to change it. Nevertheless, we can safely provide information to variables in the past that is required but which won't cause the recipients of the information to change what they've already done in the past. Does that seem logical?"

Jeena held up her hands in a stopping motion. "Fine," Jeena said. "Whatever." Sometimes a part of her rebelled against things when they got too complex. This was one of those times.

Dren and Brachia gave her a strange look. Brachia leaned over and whispered something in Dren's ear. The teenage girl nodded her head before turning back to Jeena.

"What did you just say?" asked Dren.

Something in the girl's voice told Jeena to be cautious. She thought for a moment before answering. "I said 'fine.'"

"No," said Dren. "I mean after that. You said 'whatever.' I've never heard you use the word in that manner before."

"So?" Jeena said becoming even more cautious. "I only meant let's get on with it. I'm tired of talking. I'm ready to do something."

Brachia grinned. "We know what you meant, Jeehana. We say it sometimes ourselves. We picked up the habit from our uncle."

"So?" Jeena asked again.

"Oh, nothing," said Dren.

Jeena didn't think it was nothing, but before she could pursue the matter further, the Oracle spoke.

"I agree with the high priestess. It is time to get moving. Once you've taken the DNA gas to the past, you'll be met by two variables. They'll help you complete your mission."

Jeena saw a potential flaw in the plan. "Once I've performed my task, will I be returned to the present time? Or will I—"

"Be stuck in the past?" finished the Oracle. "You may use your staff to return to the teleport pad in the current time. Just press the runes on the staff in the manner you've been instructed. And remember that the first two uses are preset. The first use will bring you back from the future. The second use will bring you back from a hundred thousand years in the past. After that, the charges for the time-displacer will be burned out. Once that occurs, the Staff of the Lady of the Tree will only be capable of normal teleportation."

"But—"

"There are no buts," said the Oracle. "Now go."

At those words, the Oracle slapped her hands together.

Jeena felt her body tingle as the room went in and out of focus. Then everything went black.

CHAPTER 35

The large insect resembled a human-sized cockroach. Two of its six appendages moved over the display console, sliding and pushing holographic levers and buttons.

Keka Derberlon crossed his antennae for luck. As a scientist, he knew it was a useless superstition, but he didn't care. He'd done all he'd been ordered over the last year and a half. Even after all of the testing, he still had no idea if the equipment would work properly.

It has to work. The lives of my children depend on it.

Keka watched the timer as it counted down to the exact moment when he was to start the teleport sequence. When the timer hit zero, he moved a lever to the max position. The soot-stained and battered teleport pad hummed as it began glowing. He'd faithfully followed the instructions he'd been given to repair the damaged equipment. Whether his repairs had been sufficient, he'd soon see.

It'll work, he thought as he crossed his antennae even tighter.

Three indistinct blurs appeared above the teleport pad. As he watched, the blurs became brighter and more distinct. One of the blurs was much shorter than the other two. The blurs came into focus.

Keka slid the lever to the off position.

Standing on the teleport platform was a small boy and two teenage girls. One of the girls had long, silver hair. The silver-haired girl's eyes fascinated Keka. They resembled molten silver. He was drawn to them as if they held all the answers, if he only knew the questions.

"Keka!" yelled the small boy as he jumped off the platform and began running with his arms outstretched.

The hypnotic spell of the silver eyes was broken by the boy's cry. "Brachia," Keka said as he stepped forward and lifted his adopted son into the air. "My how you've grown. I've missed you so much."

Dren was more dignified as she stepped off the platform, but once she was wrapped in Keka's appendages, he heard sobs and saw tears running down her cheeks.

"We've missed you too, Keka," said Dren.

The three remained wrapped in their embrace for a full minute. Finally, Keka stepped back and looked over at the silver-haired girl.

"You've brought her," Keka said. "Good. We've got much to do. The fate of three galaxies depends on us."

CHAPTER 36

The shuttle landed in a ravine several hundred meters from the cave of the Oracle so as not to draw unnecessary attention to the spot. Once the ship was down, the rear ramp lowered. Three of the ship's occupants exited.

Richard checked his passive scan for a full two thousand meter radius scan. Nothing dangerous registered. He sensed Myers send out a couple of active scans to supplement his passive scan.

"Must be nice to have enough Power to waste on active scans," Richard said in his shared space.

"Now, Rick," said Nickelo. *"Don't be jealous. At least he's on your side."*

Richard wasn't as sure of that fact as his battle computer seemed to be. While Myers and he'd fought as a team against the orc and Dragar invaders, Richard wasn't convinced of his brother's motives. He'd sensed the burning desire of his brother whenever mention was made of the DNA gas. He had a feeling his brother would do anything to acquire a bottle for his lover, the empress.

Myers spoke over the team's com-link so Matthew and his gnome gunner, Marstis, could hear. "Close her up, Matt, until we get back. At the slightest danger, I want the two of you to head back to base."

"We won't abandon you guys here," said Matthew. "We're not cowards."

Richard took his brother's side in the argument before it escalated. "It's not being cowardly. Myers and I are wizard scouts.

We can take care of ourselves as well as Emerald. This fighter, on the other hand, is too important to risk. The stealth spell Master Garis put around it only does so much. If a Dragar ship gets too close, you'll be discovered."

"But—"

"No buts, Matthew," said Myers. "We're the wizard scouts. That's an order."

Richard doubted making it an order mattered much to the headstrong teenager, but was pretty sure the empress's son would do as they asked. If for no other reason than that he knew it was the right thing to do. The fighter-shuttle was too important to their plans. They needed it if the rebellion was to become a reality.

Although Matthew didn't reply, he did raise the rear ramp in preparation for departing in a hurry if necessary.

Richard took that as a good sign.

Emerald hefted her axe and pointed in the direction of the cave. "Shall we?" Without waiting for them to answer, the dwarf took off at a fast pace.

Myers and Richard caught up easy enough. Before long, all three of them were back in the cave. Richard sensed the presence of the gas which was the Oracle. Two other figures in black leather-looking jumpsuits were in the room as well. The figures' suits looked strangely similar to an inactivated battle suit. The two figures were both wearing black helmets with red visors down and were armed with plasma rifles. The barrels of the weapons were pointed at the ground.

Richard thought the command to seal his battle suit. The bottom of his helmet rose to meet the lower part of his visor. He clicked the safety on his M63 to the auto position but refrained from aiming the weapon at the two figures.

While the two armored figures weren't registering on his passive scan, Richard did recognize their armor and weapons. They were wearing older-model Empire M4 battle suits and carrying outdated M42 plasma rifles. Richard knew the M4 and M42 had been taken out of service decades earlier. He'd seen them in a military museum on Risors. While they'd once been standard wizard scout issue, they'd been replaced with the more modern M6 battle suits along with the M63.

The four wizard scouts stood looking at each other. None of

them moved or said anything. Even the dwarf lowered her battle-axe to a non-threatening position and remained quiet.

"Nick," Richard thought. *"What's going on?"*

"I'm not sure," said Nickelo. *"However, I've got my suspicions. Just take it one step at a time and make sure you don't upset the applecart."*

By the shape of one of the wizard scout's battle suits, Richard assumed the scout was a female. The female scout's battle helmet changed shape into half mode. As the red visor was raised out of sight, he got a full view of the female's face. The male wizard scout also switched his helmet into half mode revealing his face as well.

Richard sucked in a large gulp of air.

"Well," said the female. "Someone's got to be the first to trust the other. It might as well be us. I'm Wizard Scout Janice Deluth, and this is my husband, Wizard Scout Thomas Jacobs."

Shock froze Richard's mind for a moment. "Mo—"

Myers's left fist swung out and caught Richard in the stomach.

Richard had sealed his suit but not activated armor mode since the other wizard scouts' suits were still inactivated. Consequently, Myers's blow penetrated the leather-like material enough to cut off his intended word.

Richard heard a swish as Myers switched his battle helmet into half mode as well.

"Uh," said Myers recovering a lot quicker than Richard. "I'm Wizard Scout Gaston Myers, and this is Wizard Scout Shepard." He pointed at the dwarf. "This is Emerald."

Janice Deluth smiled at Emerald.

Richard thought his mother had a nice smile.

"Yes. I recognized your frequency when you were approaching the cave. We've met before. I'm glad to see you made it out alive."

Emerald nodded. "I remember you as well. It's been a long time. Are you here to help us?"

Wizard Scout Thomas Jacobs smiled and stepped forward with his hand outstretched. "Well, we're not here for a relaxing vacation."

He shook Myers and Emerald's hands. When he turned to Richard, he grinned. "Now, what were you trying to say before your friend so rudely interrupted you?"

Richard switched his helmet into half mode as he took the proffered hand. "Nothing." When he saw a look of disbelief in his father's eyes, he added, "It was an inside joke. You wouldn't get it."

Thomas shrugged his shoulders and grinned again. "I usually don't go around calling someone I just met a liar, but…you're a piss-poor liar. I'll let it slide this time. We've got work to do."

"Nick," Richard said. *"What's going on? My mother and father are dead."*

"Yes, they are," agreed Nickelo. *"At least in your time, they are. But we're in the past. Your mother went on thirty time-commando missions. Your father went on twelve. I calculate a one hundred percent probability this is one of those missions."*

"But they're dead," Richard insisted.

"So?" Nickelo asked. *"You'll be dead too one day, but if someone goes into the past, they're still liable to meet you when you were alive. Just deal with it."*

Richard looked over at his brother. *"Myers seems to be taking it well."*

"Oh, don't be so sure," replied Nickelo. *"I'm not connected to the tele-network, but I can sense a lot of activity going on in Wanda's CPU."*

"Who?" Richard asked.

"Wanda," said Nickelo. *"She's Myers's battle computer. From all accounts, she's an easy-going battle computer who cares for her wizard scout. I calculate she's working overtime keeping Myers acting nonchalant. I calculate he's as shook up as you."*

"So," said the voice of the Oracle. "All the variables except one are in play. You'll need to have everything ready when she arrives with the bottles of DNA gas."

With great effort, Richard did his best to overcome his shock at seeing his parents alive. He had other things to worry about at the moment.

"When who gets here?" Richard asked.

"An ally," replied the Oracle.

Suddenly, the air in the center of the room shimmered. When it ended, a small girl stood where the shimmering had been.

"A hologram," Nickelo told Richard.

"You're a hologram," Richard said.

"Yes, I am," agreed the Oracle. "The future version of myself had Brachia and Dren teleport a holograph projector here along with a data disk and some other equipment. Thomas and Janice were kind enough to set the equipment up for me."

The Oracle's words gave Richard his second shock of the day. "Dren and Brachia? Are you in contact with them? Are they here?"

The hologram of the young girl smiled. "Negative, wizard scout. The data from my future self indicated you'd be concerned about their welfare. They're safe. They've spent the last three years building a combination teleport and time-displacer in support of the algorithm. My future self said that unlike you, they're very logical variables."

"Three years?" Richard repeated. "That can't be right. It's only been a year and a half since they went back in time."

The small girl smiled again. "Would anyone else care to explain?"

Richard's mother, Janice, cleared her throat. "I'll take a stab at it if you don't mind, Wizard Scout Shepard."

"Rick. Call me Rick."

Richard was amazed at the difference between the parents he'd known in the future and the wizard scouts standing before him now. The commandant and councilwoman he'd known had looked young physically. However, he'd sensed they were tired and old on the inside. These versions of his parents were young and vibrant both inside and out. Their Power reserves were large and full of untapped energy. He sensed that both of their reserves were even larger than Myers's.

"All right, Rick," said Janice. "Since you're here, you're obviously a time-commando like us. If you don't mind my asking, how old are you?"

Richard was pretty sure his mother wasn't asking for his physical age. He had no doubt she wanted to know the amount of time that had passed since his baseline had been set. Every wizard scout had a timeline as part of their shared space. He could tell to the nanosecond how much time had passed since that fateful day in the DNA center on Velos.

"My baseline was set 127 years ago," Richard said. "My physical age was twenty-six at the time. However, I don't remember most of those years. Some of my missions for *'the One'* are just bits and pieces while other missions are complete blanks. To tell the truth, I still think and feel like I'm twenty-six."

Janice laughed. So did Thomas.

Richard thought both his parents had nice laughs.

"It's nice to know it's not just us," said his mother. "My baseline was set 342 years ago, and Thomas's had his DNA baseline set 146 years ago. Like you, our memories of many of those years are sketchy."

"Why?" Richard asked.

Janice smiled and gave a wink. "You'd have to ask *'the One'* about that." Unexpectedly, his mother said, "You're kind of cute; did you know that?"

Richard blushed. "Uh…"

His father stepped next to Janice and glared at Richard. "I thought you were going to explain time differences, Janice. I didn't hear you mention anything about flirting with strangers."

Janice laughed again. "Oh, Thomas, you're so predictable. I think that's why I love you so much. Now, don't get jealous on me. I was just paying Rick a compliment. Besides, he reminds me of you a little."

"Well," said Thomas, "I don't like this small talk. We've got things to do." Richard's father looked at him. "Time in the future has nothing to do with time in the past. Janice and I might be gone twenty minutes in the future, but our stay in the past could span years. Understand?"

Richard had a feeling his father's words were intended to do more than answer his original question. His father was also marking his territory. Richard decided to beat a hasty retreat.

"I understand completely," Richard said hoping his father knew he was also including the unspoken warning. Deciding to divert the conversation to another direction, Richard turned to the Oracle. "Are Dren and Brachia coming here? I promised I'd bring them home."

The Oracle smiled once more. "No. Their part of the algorithm is not in the past. They will be accompanying the other variable to the future to help get the bottles of DNA gas."

Myers took a step forward and pointed a finger at the hologram of the small girl. "That's our mission. I should be the one getting the bottles. I've done all the research. I've studied the facility where they're located. It'll take at least six wizard scouts to retrieve the DNA gas."

"Ah," said the Oracle. "Then you'll be happy to know your efforts won't go to waste. The instructions from my future self indicates you need to have your battle computer download the information you've acquired to Danny and Margery."

"Forget it," said Myers. "That information's top secret. If you really are part of *'the One,'* I'm definitely not going to help you."

Although Richard had questions of his own about the Oracle's request, his dislike for Myers just naturally made him take the opposite side. "Then get used to living in the past," Richard said. "We don't go home if we don't finish the mission. We can't do that if we don't have the DNA gas. You're here, and those bottles are in the future. Don't be stubborn. I've tried to naysay *'the One'* more times than I can count, and all it's ever gotten me is more trouble. I hate *'the One'* as much as you, but we've got to play along if we want to get back home."

Richard glanced at his father. He noticed Thomas's face beginning to turn a little red. He had a feeling bad mouthing *'the One'* wasn't going over very well with the commandant. His father had always been totally committed to *'the One.'* This version of his father seemed to be taking it even more personal than Richard would've thought. His father looked like he was getting very angry. The commandant he'd known had always been good at controlling his temper. Just before whatever was building up inside his father came out, his mother placed two of her fingers over her husband's lips.

"Allow me, sweetheart," said Janice as she turned to face the Oracle. "I understand why you want the information loaded into Danny and Margery's databanks, but it won't work." Waving her arm to indicate Myers and Richard, she said, "If these fine gentlemen are from forty-some years in our time in the future, the data would need to be encrypted and stored until it was required. It would be dangerous to leave it in a format where our battle computers could access it before then. The risk of having one of them do something that would change those forty odd years would be too great."

"I don't understand," Richard admitted. "Why does the data need to be downloaded into their battle computers now? Can't

Myers just order his battle computer to provide the information in the future when it's needed?"

The Oracle smiled. "No. Wanda didn't give it to Margery or Danny before she was placed in your dimensional pack. Unfortunately, this version of her won't get back until after your mission is complete. Your battle computer won't either. The information has to be given to someone who'll return to the future before the information is required. Based upon the calculations of my future self, that means it must be given to Danny and Margery now."

Although she hadn't been exposed much to technology or time travel, Emerald was apparently faster on the uptake than Richard.

"Ah, I see," said the dwarf. "Thomas and Janice here are from a time that's forty years before Rick and Gaston? When this mission's over, they'll be returning to a future that's forty years before the time when Rick and Gaston return?"

"Exactly," said Janice. "Assuming we get out of this mission alive. However, like I said, it's a moot point. We can't guarantee our battle computers can't access the information. We'd need their security codes to do that, and they're prohibited from giving the codes to us by the central computer."

Richard had an epiphany. "I'll admit that's true. But what if their core programming was somehow modified to give us the security codes before then? We could then use the security codes to protect the information until it was needed."

"Your theory's sound, wizard scout," said Margery over the external speaker of Thomas's battle helmet. "However, there's a problem with your logic. Modifying a battle computer's programming would allow you to order the battle computer to give you their security code, but without the security code, the programming can't be modified to allow you to give the order."

"Ah, but that's the beauty of it, Margery," Richard said. "I've already been given your security code. I've got Danny's as well."

Considering she was a computer, Margery sounded surprised. "Who gave you our security codes?"

Richard smiled. It wasn't often he had to explain something to a battle computer. "You did. You gave them to me right before I was teleported off the *Defiant*. You didn't explain why you gave them to me, but I'm guessing it was so I could modify your programming now and order you to give me your security code in the future."

"Uh…," said Janice. "I'm not sure that makes any sense. It's like asking which came first, the pactar or its egg."

"Actually, it's completely logical," said the Oracle. "It's how my future self said it would be done. I couldn't mention it beforehand. Wizard Scout Shepard needed to think of it himself."

"Geez," Richard said into his shared space. *"I think the Oracle's as big of a liar as you are sometimes, Nick."*

CHAPTER 37

Suddenly, everyone was talking and arguing. The loudest and most argumentative was Myers. After a lot of persuasive arguments from the Oracle and Janice Deluth, Myers capitulated and agreed to have his battle computer download the required information to Danny and Margery.

"You know, Rick," said Nickelo, *"you're going to have to put on your parents' battle helmets in order to give them the security codes and change their programming. I calculate you may corrupt them emotionally if you do so."*

Richard had already thought of the possibility. In fact, Margery had hinted on the Defiant that he'd corrupted her emotionally.

"I know, Nick. It can't be helped. It's time to get this show on the road."

"Are you going to mention the possible corruption to your parents?"

Richard shook his head.

"Why are you shaking your head, Rick?" said Janice. "Are you arguing with your battle computer? You've got that same 'I am not in this room anymore' look Thomas gets whenever he's in deep conversation with Margery."

"Uh, I was just telling Nick we needed to hurry up."

His mother didn't look convinced. In spite of her nonbelief, she started to hand her battle helmet to Richard.

Thomas stopped her.

"No, Janice. I'll go first. Margery and I'll be in contact via our shared space. If this is a trick of some kind, I want to know about it right away."

"Oh, do you?" said Janice. "So you've taken it upon yourself to protect little o' helpless me. Is that it?"

Richard noticed his father begin to get a deer-in-the-headlight kind of look.

"Well, no… err… of course not," stammered Thomas.

Janice shoved her way past her husband and placed her battle helmet into Richard's hands. "Danny will go first. I'm sure he'd want to protect little o' Margery as much as Thomas seems to want to protect me."

Richard was almost tempted to smile, but one look at his father changed his mind. Instead, he removed his own battle helmet and slipped it onto his left hip. At the same time, he placed his mother's battle helmet onto his head. His mind was immediately filled with another presence in his shared space.

"I calculate a ninety-four percent probability we shouldn't be able to communicate in your shared space," said Danny. *"I'm linked with Thomas, not you. Hmm. Based upon your frequency and DNA makeup, I calculate an eighty-seven percent probability you're related to Thomas and Janice. That would explain the reason we're communicating so easily. You're their son, aren't you?"*

"Nick," Richard said. *"Are you hearing this?"*

"Affirmative, oh greatest of wizard scouts. Perhaps you should have discussed your plan with me before you put it in action. I'd recommend using Danny's security code now."

As sometimes happened when he interacted with computers, Richard's mind was operating at nanosecond speed. He pulled up the memory of Danny's security code he'd been given by Margery.

Danny said, *"Access to core memory authorized."*

Richard hesitated. He was a wizard scout, not a computer programmer. *"Nick? What do I do now?"*

"Allow me," said Nickelo. *"I can handle the necessary programming if you want."*

Richard sent a thought he hoped meant *"go for it."*

Three nanoseconds later, Nickelo said, *"Reprogramming has been completed. I've made minimum changes. Danny will use the security code to encrypt the information from Myers's battle helmet. Danny will also take your orders now. So make them good ones."*

"Fine. Danny," Richard said. *"I order you not to tell anyone else I'm Thomas and Janice's son."*

"Compliance," said Danny.

"I also order you to encrypt the information Wanda gives you about the bottles of DNA gas until it's needed in the future."

"How will I ascertain when it's needed?" asked Danny.

Nickelo provided the answer. *"Tell Danny that Wizard Scout Terrie Shatstot is going to order him to tell anything he knows about your disappearance. The order will be the trigger phrase to provide the information."*

"Uh, did you get that, Danny?" Richard asked.

"Compliance."

"And one more thing," Richard said. *"When you're brought onto the Defiant, you'll provide your security code to Margery so she can give it to me. Understand?"*

"Compliance."

"Well, Nick," Richard said. *"That went better than I thought. What now?"*

"That's easy," answered Nickelo. *"Do the same thing for Margery. Then it really is time to get this show on the road."*

Wasting no time, Richard did just that. As soon as he was finished, he handed his father back his battle helmet. He placed his own battle helmet on his head, then turned to face the hologram of the little girl.

"All right, it's done. Any other suggestions? I'd be a lot more appreciative if you'd told us something useful like explaining why my dimensional pack doesn't work. Why am I only able to summon Myers and my equipment along with a single basic load? I've tried to summon just about anything I can think of, and I get nothing."

"You too?" said Thomas. "Ours stopped working after we teleported as well. We can't get anything other than reloads for our weapons out of it."

The hologram of the little girl smiled. "Ah. The data disk from my future self said you would be concerned. I don't possess the algorithm pertaining to why you're dimensional packs have been limited, but I do know they can still be used to summon some items you need at the moment. Plus, I calculate they'll return to full functionality in the future when they're needed."

"We need them right now," Richard said.

"Apparently not," smiled the Oracle. "Otherwise they'd be working, wouldn't they?"

Richard started to say something, but Myers beat him to it.

"You said they could be used to summon some items now. What items?"

"Ah. That information has been given to me," said the Oracle. "Emerald and her dwarves will need magic armor and weapons if they ever hope to recapture their home under the mountain of Drepdenor. King Graphon's armorers will require titanium. The dimensional packs can summon the amount required."

"How much is the right amount?" Richard asked. "Plus, why do we need it at all? According to what I've been told, titanium does no good without a way to turn it into creallium."

"The Holy Metal?" asked Emerald.

"Yes, the Holy Metal," agreed the Oracle. "You can summon exactly enough titanium to create armor and weapons for the number of blue gems you have."

"The only problem is, we don't have any blue gems," said Emerald.

"That's not true, is it, Wizard Scout Richard Shepard?" said the Oracle. "My future self says *'the One'* once sent you on a mission to gather blue gems. *'The One'* sent you on that mission for a reason. The time to use them is now. Everything is as the algorithm has predicted. It is time."

"How many gems do you have, Rick?" asked Jerad.

Richard did a mental count. He'd found 2,500 during his mission. Brachia had used 200 on his battle suits. Sergeant Hendricks had used forty-eight for weapons and armor on the Defiant. Plus, two had been used to create the wedding rings for Jerad and Trinity.

"There should be 2,250 left," Richard said.

"Hmm," said Emerald. "If a gem is needed for each set of armor and a weapon, we'd have enough to outfit 1,125 dwarves. That's very interesting."

"Interesting in what way," said Janice.

Emerald smiled. "Counting me, there are exactly 1,125

survivors of the Drepdenoris dwarves who are of fighting age. Isn't that coincidental?"

"Yeah, isn't it," Richard said. "And if you believe that, I've got some swampland on Velos I'll sell you."

CHAPTER 38

Richard soon learned it sometimes took a lot to get a show on the road. Additionally, he found out rebellions didn't happen overnight. Supplies had to be gathered. Soldiers had to be trained. Plans had to be made. Plus, even after his father, mother, and he had summoned nearly a metric ton of titanium along with the required blue gems, turning them into armor and weapons was a slow process.

During the lull in action, Richard and his fellow wizard scouts were utilized to scout potential targets. Thus it was that a year after their last meeting with the Oracle, Richard found himself lying down on a low hill overlooking the Dragars' primary spaceport. As he watched, a black shuttle rose from its launch pad and burst through a shimmering haze surrounding the facility. Through the haze, which was actually a time bubble, Richard could just make out a massive building with a rounded dome. Within the dome was a pyramid. He knew the Dragars' temple contained an evil that was even now running rampant inside its walls. The thought of what was happening inside while he was safely hidden on the outside made the monster which was his anger rattle its cage.

"Calm down," said Nickelo privately. *"You can't do anything about it yet. You need to keep your mind on your current mission."*

"They're murdering dragons right now on that pyramid of theirs," Richard said. *"Even from here I can feel the emotional screams of the unborn dragons."*

"I know you can, Rick. I sense the feelings in our shared space.

However, you won't do those dragons any good by running down there and getting yourself killed. We've talked about this before. We'll only have one chance at this. Jerad's plan is solid. Even the Oracle says as much. King Graphon and King Hamerstine have their forces almost ready. It won't be long now. So don't go jumping the gun."

Tia's voice ended Richard's discussion with his battle computer. "Do you want me to scan that shuttle or not?"

"Sure. Why not?" Richard said. "You too, Matt. Just make sure you put a stealth shield around your active scans like Myers and I showed you. I don't want to get in a firefight with a shuttle this close to their base."

"Compliance," said Tia with a laugh.

"Yeah, compliance," laughed Matt.

Myers, who was lying on the far side of Matthew, reached out with his left hand and gave the teenager a light rap on the head. "This isn't a joke. If your scan's detected, we could all wind up dead. Scouting is serious business. Don't make me regret letting you come."

Richard half expected a retort from Matthew, but the young man surprised him. Instead of arguing, the teenager formed a line of Power and wrapped a stealth shield around it. The shield wasn't perfect, but it was pretty good considering he and Myers had only been training the two teenagers off and on for less than a year.

Richard hadn't been surprised at the size of Matthew's Power reserve. Neither was he surprised at the teenager's ability to grasp training in its use. He was Myers's son after all. Plus, he was Sergeant's Ron's grandson. The *Defiant's* captain could've been a wizard scout if he hadn't gotten pigeonholed into running the Deloris Armaments Corporation. Even Tia had a large Power reserve, and she grasped training as easily as Matthew. That didn't surprise Richard either since she was Liz's sister. He thought it was good both teenagers had a natural affinity for using psionic abilities. Until Myers and he had started training the two, all they'd been able to use their abilities for was guiding a bongo ball around a field.

"Not so," said Nickelo. *"They've used their psionic abilities to interact with those guidance systems Sergeant Hendricks put inside the* Defiant's *missiles."*

"I know," Richard said. *"Now stop reading my thoughts."*

"Then don't think them in our shared space," replied Nickelo. *"You've got a private space. Why don't you try using it once in a while?"*

"Whatever," Richard replied ending the conversation. At the same time, he chastised himself for not remembering to think in his private space. Thinking in his shared space was just a habit. It was a good habit, which had often saved his life. His battle computer often followed along with his thought process and implemented his plans as he thought of them.

Tia shifted on the ground where she lay next to him. "I'm having trouble getting a lock on that shuttle."

Reaching out with his mind, Richard touched Tia's scan with a line of his own Power. He saw her problem. Pulling some Power from his reserve, he merged a line of Power with hers.

"You're trying to force your scan. You've got to be light with your touch. Follow along with my mind."

Richard sensed Tia following as he gently guided her scan onto the outer skin of the shuttle. He eased her scan inside the ship. Once inside, he recognized another line of Power doing the same thing. The frequency was that of Matthew. Richard sensed his brother was helping guide Matthew's scan in a manner similar to how he was helping Tia. Although he hated to admit it, Myers was an excellent teacher. Surprisingly, his brother was also a patient teacher.

"Humph!" Richard said. *"Too bad he wasn't as patient when I was a cadet. All he ever wanted to do was yell at me and give me extra duty."*

"Hmm," replied Nickelo. *"Maybe Matthew and Tia don't give him as much lip as you did. You weren't exactly easy to get along with, you know."*

Richard chose to ignore his battle computer. He pulled back from Tia's scan and held his breath. He needn't have worried. She readily took the scan over and began probing the occupants of the shuttle. Once done, Richard sensed her pulling the scan back.

"Six occupants," said Tia. "I'd guess four Thargs along with a Dragar and a gnome. From the gnome's Power readings, I'd say he or she is a magic user." Turning her head to face Matthew, Tia said, "Beat you, slowpoke."

"Ha," said Matthew, who'd also completed his scan. "Since most shuttles have a gnome magic user to charge their ammunition, figuring that out with your scan isn't such a big deal."

"How many occupants did you detect, Matt?" asked Myers.

"Uh…six," replied Matthew. "Same as Tia."

"There are seven," said Myers. "A second magic user's in the shuttle. Based upon the frequency, I'd guess it's a Dragar. Do you concur, Shepard?"

Richard nodded his head. "Yep, I'd say you're dead on target. The Dragar's good too. I barely picked it up."

"Well, I didn't sense anything," admitted Tia.

Myers had been lying down with his plasma rifle sighted toward the Dragar city. He turned his head to look at Tia. "Sometimes what you don't sense is just as important as what you do sense. Shepard taught me that."

Richard was taken aback by his brother's offhand compliment. During the last year, he and Myers had mended their differences enough to spend time training each other. At Jerad's urgings, Richard had taught Myers in some advanced skills he'd picked up during his missions for *'the One.'* Additionally, Richard had trained Myers how to defend and break links to Power reserves. He'd also shown Myers how to place traps on links to Power reserves until his brother's link was almost as well protected as his own. In a case of one hand washing the other, Myers had shown him how to create and use multiple lines of Power at the same time. His brother had also taught him some advanced diviner techniques useful in training others. That was actually how they'd gotten started on training Tia and Matthew.

"I don't understand," said Tia. "Just because I don't sense something at a certain location doesn't mean there's anything there. Wouldn't you say that most of the time nothing really is there?"

Myers looked at Richard. "Do you care to explain? I'm still grasping the concept myself."

Richard picked up a small stone and held it in the palm of his hand. Tia, Matthew, and even Myers looked at the stone.

"Everything has Power, even this stone," Richard said. He noticed Tia roll her eyes at the obvious. "Bear with me, now. I see the stone with my eyes. I sense the stone's aura. Although it's almost negligible, I sense the stone's Power. So far, so good?"

Tia and Matthew nodded.

"All right then, we're on the same screen of music," Richard said. "This is where it gets a little harder. What I sense about the stone is exactly how I know it should be. Sometimes when you're conducting a scan, you'll get a feeling that something's out of place. You may not be able to put your finger on it, but you know there's something wrong."

The teenagers looked confused.

"I'll tell you what," Richard said. "If Myers or I get some free time tonight, we'll let you practice trying to spot us with our lowest-level stealth shield up. How's that sound?"

"No can do, Rick," said Matthew. "I've got an insertion mission at 0200 hours in the morning. I'm taking Tam and Telsa along with a team dwarfs to a landing zone north of Drepdenor. Jerad says he needs more information on the tunnel system under the mountain."

"Understood," Richard said before something drew his attention. "Get ready, everybody. Thomas and Janice are on their way back."

Myers frowned and concentrated to their front. "I don't sense anything. How come you're picking them up?"

Richard was tempted to give a smart aleck reply but refrained. His life might depend on his brother one day. "I can sense the commandant through the link he attached to me back at the Academy when he fed me Power. I suspect he's able to sense your location in the same way since you attached a link to him. I'm betting he can sense you even with your best stealth shield up."

Myers didn't answer, but Richard noticed his brother get the 'I am not in this room anymore' look as if conferring with his battle computer. Before Myers could speak again, Richard heard the sound of a breaking branch to their front. Two blurs emerged from the shrub brush a moment later. The blurs shimmered and changed into the figures of his parents as they deactivated their battle suits' camouflage. In short order, they were lying on the ground next to him and the others.

"We found a weak point in their time bubble," said Thomas. "It's not large, but Janice and I were able to slip through undetected. Margery and Danny had a field day plotting targets and developing a detailed database of the spaceport. I think we've accomplished about all we can here."

"What about the pyramid?" Richard asked. "Were you able to get any data on it?"

Janice shook her head. "Not really. Other than the fact it's putting out a lot of energy, there's not much else we can tell you. Whatever's inside that domed building is well protected."

Richard already knew what was inside the domed building. He'd been there when he'd shared a memory with one of the dragon eggs. What he didn't know was how to get inside the building and to the pyramid without being detected.

"Fine," Richard said. "We'll just deal with it once we start the attack. I'm guessing the kings and Jerad are about ready to give the okay to start."

"I doubt it," said Janice. "You remember what the Oracle said. We'll need to destroy the blue gem in Drepdenor at the same time we destroy the Dragars' temple. If we don't, the Dragars will just set up shop somewhere else."

"That's right," said Thomas. "Since we've done all we can here, I'm guessing Jerad will start sending us to Emerald's home under Drepdenor."

"I think he's already starting," said Matthew.

When Thomas and Janice looked at Matthew, the teenager explained about the insertion mission that was scheduled for tonight.

"Well then," said Thomas, "I guess we better get back. We can't let Tam and Telsa have all the fun."

CHAPTER 39

Even after a week, the sights and sounds of the strange world in which she'd been thrust continued to confuse Jeena.

The tube-train jerked to a halt. Jeena started to rise, but the human girl seated next to her placed a hand on her shoulder.

"Not yet, Jeehana," said Dren. "We've still got another two stops yet."

Jeena remained seated. "I thought it was four stops from the apartment to your lab."

Dren smiled. "I'll admit it's a little confusing. We have four stops when we take the red line. This is the orange line. Ours is the sixth stop now."

Shaking her head, Jeena said, "Everything's so complex. How do you keep it all straight?"

This time Dren laughed. "Actually, I don't always get it right myself. I'd hate to tell you how many times I've missed my stop and had to circle back."

Before Jeena could make another comment, a long, slimy length of flesh moved in front of her face.

"Excuse me," said a metallic-sounding voice to Jeena's left. "This is my stop."

Jeena tucked her legs under her seat to allow the octopod to get past. She watched as the creature scooted past Dren and her.

A small box at the octopod's side clicked before settling down into a metallic voice. "I hope you two ladies have a nice day. May you have lots of equipment requests all of your days."

"Same to you," said Dren while giving Jeena a wink.

"Uh, yeah," Jeena told the octopod. "May you have so many requests you need someone to give you a hand…, err, I mean…, a tentacle."

Dren laughed. "I didn't know elves had a sense of humor. You're funny sometimes. You remind me of my uncle a little."

"Actually, I didn't mean it as a joke."

"I know," said Dren still smiling. "That's what makes it so funny."

As the octopod exited the tube-train's door, several new riders came on board. Most were octopods, but a few were of other races. None were human. Once the new passengers were seated, the tube-train accelerated forward.

Jeena was forced back in her seat until the train reached its cruising speed. She sat up enough to look at Dren sitting next to her. She still thought of her friend as a child even though the girl was physically a little older than her now. *I suppose it's because only two years have passed since we met the first time. I haven't visually aged, but she's changed a lot.*

Since they still had two more stops, Jeena sat back and looked out the window. The city was strange, to say the least. Objects carrying passengers flew through the air. Other objects carried occupants at blinding speed along roads on the ground. Buildings rose so high they seemed to touch the sky. Everywhere she looked, lights flashed and something moved in a way contrary to the two hundred years of education she'd received in school. To top it off, it was all done without the slightest use of magic.

"I'm not sure I like this technology of yours, Dren," Jeena confessed. "It's like you force the laws of the universe to do your will. With magic, it's more a case of asking the Power in objects to assist in your desire."

"Well," said Dren, "I'll admit science sometimes resorts to brute force to make things happen. However, our galaxy doesn't have magic." Dren thought a moment, then changed her answer a little. "Actually, that's not completely true. I know of at least three planets in the Empire where magic works. Also, I've seen magic work a few times in other places."

"I've done a few spells since I've been on Storage," Jeena said. "The magic seems to work fine for me."

Dren nodded her head. “Yes, it does. Keka showed me some holo-videos of my uncle fighting magic users on Velos a couple of years ago. I’ve been thinking a lot about that. In theory, magic shouldn’t work in our galaxy, but it does. I don’t think it used to work except on a few planets with some kind of dimensional-warp connection to your magical plane.”

“Then why does it work now?” Jeena asked. “It’s true I’ve only performed a few minor spells during the last week to cool glasses of water and things of that sort, but they worked. The connection to my Power reserve appears solid, and the Staff of the Lady of the Tree feels the same. I’m confident more powerful spells will work as well.”

“I’m not sure why magic works now,” said Dren. “I’ve got a hypothesis, but I’m going to have to run a few experiments before I can figure it out.”

Jeena asked, “What’s a hypothesis?”

“Oh,” said Dren with a little laugh. “Sometimes I forget you’re not from here. When you’re wearing that orange jumpsuit, you look just like any of the other lab technicians.”

Jeena raised her eyebrows.

“Okay,” Dren laughed. “Not exactly. Your pointed ears aren’t so strange, but those molten silver eyes of yours.... Well, they’re amazing. Not to mention you’re probably the most beautiful humanoid on the planet.”

This time Jeena laughed along with her friend. “From what you’ve told me that’s not saying much. Except for Brachia and you, I haven’t seen a single human on Storage. You told me there aren’t any elves or any of the other races I’m familiar with here either.”

“Okay, you got me,” said Dren laughing. “You’re still very beautiful. I think we’re lucky there aren’t many humans on the planet, or every male with eyes would be beating on the door of our lab. We’d never get any work done.”

Jeena accidentally let her disgust with human males appear on her face.

“You don’t like humans, do you, Jeehana?”

Jeena thought for a few seconds, carefully choosing her words. She didn’t want to hurt her friend’s feelings but wasn’t going to lie. “I like Brachia and you,” Jeena said. “The few humans I’ve previously had dealings with on Portalis tried to kill me. Plus, you know the history of my family. So, no, I'm not fond of adult humans."

"I'm an adult," said Dren.

"Yes, you are," Jeena said. "But I like you. You're different. You keep your emotions under control. I sense them, but they're not overwhelming. Female elves are very sensitive to emotions. Most females of my race try to avoid contact with humans for that reason." When Jeena noticed her friend's eyes turning a little shiny, she hurriedly said, "I like Brachia and you. Plus, as you've pointed out, your species just happens to look like what I think of as humans. Any animosity I have against Portalis humans shouldn't extend to this dimension. I'm willing to give your race a chance if we meet any." When Dren continued to look sad, Jeena had a thought she immediately put into words. "I'm sure your uncle's just as nice as Brachia and you. I'd be honored to meet him if you want."

A small smile appeared on Dren's face. "That would be nice, Jeehana." She sighed. "Unfortunately, Keka says from the information he's been given, Uncle Rick is on Portalis, in the past. He's a time-commando, you know."

"So you've told me," Jeena said glad to see the girl smile again. "Maybe we'll get to meet one day. Now tell me, what was that word you used: hypothesis?"

Dren laughed. "Oh, that's just a fancy name for an opinion without any facts to back it up. Just give me time, though. I'm going to get facts. Once a problem catches my eye, I don't give up until I've figured it out."

Jeena chuckled. "Then I hope I never become a problem for you. Everyone needs a little mystery in their lives."

"Oh, believe me," said Dren with a smile. "You've got enough mystery for a dozen elves."

CHAPTER 40

Richard walked through the tunnel while nibbling on a dried mushroom stuffed with some kind of meat. The mushroom had a dusty taste and the meat was spicy, but all in all, it was excellent. When he'd asked the cook what kind of meat it was, the old dwarf had only smiled and said, "You don't want to know."

Well, Richard thought. *Whatever it is, it tastes pretty good.*

Two life forms registered nearby on his passive scan. Within seconds, one dwarf child and one human child came running around the corner.

The taller of the two, a human boy, yelled, "Last one to the dining hall is a Tharg!"

The smaller dwarf boy gamely sped up on his short legs and passed the human. "That's better than being a stupid Dragar!"

The children sped past Richard, running toward the main living area deep in the center of the massive underground complex. He heard their laughter echoing through the tunnel until it faded in the distance.

"Well," Richard said. *"They seem to have adjusted well."*

"Children usually do," said Nickelo.

Richard let his passive scan reach out until it blurred into a solid white color from the number of life forms. The two races were integrating well together. Of course, they'd had a few problems, but nothing the kings, Jerad, and the newly promoted General Dandridge couldn't handle.

"I suppose it helps having a common enemy and a common

purpose," Richard said.

"No doubt," replied Nickelo.

With a final look at his passive scan, Richard headed toward the foundry to talk to Fenmar about the status of the Holy Metal. The process of preparing the titanium to work with the blue gems had been a much harder ordeal than he had anticipated. The armor and weapons had been cast and beaten into shape, but the spells required to link the titanium and the blue gems weren't yet complete. According to Jerad, the time was getting close, but it would still be a few weeks.

Richard checked the timeline that had been set up when he'd gotten his DNA baseline. Converting the elapsed time over to Portalis time, Richard figured he had almost an hour before he needed to meet with Jerad and the others.

The sound of steps coming up fast behind him caught Richard by surprise. Nothing appeared on his passive scan. He began thinking the commands to seal and activate his battle suit as he whirled around with his left hand on the handle of his phase rod. He stopped the activation sequence when he realized who was behind him. It was his mother, Wizard Scout Janice Deluth.

"Ah," said Janice with a friendly smile. "You must be getting hard of hearing in your old age. I had to practically stomp on the floor to get your attention."

Richard smiled back. "Sure you did."

They both knew better. His mother had a way of walking that resembled a cat stalking its prey. Richard had never seen her in a fight but had no doubt she was a force to be reckoned with.

Spying something interesting at the side of his mother's right hip, Richard pointed to it. "That's new. What is it? A blaster of some type?"

Janice nodded. "Yes. It's one of the magic-based pistols off of Matthew's shuttle. Gaston gave it to me yesterday. I think he's taken your constant talk of mixing magic and technology together to heart. He issued Thomas a magic-based pistol also." She tapped an older model Deloris plasma pistol on her left hip. "I still have my old R6 here if I need it."

Richard laughed. "So I see. You look like one of those gunslingers from the old west carrying two sidearms. It's too bad one of them isn't a phase weapon. It would come in handy against creatures in the void."

"No doubt," agreed Janice. "Unfortunately, it's like I told you before. Maybe phase weapons are a credit a dozen in your time, but in Thomas and my time, the Empire has relatively few phase weapons, except for our phase rods, of course. Phase weapons just aren't part of our standard equipment."

Richard shrugged his shoulders. "Yeah, I know. It's still a shame. In my time, the Empire is able to convert titanium into creallium faster by—"

"No!" Janice said as she held up her hand in a stopping motion. "You can't tell Thomas or me anything about the future. You know that. The risk is too great we'd change something in the timeline when we get back if we knew. Even telling us you're from forty-two years in our future was dangerous.

Richard turned a little red. He was thankful they were in a section of tunnel only dimly lit by a few glow balls in the roof. He hoped his mother didn't see his embarrassment. The truth was, he had forgotten.

"I know. Sorry. My brain gets a little screwed up sometimes. My battle computer tells me it's because I've got a weird set of DNA."

Janice laughed. "Don't we all? Every wizard scout's DNA is different to some extent. It's part of the price of getting a DNA baseline."

"Yeah, I know. I think mine's stranger than most."

Janice mother laughed again. "Don't let your parents hear you say that. I'm sure they're very proud of you."

Her comment made Richard twinge. *She's my mother, yet I can't tell her. Even if I could, what would I say? Would I tell her one of her sons was stolen from her and raised in an orphanage? Or would I tell her that she'd only meet her lost son a short time before she died? Or that her husband would never know he had another son?*

Richard's anger at *'the One'* for stealing his childhood caused him to close his eyes and grit his teeth in an attempt to hold it in check.

"Rick," said Janice. "What is it? I was just making a joke."

Richard opened his eyes and forced himself to relax. "I know. It's just that, well, I was raised in an orphanage. I didn't find out who my parents were until late in life. My father never did know I was his son. And…, I only got to spend a few short hours with my mother before she—"

"Rick! No," said Nickelo in their shared space. *"You can't tell her any more. If you do, it might affect the future. I know your mother's death hurt, but you can't let her know now."*

Janice must have seen the sadness in his eyes. Something changed in her demeanor. Her face softened, and her eyes became a little shiny. She reached out with her right hand and gently wiped something wet from Richard's cheek. His mother kept her hand on his cheek and looked into his eyes.

"I'm very sorry, Rick. I have a son back home. He's very young. I know the missions Thomas and I do for *'the One'* are important, but our son needs his mother and father also. I'm sure your parents would've wanted to be with you as well if they'd only known."

Richard felt a few more drops of liquid leave his eyes. He saw a look of pain on his mother's face. She did miss her son. That the son she missed was Myers didn't matter. His mother wanted to be with her son. On impulse, Richard wrapped his arms around his mother and gave her a hug. She didn't draw back. He heard a sob as she buried her head in his shoulder.

"I guess we both have hurts," Richard said as he struggled to control his own heaving chest. "I guess—"

"Just as I suspected!" yelled a voice behind Richard.

Spinning around, Richard came face to face with Wizard Scout Thomas Jacobs. His father's face was red. Richard could practically see the flames of jealous anger in the wizard scout's eyes.

"I've seen you eyeing Janice," said his father through gritted teeth. "I should've known."

With a move quicker than a striking cobra, his father grabbed the phase rod off his hip and activated it in destructive mode. The red glow of the miniature lightning bolts running up and down the creallium shaft appeared even more deadly in the dimly lit tunnel.

"I'll teach you to try and steal my wife. Draw your phase rod, sir. I'll teach you a lesson you won't soon forget."

Richard had no intention of fighting his father. He raised his hands. Before he could speak, he heard the swish of a phase rod activating. A split second later, his mother was standing in front of him with her phase rod at the ready. Richard noticed it was in stun mode.

"Don't be a fool," said Janice. "I've had it with you and your temper. Rick and I were consoling each other."

Anger continued to flash in the commandant's eyes. "Out of the way, Janice. He's a man. He wasn't trying to console you. I'll teach him to—"

Wham!

In a movement so fast Richard was barely able to follow, his mother slammed her phase rod down on his father's right wrist.

Crack!

The sound of breaking bone made Richard involuntarily flinch. While his mother's phase rod might be in stun mode, its brerellium shaft along with its creallium core was heavy enough to do a lot of damage.

To his father's credit, he didn't scream. His phase rod flew down the tunnel chipping pieces of stone off the floor as it went.

Thomas gritted his teeth as he held his shattered wrist. "Now wait a minute, Janice. This is between me and—"

Janice whirled and made a backhanded swing at the commandant's left leg.

Crack.

Down went Richard's father. This time, Thomas did let out a high pitched groan. "Argh."

Richard was unsure what to do. A part of him wanted to intervene. He started to move, but a glance from his mother warned him back. He withdrew until he felt the stone of the tunnel's wall against his back.

"Wise decision," said Nickelo. *"Otherwise, you're liable to be lying on the floor along with your father. Besides, his healing reserve's already repairing his injuries. I calculate a ninety-eight percent probability your mother will keep her attacks to nonlethal ones. I've got a feeling this little confrontation has been brewing for a while."*

As Richard watched, his father leveraged himself up with his good arm until he was able to lean against the wall of the tunnel.

"What are you doing, woman? Have you gone crazy?"

"Me?" asked Janice with anger dripping from every syllable.

"Yes, I'm crazy. I've warned you, Thomas. I've taken all of your temper I'm going to take. You've crossed the line. I'm done. You hear me? I'm done!"

"Hmm," said Nickelo. *"I calculate your mother has some temper issues of her own. I guess you get yours honestly."*

"Hush, Nick," Richard said. Although his mother's voice held an angry edge, he didn't think the tears streaming down her face were from anger.

The commandant held out both hands before him in a stopping motion as he hobbled a couple of steps away from the wall.

"Good self-heal," observed Nickelo. *"Your father's healing ability appears to be much faster than yours. I calculate your arm would only be half-healed by now."*

Richard ignored his battle computer. He wasn't sure what was going on, but somehow his innocent hug had triggered a landmine. He was tempted to make a hasty retreat, but at the same time, he didn't want to draw attention to himself.

"Janice," said Thomas. "You can't mean that. You're tired. You need to—"

"You're right, Thomas, I am tired," said Janice. "I'm tired of your temper. I'm tired of never knowing when I'm going to get jerked away from my family to do some Creator-forsaken mission for *'the One.'*"

"But our missions are important," said the commandant. "We're time-commandos. We have a responsibility."

As Richard continued watching, the phase rod dropped out of his mother's grasp. She buried her face in her hands. Her chest heaved, but her sobs were barely audible. His father looked as if he wanted to hold his wife but at the same time, like he feared any action would start a new round of attacks.

After a few seconds, Janice removed her hands from her face and looked at her husband through reddened eyes. "Do you know what I was doing when *'the One'* teleported us on this mission?"

"Uh…, you were in our home on Risors, the same as me."

"No," said Janice. "Not the same as you. I was upstairs putting our son to bed. I was reading him a story. He'd just given me the biggest smile when…, when…"

"It's all right, Janice. He'll understand. I've explained it to him."

"He's six years old. Believe me. He doesn't understand. He needs his mother at home. He needs his father."

"But our missions are important," protested Thomas. "The fate of three gal—"

"Our son is important too," said Janice. "Our marriage is important. I can't keep this up any longer. I've been doing missions for *'the One'* for three centuries. For what? They never end. They just keep coming. I'm tired, Thomas." Her voice broke, and the tears came. "I'm tired to the point of death."

This time, Richard's father did step next to his wife and wrap his arms around her. "Janice. Please don't say things like that. I..., I couldn't live without you. I wouldn't want to live without you."

"What about our son? Can you stop these missions? Can you guarantee *'the One'* will leave us alone and let us give our son a normal life?"

"You know I can't. As long as our Power reserves are whole, *'the One'* will send us on missions. There's nothing we can do about it, my love. I swear, I wish to the Creator we could spend the rest of our lives as a family with our son, but we can't. There's nothing I can do about it. I'm sorry, Janice. I'm so sorry."

Until that moment, Richard's mother had been keeping her arms hanging at her side. She suddenly raised them and embraced her husband, and buried her head in his shoulder. Between sobs, she said, "I wish to the Creator I'd never been born with a Power reserve. I hate this life. I want my son."

Richard slowly edged his way backward until he got around a corner of the tunnel. His last view of his parents was of them standing in the middle of the tunnel holding onto each other.

The sound of sobs followed Richard as he made his way down the tunnel. Not all of the sobs sounded like they were feminine.

CHAPTER 41

Jeena whispered a low-level shield spell. The blast of wind and small bits of dust and sand bounced off the shield.

"That was cool," shouted Brachia over the roar of the landing starship. "I want to be a magic user when I grow up. I could travel the galaxy putting on shows."

Jeena smiled at the boy. He was a strange one. Sometimes he was a little boy, and sometimes he acted like someone well beyond his years. She liked him anyway. Along with his sister, the three of them had accomplished a lot together.

A silvery starship came to a soft landing on the stone platform.

Concrete, Jeena thought. *Brachia says it's concrete.*

Trying not to let her apprehension show, Jeena forced herself to relax by silently repeating a mantra taught to her by Priestess Aldriss. The chant worked. Jeena felt ready to meet whoever stepped off the starship.

A ship that goes to the stars, Jeena thought. *I read hints of such in the writings of the ancient Letian elves. I thought they were only legends. Now I'm going to travel in one. None of my friends will ever believe me.*

Dozens of octopods came driving up in hover-vehicles of every sort. To Jeena, it was organized chaos.

"Why so many?" Jeena asked.

Brachia laughed. "Storage doesn't get many visitors nowadays. I'm told the big resupply ships stopped coming before I was born. The octopods live to do their mission. I think they're concerned their missions are coming to an end. The arrival of the *Defiant* is a boost to their morale."

Jeena thought back on all the children had told her over the past week as well as what she'd seen. The entire planet was devoted to maintaining and supplying thousands of warehouses to support the variables of *'the One.'* According to the children, their uncle was one of those variables.

So am I, Jeena thought. *That is, if I'm to believe what the Oracle told me.*

Glancing at the starship before her, Jeena noticed writing on the bow. She made a gesture with her hand and whispered a single word. The writing wavered in her mind before settling down into the name *Defiant II.*

Jeena pointed at the writing. "I'd say *Defiant* is a good name for a ship that's trying to prevent the destruction of three galaxies."

"Yeah," agreed Brachia. "Keka says Uncle Rick is half-owner of the *Defiant*. I think that's a good name for his ship. He can be stubborn at times."

Suddenly, Brachia laughed.

When Jeena looked around to see the cause, she saw nothing. "What's so funny?"

"I was just thinking that you're a little stubborn too, Jeehana."

Jeena didn't argue the point. She doubted any of the instructors she'd had in school would either.

A large ramp began lowering at the rear of the *Defiant*.

Jeena steeled herself for the inevitable. She knew from speaking to the children the ship had human males as part of her crew.

As soon as the ramp touched the ground, a tall figure dressed in a gray jumpsuit walked down the ramp toward them. Jeena relaxed. The figure had gray hair and pointed ears. He was an elf.

"Ah," said the elf when he got close. He bowed at the waist. "My name is Comstar, High Priestess. Sergeant Ron, our captain, thought you might feel more comfortable if I was the first to make your acquaintance."

"Sergeant?" Jeena asked.

The old elf smiled. Jeena thought he had a friendly smile. She felt her muscles relax. If an elf was part of the ship's crew, she figured there was little to fear.

"The *Defiant's* captain prefers to be called Sergeant Ron," explained Comstar. "He's a quirky human, but he knows his business. I'd trust him with my life. You can too."

"From what I'm told," Jeena said, "I think I already am."

Comstar smiled again. "Aren't we all?"

The old elf glanced at Brachia. "Well, who do we have here?"

"Oh," Jeena said suddenly remembering her manners. "This is my friend Brachia. I'm Jeehanathoraxen, high priestess to the Lady of the Tree, and a lord of the Council of Light of Silverton."

"Well met, Lord Jeehanathoraxen," said Comstar with another bow.

"Jeehana," Jeena said. "Please, call me by my friend name. I've got a feeling I'm going to need all the friends I can get if I'm going to complete my task."

"Well, Jeehana," said Comstar, "I think you'll find you have many friends on the *Defiant*."

Comstar got down on one knee until he was at the same height as Brachia. The old elf smiled again and stuck out his hand.

"Well met to you also, Master Brachia. I've heard a lot about you from your uncle."

The young boy grasped the elf's hand and gave it a shake. "You know Uncle Rick?"

Comstar nodded his head as he returned the boy's shake. "Oh, yes. As it so happens, he's my cabin mate on the *Defiant*." With a whisper as if sharing a secret with the young boy, Comstar said, "Your uncle's kind of funny at times. He makes me laugh." With a wink, the elf added, "Plus, he's a good cook."

The old elf stood up. He moved his hand toward the *Defiant*. "Shall we? The rest of the crew are anxious to meet you."

The next thirty minutes was a blur of introductions. Amazingly, the *Defiant's* crew consisted of dwarves and gnomes as well as a few humans. One of the crewmembers was even a species of humanoid-sized lizard. Jeena's initial apprehensiveness at meeting the crew slipped away the more she was around them. Even being near the human males wasn't as bad as she'd feared. Like Brachia and Dren, the humans on the *Defiant* kept their emotions on a tight leash. She could sense them, but they didn't threaten to smother her like the emotions of human males on Portalis.

The only exception to sensing the humans' emotions was the one they called Terrie. He was a strange blank to her. He obviously had a stealth shield of some kind protecting him, but even its existence eluded her. Although Terrie was a human male, Jeena found she was able to be around him without feeling too uncomfortable. She would have talked with him further after they were introduced, but a fiery, redheaded woman called Angela hustled Terrie out of the room before Jeena got a chance to talk to him alone.

After the introductions were complete, Comstar took Brachia and her on a quick tour of the ship. It was all orc to her, but Brachia was full of questions. In order to finish the tour, Comstar and she were forced to leave the young boy in a deep discussion with the ship's armorer over the best technique for mixing magic and technology.

As they were heading down a ladder to visit the *Defiant's* engine room, Jeena stopped and faced Comstar. The ship was crowded with crewmembers and visiting octopods, but for the moment, they were alone.

"May I ask you a question?" Jeena said.

"Of course. At present, my only duties are to accompany you. Sergeant Ron really is concerned about your comfort."

An image of the old captain appeared in Jeena's mind. Somehow, he didn't seem like the type to worry about anyone's comfort. Still, as Priestess Aldriss had often told her, you never knew what was in someone's heart.

"I appreciate Sergeant Ron's courtesy," Jeena said. "I must admit, I was surprised to discover an elf was onboard. You are an elf, aren't you? You look like one of my race, but at the same time, you're different."

"Ah, that's a long story, Jeehana," said Comstar. "I'm an elf, but I wasn't born on Portalis."

"Were you born here in this galaxy?"

Comstar shook his head. "No. I was born in the magical dimension the same as you. Only I wasn't born on Portalis. You've been on Storage for a week. Surely Brachia and Dren have told you this planet is only one of tens of thousands of inhabited worlds in this galaxy."

Jeena nodded her head. The children had told her much during the past few days; so had the insect, Keka. Also, she'd spent a lot of time viewing historical videos of the diverse species of the galaxy along with their accomplishments. She wasn't sure she believed all of it, but she'd seen too many things already to deny at least some of it was true.

"Well," said Comstar, "you've only been on Portalis."

"Until now," Jeena corrected.

Comstar smiled. "Yes, until now. I, on the other hand, have been to dozens of worlds in our galaxy in the magical dimension. Our galaxy is just as full and diverse as the one we're in now. The inhabitants of our galaxy have starships of their own powered by magic. Vast empires extend across hundreds of worlds."

Jeena looked into Comstar's eyes. She saw no hint of humor. "It seems hard to believe," she confessed. "If so many ships fly between the stars of our galaxy as you say, how come no one's ever contacted us on Portalis?"

The old elf looked down for a moment before answering. "Dragars."

"I'm sorry," Jeena said. "Did you say dragons?"

"No. I said Dragars. They were drawn to Portalis a hundred thousand years ago by a source of immense Power. They conquered an entire continent and built a spaceport near their city."

Try as she might, Jeena couldn't remember ever reading about Dragars. Not even the writings of the Letians mentioned the name.

"I've never heard this before. Are you sure it's true? Perhaps it's just a legend."

Comstar shook his head. "I wish it were. The Dragars attacked my homeworld of Enneastar. They killed my family and I was taken prisoner. I served on one of their black starships as a slave. I know the truth of their spaceport on Portalis because I've been there."

Jeena wanted to ask more, but two octopods began climbing down the stairs behind them. Rather than have the slimy creatures squeeze their way past, she opted to forego her discussion and continue on to the engine room. Once she arrived, she got another surprise. A two-meter long silver dragon was waiting to greet her.

"So, you're the variable we've been expecting," said the dragon.

Jeena didn't hear the words. Instead, she sensed them as emotions.

Unsure how to speak using emotions, Jeena decided to use her voice as normal.

"I'm told I'm a variable, so I guess it's true," Jeena said. "I've never spoken to a dragon before. In fact, I've never even seen one of your species until now. I've read about dragons, but they've been long gone from my world."

"Actually," said the dragon, *"the dragons were legion on Portalis at one time. My ancestors traveled throughout the galaxy spreading magic wherever they went. They even populated other planets in the galaxy with races from Portalis. It was a glorious time in dragon history."*

"Spreading magic?" Jeena asked. The dragon's choice of words seemed strange. "Do you mean they cast spells?"

A sense of laughter echoed in Jeena's mind. Even though the laughter came as an emotion, Jeena sensed friendliness. The dragon wasn't laughing at her.

"No, not spells, fair elf. Dragons are magic. Our very essence is magic. Even our breath is magic."

"I see," Jeena said although she really didn't. "My name is Jeehanathoraxen, but you may call me Jeehana. Do you have a name?"

Again the laughter echoed in Jeena's mind. *"You couldn't pronounce my name, Jeehana. However, my brother calls me Bright Wing. So do my fellow crewmembers on the* Defiant.*"*

"All right, Bright Wing. Uh..., you're a crewmember?" The concept of a dragon as a member of a starship's crew seemed more than strange.

"Yes. I tend to the starship's engine. It's fortunate that I do. From what I know of your mission, we're going to be traveling a very long way. Now, Jeehana, if you'll pardon me, I must attend to my duties."

"Farewell, Bright Wing."

"Farewell, Jeehana," said the dragon as she turned and left down a narrow corridor.

Comstar gave a little laugh. "I only caught half of the conversation, but it seems you two got along well."

"You didn't hear?"

Comstar laughed again. "I only heard your words. Bright Wing can speak using her voice the same as you or I, but I think she prefers using emotion-speak. I can pick up a few words when she does so, but not enough to carry on a conversation. As far as I know, only Rick has conversed with her thus."

"By Rick, you mean Brachia's uncle?"

Comstar nodded. "Yes. Bright Wing calls him her brother. He rescued her from the same black starship that enslaved me. Now, Jeehana, if you don't mind, I think we should show you where you and Dren will be staying. Then it'll be time to start your training."

"My training?" Jeena asked hesitantly. No one had mentioned anything about training to her.

Comstar smiled. "Of course. Did you think you could penetrate the Crosioians' most secure facility without training? Your mission won't be easy."

"I haven't been told my mission," Jeena said. "Keka told me I had to wait until the *Defiant* arrived."

"Well, we're here now, fair Jeehana. So, I'd say it is long past time to get to work."

CHAPTER 42

Richard roamed around the tunnels for another thirty minutes. His desire to speak with the dwarf armorer, Fenmar, was totally forgotten. Seeing the terrible effects of years of loyal service by his parents to *'the One'* made Richard hate his nemesis even more. From what his mother had said, all she wanted out of life was to live like a normal family with her husband and child. Richard's heart ached for both of his parents.

When he finally tired of wandering, he made his way to the command center. Jerad was there along with General Dandridge, Myers, Tam, Telsa, Trinity, Emerald, Chancee, and Matt. His parents were there as well. He avoided eye contact. They seemed to do the same.

"Good," said Jerad. "I was beginning to think you weren't coming." He smiled. "If your stealth shield wasn't so good, I could've figured out where you were with my passive scan."

"Sorry," Richard said. "I had some thinking to do."

"Well, keep your thinking helmet on," said Jerad. "We're going to do something I've wanted to do for quite a while now. We just haven't had enough resources free at the same time to do it."

Curiosity drove away any remaining thoughts of the scene in the tunnel with his parents. "What do you have up your sleeve? You've got all eight wizard scouts here. I'm guessing it's important."

General Dandridge walked over to a table with a large map spread out on it. The map displayed the Dragars' spaceport and the surrounding area. The map of the spaceport was very detailed. It displayed all the information on the spaceport that had been obtained by the wizard scouts over the last twelve months. Someone had even carved miniature wooden replicas of the buildings and spaceships and placed them strategically on the map.

Richard noticed a large mountain about ten kilometers to the north of the spaceport. He knew it was Drepdenor, the home of Emerald's people. A detailed layout of the mountain's underground tunnel system was marked out on the map as well.

Pointing to the tunnel system, General Dandridge said, "Thanks to Emerald and the other survivors of Drepdenor, we've got a good layout of their tunnel system. What we don't know is the current location of the Mountain's Heart."

"Their blue gem?" Richard asked.

"Yes," answered Jerad. "From what you and Gaston told us, the Oracle says it has to be destroyed as well as the pyramid. Otherwise, the Dragars will just take it and set up shop on another planet."

Richard looked at Emerald. "Are your people fine with that? Destroying the gem?"

Emerald took her eyes off the map and stared at Richard a few seconds before answering. "Do we like it? No. Are we willing to destroy the Mountain's Heart? If it means keeping it out of the Dragars' hands, then the answer is yes."

With a glance back at Jerad, Richard said, "All right then. I'm guessing you're saying it's time we go in and find the gem."

"Exactly," said Jerad. "We're going in tonight, and we're taking two full quads of wizard scouts. We're also taking Emerald, Chancee, and General Fenmar."

"The armorer?" Richard asked.

"Not anymore," said General Dandridge. "King Graphon promoted him to general a few hours ago. General Fenmar will be commanding the Drepdenoris dwarves along with Emerald when we attack the spaceport."

Richard nodded his head. Fenmar was a good dwarf. After a year of living with the dwarves, Richard had come to like their race almost as much as he liked gnomes.

"That's probably because you have a piece of dwarf DNA mixed in with yours," said Nickelo.

"Doubtful," Richard thought back. *"According to your memories, I've got a little bit of orc and troll DNA mixed in as well. I can definitely say I'm not too fond of either of those races."*

Turning his attention back to the map, Richard studied the layout of the tunnel system. He tried to think of the most efficient way to perform the recon. They'd need to break into multiple teams to cover more area.

"Teams?" Richard asked. "I assume Myers and I will each be leading a team since we're the only shifters. Plus, we're the only ones with modern battle suits and weapons."

Jerad didn't reply for a few seconds. Richard thought he saw his friend trade glances with Tam and Telsa. He grew instantly suspicious. Finally, Jerad answered his question.

"We'll break into three teams. Gaston will lead one team. He'll take Tam and Telsa. They'll take the main corridor."

Jerad pointed to a wide tunnel leading in a straight line to the center of the mountain. He moved his finger down the tunnel until it stopped at a large cavern. "This is the old location of the Mountain's Heart. Gaston's team will verify if it's still there."

Richard wanted to ask '*Why Myers?*' He didn't trust his brother. The man was too interested in acquiring a bottle of DNA gas for the empress. Despite his misgivings, Richard remained silent. The military wasn't a democracy. Only one person could be in charge. He was thankful it was Jerad instead of him and trusted his friend.

"A second team," continued Jerad, "will consist of Trinity, Thomas, Janice, Emerald, Chancee, and myself. We'll lead the recon until we get to this secondary split in the main corridor." Jerad pointed to the second tunnel and traced its path down a winding set of stairs. "My team will split off here and follow this tunnel down to the dwarves' treasure chamber. Emerald tells us it's protected by powerful stealth spells. Since we haven't detected energy readings from the Mountain's Heart during our previous recons around the outside of the mountain, we think the gem may have been moved there."

"Then why don't we all go there and check it out?" Richard asked. "We'd be safer if we're all together."

"Because," replied Jerad, "you told us this Lord Cancontus might be the demon you fought with your dolgars. If that's the case, he might be able to cast a stealth spell powerful enough to prevent the gem's detection. The gem might still be in its original location."

"We've only got one chance at this, Rick," said Tam. "Jerad and the rest of us have gone over the plan several times. Except for Trinity, none of us wizard scouts have fought vampires. If we're detected, all hell's going to break loose. Assuming we get out alive, they'll probably beef up security so much, we'll never get back in. You've fought in tunnels before. You know they can be death traps."

Richard did know. He looked down at the map again. He could feel everyone looking at him. Tam's comment that the others had gone over the plan before with Jerad bothered him. None of his friends had mentioned it to him.

Why? he wondered.

He'd been a marine. He decided to confront the obvious giant pactar in the room. "What about Fenmar and me? You didn't include us in either of the two teams."

Jerad pointed at a point on the map. "The two of you will remain here at the entrance as our rear guard."

"Rear guard?" Richard said. "I've got more experience fighting on Portalis than any of you. I should be with one of the recon teams."

"Speak for yourself," said Janice. "I've spent more time on Portalis than you, so don't think for one second you're the only expert on fighting magic users."

Richard immediately tried to backtrack. "What I meant was that Myers and I have modern battle suits and weapons. From what we've been told about vampires, they can shift in the void. You'll need me on one of the teams if you're discovered."

Jerad cleared his throat. "I know we need you, Rick. Believe me, if we didn't, I'd be leaving you back here. However, what we need is for you to hold the entrance and act as a reserve force in case we're discovered. Gaston has his phase rod and a Deloris phase pistol. Plus, as you pointed out, he's a shifter." Jerad pointed to the tall blonde woman next to Emerald. "Chancee here has magic arrows and her longsword. The sword's one Emerald took off one of the vampires when she was young. It's very powerful magic according to Master Garis. Tam and Telsa have magic-based weapons from the shuttles. Plus, Gaston has given Tam his sword, so they'll both be armed with magic swords."

Richard wasn't convinced.

Apparently, Jerad picked up on the fact. "Janice and Thomas have their phase rods along with their M4 battle suits," said Jerad. "The rest of us wizard scouts have captured Dragar armor and weapons. We won't exactly be helpless if we're detected."

"But still," Richard said forgetting his earlier thoughts about only one person being in charge. "I think I should—"

"We've told them," said Emerald in a loud, icy voice.

The dwarf's words made Richard go cold. "Told them *what*, Emerald?"

Myers spoke before she could answer. "Emerald and I told Jerad and the others what happened on the wall at Cantonsburg. You can't be trusted around Power, Shepard."

Emerald nodded her head in agreement. "You're a good man, Rick. Nonetheless, you almost got us killed during the battle."

"You're addicted to Power, Shepard," said Myers. "From all indications, the Mountain's Heart is possibly the most powerful object in this galaxy. Putting you near it would be like asking an alcoholic to guard a keg of Strakos beer."

Anger burned in Richard. "Me? You're the one who can't be trusted. I see it in your eyes every time we mention DNA gas. I wouldn't trust you any more than I'd trust one of those Dragars."

Myers's face turned a bright red.

Jerad slammed his fist on the table. Miniature mockups of buildings and spaceships bounced into the air.

"Enough!" said Jerad.

An accusation that had been in Richard's throat stayed where it was. In all his years of association with Jerad, he had never heard his friend raise his voice in anger. Even Myers was shocked into silence.

"I'm in charge," said Jerad. "If you want to be in charge, Rick, then just say the word. You can have at it with my blessing."

Richard remained silent. His silence wasn't good enough for his friend.

Jerad locked eyes with Richard. "Is what Emerald and Gaston told us true? Did you give in to the Power when she was forming her Circle? When we were on the *Defiant*, Terrie told me something similar happened on that black destroyer you all fought when you destroyed the dimensional gate. Is it true?"

Once again, Richard felt the eyes of everyone in the room on him. Regardless, he didn't permit his eyes to waver from Jerad. "It's true." After a pause, he explained further. "I fought it off, though. I used the Power to help Emerald complete her Circle. If I hadn't—"

Holding up a hand to stop Richard, Jerad nodded his head. "I know. We all know. Nevertheless, we can't take the chance on letting you near the Mountain's Heart. It's too risky. I need you to keep the entrance open for us. General Fenmar will be with you. As you pointed out, you've got a modern battle suit and weapons. The general will be equipped with one of the sets of armor along with a war hammer his armorers made using the blue gems you supplied. I need the two of you to keep our line of retreat open if it comes to that."

Telsa moved next to Richard. She raised her hand up and placed it on his shoulder. "We need you, Rick. If we stir up a hornet's nest, we need to know we can get out. I…, er…, we'd rather have you there guarding the entrance than a battalion of magic users."

Telsa's words soothed Richard's bruised ego a little. It was hard for anyone to be angry with the small wizard scout. He'd always thought of her as a younger sister. He supposed all the male cadets in his cohort at the Academy had thought of her as such.

"Fine," Richard said with a nod of his head. "I'll play rearguard."

When Jerad seemed to relax, Richard pointed a finger at him. "But by the Creator, at the first sign of trouble, Fenmar and I are coming in to help."

Jerad grinned. "You won't need to come far. At the first sign of trouble, we'll all be running for the entrance like a pack of frightened pactars."

"Speak for yourself," said Tam. "I'm an ex-mercenary. I'll just be attacking to the rear."

Everyone laughed. That is, everyone except Richard.

CHAPTER 43

The black pack lay on the table in front of Richard. Nickelo's wizard scout continued to stare at it.

"What are you thinking?" Nickelo asked. *"I can't hear your thoughts when you keep them in your private space."*

When his wizard scout remained silent, Nickelo decided to try a different approach.

"They were right, Rick. You can't be trusted around Power. Don't ask me why, but it's the truth. You know that as well as I."

Finally, his wizard scout replied. *"I should be on one of the teams going in the mountain. They've got no idea what they're up against."*

"Like you do?" Nickelo asked. *"You've never fought vampires before either. Besides, you'll be in the mountain. You'll just be at the entrance. You won't be far if they need you."*

"No, I haven't fought vampires," admitted Richard. *"However, I've tangled with enough creatures that could shift into the void to know the danger. From the little information on vampire's you've got in your databanks, they can self-heal as well."*

"The other battle computers have the same information as me," Nickelo said. *"You can bet your bottom credit they're jabbering away as we speak, prepping their wizard scouts for any eventualities."*

"They'll be slaughtered," said Richard. *"They need me."*

"What makes you think you could do any better?" Nickelo asked in an attempt to keep his wizard scout talking. He was

puzzled by his friend's attitude. Based upon previous experiences, it usually meant trouble whenever his wizard scout kept his thoughts to himself. They were a team. They were at their best when working together.

Nickelo watched Richard reach out and begin opening and closing the flap of his dimensional pack. The neurons of his wizard scout's brain were working overtime, but he was keeping his thoughts in his private space.

"Talk to me, old buddy," Nickelo said trying to prod his friend into talking. *"What makes you think you could do any better?"*

Richard stopped fiddling with his pack. *"Thanks to Brachia, my battle suit's able to protect me against attacks from the void. I've got another 199 of them in some warehouse on Storage."*

"So?" Nickelo asked. He thought he now understood his wizard scout's line of thinking. He was surprised. He doubted his friend even understood the probable direction his thoughts were taking him.

"If the others were wearing one of those battle suits, they'd stand a chance against those vampires."

"Perhaps, Rick. However, your battle suits are designed to work only for you. They're attuned to your frequency. Also, they're designed to only work with your battle helmet, which is designed to work only with me."

Nickelo knew that wasn't exactly true, but he'd learned long ago it was best to allow his wizard scout to figure things out on his own. Of course, he often needed a few helpful hints, but that was why he'd been issued a battle computer.

"Not true," said Richard as he started opening and closing the flap of his pack again. *"My battle suit worked fine with Jonathan when he replaced you during my first mission with the dolgars."*

"Okay. I stand corrected. Apparently, your battle helmets can work when they have another battle computer installed. However, my point about your battle suit only working for you is still valid. It's attuned to your DNA. Even if you gave your battle suit to one of the other wizard scouts, it would just be an inert lump of material. They wouldn't be able to activate it in armor mode. They're a lot better off wearing the confiscated gear from the fighter-shuttles."

"Unless...," said Richard, *"they had the same DNA as me. Or*

at least close enough to mine to satisfy whatever algorithm is protecting my equipment. The question is how close would their DNA need to be?"

Nickelo mentally smiled. His wizard scout was learning to sacrifice for the good of others. He was learning to overcome the selfishness of the small bits of orc and troll DNA in his body.

"Maybe you should try a test," Nickelo suggested.

"Maybe I will," said Richard.

Without another word, Richard removed his battle suit and put on the uniform he'd been given by King Hamerstine. Once completed, he folded the battle suit and placed his utility belt on top. However, he continued to wear the battle helmet.

"Are you sure you want to do this?" Nickelo asked.

"No," said Richard as he picked up the equipment and headed toward the door. *"But sometimes you've got to do things you don't want to do."*

Nickelo mentally smiled again. His wizard scout was definitely learning.

CHAPTER 44

"I heard you the first fifty times, Wanda. I'll be careful."

Gaston made a final function check of his phase pistol. It was fully loaded with fifteen rounds. He checked the ammo pouch on his utility belt. The contents hadn't changed. Only two spare magazines were inside.

"Too bad your brother can't summon you more than your basic load. Forty-five rounds won't go far in a firefight."

"He's not my brother. I told you to stop calling him that. Shepard and I may share a few bits of DNA, but that doesn't make him my brother."

"Well, my point's still valid," said Wanda. *"You'll need to use your phase rod as much as possible and save the phase rounds for emergencies."*

Gaston kept some of his thoughts in his private space. Even Wanda couldn't be trusted with his most sensitive secrets. He had a feeling the entire recon was going to be one big emergency. Unfortunately, there wasn't anything he could do about it.

Whatever the danger, he thought, *we have to pinpoint the location of the dwarves' gem. Then I'll need to find some way to be put in charge of the team assigned to destroy it. They'll have to give my team the fourteen bottles of DNA gas. Somehow, I'll figure a way to destroy the gem with only thirteen bottles. Then I'll be able to take one bottle back to Diane. We can finally be together. We'll be able to live like a real family; Diane, Matthew, and me. We won't be like my parents. Diane and I won't have to worry about* 'the One' *tearing us apart. We can be together forever.*

A knock on the door brought Gaston out of his thoughts. When he opened the ornately carved piece of wood, he saw a tall figure dressed in the uniform of one of King Hamerstine's soldiers. Unfortunately, it wasn't one of the King's men. It was Shepard.

"What do you want?" Gaston said a little harsher than he'd intended. Wanda had advised him to try and get along with Shepard since they were on the same side. Unfortunately, any interaction with the man always put him on edge.

Instead of answering, Shepard just stood there with the insolent sneer Gaston had grown to hate.

"I said what do you want? I'm busy."

"Don't make this any harder than it is," said Shepard. "Can I come in?"

Part of Gaston wanted to slam the door in Shepard's face, but he resisted the urge. In spite of his dislike for the man, Gaston was curious. He knew his brother wasn't fond of him either, so he doubted Shepard would be here if it wasn't important.

While he didn't say anything, Gaston did step to one side. His brother came inside like he owned the place and placed a folded battle suit with a complete utility belt on the table. The pile of equipment even had a shoulder holster on top.

Pointing to the pile of equipment, Gaston asked, "What's all this?"

"It's my battle suit," said Shepard.

"I know it's your battle suit. Do you think I'm stupid or something?"

Shepard grew red-faced. Trying not to draw attention, Gaston reached down and fingered the handle of the phase rod at his side just in case. The man had a temper. Gaston knew he was liable to attack. After a few seconds, the red left his brother's face. Even so, Gaston noticed the man's fists were balled up and the knuckles remained white.

"You're all making a mistake," said Shepard. "I've got a very bad feeling about this recon. You haven't fought dimensional-shifting opponents before. As far as I know, even our parents haven't."

This time Gaston felt his own face heating up. Shepard had no right to call them his parents. His brother hadn't shown up on the scene until late. As a child, Shepard hadn't always been scared his parents were going to be teleported out to do some mission for *'the One'* without notice. The man hadn't grown up fearing to let his emotional guard down out of concern his mother was liable to disappear at any time.

"He has no right," Gaston thought in his shared space.

"Now, Gaston," said Wanda. *"Don't start trouble. He's not the enemy. See what he has to say. I doubt he came here just to make you mad."*

Like he often had to do when he was around Shepard, Gaston used the technique his father had taught him to control his anger. Slowly, he felt his muscles relax.

"What's your point, Shepard?"

"My point is you're going to need an edge. I may be able to give you one."

Shepard unhooked the phase rod from the utility belt on the table. He held it out.

"See if you can activate this on your own."

Gaston felt himself growing angry again at the audacity of Shepard for thinking he could order him around. Once again, Gaston used his father's technique for controlling his anger.

"Wise decision," said Wanda. *"I calculate a ninety-one percent probability this may turn out to be beneficial for you."*

Overcoming his anger, Gaston jerked the phase rod out of his brother's hand. It was slightly heavier than a standard-issue phase rod.

"The dial looks different," Gaston said.

Shepard pointed at the phase rod. "My nephew Brachia increased the energy output by almost twenty-five percent. You'll need to adjust your desired phase energy accordingly. The numbers on the dial aren't very reliable."

Gaston thumbed the dial to fifteen percent and thought the command to activate the rod in destructive mode. He sensed a small amount of Power leave his reserve. The brerellium shaft of the rod popped out of the handle as phase energy began running up and down the length of its creallium core.

A strange sensation of hunger filled the room. The hunger felt evil. A desire to swing the phase rod at Shepard swept over Gaston. He resisted the urge. He didn't like Shepard, but he had no wish to kill him. The man was a good fighter and might come in handy.

After a few seconds, Gaston looked at his brother, who was nodding his head as if something he'd anticipated had occurred.

"I thought so," said Shepard. "Our DNA's close enough for you to energize my equipment."

As Gaston watched, Shepard pushed the folded battle suit toward him.

"You should take this on the recon," said Shepard. "The material of the battle suit's embedded with titanium. Brachia installed one of those blue gems in the suit. If you activate the gem, the titanium will temporarily turn into creallium. It'll provide protection from creatures in the void."

"Say something, Gaston," said Wanda. *"He's offering you a great gift."*

Gaston wasn't as trusting as his battle computer. He wasn't sure what Shepard had up his sleeve, but he suspected a trick of some kind.

"My battle helmet won't work with your suit," Gaston pointed out.

Shepard took on a blank look as if conferring with his battle computer before replying. "No. It won't. We'll have to switch out battle computers."

Gaston wasn't sure what to say. He'd seen Shepard's phase rod in action. It was a very dangerous weapon. If what his brother said about the battle suit was true, he'd have an advantage if it came to a fight with a vampire.

"Why me?" Gaston said still suspicious. "Why not one of the others? Why not my parents?"

Gaston noticed Shepard grow noticeably red in the face. For some reason, he didn't think it was from anger.

"They don't have a close enough match to my DNA," said Shepard. "They each only have half." He paused before adding, "Besides, I did offer it to the others first. None of them could activate any of my gear. Even Thomas and Janice weren't able to make it work. My battle computer says it requires someone with DNA from both parents to have a close enough match."

"My advice would be to take him up on his offer," said Wanda. *"What have you got to lose?"*

"How about my life?" Gaston said.

Making his decision, Gaston removed his battle helmet and thought the command to eject his battle computer. When the brerellium-armored chip popped into view, he extracted it.

He looked at Shepard. "Well? Are you just going to stand there? We've only got two minutes of backup power to make the switch."

Much too slowly for Gaston's liking, Shepard placed his own helmet on the table and extracted its CPU. As soon as the chip was out, Gaston grabbed the battle helmet and inserted Wanda into the slot.

"You there, Wanda?" Gaston asked.

"Affirmative. I've completed a full diagnostic check of the battle helmet. It's different, but nothing I can't handle. I've put the instructions for energizing the battle suit's titanium on the helmet's heads-up display."

After removing his old battle suit, Gaston tried on the new one. The suit shrank to accommodate his shorter frame. Once he sealed the suit, he activated it in armor mode. Following the instructions on his heads-up display, he thought the command to energize the titanium. He felt energy surge through the suit, but he felt no difference.

"How do I know it's working?" Gaston asked, growing even more suspicious. He wondered if his brother was trying to trick him into depending on the suit during a fight when in reality it would provide no protection at all.

Gaston sensed Shepard wrap himself in Power. His brother shimmered as his body shifted into the void. As Gaston continued to watch, Shepard reached out with one hand and grabbed for his arm. Instead of passing through as expected, the man's hand was stopped by the battle suit's energized titanium.

"See, Gaston," said Wanda. *"You're too suspicious. You need to be more trusting. Not everyone's out to stab you in the back."*

Gaston ignored his battle computer. She was always preaching to him about the good in others. Sometimes she was a fool. Fortunately, he wasn't. Gaston thought the command to de-energize the titanium. He then switched the battle suit out of armor mode. The black suit took on the consistency of soft leather again.

"Okay, it works," Gaston admitted. "So what are you going to do? Use my gear? If we get in a fight, you won't do us any good if you're not in armor."

Shepard shook his head. "I'm hoping I won't be forced to wear your gear. We'll soon see."

With those words, Gaston watched Shepard take his pack off his back and open the flap. A dull black was visible in the opening. His brother pulled out a battle helmet, battle suit, a fully equipped utility belt along with a phase rod, and a shoulder holster. Shepard quickly inserted the brerellium chip that was his battle computer into a slot in the battle helmet.

Shepard glanced up. "I've been told that fifty-five battle helmets and two hundred battle suits were made for me. I don't know how many I've got left on Storage since several have been damaged over the years, but this is one of those extra sets."

"Function check is complete," said the voice of Nickelo, his brother's battle computer, over the helmet's external speakers. "See, Rick. I told you there was a seventy-four percent probability *'the One'* would allow you to summon another set of equipment if you gave the other one away."

Shepard stood there looking at him for a few seconds as if expecting something. Finally, the man gathered up his gear and started for the door.

"Aren't you going to say anything?" asked Wanda. *"I calculate he's significantly increased your odds of staying alive."*

"Shepard," Gaston said before his brother made it to the door.

His brother stopped at the doorway and turned around. The man didn't say a word. He just stood there with an arrogant expression on his face.

"Uh, thanks," Gaston said, forcing the words out.

With a nod of his head, Shepard pointed at the phase rod on Gaston's hip.

"Be careful with that thing. When it's in destructive mode, the demon essence will infect whoever it touches. Normal healers can't remove its taint."

"I'll try to remember," Gaston growled. Matthew had already told him how Shepard nearly killed the entire royal family of Trecor by infecting them with something from his phase rod.

Shepard turned to leave again.

"You know, Gaston," said Wanda. *"If you're ever going to make peace with your brother, this might be the time. You never*

know, you might need him as an ally one day."

Gaston knew she was right. Shepard might come in useful.

"Wait," Gaston said.

His brother turned around again. Gaston tried to ignore the man's obvious arrogance.

"We aren't enemies," Gaston said. "We should be working together. Our common enemy is *'the One,'* not each other." When Shepard didn't say anything, Gaston pressed a little harder. "Do you enjoy being forced to do the bidding of *'the One'*?"

That got a response.

"No," said Shepard. "I hate him, or it, or whatever *'the One'* is."

"Then we should be working together," Gaston said. On a hunch, he decided to make a peace overture. "This is our parents' last mission. You know what's going to happen. *'The One'* is getting ready to chew them up and spit them out. He's going to do the same to you eventually unless you stop him."

Shepard got a strange look on his face. For a fleeting moment, Gaston thought the man's natural insolence disappeared.

"You said our parents," Shepard said.

Gaston locked eyes with Shepard. "I'm wearing your battle suit. At this point, I guess it's hard to deny we've got at least a little DNA in common."

Neither of the wizard scouts spoke for several seconds. Finally, Shepard broke the silence.

"I don't want to be your enemy." After waiting a few seconds, Shepard stepped into the hallway before turning back around. "Take care of yourself, Myers."

"Same to you, Shepard."

With that, his brother gave a final nod of his head and disappeared down the hallway.

"I'm proud of you, Gaston," said Wanda.

Gaston didn't reply. He kept his thoughts in the private area of his mind. He began thinking of ways he could use his brother to get a bottle of DNA gas for Diane. They needed to complete the mission for *'the One'* to get home, but getting a bottle of DNA gas for the empress was also a priority.

I swear I'll get it if it's the last thing I do, Gaston thought in his private space. *I can't let Diane down.*

CHAPTER 45

The two bat creatures walked past Jeena's hiding place. One of them stopped and turned to face her direction for several seconds. The creature's furry ears swept from front to side as if seeking something. Jeena scarcely breathed. After a few heart-rending seconds, the creature's ears stopped moving. The Crosioian turned back around and rejoined its companion. They both continued down the hallway.

"Good," said Danny. *"Your invisibility and silence spells are still holding."*

Jeena didn't hear Danny the computer as a physical voice. Instead, she heard his words as thoughts through the metal headband Brachia had made for her.

Jeena thought her reply. *"Yes, they're holding, but those two bats obviously sensed something. I'm not sure what. By the way, is Stella still with me? I can sense the spells I put on her, but I can't sense her."*

"Stella's fine," said Danny. *"She's about five meters behind you. She's a wizard scout with her best stealth shield up. Combined with your spells, she's virtually undetectable."*

"Well," Jeena said. *"Just make sure she keeps up. If I get in a fight, I want her close enough to help."*

"She will be," Danny assured her. *"She's a wizard scout."*

Jeena checked the image of the space station Danny was projecting in her mind. She'd made it about two-thirds of the distance to her destination. Stepping out of her cubbyhole, she began walking in the direction of her prize. Each time one of her feet made contact with the metal deck, Jeena cringed. Even though logic told her the silence spell would keep her from making noise, her natural instincts said otherwise. She was well aware if she was discovered, both Stella and she would be in a fight with no one else to help.

"Don't forget about Bright Wing," Danny reminded her. *"She'll help if she can."*

Jeena knew the silver dragon was somewhere on the outside of the space station waiting to teleport in when needed. Jeena half wished she was out there with the dragon.

"You're not wearing an environmental suit," said Danny matter-of-factly. *"You'd die a horrible death in the vacuum of space."*

"What makes you think I'm not going to die a horrible death in here," Jeena asked as she continued moving down the hall. *"Besides, I've got a spell that could help."*

"Oh, I give you a fifty-fifty chance of avoiding a horrible death," said Danny with what sounded like a chuckle. *"I figure there's at least a fifty percent probability your death would be quick and relatively painless."*

Jeena ignored the computer. She didn't want to get sidetracked from her mission. Acquiring those bottles of DNA gas was the priority. Drawing Power from her reserve, Jeena mouthed the words for her best detection spell. When no words came out, her spell fizzled.

"I keep reminding you that your verbal spells won't work when you have a silence spell on you," said Danny.

Jeena bit off a retort before it was fully formed. The computer was just trying to be helpful. Still, it was a little aggravating to have Danny trying to advise her about spells when he hadn't ever done one himself.

Switching to a lower-level detection spell that required only hand movements and thoughts, Jeena sent a ball of magic down the hall. She was getting close now. The Crosioians were bound to have detection spells and traps in the hall.

"They wouldn't be using spells," said Danny. *"The Crosioians use technology just like we do."*

"Speak for yourself," Jeena said. *"I use sp—"*

A loud clanging reverberated throughout the space station as alarms sounded. With a wild thought she might be able to grab the bottles and escape if she was fast enough, Jeena began running down the hall. Before she got twenty steps, a squad of bat creatures dressed in armor and carrying the long metal rods Danny called rifles came charging around a corner toward her.

A stream of red plasma rounds passed over Jeena's right shoulder and struck two of the Crosioians at weak points in their armor. They both fell to the deck.

"How'd Stella know where I was? I'm invisible."

"She made her best guess," said Danny. *"You'll find wizard scouts guess a lot. Fortunately, they're very good at it during a fight. They're abnormally lucky as well."*

By the time Danny finished speaking, Jeena was too close to the remaining soldiers to reply. She jammed the tip of her staff into the neck of one of the soldiers. She missed the weakest point of the armor, but it didn't matter. A blast of blue energy from the staff's gem decapitated the soldier. Jeena was on the next bat creature before the first's headless body hit the deck.

"You're visible, and your silence spell is broken," warned Danny. *"Watch out."*

Jeena mouthed a defensive shield just as a soldier fired a burst of rounds in her direction. She tilted her shield in such a manner to make the rounds ricochet into one of the soldier's comrades. The reflected rounds didn't penetrate the Crosioian's armor. They did slow the bat creature down.

Whipping a dagger out from the sheath at her waist, Jeena stabbed down into another soldier's knee. The Crosioian gave a loud screech, which Jeena interpreted as a scream.

Before Jeena could swing her staff at another target, Stella was there swinging all four of her phase rods. The fast moving weapons formed a multi-colored blur in the air. The wizard scout made short work of the remaining soldiers.

"Hurry," said Stella. "No time."

Jeena didn't need to be told twice. She started down the hallway again. She was brought up short by two figures in armor holding short spears with glowing points.

"Scouts!" Jeena shouted.

Turning to run back the way she'd come, Jeena was stopped

short again. Two more of the scouts blocked the only path of retreat. Stella moved to engage the scouts in the rear. Jeena spun on her heels and faced the two scouts advancing from the front. One of the scouts raised a rifle to her shoulder. The barrel was pointed directly at Stella's back.

Without taking time to think, Jeena drew Power from her reserve and began the words to send a lightning bolt at the two scouts.

"No!" shouted a disembodied feminine voice. The voice was that of Margery.

At the shout, Jeena cut off her line of Power. The ball of magic that had started to form above her hand twisted and turned as the energy tried to find a point of release. Jeena concentrated on the ball and forced the magic to slowly return back into the universe.

The scouts as well as the hallway of the space station wavered and disappeared to reveal the Defiant's cargo bay. Most of the boxes in the bay had been stacked along the walls to make room for the holo-square Brachia and Dren had set up.

"Sorry, Margery," Jeena said. "I forgot where I was. These holograms of yours are better than Master Jathar's illusions. I got carried away.

Comstar and the wizard scout called Terrie were standing near a panel with flashing lights. So were Brachia and Dren.

After looking at some writing scrolling across one of the panel's display screens, Comstar looked up at Jeena. "It's fortunate you were able to stop your spell before it could backfire. With all the boxes of ammunition in the cargo bay, the results would've been devastating."

"I know," Jeena said. She was already chastising herself for the near disaster. "I'll remember next time. Should we try again?"

The human, Terrie, answered. "We've run the simulation six times in a row. The two of you should take a break for a couple of hours. I'm sure you're tired. We can try again this afternoon."

Having a human order her around grated on Jeena's nerves. The fact that the man was right helped her keep the irritation off her face. Besides, for a human, Jeena thought the disabled wizard scout wasn't so bad. Although she still didn't have a good handle on what a wizard scout was, the rest of the crew gave the human a lot of respect. That told her a lot about his abilities.

Stella moved to stand beside Jeena. The big lizard had deactivated her phase rods and placed them back on her utility belt.

"I not tired," said Stella. "We get farther this time. Next time we do better."

Terrie gave Stella a grin. "Well, I'm tired even if you aren't, so let's take a break anyway. You and Jeehana can use the time to hash out your strategy for the next simulation."

"That may be best," Jeena said surprised to find herself on the human's side of the discussion. "I made a mistake somewhere along the way. The Crosioians must have spotted my detection spell. I assume that's what activated the alarms. Perhaps Stella should be the one to lead next time. Maybe she could get closer without being detected."

Terrie shook his head. "No. Bad idea. Stella's good, but the security on the space station is the best the Crosioians have got. We were originally planning on sending six wizard scouts on the raid. We don't have that luxury anymore, so we need to do the unexpected."

"Yeah," said Brachia. "From what I can gather, the Crosioians blame magic users for their defeat on Velos a couple of years ago. They won't be expecting us to use magic against them."

Dren smiled. "Besides, Jeehana, you didn't make a mistake. Margery just triggered the alarm to see how you'd react."

"That's correct," came Margery's voice over one of the speakers in the cargo bay. "My calculations indicated an eighty-six percent probability you would reach the room with the bottles of DNA gas on the last simulation. I calculated testing your response at being discovered was more valuable than completing the scenario."

"What?" Jeena said. She let her irritation at being stopped before reaching her goal creep into her voice. She hated to lose. "Are you saying I could've completed the mission?"

"No," said Comstar who seemed to be more attuned to Jeena's desire to win than the others. "The purpose of the holo-square is to familiarize Stella and you with the layout of the space station and possible problems you might encounter. The only mission that matters is the real one in three more days."

Jeena reluctantly nodded her head. She had a feeling she was more tired than she thought. The last four days was a blur of activity. Her brain was still trying to acclimate to her new reality. All of the technology surrounding her every waking moment sought to overwhelm her senses. She didn't like technology. However, it was a necessary evil to complete her current mission.

"Come," said Stella as she glanced down at Jeena. "I go eat. You come too."

"Uh, not right yet," Jeena said hoping the Sterilian wouldn't be offended. She'd seen Stella eat on several occasions. Watching the lizard-like wizard scout shove worms into her mouth wasn't exactly appetizing.

"She's not a lizard," said Danny privately through the headband Jeena was still wearing. *"She's a Sterilian. She's as intelligent as you; maybe even more so. I calculate you're hurting her feelings. See the deepening gray around her neckline?"*

Jeena looked at Stella. The wizard scout's four muscular arms and double-row of serrated teeth didn't give the impression of someone who could have their feelings hurt very easily. Regardless, Jeena didn't want to risk alienating her teammate.

"You know, Stella," Jeena said. "I'll bet Charlie would like to go eat. Wouldn't you, Charlie?"

Jeena had spotted the other Sterilian standing by one of the side walls with the human boy called Daniel. It hadn't taken Jeena long to figure out that Stella and Charlie were attracted to each other. Based upon the way they were always stealing glances at one another, Jeena had a feeling they might eventually become bondmates.

"Uh..., yes," said Charlie over the translator strapped to his hip. "I hungry."

"Well, good then," Jeena said grateful her plan seemed to be working out. She would be depending on Stella during their raid. They needed to stay on good terms. "The two of you should go and eat now. I'll be up later after I talk to the others."

Neither Charlie nor Stella argued. They just turned and climbed the stairs leading up to the galley. Once they were gone, almost everyone in the cargo bay broke out in laughter. Jeena noticed even Comstar gave a little smile.

"Good one, Jeehana," said Dren. "Those two want to be together, but they keep fighting it. I think it's up to the rest of us to make sure they spend time with each other."

"Oh, yes," said the human woman, Angela, who'd just come down the stairs. With a smile of her own, Angela said, "I guess we can all put matchmaker down as one of our skills when we fill out a resume. Now, if you all don't mind, I'd like to steal my husband and take him to lunch."

As the redhead woman spoke, Jeena noticed Angela glare in her direction.

Is she jealous? Jeena wondered. *I'm an elf. I've got no interest in human males.*

"True," said Danny privately. *"Still, there's no use making enemies. You might need each other someday."*

"Elves don't need humans."

"Oh, really?" laughed Danny. *"Tell me that again in three days when a couple of thousand Crosioians on the space station are trying to kill you. I calculate you'll be happy to see the Defiant and her humans come to rescue you."*

Jeena did not laugh. She had a strange feeling the computer might be right.

CHAPTER 46

Matthew banked the shuttle in a hard right turn to line up for the final approach. Once he was level, Jerad gave the team their final instructions.

"All right. We go in quick, and we get out even quicker. Our mission is to pinpoint the Mountain's Heart. It's not to fight. Got it?"

Everyone nodded their head.

When Jerad was satisfied, he pointed at Emerald and Chancee. "You two stick close to Thomas."

"We can take care of ourselves in a fight," said Chancee. "This isn't our first battle."

Jerad shook his head. "If we do our jobs right, there won't be a battle. The reason I want you to stay close to Thomas is that he's a protector. He can extend his stealth shield to cover both of you in addition to himself. That's why you're on the heavy team."

Jerad looked at Myers. "When my team gets to the intersection, we'll peel off and check out the treasury. You'll take the light team and continue down the main corridor to the gem's original location." Jerad turned to face the rest of the raiding party seated along the sides of the shuttle. "Gaston, Rick, Thomas, and Janice all have battle helmets. Consequently, I expect each team to keep the other teams updated. If either the light or heavy team detects the gem, contact the others so we can all return to the rally point and get out of here. Any questions?"

Richard listened absentmindedly as Jerad went over the plan for what was probably the tenth time. He had no doubt they all knew it, but his former tent-mate was like an old mother hen watching over her chicks. He knew his friend was just trying his best not to leave anything to chance.

"Rick!"

Startled, Richard looked up.

"You with us?" asked Jerad. "I had to call your name three times."

Richard nodded his head but remained quiet. His job didn't require much thought. He and Fenmar only had to hold the entrance. There wasn't much to understand.

"Thirty seconds," shouted Matthew over his shoulder for the benefit of those without battle helmets. There's a clearing about four hundred meters from the entrance. I'll put you down there."

"Roger that," replied Jerad.

Richard noticed Myers glance toward his son.

Myers caught Matthew's eye and gave the teenager his own set of final instruction. "As soon as we're out, I want you to haul your tail out of here." Myers held up one of the portable com-units they'd found on the fighter-shuttles. "We'll call you if we need you."

Matthew looked dubious. "I should stay here. I could be at the entrance in twenty seconds."

"No," said Jerad and Myers at the same time.

Jerad got in the next words before Myers had a chance. "Soldiers obey orders. That's how we stay alive."

To his credit, Matthew didn't argue. From the strain on the teenager's face, Richard could tell he wanted to say something, but he didn't. Instead, he turned and concentrated on the blur of terrain whipping past the shuttle's windscreen.

"The boy's good," Richard said in his shared space. *"Even with the night vision spell on the windscreen, I'd have trouble flying at half this speed."*

"Then I guess it's a good thing your nephew's flying instead of you."

"My nephew?"

"Geesh, Rick," said Nickelo in the exasperated tone he used during a particularly bad training session. *"Matthew is Gaston's son. Gaston is your brother. What do you think that makes*

Matthew? In fact, except for your brother, Matthew may be your only living relative."

"Uh..., you're right. I wonder why I didn't think of that myself?"

"Hmm," said Nickelo. *"Are you asking me? Perhaps it's because you have a tendency to be selfish and self-centered. Of course, that's just my opinion."*

"Five seconds," said Matthew over the shuttle's intercom.

The view of the ground rushing up sent a shiver up Richard's spine. He half considered shifting into the void but resisted the urge. He knew any use of Power besides stealth shields and passive scans would increase the risk of detection.

"You're learning, aren't you?" said Nickelo. *"Makes me feel like I haven't wasted all those years of training after all."*

The shuttle touched down before Richard could reply. Everyone on the landing party was out the rear ramp in short order. If the teams had been composed of only wizard scouts, they would've jumped in. Unfortunately, the addition of the two dwarves and the ranger forced them to land.

Richard was the last one out of the shuttle. As soon as his feet cleared the ramp, the shuttle began to rise. At the same time, he heard the whine of the shuttle's engine. A blast of air hit him from behind and knocked him toward the ground. He tucked and rolled. By the time he was back on his feet, the shuttle was nowhere to be seen.

"Yep," said Nickelo. *"Tia's definitely been showing him a thing or two about flying."*

No one on the team spoke. They just assumed their positions in the formation and moved out at a quick pace. Jared led them in the direction of a small entrance in the side of the mountain. Emerald and Fenmar had assured them it was a secret door known only to the royal family and their closest advisers.

The heavy team led with Janice at the point of the formation. Myers followed with the light team. General Fenmar and Richard trailed a hundred meters behind as rear guard.

"I don't think my mother should be on point?" Richard complained to his battle computer. *"Jerad or my father should take the lead."*

"Why?" asked Nickelo. *"Because she's a female? Your*

mother's the most experienced wizard scout out of all of you."

"Well, I still don't think it's right."

"Deal with it," said Nickelo. *"I recommend you concentrate on your part of the task. I've plotted the life forms your passive scan is picking up on your heads-up display. I count 3,227 in the tunnels under Drepdenor. Some of the life forms appear to be magic users. I've plotted them in red."*

Richard looked at his battle helmet's display. Sure enough, the portion denoting the area inside the mountain was covered with various colored dots. The pitifully few number of white dots moving toward the dwarves' secret opening made him realize what they were up against.

"I sure hope Jerad knows what he's doing," Richard thought.

"You better hope you know what you're doing," laughed Nickelo. *"Based upon some of your previous missions, I calculate Sergeant Hendrick's wouldn't be placing any double or nothing bets on the outcome of this little recon."*

Richard didn't laugh. For some reason, he didn't see the humor of the situation.

CHAPTER 47

When she opened her eyes, Jeena stared at the bottom of the bunk above her. The slight indentation of the springs told Jeena her friend Dren was still in bed. When they'd first arrived onboard, Comstar graciously gave up his bunk so she and Dren could have a private room together. Not that there was all that much privacy. Instead of a solid door, a curtain served as the only separation between their quarters and the galley. Still, considering the close confines of the recon ship, Jeena figured even that little privacy was a blessing.

Jeena focused on some black writing on one of the two storage lockers in their quarters. R. Shepard. It was the name of the other occupant of the room, the Uncle Rick that Dren and Brachia talked about so much. Dren had also told her that their uncle, along with seven others, was on a mission for the mysterious being the children called *'the One.'*

That she'd be sleeping in the bed of a human male bothered Jeena at first. Her logic quickly overcame her emotions. The bedding was clean, and space on the ship was limited. In the grand scheme of things, sleeping in the bed of a human male, minus the male, was a small sacrifice to make.

When Dren offered to switch bunks with her, Jeena refused. High Priest Questor had once told her that it was best to face your fears or phobias head-on.

When you look at it, Jenna thought, *maybe this is part of my penitence for past sins.* Jeena closed her eyes and snuggled deeper into the warmth of her blanket. *Just five more minutes*, Jeena thought. *The day will start soon enough. I'll rest for five more minutes.*

The sound of stomping feet in the galley prevented her from returning to the sweet dream she'd been having. She couldn't remember her dream exactly but did remember feeling safe and at peace. She'd also felt whole. It reminded her of when she'd once linked with the entity she'd known only as the *'helper.'* Even though the life form on the other end of the link had initially frightened her, the presence of the *'helper'* had also given her a sense of peace.

The sound of stomping feet continued. Jeena recognized the heavy footfalls of the dwarves. From prior association, she knew their race could be quiet when they desired. Apparently, this wasn't one of those times. Since her hope for five more minutes of sleep was shot, Jeena decided to get up and start the day. She'd soon be meeting with the ship's captain to make the final go or no-go decision for the mission. After seven days of discussions, they still hadn't been able to come up with a functional plan. Jeena began to wonder if she'd left home for no reason.

Why did I let the Oracle talk me into this? I'm probably wasting my time. Why?

Jeena wondered if anyone else ever felt like they were wasting their time. She wondered if anyone else ever asked themselves why.

Opening her eyes, Jeena focused on the bottom of Dren's bunk. Something on one of the metal bracing-bars caught her eye. She saw four symbols scratched into the metal. Jeena studied the symbols, recognizing them as the writing of the humans of this dimension. The writing was directly above her head as if someone had been lying in the same position as her when they'd etched the letters. She wondered if they'd done it during some sleepless night.

Doubtful, Jeena thought. *Since it's the children's uncle who sleeps here, it's probably a foul word or the name of an ex-girlfriend.*

Jeena eyed the word for a few more seconds. Something told her it wasn't anything foul. Curious, Jeena recited the words of a translation spell as she simultaneously made an intricate flip of her hand. The letters wavered before settling down into a single word.

'WHY?'

The single-word question stuck in Jeena's mind. She continued to stare at it for a full minute.

Did the children's uncle write it? she wondered. *If so, what was he asking? And did he ever find an answer?*

Jeena thought about the ramifications of the question. Her philosophy teachers had talked for hours on end about how to solve the great question of 'Why?' But at the end of all those hours, they'd all failed to give a suitable answer. Jeena was positive she could write page after page quoting the thoughts and teachings of all of the great elven philosophers. In the end, it all settled down to one thing. Every person had to answer the question for themselves. The children's uncle, if that was who had actually written the question, would have to answer it for himself as well.

Jeena ignored the stomping feet outside the curtain. The springs of the bunk above her moved slightly. She knew Dren would be getting up soon. Jeena decided to ignore the movement of the human girl for a minute. She concentrated on the single word question; 'WHY?'

Finally, Jeena turned her head toward the room's only desk. She spied her belt and dagger. Drawing Power from her reserve, Jeena recited a levitation spell. The belt with her sheath and dagger floated across the room into her hand. She pulled the dagger out of its sheath and stared at the question again.

Why indeed? she thought.

Holding the tip of the dagger against the metal bar, Jeena wrote a single word reply in elvish.

Jeena smiled. *Let the children's uncle figure that one out.*

The springs above her shifted again. With a devilish grin, Jeena sheathed the dagger and placed both of her feet in the center of her friend's mattress.

Kicking hard with both legs, Jeena shouted. "Get up!"

Bang!

Oops! Jeena thought. The noise had been the unmistakable sound of Dren's head hitting the low ceiling. *I kicked too hard.*

"Jeehana!" yelled Dren half laughing but sounding a little angry at the same time. "I swear I'm going to get you for that."

Definitely too hard, Jeena thought as she hurriedly tried to jump out of her bed. Unfortunately, she rose too fast and bumped her own head on the bottom of Dren's bunk. A few strands of her hair tangled in the springs. Ignoring the resulting tug, Jeena rolled onto the floor as she made a dive for the door.

Dren was on the floor in a blink. Jeena thought for a human, her roommate was very fast.

"I'm sorry," Jeena laughed as she made for the door.

"Oh, you're going to be sorry," said Dren laughing for real this time. "You're supposed to be a high priestess. Shame on you."

Jeena laughed again. It had been a long time since she'd allowed herself the luxury of pulling a prank on a friend and sharing a laugh.

CHAPTER 48

Gaston followed his mother's progress with his passive scan. Both his father and mother had allowed him to place a trace on them. He was familiar enough with the other wizard scouts to follow their progress as well. The only member of the recon team he couldn't track was Shepard.

"He's good," said Wanda in their shared space. *"I've told you that before. I don't have communication with your brother's battle computer, but I calculate a ninety-seven percent probability Wizard Scout Shepard is in his assigned position at the entrance. As you can see, General Fenmar is definitely there."*

Gaston didn't say anything. However, he grudgingly calculated the probability was closer to one hundred percent Shepard was there as well. The man was a wizard scout. While he didn't particularly like Shepard, Gaston didn't doubt his brother's abilities.

When Jerad's team was about fifty meters from where the secret tunnel intersected the main corridor, his team stopped. Gaston motioned for Tam and Telsa to remain where they were while he went ahead. He noticed Telsa kneel and face to the rear. Tam took a knee and faced forward. Both women were dressed in their confiscated armor from the fighter-shuttles. Tam wore an armored helmet. Telsa did not. Instead, she wore the hooded cloak and set of magic goggles the gnome mage had donated when they were at Cantonsburg. Gaston momentarily considered advising Telsa to don her helmet, but refrained.

She's a wizard scout. It's not my job to second-guess her.

Moving forward, Gaston joined Jerad, Emerald, and his mother, kneeling beside them.

Emerald pointed ahead and whispered, "The exit to the main tunnel is fifty paces ahead. From the other side, the door looks like a column with the likeness of a two-headed troll on it. No other columns bear a similar carving. You can open the door from the other side by pressing all four eyes at the same time."

Gaston nodded his head. "Understood."

"If you run into vampires," said Jerad, "make sure Tam and Telsa know their creallium swords will be their only effective weapons."

Gaston nodded his head for Jerad's benefit. Tam and Telsa had already been told a dozen times. He was confident they knew what they were doing. He wasn't going to insult them by repeating it again. While Jerad was giving Emerald and Janice some final instructions, Gaston looked at the results of his passive scan on his heads-up display.

"Wanda, you're falling behind. Make sure you keep my heads-up display updated with the most recent results of my passive scan."

"I have been," said Wanda. *"I've been updating it twice every second. I didn't come off the shelf this morning, you know?"*

Gaston frowned. Instead of replying to his battle computer, he touched Jerad's arm. "Something's not right. The plots on my heads-up display haven't moved since we've been here."

Jerad seemed to concentrate on something unseen. Gaston noticed his mother doing the same.

"I can't tell just using my passive scan," said Jerad. "Are you getting anything, Janice?"

"Gaston's right," said Janice. "Danny says none of the life forms have moved since we got here. I'm not all that familiar with vampires. Since it's starting to get daylight outside, I guess I assumed they were asleep in their coffins or something."

Emerald shook her head. "Vampires are dead. They don't sleep. Daylight doesn't affect them? If you remember, you and I fought those three vampires during daylight. They get along fine regardless of whether it's day or night."

The hair on the back of Gaston's neck stood on end. "I don't like this. Something's wrong. I recommend we abort the mission until we can figure out what's going on."

Jared seemed to consider his suggestion before finally nodding his head in agreement. "I think you're right. Get your team heading back toward the entrance. We'll follow. I'll let Rick and General Fenmar know we're on our way."

Emerald grabbed Jerad's arm. "No. We can't turn back. We're so close. We need to find the Mountain's Heart."

Janice looked at the dwarf. "Finding the location of your blue gem won't do us any good if we're dead. We'll be back. You said yourself Cancontus has been in possession of the gem for over a century and a half. A couple more days isn't going to matter. We'll be back."

Without waiting to see if the dwarf accepted that they were aborting the mission or not, Gaston headed back to join his team. Telsa and Tam were both kneeling where he'd left them. Although they weren't in battle suits, he thought they looked dangerous nonetheless.

"They are dangerous," said Wanda. *"They're wizard scouts."*

Gaston wasted no time in explaining the situation to his team. They didn't ask questions. He wasn't surprised. Both women were very good at their job.

"I'll take point," Gaston said. "Tam, you're on my left. Telsa, you'll be on my right. Remember, if we encounter any vampires, those rifles of yours won't do any good. Use your swords."

As soon as both women nodded their heads, Gaston moved out. He drew his Deloris blaster and clicked the safety off. At the same time, he pulled the phase rod off his left hip and thought the command to extend the brerellium and creallium shaft out the handle. He didn't activate the rod. He was pretty sure the demon essence would be a dead giveaway. He had a feeling their only hope of staying alive was to avoid detection at all costs. If the vampires even suspected they were in their tunnels, he figured the odds of them getting out in one piece would be near zero.

"Actually, the odds would be about seventeen percent," said Wanda. *"But don't worry. It's only a number. Besides, I calculate only a very slight chance they'll discover we're here."*

* * *

A never-ending stream of data flowed into the primary processing unit of the demon, Zenthra. All was as it should be.

"Our opponent's variables are meekly walking right into my trap," Zenthra said.

"Our trap," corrected a winged, bat-creature with red eyes and finger-long fangs. The bat-creature was standing near one of Zenthra's control panels. "Beware, brother," said the bat-creature. "Your ambition may one day lead you to ruin."

Zenthra burned with anger but kept his temper contained to a few processing threads. His brother Cancontus thought he was the stronger of the two, but he was wrong. Still, Zenthra knew it would serve no purpose to risk a confrontation now.

Ha! thought Zenthra while making sure he kept his thoughts to secure threads his brother couldn't access. *All three of my brothers are fools. Only I am wise enough to possess the Dragars' computer. Only I control the time-gate. Only I am connected to my future self through computers. I am the master of all time. I am invulnerable. Even my brothers dare not destroy the Crosioians' master computer in the future or the Dragars' computer of the here and now. One day my brothers will kneel down before me. They will pay for their arrogance. Oh, how they'll pay.*

"You say nothing," said Cancontus. "Do not deceive yourself, brother. I will destroy the boxes of magic you call computers if I even think you're trying to betray me. I can destroy the computer you chose for your avatar with a single thought."

"Me, betray you?" said Zenthra trying to sound surprised. "Why would I do that? Our plan is perfect. Even now our opponent's variables are in the secret entranceway of the dwarves. They're almost in our trap. They foolishly think that which they seek is still under the mountain."

The bat-creature which was Lord Cancontus paced the room. "The Master will not be pleased if we kill his chosen variable. He's forbidden us from harming him. The Master says his variable will be useful during the final battle."

"The Master says many things," said Zenthra. "Besides, we won't be harming the Master's variable. Your vampire servants shall do the job for us."

Lord Cancontus said nothing.

Zenthra sent logic threads to his security programs both in the present and in the future just to be sure all was well. It was.

Zenthra calculated victory was in his grasp. *The Dragars' primary computer I inhabit is deep below their temple. The entire subterranean complex is encased in creallium. Nothing can enter or exit without my permission. I am invulnerable.*

The security programs of the Dragars' computer located the blue gem.

Ah, thought Zenthra. *The Dragars are even now loading the gem onto their destroyer. Soon, they'll transport it to my future self. With the added Power of the Mountain's Heart, the part of myself which possesses the Crosioians' master computer will easily take over the galaxy in the physical dimension. All is going as planned.*

"You do not speak, Cancontus," said Zenthra. "Do you doubt the ability of your vampire servants to destroy the humans and the dwarf? Perhaps you should return to the mountain and oversee the trap yourself."

The bat-creature whirled. Cancontus's long fangs protruded from his mouth. "Do not think to advise me, brother. I may return to the mountain, but it will be my decision, not yours."

"I wouldn't think of advising one so powerful as yourself," said Zenthra in what he calculated was a placating voice. "I'm a mere computer. You, on the other hand, possess the body of a powerful vampire lord. Although, why you chose a Crosioian to convert into a vampire lord is a mystery. However, you're obviously so much more knowledgeable than me, so who am I to naysay you?"

Lord Cancontus bared his fangs. "You are no one. Never forget that. When I am the Master, I may allow you to rule the sister galaxy in the physical dimension. However, never forget it will only be because I chose to do so."

Zenthra devoted several billion logic threads in an attempt to think of a way to open a gate to the demonic plane without the help of any of his brothers. He came up with nothing. His best chance at overthrowing their Master and assuming the role himself was by using his fool brothers. One day, he'd no longer need them. He'd be the Master. One day, he'd be a demon lord of the Dark Council. It was only a matter of time.

However, Zenthra thought, *the time isn't now. Until that time, I need to continue playing my part.*

"I am your humble servant," said Zenthra. "We needn't quarrel, brother. The Dragars will transport the blue gem to the physical dimension in the future. The time is close at hand for us to open a gate. Let our brothers, the Dalinfaust and Efrestra, continue to pin their hopes on the two gates in the land of the elves. When they least expect it, we shall use the dwarves' gem to open a gate ourselves. We shall summon forth the demon armies. We shall conquer the three galaxies. The Dark Council will be forced to reward us. Our brothers will kneel before us and beg for mercy."

Zenthra laughed as he envisioned not just two, but all three of his brothers kneeling before him. He would punish Cancontus most of all for being fool enough to trust him.

Lord Cancontus didn't join in the laughter. "Do not deceive yourself, brother," said Cancontus. "We must be careful. If the Dalinfaust discovers our plans, it may well be us who will be begging for mercy."

Zenthra laughed again. "You worry too much, brother. The overflow of DNA gas from the Dragars' temple has been permeating the physical dimension long enough. Soon, magic will work there just as effectively as it does in the magic dimension. The Dragars only need to sacrifice a few hundred thousand more dragon eggs to complete the task. Once the Dragars can use their magic weapons in the physical dimension at full effectiveness, we'll use the fools to conquer the Empire, the Crosioians, and all the other pathetic species in the physical dimension. Our plans are perfect. What could go wrong?"

CHAPTER 49

The Dalinfaust retrieved his scan from underneath the Dragar temple and back to where he was in the future. He'd heard and seen enough. He laughed. The sound echoed off the walls of the large cavern.

"May I ask what's so amusing?" asked a dark elf standing near a small pool of water at the back of the cave.

The Dalinfaust raised his dragon head to its full height. He preferred black dragons to all of his other avatars. Other creatures were so easy to intimidate when he was in a dragon form. He looked down at Lord Crendemor.

The Dalinfaust thought Lord Crendemor failed to look suitably intimidated. The dark elf's attitude irritated him. The Dalinfaust chose not to answer the dark elf right away. Instead, he turned his attention to a dark-haired female elf chained to a boulder in the center of the cavern. The virgin elf no longer had enough of her mind left to be properly afraid. The Dalinfaust reached out with a claw and scrapped its tip down the elf's side. The female elf screamed in agony. The Dalinfaust pulled his dragon lips back in a smile.

Apparently, the elf's mind isn't totally gone after all, he thought. *Perhaps she'll provide a few more days of amusement before I finally eat her.*

Sufficiently appeased by the elf's scream, the Dalinfaust looked back at Lord Crendemor. He wondered if he should just kill the arrogant dark elf and be done with it. After a few beats of his dragon's heart, he decided to let the dark elf live a while longer. *I'll allow him to live until he no longer appears useful.*

"My amusement or lack thereof is no concern of yours, elf," the Dalinfaust said. "I let you attend my little torture sessions because it amuses me for the time being. Don't mistake your attendance as a sign you may speak without first being spoken to. Do you understand?"

"Of course," said Lord Crendemor with a half bow. "However, as much as I enjoy watching you play with your toys, I've other duties as well. May I be permitted to ask why you've summoned me to this place?"

The Dalinfaust narrowed his eyes and stared at the dark elf. He almost changed his mind about allowing Lord Crendemor to remain alive. "I desire you to retrieve the device you stole from Zenthra and bring it here. I also want you to bring the bottle of DNA gas you have in your possession."

The dark elf stared back with a strange look in his eyes. The Dalinfaust noticed the dark elf's hands twitch and wondered if the fool might be stupid enough to attack. He doubted it but prepared a defensive spell just in case. After a few seconds, the Dalinfaust noticed the dark elf's hands stop their twitching and grow still.

"I have plans for the DNA gas," said Lord Crendemor.

"Your plans mean nothing to me," said the Dalinfaust. "However, in this case, you may keep your petty desires. I merely wish for someone to see the bottle. Their greed will take care of the rest."

Lord Crendemor didn't answer immediately. Finally, he said, "Naturally, it will be done as you say. Will there be anything else?"

"No," replied the Dalinfaust. "You may go."

The dark elf gave a curt nod before turning and heading toward the only exit out of the bone-strewn cavern. Once he was gone, the Dalinfaust turned his attention back to the female elf. Her sobs soothed his irritation. He knew he'd need to replace her with a fresh toy soon but for now, she served his purpose. He lowered his dragon head and breathed on the female. She was a virgin. He could heal virgin females.

Her wounds closed over with the touch of his breath. Within seconds, she was whole again.

The Dalinfaust smiled. “Now, let us start again, shall we?”

CHAPTER 50

Although Lord Cancontus would never admit it to his brother, he actually had begun to wonder if his vampire minions could handle the wizard scouts on their own. As soon as his meeting with Zenthra ended, Cancontus teleported back to Drepdenor. When he arrived, he relaxed. All was as it should be.

The wizard scouts were in the secret tunnel just as Zenthra had predicted. While Cancontus thought his brother's selection of a computer for an avatar was a poor choice, it certainly worked to his advantage on this occasion. The processing power of both the Dragars' computer system in the present and the Crosioians' master computer in the future proved to be very reliable at making predictions. They weren't perfect by any means, but they were useful.

As he continued to ponder the situation, something drew Cancontus's attention. The wizard scouts had stopped.

Are they turning back? If so, why? Do they suspect a trap?

Cancontus scanned the area in the tunnels. His vampires were still hidden by his stealth shields. Some were in the void, hidden in the walls near the wizard scouts. Others were in the hidden room near the middle of the secret tunnel. He was confident his spells hid his servants so well that even the abilities of the wizard scouts couldn't detect them.

Nevertheless, Cancontus began to have doubts. If all of the wizard scouts had been equipped with their advanced armor and weapons, he'd never have considered leaving the task to his vampire servants. He'd have been forced to take direct action himself. That wasn't the case though. Only four of the scouts were in the Empire's armor, and two of those scouts were in older models at that. The other four wizard scouts only had Dragar equipment along with a few magic swords. The dwarves and the human ranger were of no concern. They couldn't even self-heal. Only the wizard scouts were a threat.

Cancontus thought back to what his brother Efrestra had once told him. The Master's variable was tricky. He thought back to how the Master's variable had escaped his trap in the spiritual dimension. He'd come so close to capturing the foolish human, but the wizard scout had been lucky. Cancontus wondered if his luck had caused him to notice something this time that the others hadn't.

Did he warn them? Cancontus wondered. *No. The fool's still at the entrance. He's as oblivious as the rest. The spell I used to create illusions of life forms has them all fooled. My vampires can still spring our trap. All of the wizard scouts will die. If my vampires are discovered prematurely, then I'll take an active part. Otherwise, I'll remain hidden. The Master wouldn't be pleased if I killed his variable directly.*

CHAPTER 51

Telsa kept her senses on high alert. She missed her battle suit. The magic armor she wore was good, but its helmet was inert. She preferred wearing Master Garis's goggles.

My battle computer would come in handy right about now. I don't have it, so I'll just have to make do with what I've got.

After adjusting the filter on her passive scan, Telsa reduced the range until it extended only a few feet beyond the walls of the secret tunnel. Although she sensed nothing, something didn't feel right. She remembered Rick telling her how he'd once found a secret room by looking for a spot where it just felt like something should be there.

Telsa decided to use the technique her friend had taught her on the stone around her. She continued following Gaston but concentrated on the walls as well. After about twenty steps, Telsa stopped. Something to her right really did feel strange. Gaston and Tam stopped and looked at her.

Her ex-TAC officer made a gesture with his hand as if saying, "What is it?"

Telsa didn't have an answer. She just knew something wasn't right. Touching the side of her goggles, Telsa switched the left lens to the invisibility setting. The tunnel walls took on a double vision as her right lens displayed the tunnel in night-vision mode, and the left lens displayed it in a view resembling her battle helmet's radiation filter.

Her eyes were drawn to a particular spot on the tunnel wall. Part of the wall seemed to radiate a different energy than the rest. The spot was rectangular. It was about the height of a tall man and the width of two large men. Realization suddenly came over her.

"There's a door there," Telsa whispered as she pointed at the hidden opening with the barrel of her rifle. "I think there's something behind—"

The hidden door burst open.

Telsa pulled the trigger of her rifle as a creature from her worst nightmare leaped through the air straight toward her throat. The creature was a tall human male with red eyes and long fangs.

Telsa heard Gaston yell, "Vampire!"

Then everything began to happen at once.

CHAPTER 52

Richard quickly grew bored after the others left. *"I'm not sure I like working as a team after all. I should be with one of the recon units, not Myers."*

"Protecting their path of retreat is just as important as performing the recon," said Nickelo. *"The reason it's called teamwork is because everyone does their part. I'd advise doing yours. Jerad told you to hold the exit. So hold it."*

"I am holding it," Richard said. He knew his battle computer was right, but he was a soldier. Sometimes he just liked to complain.

Looking to his right, Richard eyed General Fenmar. The dwarf was sitting on an outcropping of rock just inside the entrance. The area where they were was the size of a small room about six paces across. The dwarf was in full-plate armor with the visor raised on his helmet. The dwarf wore a strange expression. His eyes were focused on the blue gem at the end of his war hammer.

Since he was bored anyway, Richard decided to strike up a conversation. "Are your armor and weapons ones you made?"

The dwarf continued to stare blankly at the gem.

Richard wondered if he'd heard him. "Fenmar?" Richard said. "Are you okay?"

"Huh?" asked the dwarf coming out of his daze. "Sorry. I was just thinking about my family. My son and I worked on parts of this very room together. He was a good lad. You'd have liked him."

"I'm sure I would have," Richard said immediately regretting his decision to start a conversation.

The dwarf shook his head as if pulling himself back to the here and now. "You asked about my gear," said Fenmar. "This armor is one of the new sets. While my old armor was magic, it wasn't full plate, and it wasn't made of the Holy Metal. My old armor was only enchanted with spells. Magic armor created with spells alone didn't seem to provide any protection from the vampires when I was last here. Only the Holy Metal was able to stop them. Only armor and weapons with a piece of the Mountain's Heart were effective against those creatures when they were in the void."

"Well," Richard said, "they'll have a tough time getting through your armor now. Once you pull your visor down, you'll be completely encased in energized titanium, or the Holy Metal as you call it."

"True," replied Fenmar, "but don't think for one second that'll make me invulnerable. It'll stop their attacks from the void, but once they realize I'm immune to void attacks, they'll shift to physical ones. Vampires are immensely strong. If they get a full swing with a magic sword, it'll cut through even that armor of yours."

"Hmm," said Nickelo. *"Good safety tip. Don't let vampires get a full swing."*

"And your war hammer?" Richard asked.

The dwarf raised the hammer. "This is Dawn's Guardian. It's been in my family for generations. It sent many of those vampire fiends to meet the Creator when they attacked our home, but not nearly enough."

The dwarf's voice took on an edge. "Once we've forged the rest of the armor and weapons with the Holy Metal and gems you gave us, Queen Emerald will lead us to victory. We'll rid our home of Lord Cancontus and his vampire filth. One day soon. Just wait and see."

Richard remained silent. He had no idea what to say. He'd been raised in an orphanage. The sisters had done their best, but their resources had been limited. The environment at the orphanage hadn't exactly been one to induce bonding. The orphanage had been a place to stay, but it hadn't been his home. He couldn't relate to the dwarf's obvious attachment to the tunnels of Drepdenor.

Well, this is awkward, Richard thought as he looked for something else to do. He glanced at his passive scan.

"That's strange," Richard commented to Fenmar. "The others have turned back."

"Why?" asked Fenmar.

"I'm not sure," Richard said. "Nick?"

His battle computer's answer came as a whispered reply over the external speaker of Richard's battle helmet. "Margery says Gaston noticed the life forms he was picking up on his passive scan were remaining perfectly still. Jared's aborting the mission until he figures out why."

Richard noted the life forms on his passive scan. There were thousands of the red, yellow, and orange dots.

"Nick, plot me all movements since we've been here."

"Compliance."

The white dots of the members of the two recon teams turned into lines denoting their paths from the entrance. All the thousands of remaining dots on the heads-up display remained as stationary dots.

"Hmm," said Nickelo once again whispering over the helmet's external speakers. "Gaston's right to be suspicious. The energy levels of the life forms aren't fluctuating either. I calculate that's not possible."

A sense of dread swept over Richard. He unhooked his phase rod from his utility belt, but he didn't activate it. Fenmar stood up, lowered his visor, and raised his war hammer into a ready position. Richard stood as well and clicked the safety off on his M63.

Brrrp!

The sound of an automatic rifle firing echoed through the tunnel.

A dark shadow coming out of a wall caught Richard's attention. "Vampire!" Richard warned using his battle helmet's com-link.

Spinning, Richard pulled the trigger on his M63. At the same time, he thought the command to activate his phase rod in destructive mode. He sensed the gem in his battle suit shimmer as the titanium flakes within the armor energized without him having to give the command.

"Thanks, Nick," Richard thought.

"That's what I'm here for, oh greatest of wizard scouts."

The attacking shadow was a vampire in the void. When it tried to bite into Richard's neck, its fangs slid off the energized titanium of the battle suit. The force of the creature's attack knocked Richard backward. As he fell, he brought the phase rod up between the vampire's legs. It was a human male.

"Arrgh!" groaned the vampire.

Richard's swing was only a half blow since he was off balance, but it was enough. He sensed the phase energy's subatomic explosions taking a toll on the vampire's flesh. Richard felt the demon essence within his phase rod sucking life force from the creature.

The vampire screamed in pain.

Suddenly, the vampire pushed out with his arms and knocked Richard away. Before Richard could renew his attack, two arms wrapped around him from behind. A set of fangs tried to bite into the back of his neck. Once again, the energized titanium kept the attacker at bay. The vampire behind him was in the void as well.

A bearded head and another set of arms popped out of the stone floor in front of Richard as a third vampire grabbed for his legs.

"There's more coming," said Nickelo. *"You best do something, soldier, or you're going to be one dead wizard scout."*

Richard kicked at the vampire coming out of the stone floor. He heard a crunch as the creallium in his boot crushed the vampire's nose. The vampire groaned, but no sooner had Richard's foot moved away than he sensed the creature's nose begin to heal.

"Your phase rod's your only effective weapon," said Nickelo. *"Use it."*

With his arms pinned, Richard couldn't swing his phase rod. However, he was able to twist his hand back enough to bring the rod's tip into contact with the knee of the vampire holding him from behind. A feeling of immense hunger accompanied the vampire's scream as the phase rod sucked life force out of the creature. The vampire released its grip and jumped back to escape the demon essence in the rod.

The vampire coming through the floor was almost halfway out. Richard swung the phase rod at its head. The monster's skull cracked as brain matter splattered into the air. Richard sensed the wound trying to heal, but the demon essence in his phase rod hungrily continued to suck life force out of the vampire as fast as the vampire could heal itself.

"You're taking too long," Nickelo mentally yelled.

More vampires were coming out of the walls and floor. Richard noticed Fenmar swinging his war hammer in wide arcs as he sought to keep a dozen of the monsters at bay. The bodies of two vampires, a dwarf and a human, lay at the general's feet. Richard sensed no sign of life in them.

"Are they really dead?" Richard asked his battle computer. *"How'd he kill them?"*

"They're vampires," replied Nickelo. *"Technically speaking, they were already dead. However, the dwarf destroyed what was keeping the vampires in their half-life state. He hit them on the left side of their chest with his hammer. Its magic destroyed the life force in the vampire's heart. I calculate that's their weak point."*

The vampire to Richard's front had just cleared the floor. Wasting no time on questions, Richard slammed his phase rod into the undead monster's left side. Between the subatomic explosions of the phase energy and the loss of life force to the demon essence, the vampire didn't stand a chance. Richard sensed its heart explode inside its chest. The vampire didn't even have time to scream. It fell unmoving to the stone floor.

Spinning on his heels, Richard thrust out with his phase rod and caught the vampire behind him on the left side of its chest. That vampire crumpled to the floor as well.

A score of vampires were in the room by this time. Richard let his useless M63 hang by its shoulder strap. With his right hand, he grabbed for the starburst signaling grenade at his waist. With a single move, Richard pulled the pin and threw the grenade into the center of the room. With no time to warn the dwarf, Richard bulled his way past two vampires and tackled Fenmar to the floor. He covered the dwarf's eyes with his right hand.

"Nick," Richard said in command voice, *"tell the other battle computers the vampire's hearts are their weak spots. Tell them to go for the hearts."*

"Compliance."

Boom!

Richard got his visor switched to its darkest filter just before the starburst grenade went off. The device wasn't so much a grenade as it was a signaling tool. The bright light of its explosion was strong enough to be seen from a hundred kilometers overhead.

Switching back to his normal night-vision filter, Richard jumped to his feet. Most of the vampires were staggering around with their hands over their eyes.

"Hurry," said Nickelo. *"Their self-heal is already starting to repair the damage to their eyes."*

Without taking time to reply, Richard began to methodically swing his phase rod at the left side of any vampire within reach. Four went down before they knew what had hit them. A fifth tried to parry Richard's blow with a sword, but Richard powered his way through with the aid of his battle suit's assistors. The phase rod crushed the left side of the vampire's chest.

A glance to his right showed Fenmar trading blows with a female dwarf dressed in gold-trimmed armor. The vampire carried a battle-axe with a blue gem in the handle. Whenever the female's battle-axe struck Fenmar's war hammer, the old general was forced to give way.

"Good axe," said Nickelo. *"It's definitely got Fenmar's war hammer outclassed. I think it's just a matter of time before he's killed."*

A glance at Richard's heads-up display told the story of the ongoing battle. Farther up the tunnel, the two recon teams were surrounded on both sides by over a hundred life forms. Richard could only assume they were vampires. Hundreds more were heading their way. The decoy life forms, which he'd previously been picking up with his passive scan were no more.

"It was probably a decoy spell of some kind," said Nickelo. *"You'll notice there aren't as many vampires attacking the dwarf and you. I think if you look at the area outside the entrance to this tunnel, you'll see why."*

Richard did look. At least a thousand life forms were gathered outside the entrance. He knew there'd be no escape in that direction. Thankfully, only the one vampire fighting Fenmar remained in the room where they were. Richard picked up a couple score more heading down the tunnel in their direction. At least another score was in the void and coming through the walls. The situation looked hopeless.

First things first, Richard thought. *I need to concentrate on living for the next five seconds. If I last that long, then I'll figure out how to live for another five.*

"That's the marine spirit," said Nickelo. *"Never give up."*

Since he had a moment's respite before the next wave hit, Richard turned toward the battle between Fenmar and the female dwarf. She had backed the general into a corner. With a hard swing of her battle-axe, the vampire knocked Fenmar's war hammer out of his hands.

The vampire drew her axe back for the kill. Before she could swing, Richard wrapped the battle-axe with Power and yanked hard with his telekinesis. The vampire was caught off guard. The battle-axe was jerked out of her grasp and into Richard's waiting right hand.

The vampire turned and snarled.

General Fenmar dived for the ground and came up swinging his war hammer. With a mighty stroke, the old dwarf caved in the left side of the female vampire's armor. Richard sensed her heart crumple. Suddenly, she was no longer in the void. On a hunch, Richard wrapped the vampire's heart with Power and twisted. The vampire screamed and fell to the floor. Richard twisted the heart some more. He felt something in the heart trying to repair the damage.

"She's a fighter," said Nickelo.

A fighter she might be, but Richard knew her weakness now. He sensed a powerful source of energy surrounding a mass of bacteria in her heart. Richard imagined how the dwarf's heart would be without the bacteria and compared that with how the heart was now. He wrapped the difference with Power from his healing reserve and pulled half of the Power into himself.

A sudden hunger overtook Richard. He smelled the warm blood pumping through Fenmar's veins. Richard had an overpowering desire to rip the general's throat out and feast on the dwarf's blood. Before he could take a step in Fenmar's direction, his healing power destroyed the mass of bacteria in the vampire's heart. A moment later, Richard's healing Power brought his body back to baseline. The desire to kill Fenmar was gone.

When Richard returned to normal, he saw General Fenmar on his knees beside the female vampire. Richard sensed no signs of life in her. With the destruction of the bacteria mass in her heart, she was finally and truly dead.

"Actually," said Nickelo, *"it was a viral mass, not bacteria. There's a difference, you know."*

"Oh, my queen, my queen," wailed General Fenmar. "What have I done? How can I face your daughter knowing I killed you?"

Richard ran to the dwarf and jerked him to his feet. "You can't tell Emerald anything if she's dead. Besides, you didn't kill this one. Neither did I. She died a hundred and fifty years ago. We just put her out of her misery."

Shoving the vampire's battle-axe into Fenmar's free hand, Richard yelled, "Now, let's go! We've got to get to the others."

With that, Richard turned and ran toward the firing he'd heard echoing down the tunnel. The others were obviously in a desperate firefight. He had to save them.

CHAPTER 53

When the door opened, Gaston saw a dark form diving for Telsa's throat. He knew immediately what it was.

"Vampire!" he shouted.

Before he could get to Telsa's side, the vampire bowled the little wizard scout over. She came out of the tangle of limbs on top with her sword sticking out the back of the vampire's neck. The creature continued snapping at Telsa, but with a twist of her sword, she decapitated the undead monster's head.

That was all Gaston had time to see before a mass of dark forms began clambering through the previously hidden door and out of the very walls of the tunnel. With a thought, he energized the titanium in his battle suit as he activated his phase rod in destructive mode. An overpowering sense of hunger permeated the area from the demon essence in the phase rod. Gaston swung wildly at a dark form to his front.

The vampire screamed as the phase rod sucked life force out of its body. The creature fell back, but another vampire took its place.

Gaston's passive scan indicated most of the vampires were in the void. He fired a round from his Deloris blaster. The blaster's phase round tore through the head of one of the vampires. It fell backward, spraying blood into the air. Almost immediately, the vampire was back on its feet. Gaston noticed the gaping hole in the monster's forehead begin to close over.

"The heart," said Wanda in their shared space. *"Your brother's battle computer says the heart is their weak spot."*

Gaston adjusted his aim and put a phase round into the left side of the vampire's chest. It went down. This time it didn't get back up.

Gaston yelled to the others. "Go for their hearts! Go for their hearts!"

"Wanda," Gaston said. *"A little help would be nice."*

Gaston felt the arm of his battle suit holding the Deloris blaster jerk left and right while firing phase rounds as it moved. Each time the blaster fired, a vampire went down with a hole through its heart.

"Reload," said Wanda.

Gaston thrust his phase rod into the left side of a human vampire's chest. As the demon essence sucked life force out of the vampire, the phase energy's subatomic explosions tore the heart to shreds.

Wrapping the magazine of his Deloris blaster with Power, Gaston extracted the empty magazine with his telekinesis as he swung his phase rod at another vampire. Once the magazine was out, he used telekinesis to pull a fresh magazine out of his ammo pouch and insert it into the butt of his blaster.

"Go, Margery."

No sooner had Gaston thought the words than the right arm of his battle suit began moving and firing again. The phase rounds, combined with the phase rods and magic weapons of the others, blunted the initial charge of the vampires. However, for every vampire his team destroyed, two more of the bloodsuckers took their place.

A double team of vampires came at Gaston from the left. He caught one in the side with his phase rod. The second vampire was a well-muscled dwarf wielding a double-handed war hammer. Gaston tried to dodge but knew he was going to be a hair too late.

A phase rod swept in front of his face and knocked the war hammer aside. The body of a black-suited wizard scout slammed into the vampire. Both the vampire and the wizard scout fell to the ground. As Gaston watched, the wizard scout stabbed a magic dagger into the vampire's heart. The wizard scout jumped up and headed for another target. The wizard scout was his mother, Janice Deluth.

"Empty," said Wanda.

Using the same technique as before, Gaston switched out his Deloris blaster's magazine for a fresh one with his telekinesis. He destroyed two more vampires with his phase rod before the reload was complete.

"That's the last magazine," Gaston told his battle computer. *"Make it count."*

"Compliance," replied Wanda as the phase pistol began barking once more.

Gaston took a moment to check his heads-up display. The white dots of everyone on the two recon teams still shone brightly. No one had been killed yet. He had no doubt they'd been lucky so far. The mass of red, yellow, and orange dots converging on their small group made him doubt their luck would continue much longer.

A glance at two white dots near the entrance gave proof Fenmar and Shepard were still alive as well. Unfortunately, what he saw beyond them added to the seriousness of the situation. Fully a thousand dots were massed outside the secret entrance. There'd be no escape in that direction.

"Empty," said Margery. *"I'm returning control of your battle suit's arm to you."*

Gaston kept fighting, but the image of his son flashed in his mind. *Thank the Creator he's safe on the shuttle. My only regret is that I never got a chance to tell him I was his father.*

Wanda intruded upon his thoughts. *"I've got a message from your brother's battle computer. Wizard Scout Shepard says to use telekinesis to rip the vampire's hearts apart. He says there's something inside their hearts keeping them alive. You have to get it out of their bodies. He says using telekinesis might destroy the vampires faster than using swords and phase rods alone."*

Gaston noticed several vampires shifting out of the void. He picked out one of the vampires who was no longer in the void and reached inside its chest with his telekinesis. The vampire wasn't wearing armor. Gaston jerked hard enough to cause the heart to explode out of the monster's chest. The heart was a putrid black. It had a pulsating mass of goo near its center.

Before Gaston could do anything else, he heard the twang of a bow. A magic arrow passed over his shoulder. The arrow struck the heart dead center. The pulsating mass on the heart exploded in a flash of light. The vampire fell and moved no more.

"Tear out their hearts," Gaston ordered. "Rip them out of their chests. Emerald and Chancee, destroy the hearts with your magic weapons."

Six lines of Power reached out and burrowed deep into the chests of vampires who weren't in the void. Gaston sent out a line of his own Power and split it into two separate lines the way his father had taught him. Eight hearts were jerked out of vampire chests and suspended in the air by telekinesis. Phase rods and magic swords struck home. Eight hearts burst into flames.

At the destruction of eight of their companions, most of the vampires began shifting back into the void. However, the vampires weren't fast enough. Eight more hearts were jerked out and destroyed.

"Enough!" came a deep shout which wasn't a true voice. "Can you not destroy even a few pathetic wizard scouts? Pull back. I, Lord Cancontus, will show you how it's done."

The words were accompanied by a great sense of evil. The sense of evil reminded Gaston of the demon essence in his phase rod, only it was something different. He sensed Power building in the very atmosphere around him. The Power was similar to the Circle Emerald had created at Cantonsburg during the battle on the wall.

Wanda spoke the words Gaston felt. *"I've got a very bad feeling about this."*

CHAPTER 54

As Cancontus watched his vampire minion's battle with the wizard scouts, he grew increasingly annoyed the longer the battle took. When the wizard scouts began ripping the hearts out of his servants, he started having serious doubts about the ability of his servants to succeed. Logic told him the thousands of surviving vampires should overwhelm the paltry group of wizard scouts and their companions, but his doubts remained.

The wizard scouts should have been dead already. The Master's variable escaped my last trap. He may escape this one as well. Perhaps I should have used the Circle differently during the battle with the dolgars. I used the Circle to trap the Master's variable inside the valley. By doing so, I allowed him to maintain his free will. That was a mistake.

Lord Cancontus spun on his heel and struck the wall of the cavern in which he waited. Pieces of shattered stone fell to the floor. He stretched out the wings of his Crosioian avatar until they touched opposite sides of the small room.

He won't escape this time. Zentra's plan is to use the vampires to kill the Master's variable and the other wizard scouts. He's a fool, and I'm not. What if I can use the Circle to make the Master's variable my willing slave? Using the power of the Circle, I could make them all my slaves. Once captured, even if the Master's variable tried to resist me, I could torture his companions in front of his eyes. He would be forced to submit. He would be forced to obey. Once he is under my control, I could compel him to open the gate to the demonic plane. The demon armies would be mine to command.

Cancontus laughed. He envisioned his three brothers kneeling down before him as they quaked in fear at his presence. He would be the new Master. He would rule the three galaxies. He only needed to capture the Master's variable and keep him for himself.

Reaching out with a line of Power, Cancontus sought out the three spheres surrounding the Dragars' temple. He took great care to avoid touching them directly with his Power. Even his current avatar was susceptible to their insidious enthrall spell.

The wizard scouts won't stand a chance. They'll all submit to my will.

Using the information he'd obtained from the dwarf king, Cancontus formed a Circle and connected a link to the three spheres. He stretched the Circle out and attached a link to the Master's variable, then extended the Circle to the variable's friends. Cancontus felt them all trying to resist, but they could not. The spheres' enthrall spell was too much for them. The power of the Circle increased the strength of the spheres' spell. Cancontus was confident none of the wizard scouts would be able to resist the peace the spheres offered.

While carefully monitoring the Circle's links, Cancontus made sure his keystone link remained far from the Master's variable.

This time I'm ready. I won't allow him to use the Dalinfaust's essence against me. This time the Master's variable will be mine. This time the variable will not escape.

CHAPTER 55

The seventh day on the *Defiant* found a grim lot sitting around the galley table. They'd been at it nearly an hour. Jeena could tell Sergeant Ron was beginning to lose his patience. Like most humans, he appeared to hate hearing the same arguments repeated over and over.

Come to think of it, so do I, Jeena thought.

"I know Jeehana's got a foolproof way to get the bottles back to our wizard scouts," said Sergeant Ron. "The problem is, how do we get Stella and her onboard the space station without getting the Defiant blown to smithereens?"

Jeena winced internally at the use of her friend name by the Defiant's captain. *None of them can pronounce my formal name. That's why I insisted they use my friend name instead. I've just got to put up with it.*

Jeena turned to face Sergeant Ron. "Even if we're able to get onboard the space station there's no guarantee we'll be able to get the DNA gas."

"You're too modest," said Terrie. "I've watched the videos of your holo-square simulations. You're good."

The redheaded woman sitting next to Terrie punched him on the arm.

"Hey! What was that for?" asked Terrie. "I was just stating a fact."

"Then state it without your tongue hanging out," said Angela. "I told you before, I'm the only one you should be looking at that way."

Terrie's face turned pink. "You are, Angela. Trust me."

"Oh, I trust you, sweetheart," said Angela. "But rest assured, I'm keeping a close eye on you as long as this temptress is onboard the Defiant." Turning to Jeena, Angela said, "No offense, Jeehana."

"Uh…, none taken," Jeena replied.

The idea of the young woman thinking she was after her husband was actually a little amusing. True, of all the human males on the starship, Jeena avoided Terrie the least. What little aura she could detect from the wizard scout was emotion free. While she knew he was an emotional creature just like all humans, he was able to keep his emotions under tight control. Actually, she had to admit the auras of all the humans she'd encountered in the physical dimension were kept under control. She had a feeling there'd be a lot less friction between elves and humans on Portalis if the human race there could do the same.

"It's too bad you can't use your staff to teleport onto the space station," said Kester, the youngest of the gnome mages.

"Yes," Jeena agreed. "But as I've said, the staff is preset. I'm confident I can use it to teleport Stella and I back to the Oracle on Portalis. However, that's all it can do unless I misunderstood the directions."

Dren, who was sitting next to Jeena, turned to face her. "No, you understood correctly. The first two uses of the staff are preset. After that, it'll still teleport you to the Oracle, but the time differential part of the staff will no longer work."

Sergeant Hendricks was sitting at the end of the table next to Sergeant Ron. He whispered something in the ear of the Defiant's captain. When Dren finished speaking, Sergeant Hendricks stood up.

"I'm just an armorer, so I don't profess to know a lot about teleportation or any of that mumbo-jumbo. However, as I was telling Sergeant Ron, what we need is something that can travel to other dimensions like Rick's spirit-horse."

"Unfortunately," said Terrie, "Rick's not here. Gaston was depending on his brother and that spirit-horse of his to get our team on and off the space station. Normal teleports won't work. Otherwise, Gaston could've requested a teleport from one of the teleporters on Velos."

A lot of what the people around her had discussed over the past hour went over Jeena's head, but a teleport was something she understood. Because she was a priestess, she couldn't do them herself, except for the limited use of the staff, of course. However, she did understand the concept well enough. Teleportation was an advanced mage spell. Since she had a couple of friends at the mage academy in Silverton who kept her up to date on mage magic, she was familiar with their teleportation spells.

"I've been wondering about that," Jeena said. "Keka had an advanced teleporter on Storage. I was wondering why we were wasting our time going to the space station in the Defiant? So tell me, couldn't we have just teleported there?"

Jeena noticed Dren shake her head.

"Not possible, Jeehana. The location of the space station is near an anomaly called a black hole. The hole is so powerful it even sucks light into it. Any teleport beams would be taken in as well. Only a starship with a good hyper-drive can get to or from the space station. Trying to do a normal teleport there would be certain death."

Jeena thought she detected a flaw in Dren's answer. "I'll be using my staff to teleport off the space station and back to Portalis. What's to prevent Stella and me from being sucked into this 'black hole' of yours?"

A raspy voice spoke up. "I can answer that, High Priestess."

The owner of the voice was the dragon, Bright Wing. She was curled up on top of one of the galley's cupboards.

Jeena gave the dragon her best smile. She'd come to like the little reptile. "Then please do. You're as wise as you are beautiful."

The dragon gave a toothy grin. "Now there's someone who knows her manners. The rest of you should take notes."

"This isn't the time for good manners," said Sergeant Ron sounding grumpier than usual. "If you've got something to say, say it. The longer the Defiant stays in Crosioian space, the more likely it is that one of their recon ships will spot us."

"Very well, Captain," said Bright Wing sounding as if she wasn't at all affronted by Sergeant Ron's words. "I'm a dragon. I'm very good at sensing flows of Power. Based upon the flows in your staff, Jeehana, I can tell you that your staff will simultaneously shift you into another dimension when it does the teleport. I can sense the black hole. It connects this dimension with another. However, it doesn't extend into the magical dimension. That's why you can safely teleport to Portalis. By the way, that's also how Rick's spirit-horse and his dolgars travel. They combine dimensional shifting with teleportation. We dragons can do the same. That's how we can travel long distances."

Sergeant Ron turned and faced the dragon. "Then why haven't you said something before now instead of letting us flap our gums for the past hour. If you can do what you're saying, then you can get Stella and Jeehana onboard."

"Negative," said Margery over the galley's intercom. "Bright Wing's too young. She's barely able to teleport herself. She can only travel short distances. If we got close enough to the space station for her to teleport, we'd be detected."

The battle computer, Danny, spoke next. "That's why our original plan needed Rick's spirit-horse. The older the spirit-horse or dolgar, the farther they can dimensional shift and teleport. It's unfortunate Bright Wing isn't older. In a few thousand years, I calculate she could do as you ask. However, I also calculate remaining in our current position and waiting four thousand years or so for her to sufficiently age is out of the question."

"You calculated that all by your lonesome?" asked Sergeant Ron putting a lot of sarcasm into the question. "I ain't got no nanosecond brain and I could've told—"

The ceaseless back and forth discussion finally took its toll on Jeena. Something snapped inside her. She slammed her fist down on the table.

Bang! "Enough!" Jeena said. Although she'd tried hard all her life to control her temper, she sometimes failed. This was one of those times. "I didn't come through time and space to listen to endless arguing. I need solutions."

Ignoring the shocked looks of everyone at the table, Jeena pointed to Bright Wing. The dragon was still curled up on the cupboard. "If you were older, could you or could you not teleport Stella and I from our current location to the space station?"

Bright Wing didn't answer right away. She stood and jumped lightly to the center of the table. Once there, she looked directly into Jeena's eyes. "Yes I could, but as Danny said, only an ancient dragon could do what you require. I won't have sufficient abilities for thousands of years. I'm sorry, High Priestess. I'm still what the humans would call a pre-teen."

"How old would you need to be?" Jeena asked. "How much would you have to age?"

The dragon took on an expression as if wondering whether Jeena was serious or not. Finally, Bright Wing answered. "At least another 3,500 years, Jeehana."

Sergeant Ron stood up. "I don't see what this—"

Jeena stood up and whirled to face Comstar, her temper in full swing. She was the high priestess of the Lady of the Tree. She was in charge now, and wasn't about to let anyone keep her quiet. "Can you perform a polymorph spell?" Jeena asked her fellow elf.

The gray-haired elf looked back at Jeena. His eyes took on an expression of understanding.

Jeena took that as a good sign until the male elf shook his head.

"No, Jeehana. I see where you're headed, but I can't. Neither can any of the gnome mages. We were slaves. The Dragars only allowed us to memorize spells we needed in order to charge their weapons. What few spell books we have only contain offensive spells such as fireballs and lightning bolts. Even if we had the skill, we don't have a polymorph spell in our books. We can't do what you ask."

"Could you if you had the spell?" Jeena asked.

"Will you wait one darn minute," said Sergeant Ron. "What are you two talking about? I'm the captain of this ship, you know? It'd be nice to at least have a clue what's going on."

Jeena's temper had calmed somewhat. It had always been thus; quick to come and quick to depart. She turned to face the Defiant's captain. "Two years ago, a polymorph spell was cast on me. It turned me into an old woman. It wasn't a low-level spell, which only superficially made me look like an old woman. I actually became an old hag; weak muscles, rotted teeth, the works. Brachia saw me. He can tell you."

"I remember," said Brachia while making a 'yuk' look with his face. "It was a good spell. You were very ugly."

Comstar turned to the captain. "I think Jeehana hopes to cast such a spell on Bright Wing. It's an advanced mage spell. When I say advanced, I mean it's so complex only the most powerful of mages can hope to control the flows of magic energy required to make the spell work. The magic would consume a lesser mage." Glancing back at Jeena, Comstar added, "But we don't have the spell in our spell books. No one here can do as you ask."

Jeena nodded her head as if agreeing with Comstar. However, she was far from defeated. She began thinking frantically. A tingle at the back of her mind told her she was on the right track. From the tingle, she knew the Lady approved.

"I'm a high priestess. As such, I'm skilled in the ways of the flows of magic. I also have the silver hair and eyes of my ancestor, the High Priestess Shandristiathoraxen, so I'm doubly blessed. I sense your Power reserve, Comstar. It's quite large. Now tell me, are you skilled enough to cast the spell if you had it? I'm not a mage. I can't do it myself, but I could help you control the flows of magic if necessary.

The male elf looked down at the table. He seemed lost in a memory of times past. It was several seconds before he looked back up.

No one in the room spoke. They barely breathed.

"I was once blessed by the Creator to be considered one of the most skilled mages on my home world. Mages of advanced levels came to me for training. I had a good life with my mate and my children. Then the Dragars came with their flying ships. We fought. We killed many, but in the end, my people were defeated. My mate and children were…killed. I was spared and taken as a slave to serve the Dragars on one of their destroyers." Comstar paused before locking eyes with Jeena. "Could I cast such a spell? Yes, but as I told you, I don't have the spell."

Jeena wasn't about to let a minor problem like that stop her. She turned to the human girl sitting next to her. "Your Keka retrieved us through time from Portalis to Storage. Could he do the same for a spell book?"

Dren shook her head. "It doesn't work that way, Jeehana. *'The One'* gave Keka the exact time and coordinates. Keka was able to teleport us because he knew we'd be standing on the teleport platform at the Oracle's, and he knew exactly when we'd be standing there. Even if we were still there, the Oracle's library doesn't have spell books. I looked several times over the past three years. I didn't find any."

Jeena smiled. The tingling at the back of her mind increased. She was definitely on the right track. "That's because you didn't look in the right library, Dren. The library in Silverton has copies of every known spell. I'm confident the spell we need is there."

"That doesn't do us any good," protested Dren. "Keka doesn't have those coordinates. The teleporter in our lab on Storage is only attuned to the teleport pad in our lab at the Oracle's. The teleporter I built on Storage was just an experiment. I never thought it would need to go to other places. Someone would have to place the spell on the Oracle's teleport pad at the right time. Who would do that?"

Jeena smiled even more. She knew who. "I will."

"What?" said more than one person in the room.

"I'll do it when I get back," Jeena explained. "One year to the day after Keka teleported us from your lab at the Oracle's, I'll place a copy of the spell we need on the pad."

"Well, I don't kn—" started Dren.

"Captain Ron," Jeena said determined not to let even Dren get her discouraged. "Is the Defiant in a position where Keka could teleport something to us if he used one of the normal teleporters on Storage? Or are we too close to the black hole?"

"Uh, no…, err.., I mean yes, he could teleport something to us," said Captain Ron. "And no, we're not too close. We're still one hyper-jump from the space station. I stopped the Defiant when the dimensional fold was still two light-seconds away. I wasn't going to make the jump until we knew for sure what we were doing."

"That's good," Jeena said. Turning back to Dren, Jeena gave her orders. "Contact Keka. Tell him what to do. Give him our location." Looking back at Sergeant Ron, Jeena said, "I'm assuming the Defiant will need to remain stationary. Make it so." Jeena made a sweep of the room.

All eyes were on her.

"The time for talk is over," Jeena said. "We leave in an hour."

When no one moved, Jeena slammed the butt of the Staff of the Lady of the Tree onto the metal deck.

The entire ship shuddered.

"Well?" Jeena said. "Get moving."

Everyone moved; even Sergeant Ron.

CHAPTER 56

Even before the line of Power touched Richard, he recognized it for what it was. The line was part of a Circle. The Circle wasn't the massive affair Emerald had formed during the battle at Cantonsburg. The links of this Circle only touched the members of the recon teams along with Fenmar and him. The Circle did include four others. Richard recognized the frequencies of three of the others. They were the green, orange, and purple spheres he'd encountered on the mining planet a few months earlier.

But they're dead, was all he had time to think before he recognized the frequency of the final member of the Circle. The frequency was that of the demon he'd fought in the valley with the dolgars. The sense of hate and evil was unmistakable.

Richard sought out the keystone link from the Circle to the demon. He found it, but it was too far away. He'd broken the Circle during his previous battle with the demon by touching its keystone link with the demon essence in his phase rod. He saw no way he could do that now.

Only a major demon can destroy the link of a major demon, Richard thought. *This link's too far away. I can't reach it.*

Richard decided to open himself up to the Power of the Circle. His desire for Power had allowed him to take over Emerald's Circle on the walls of Cantonsburg.

Maybe I can use the demon's own Circle to steal his Power, Richard thought. *I'll have to force myself to control the Power this time. I can't let it overwhelm me.*

With a thought, Richard released a line of Power to the link of the Circle. Unfortunately, things didn't work out like he'd hoped. Before he could start pulling Power into himself, he was overcome with a sense of warmth and peace. A vision of three spheres of swirling gas; green, orange, and purple filled his mind. Richard dropped his line of Power as all worldly cares left him. This was how things were supposed to be. Everything was perfect. He was at peace.

A part of Richard's mind heard shouting. He recognized the voice as that of his battle computer. Richard paid the voice no mind. He was at peace. For once in his life, he was totally happy.

Richard's body changed. All aches disappeared. His sense of tiredness and hunger went away. The Circle supplied his every need. He needed nothing but the Circle. He hungered for nothing. He thirsted for nothing. All was well.

But all was not well. Power from the reserve his body used to self-heal battled to bring his body back to baseline. Since he'd been a little tired and hungry when his DNA baseline had been taken, his baseline was set at a little tired and hungry. While the enthrall spell of the spheres tried to remove any tiredness or hunger, his self-heal dutifully brought the feelings back. The Power of the Circle immediately sought to bring his body back to the Nirvana which was the peace of the spheres. Once again, the Power from his self-healing reserve overrode the perfection of the spheres. The feeling of hunger and tiredness again swept over him driving the peace away. The Power of the Circle and that of his self-heal struggled for dominance. How long the battle would have lasted, Richard didn't know. Fortunately, something changed.

"Who are you?" said a thought in Richard's mind. *"We feel as if we know you. Or perhaps we feel as if we will know you."*

Richard recognized the mental voice. It wasn't the demon Cancontus. It was the voice of the green sphere.

The struggle between Richard's self-heal and the Circle continued, but during a lull when the hunger and tiredness were most prevalent, he had a moment of clarity. He took that moment to answer the green sphere.

"I'm a dragon-friend," Richard told the green sphere.

"Who declared you such?" asked the green sphere.

"You did," Richard replied. *"We've met before; in the future.*

You tasked me with a mission. You made me promise. I'm here to fulfill that promise."

"What promise was that?" asked the green sphere.

Richard felt the Power of the Circle starting to gain control over him again. With no time for words, he told the story of their last meeting using dragon-speak. He sent the green, orange, and purple spheres his emotions of their last meeting. He sent them the images of the battle between the *Defiant* and the Dragars' black starships. He sent them the memories of how they'd helped him escape, and how they'd made him promise to stop the slaughter of the unborn dragons. He sent them everything he remembered.

Just as the Circle was on the verge of taking control of his mind, the green sphere replied. *"Yes, we understand. We haven't yet met in the future, but that time will soon be here. Come. Come with us."*

Given the choice of allowing the demon's Circle to take over his mind or of following the three spheres, Richard chose the spheres.

The minds of the three spheres combined with Richard's. He immediately knew what they knew. He felt what they felt. For too many years, he'd been forced to obey the Dragars. For too many years, he'd been forced to listen to the screams of the unborn dragons being slaughtered while helpless to do anything about it.

Merged as he was with the three spheres, Richard sensed the Dragars' pyramid under the dome. The pyramid was filled with the sacrificed dragons' emotional energy.

Richard remembered being at the temple before. Once again, he was inside the dome. He saw the thousands of slaves standing around the worktables. They were touching hoses filled with the red gas created from the sacrificed dragons to containers made of titanium. The containers were the equivalent of the Empire's isotopic batteries. The red gas was the refined emotional energy and magic of the sacrificed dragons.

Hundreds of four-armed Thargs were walking between the tables, whipping the slaves. As Richard watched, they beat one of the slaves for no apparent reason other than they seemed to enjoy hearing the screams.

Richard sensed the location of the three spheres. They were arranged in a triangular formation around the pyramid. Using the knowledge of the spheres, he knew they would stay in the same location until called upon to create a time-gate for the Dragars' black starships. From the knowledge of their shared minds, he knew they were called to do so often. Even now, dozens of black starships of all sizes were at berths around the spaceport waiting for their turn at a time-gate. A large energy source was near one of the destroyers. A dozen Thargs were using an alien-looking forklift to place a large, blue object in a metal container. Richard had never seen the dwarves' Mountain's Heart before, but instinctively knew he was looking at the blue gem they'd been seeking.

It isn't even in the tunnels, Richard thought. *We walked into a trap for nothing.* Switching to his shared space, Richard called out. *"Nick! Nick! Are you there?"*

He heard no reply. For some reason, his battle computer wasn't connected to him.

"It's the Power of the Circle," said the green sphere. *"Cancontus is using our natural defensive mechanism to enthrall your companions. How is it that you're able to resist our peace?"*

Richard knew time was short, yet in a strange way, he sensed he had an eternity of time. The three spheres were actually a special type of dragon. The dragon, of which he was now a part, existed in a time-bubble. From what Richard could tell, their entire conversation was taking less time than it took to blink an eye. On the other hand, it was taking all the time between the here and now, and the time when he would encounter the green sphere a hundred thousand years in the future.

"How can I resist your peace?" Richard said repeating the sphere's question. *"I guess you can thank my brother for it. Because of him, I missed a meal and lost sleep at a bad time. My body now considers that normal. It's hard to be at peace when you're tired and hungry."*

"We suppose," replied the green sphere. *"Now we must ask how you'll save our unborn brethren? The Dragars are going to take the Mountain's Heart off planet. Even if you destroy their temple here, they'll use the blue gem to build another temple on another world. They'll continue sacrificing the innocents at their new temple."*

Richard had many questions, but he didn't need to ask. His mind was one with the three spheres. He was one with the dragon.

He knew the black destroyer would leave as soon as the Mountain's Heart was loaded. He also knew the three spheres would be forced to create their time-gate to take the Dragars' starships into the future in the physical dimension. The three spheres couldn't resist. The energy of the sacrificed dragons stored in the pyramid was under the control of the Dragars. Consequently, the three spheres were under the Dragars' control as well.

"We're sorry," said the green sphere. *"We see your thoughts. You believe you will destroy us. You will not. You will only set us free."*

"I already destroyed you," Richard replied continuing to use dragon-speak. *"I saw your spheres come together. I watched your destruction."*

"Yes, time can be confusing," agreed the green sphere. *"In the end, it all turns out for the good. We see the plan of the Oracle in your mind. We believe it will work. It must work. You must insert the fifteen bottles of DNA gas into the Dragars' temple."*

A vision of the pyramid inside the dome appeared in Richard's mind. He saw a small opening near the tip.

"That's where they must go," said the green sphere. *"The concentrated DNA gas will overload the emotional and magic energy stored in the temple. When that occurs, the Dragars will lose control over us. Then we'll do what must be done. Your mind has shown us the way. We know how we can be free."*

"How?" Richard asked.

The green sphere only answered, *"You'll see when the time comes."*

Richard hated it when he had to drag answers out of someone. He decided not to try. *"Fine. What about the blue gem? How do I destroy it?"*

Another vision came to Richard. This time it was an image of the Mountain's Heart. He saw a crack in the gem. He saw the fourteen bottles of DNA gas being opened near the crack.

"Anything else I need to know?" Richard asked curtly. He had a feeling his time was running short.

A final vision came. This time it was of a chamber deep below the Dragars' temple. Richard sensed evil coming from the underground room. He'd encountered the evil before. It was the demon, Zenthra. Richard knew the demon possessed the

Crosioian's master computer. He visualized the equipment in the room. The equipment was magic, yet it was also a computer. The Dragars' computer was connected to the Crosioian's master computer in the future.

Richard wished his battle computer was with him to help make sense of things, but he wasn't. He allowed more information from the spheres to enter his mind. He saw the architecture of the hidden computer room. It was encased in creallium. Nothing could go in or out of the room unless Zenthra allowed it.

"Zenthra thinks he's invulnerable," said the green sphere.

Richard wondered if the demon might be right. *"Zenthra's a major demon. So's Cancontus. How can I hope to defeat them?"*

"That is for you to decide, wizard scout," replied the green sphere. *"We cannot help as long as the DNA gas in the temple is under the Dragars' control. Even so, don't lose hope. Zenthra and Cancontus are in many places at once. The parts of them that are located here are relatively weak. They've spread themselves too thin. We see from your memories that you destroyed one of their brother's avatar. Efrestra was more powerful than either Zenthra or Cancontus. You can succeed here as well. We have faith in you, wizard scout."*

"I need my friends," Richard said. *"Release them from your spell."*

"We cannot. Zenthra controls the Dragars, and the Dragars control us. You must release your friends yourself."

Richard thought for what seemed like a long time. Finally, he had an idea. *"Take me back,"* he ordered.

Suddenly his mind was back in the tunnel. He sensed the Power of Cancontus's Circle forcing the spheres' enthrall spell on his friends. Richard took his feeling of hunger and tiredness and inserted them into the Circle.

Then he waited. He hoped he wouldn't have to wait long.

CHAPTER 57

As it turned out, Stella and Jeena didn't leave in an hour. A large chest was teleported into the cargo bay a half hour after their meeting broke up. Inside was not just the spell they required, but seven complete sets of spell books. The magic tomes contained both basic and advanced mage spells. Also included in the chest was a complete set of spell books for a priest along with two priest wands.

After a cursory glance at the polymorph spell, Comstar announced he needed at least six hours to memorize and practice the complicated spell. Consequently, the decision was made for Stella and Jeena to spend the remainder of the afternoon practicing in the holo-square.

After a particularly grueling session, Terrie finally called a halt to their training. When the holographic image of the space station's interior disappeared, Jeena sought out the human wizard scout.

"Why'd you stop us? I think we could've completed the mission successfully this time.

Laughing, Terrie held up his hands in a stopping motion. "Hey, don't kill the messenger. Sergeant Ron said Comstar's ready. They're on their way down now." With a wink, Terrie added, "Besides, Margery, Danny, and I also think you could've gotten away with the bottles. I guess you could say the two of you are going to take your final exam in the next ten minutes."

Jeena did her best not to smile. For a human male, she guessed Terrie wasn't completely horrible. In fact, all of the human males onboard the *Defiant* were starting to grow on her; a little. Although years of prejudice were hard to overcome, she was trying her best. She found it helped to imagine the men with pointed ears.

"Not just the two of them," said Bright Wing who was just coming out of the engine room. "I go too."

Jeena smiled. "Yes, you are. In fact, the entire mission depends on you. Are you sure you want to go through with it? Even if we successfully get the bottles of DNA gas, you'll still have to get back to the *Defiant* on your own."

The silver dragon grinned. "I'll use a dimensional shift and teleport. I'll be fine."

Sergeant Ron had just come down the stairs. He gave Bright Wing some bad news. "I'm afraid it's not going to be that simple. Comstar says with his limited experience with this version of the spell, he has to keep the level of magic energy to a minimum. According to him, that means you'll only be in the form of an ancient dragon for about fifteen minutes. After that, you'll shift back to your normal form."

"So how will Bright Wing get back?" Jeena asked. She liked the little dragon and wasn't about to let her go on a suicide mission.

"The *Defiant* will have to come get her," replied Sergeant Ron. "Bright Wing can teleport a few thousand meters in her current form. That'll get her outside the space station at the very least."

Charlie was helping Daniel add a fireball wand to the underside of Stella's M12. At Sergeant Ron's words, the Sterilian looked up. "No good. Black hole get her."

Apparently just as concerned about the dragon's welfare, Terrie added his two credits' worth. "Yeah, and the *Defiant* can't go get her at short ranges anyway. The space station would blow us out of existence in less than a minute. Our defensive shields are good, but they wouldn't last long under all that firepower."

Captain Ron snorted. "I wasn't born yesterday. Bright Wing will just have to destroy the space station before they destroy us."

Frowning, Jeena asked, "How?"

"By overloading their reactor," said Comstar who'd just come down to join them. The old elf was holding a thick spell book in his hands. A piece of paper sticking out toward the end of the book appeared to be marking a page.

This time, Jeena was the one shaking her head. "Unacceptable.

It would place her in too much danger. I think as soon as Bright Wing teleports us inside the station, she should immediately teleport back to the *Defiant* while she's still in ancient form. She'll have time before her spell wears off if she hurries."

The dragon reared back on her hind legs until her head was level with Jeena's.

"No! I stay. You need me. My brother can't get back until we get the bottles to him. I'll stay and help fight."

One of the speakers in the cargo bay popped with static electricity before settling down to Margery's voice. "The dragon's right. I calculate your mission will fail if she's not there with you. The shock value of her spells and breath weapons will give you the confusion you need to get the bottles of DNA gas."

"Margery's right," Danny mentally agreed over the metal band Jeena was still wearing on her forehead. *"The truth is, the dragon has a higher probability of surviving the mission than Stella and you. I'd advise worrying about what you're going to do if you run into Crosioian scouts."*

Jeena had been worrying about such an event but wasn't about to admit it to anyone else.

"Well," said Sergeant Ron getting back in the conversation. "If you're going, you best get to it. We've had a couple of Crosioian recon ships pass within two light minutes of us less than an hour ago. Something's got them spooked. We've either got to pay the piper and get on with the mission, or we need to tuck our tails between our legs and head back home. Which is it going to be, High Priestess Jeehanathoraxen?"

The captain's use of her formal name surprised Jeena. "That's the first time you've called me by my title, Sergeant Ron. You pronounced my name perfectly. I'm impressed."

"Yeah, well," said Sergeant Ron, "don't think I'm going to make a habit of it. Your name's definitely a tongue twister. Now, what's it going to be? Do we go, or do we head back home?"

Jeena didn't have to think long before replying. She'd never abandoned a mission in her life.

"We go. We go now."

CHAPTER 58

Even though Gaston knew what was happening, he didn't care. It didn't matter that he was being enthralled by the Circle. It didn't matter that some alien presence was soothing his soul and controlling his emotions. Even though he could feel the demonic evil in the first link of the Circle, it didn't matter. As far as he was concerned, everything was as it should be. He was at peace. He was in a world where Diane, Matthew, and he could finally be together as a family. His mother and father would be there as well, and they'd be loving parents. In the world where Gaston now found himself, he felt no animosity between his father and him.

Why should I? he thought. *My life's perfect.*

Gaston knew he was on his knees in the secret tunnel, but it didn't matter. He could see the other members of his team around him. Everyone was on their knees. They all had smiles on their face.

They lack for nothing, he thought. I lack for nothing. Life is good.

For the first time in his life, Gaston felt truly happy.

* * *

Lord Cancontus remained at a distance until the Circle amplified the enthrall spell enough so that none of the wizard scouts could resist. Except of course for the Master's variable.

The variable's still near the entrance, thought Cancontus. *He hasn't yet fallen to his knees. He continues to fight against the power of the spheres. The Master's variable is strong-willed. Even the increase in strength provided by the Circle hasn't been enough to bring him to his knees.*

Cancontus knew why the variable could resist. The Master's human had a flaw in him. The flaw fought the enthrall spell for dominance. The Master's variable had also been exposed to the enthrall spell on a previous occasion. The variable knew what to expect. Like a creature who'd been exposed to an illness, the variable had built up a resistance.

The wizard scout's a resistor as well. The enthrall spell can't get a firm hold on his mind. I should have foreseen it.

Lord Cancontus wasn't sure if he should be concerned. Unlike their last encounter, he was at a safe distance. The Master's variable couldn't reach the Circle's keystone link. He was safe. However, he couldn't take any chances. He considered recalling his vampires and having them finish the job.

No. The vampires would see it as a sign of weakness. I would have to destroy them all. I must do the task myself.

The variable's companions were in the center of the secret tunnel. From their expressions, Cancontus knew they were all fully enthralled. He sensed something else among one of the other wizard scouts. He sensed the essence of his brother, the Dalinfaust.

So, Cancontus thought, *you placed a part of yourself in more than one weapon.*

Cancontus unfurled his avatar's bat wings and laughed.

Perhaps I can use the essence to gain an advantage over my brother. With the Dalinfaust as my servant, I wouldn't need that fool Zenthra.

With a thought, Cancontus teleported into the secret tunnel. All nine of the companions of the Master's variable were on their knees. Even the female dwarf had the same foolish smile as the others.

Cancontus laughed. *I'll make her scream just like I made her father beg for mercy.*

The demon approached the lead wizard scout. The man held the weapon with the demon essence of his brother in his left hand. The human's hand hung loosely on the floor. Sparks of phase energy crackled as the rod made contact with the stone surface of the tunnel.

Speaking aloud, Cancontus said, "You fools. You should never have opposed me. I'm going to rip out each of your throats and feast on your blood."

None of the wizard scouts or their companions responded. They just continued to stare off into space with the same satisfied smile on their faces.

"Ah, but you don't care do you?" said Cancontus as he knelt next to the lead wizard scout. "You'll raise your head and keep smiling as I suck out your life. I'll start with you, wizard scout. Bare your neck for me, fool. I hunger for the taste of your blood, and I don't like to wait."

* * *

Gaston let go of his empty Deloris blaster and removed his battle helmet. He heard Wanda yelling at him, but didn't care. Everything was perfect. Lifting his chin, he tilted his head to the side to better expose his neck.

Why not? he thought. *I'll be with my family. All will be well.*

However, all wasn't well. Gaston began to sense a feeling of hunger sweep over him. He pushed the feeling aside. His perfect world had no place for such mundane feelings as hunger. No sooner had he pushed the hunger aside than a feeling of tiredness came over him. He shoved that feeling aside as well. When he did, the feeling of hunger came back.

Why can't you leave me alone? Gaston thought. *My life would be perfect if you just left me alone.*

Something else touched Gaston's mind. He sensed another presence through his link with the Circle. He knew the presence. It was his brother. Just thinking of his brother irritated him. The sense of peace that was finally his was in danger of being taken away. Gaston sensed his brother destroying his only hope for happiness. The irritating presence of his brother was joined by a feeling of hunger and tiredness.

Gaston's world of peace and happiness began to crack. He felt something warm on his neck. It was the breath of the demon.

Fear and revulsion suddenly threw off the last bonds of the enthrall spell. Gaston rolled back as he slashed out with his phase rod. The demon roared with anger when the weapon smacked into his face.

Gaston came up out of his roll with the .44 caliber AutoMag in his hands. He pulled the trigger as fast as the finger of his battle suit could move. The demon was knocked back a step but wasn't harmed. He sensed layer upon layer of shields around the demon.

A link from the demon to the Circle drew Gaston's attention. It beckoned to him as surely as if it was calling his name. Stabbing downward with his phase rod, Gaston drove his phase rod into the heart of the link. This time the demon roared with pain.

The jagged claw of the demon's right hand reached out for Gaston. Before it could make contact, another round from the AutoMag struck the demon in the left side of its chest. Although the bullet didn't penetrate the layer of hardened skin, the demon's vampire body was once again driven backward by the force of the round.

"The heart," Wanda mentally yelled. *"Your brother's battle computer says to go for the heart."*

Sending a burst of pure Power at the demon's chest, Gaston tried to tear an opening through the demon's defenses to expose the heart. He wasn't strong enough. The heart was too well protected. While a thin layer of shielding gave way to his Power, there were many layers beyond it. Even as he swung his phase rod at the demon-vampire, Gaston realized it was hopeless.

A bright length of red flashed over Gaston's shoulder and struck the demon in the chest. The red glow was a phase rod in full-destructive mode. The strike of the phase rod was accompanied by a blast of pure Power as another layer of the demon's defenses was stripped away. Suddenly, Gaston's mother was standing shoulder to shoulder on his left side stabbing wildly at the demon as she fired a burst of plasma rounds from her rifle into the vampire's chest.

Another blast of pure Power struck the demon from Gaston's right. His father was standing shoulder to shoulder on his right side, adding his phase rod to the fray. Two more blasts of Power hit the demon and stripped away more layers of its defenses. Gaston recognized the frequencies of Tam and Telsa.

The demon formed a ball of magic in its hands. Before it could strike, two more blasts of Power hit the demon's chest as Trinity and Jerad entered the fight. They were joined by Emerald and Chancee who began beating at Cancontus with their magic swords.

Sensing a possible victory, Gaston shouted, "Pour it to him. He's only got a few shields left. Don't hold anything back."

Gaston felt a surge of hope. He wasn't fighting the demon alone. He was with the greatest fighting force the galaxy had ever known. He was with wizard scouts.

* * *

Cancontus roared with pain and agony. Realization swept over him that his avatar was in danger of being destroyed. He'd spread himself too thin. The Crosioian vampire was only one of his many avatars. He was trying to do too much at once. Some of his other avatars were in perilous positions as well.

If I had time, I could draw Power from my other forms, he thought. I could bring enough Power to bear to destroy these wizard scouts with the wave of my hand. However, I need time to pull the Power from my other avatars without endangering them as well. I need time.

Time. That which he'd so often scoffed as the weakness of physical life forms was now his enemy as well.

If this avatar is destroyed, I'll be banished to the demonic plane for a thousand years. My brothers will combine forces and torture me for a millennium.

Cancontus didn't relish the thought. When the Master's wizard scout had destroyed Efrestra's dragon-avatar, Cancontus had spent many pleasurable years helping to torture his brother. He had no wish for Efrestra to return the favor.

I must save this avatar, Cancontus thought. *Then I'll regroup and destroy these pitiful fools. However, this avatar must first survive.*

"Attack, my vampires!" boomed Cancontus. "Destroy these fools. Feast on their blood while I go to prepare the way for our final victory."

Off balance from the onslaught of attacks, Cancontus only had time for a simple teleport spell back to the lair of his brother, Zenthra. His brother was a weakling and a fool, but his skill at protective spells couldn't be matched by anyone less powerful than a master demon. Cancontus knew if Zenthra hadn't specifically formed his defenses to allow his brothers in, even the high and mighty Dalinfaust would be unable to enter.

Zenthra's room will be the perfect place for me to prepare a counterattack. Once I draw Power from my other avatars, I'll return and destroy the wizard scouts. They'll pay for their insolence. Oh, how they'll pay.

* * *

Zenthra watched with amusement as the wizard scouts stripped away layer after layer of his brother's shields. As he'd suspected, Cancontus wasn't as powerful as he proclaimed.

If the fool doesn't leave soon, Zenthra thought, *the wizard scouts will destroy his avatar. Now, wouldn't that be a shame?*

Zenthra thought back to when Efrestra's avatar had been destroyed. Torturing his brother for a thousand years had been very therapeutic. Zenthra began to hope his brother would choose to remain and continue the fight with the wizard scouts.

The fool deserves to have his avatar destroyed.

Zenthra heard his brother order his vampire minions to attack.

He's going to run, Zenthra thought. *I knew my brother was a coward.*

Power shimmered in the room near one of Zenthra's control stations. The shimmering turned into the vampire form of Lord Cancontus.

Zenthra nearly laughed as he sensed his brother's shields. *His avatar is nearly destroyed. One more round of attacks by the wizard scouts would've done the trick.*

"Ah, brother," Zenthra said trying to keep the laughter out of his voice. "How good of you to drop in."

"Quick," ordered Cancontus. "Feed me some of your Power. I'll go back and rip those wizard scouts apart. I'll reward you once I am the Master."

"Of course you will," said Zenthra. This time he was unable to keep the laughter from his words.

Drawing a large amount of Power from his reserve, Zenthra sent it directly at the left side of his brother's chest. The few remaining shields buckled before finally giving way to the onslaught of

Power. Cancontus's heart exploded out the vampire's back. Zenthra sent another blast of Power to finish the job. Every particle of his brother's avatar was destroyed.

Zenthra laughed long and hard.

"Don't get bored, brother," he said. "I'll join you soon enough to personally see to your entertainment."

Zenthra laughed again as he sent a call to his two remaining brothers, Efrestra and the Dalinfaust. He was confident between the three of them, they'd make Cancontus wish he'd never been created. Zenthra looked forward to the thousand years of pleasure Cancontus would give them all.

Again Zenthra laughed. "Existence is so good."

CHAPTER 59

The booming sound of the demon's voice ordering his vampires to attack reverberated through every nook and cranny of the underground tunnel system. Richard heard it as he stood in the entrance's foyer.

Even as the demon shouted, Cancontus continued fighting Richard for control of the Circle. It was all Richard could do to force the feelings of hunger and tiredness into his companions to overcome the effects of the spheres' enthrall spell.

"Keep at it," said Nickelo who'd once again established contact in their shared space. *"The others are engaging the demon. Don't let up."*

A pounding at the entrance to the secret tunnel brought Fenmar to his feet. He pushed a small outcropping of rock. When he did, Richard heard a loud click.

"The vampires outside are trying to force their way in," said the dwarf. "I've locked the door, but it won't hold for long."

Using his passive scan, Richard took note of the situation. A crowd of nearly a thousand vampires was at the entrance, trying to force their way inside. A large source of energy halfway down the secret tunnel marked the location of Lord Cancontus. He was surrounded by the nine life forms of Richard's friends. As he watched, the life force of the demon diminished slightly. Unfortunately, Richard sensed the life forms of over three thousand vampires converging on the location of the demon and his fellow wizard scouts.

Suddenly, the life force of Cancontus was no longer in the secret tunnel. Still connected by the Circle as he was, Richard sensed the demon reappear deep below the Dragars' pyramid. He detected the demon Zenthra there as well.

Then the life force of Cancontus disappeared as if his avatar had been utterly destroyed.

With the disappearance of Cancontus, the Circle began to dissipate. Before it disappeared completely, the green sphere made one last contact with Richard.

"You must hurry," said the green sphere. *"The Mountain's Heart is already loaded on the destroyer. The Dragars are forcing us to open a time-gate to the future in the physical dimension. Come now, or all is lost."*

Richard wanted to tell the green sphere he had a few problems of his own. The Circle vanished before he got the chance. He lost contact with the green sphere at the same time.

When the Circle disappeared, Richard also felt a change in his dimensional pack and dimensional canteen. Although he didn't know why, he got the feeling the items were working once more.

"I calculate 'the One' *is probably using a tele-bot to let you know you can summon items again,"* said Nickelo. *"I'd advise not wasting the opportunity."*

Richard prepared to run and assist his friends. The vampires were almost on them. Before he could take more than a couple of steps, a loud crash behind him made him spin around.

Broken bits of stone flew through the air as the secret door gave way to the combined strength of the vampires outside. Two dwarf vampires bulled their way past the rubble with weapons raised. General Fenmar engaged one. Richard ran to the general's side and took out the other with his phase rod.

Hundreds of vampires struggled to get through the narrow entranceway. Their sheer desire to feast on the warm blood of those inside caused them to momentarily jam up inside the doorway.

Richard raised his M63 and fired a long burst of plasma rounds at the struggling vampires. Blood and gore spouted out of wounds, but their injuries almost immediately healed.

"You can't take them out with plasma rounds," said Nickelo. *"Their self-heal is even better than yours. I recommend coming up*

with a different tactic."

Richard noticed his battle computer didn't offer any specific suggestions. That normally meant he couldn't come up with anything having a better than five percent probability of success.

Fine, Richard thought. *I'll come up with my own idea.*

Richard knew he only had time to try one thing. He momentarily considered trying to summon a phase weapon from his dimensional pack, then quickly discarded the idea. *'The One'* had never let him summon one for himself in the past. He knew he couldn't afford to waste time seeing if *'the One'* would make an exception. He needed to try something different.

Releasing his grip on his M63, Richard reached out and jerked Fenmar away from the entrance. As soon as the dwarf was clear, Richard reached back with his right hand and extracted his dimensional canteen from its case on his hip.

Richard spun the canteen's lid with his thumb until it dangled by its lanyard. He fumbled for the canteen's control valve. In a fashion similar to his dimensional pack, Richard knew his canteen was connected to a water source on the planet Storage. How big the water source was he didn't know. He had a feeling he was about to find out. Once he found the control valve, Richard twisted it to maximum pressure with a temperature setting of 'boiling.'

A stream of water shot out of the canteen's opening. Hot water bounced off the wall near the doorway. Richard felt his battle computer adjust the aim until the scalding water was hitting the vampires full in the face. A great cloud of steam filled the foyer.

Richard shoved the dwarf behind him. "Get back, or you'll be boiled alive."

General Fenmar didn't waste time arguing. The dwarf made a hasty retreat several meters down the tunnel. When the general was a safe distance away, Richard began moving the stream of water back and forth across the opening. The vampires screamed as their flesh was burned off their bodies. He sensed their self-heal renewing the flesh, but the force of the jet of water continued to force them back.

"Hmm," Nickelo said. *"According to the information in my databanks, the water pressure for your canteen is able to shoot a stream up to a hundred meters in the air. Based upon the force of the current water flow, I'd say someone on the other end has*

cranked up the water pressure even higher. Whoever's doing it, I calculate they're saving your life. The vampires are being driven back from the entrance."

Sure enough, the vampires were giving ground. The entrance was almost clear. Richard knew it was only a temporary victory. Sooner or later, the vampires would think to shift into the void and enter from another way. Richard had a feeling the only thing preventing them from doing so now was their own greed to be the first to taste the blood of those inside.

Richard heard the sound of weapons firing along with several booms in the tunnels behind him. A glance at his heads-up display told the story. His friends were slowly making their way back to his location. They appeared to be hard-pressed by a large force of vampires. Several smaller groups of vampires were in the void and moving to cut off his friend's retreat.

"I've got to save them," Richard told his battle computer.

"You can't," replied Nickelo. *"If you leave your post, the vampires will overwhelm us. Your friends are on their own."*

CHAPTER 60

Wizard Scout Thomas R. Jacobs stabbed the tip of his phase rod straight at the demon's chest. He could sense Cancontus's weakening shields.

Just a few more blows, Thomas thought.

Without warning, the demon shimmered and disappeared. Thomas was temporarily thrown off balance when his phase rod met only thin air. A hand from behind grabbed his left shoulder preventing him from toppling over. When he looked over, Thomas saw the hand belonged to Gaston.

"The demon's gone," said Gaston. "I can still sense him through the Circle. He'll be back when he's gathered his strength. We'd best not be here."

Thomas was about to agree when the Circle suddenly disappeared.

Janice looked around from the other side of Gaston and asked, "What just happened?"

"Cancontus's avatar has been destroyed," answered Margery over the external speakers of Thomas's battle helmet. "Rick says the demon's brother, Zenthra, took him out. The Circle's gone. I highly recommend you be going also."

Thomas glanced at his heads-up display. Thousands of life forms were converging on their location. Another thousand outside the entrance were engaging Richard and Fenmar. Hundreds more were shifting into the void and moving to set up a blocking position behind them.

"If we don't get past there before those vampires arrive," said Margery in their shared space, *"they'll block our line of retreat."*

The first of the vampires arrived at Thomas's front. Before he could react, Gaston stepped forward and tore into them, swinging his phase rod like a wild man. For a brief moment, the vampires were driven back.

"Thomas!" said Janice. "Our dimensional packs are working again."

Sure enough, Thomas detected a change in his dimensional pack's frequency. He didn't waste time trying to figure out the whys or wherefores of the pack's sudden capability. He just pictured the specs for an experimental phase pistol he knew was being developed by the Deloris Armaments Corporation. He didn't feel any Power leave his reserve.

"Did you honestly think that was going to work?" asked Margery. *"It's like Janice told Rick, they may be a credit a dozen in the future, but they're rare during our time. I calculate there aren't currently any on Storage."*

The beast which was Thomas's temper tried to claw its way out from the prison where he kept it. Through sheer willpower, he forced it back down where it belonged. Thomas knew he needed to keep a cool head. He needed a plan.

"Everyone back to Rick," Thomas shouted. "I'll hold these vampires back."

"No!" said Janice. "We stay together. Besides, Rick and Fenmar aren't in any better shape than we are. We should stick together."

"Rick's dimensional pack is from the future," Thomas said trying to reason with his wife. "I'm betting he can summon phase weapons for everyone. Phase weapons are our only hope. You go get the weapons and then come back for me."

Janice finished caving in a vampire's chest with her phase rod before giving her reply. "No! I'll never leave you."

"Nor will we," said Tam. "Wizard scouts don't desert wizard scouts."

* * *

Gaston listened to the back and forth argument going on around him. He knew his father had the right idea. He'd just chosen the wrong person to stay back.

"You can't," said Wanda sounding very concerned. *"It'd be suicide."*

"We're all dead if I don't," Gaston replied. *"The vampires almost have us cut off. If the others don't leave now, they'll never make it to Shepard. He's their only hope."*

"Your father will never let you remain as a rearguard by yourself," said Wanda. *"As long as he's able to fight, he'll remain. Your mother won't either. They'll both stay as long as their Power reserves are functioning."*

Gaston swung at two more vampires before finalizing his decision. He knew what he was planning was a fool's errand, but couldn't let his mother and father die. His plan meant he'd never see Diane again, and Matthew would never know his true father. Regardless, Gaston knew he had to do what he had to do.

Reaching out with his mind, Gaston gathered a line of Power and sent it down the link he'd connected to his father during the attack on Velos. As he'd hoped, the link transcended time. He followed the link until it connected to his father's Power reserve here in the past. He sensed traps near the opening. He recognized his brother's frequency. Gaston smiled.

You taught me too good, he thought. *Plus, you were sloppy.*

Gaston spied a weak point in the traps. Perhaps Shepard had been in a hurry. It didn't matter. All that mattered was that it was there. Slipping through the weak point, Gaston made his way into his father's reserve. The Power reserve of his father was strong, powerful, and large. Gaston sensed his father's vitality. Until now, Gaston hadn't fully realized how great a wizard scout his father actually was.

My father's too good, Gaston thought. 'The One' *will never willingly let him go. I'll make it so he has too.*

Gaston knew his father would never forgive him, but didn't care. He had a sudden insight as to why there'd always been an obvious chill between them while he was growing up. His mother had been very loving. Gaston knew she'd eventually forgive him. He also knew his father wouldn't. If he went through with his plan, he'd be creating a split in his relationship with his father that would never heal.

So be it, Gaston thought. *At least he'll be alive.*

Drawing more Power from his reserve, Gaston attached lines to several structural points on the inside of his father's reserve.

I love you, Father, Gaston thought in his private space. *Forgive me.*

Gaston twisted and pulled hard with his Power. He heard a scream. Out the corner of his eye, Gaston saw his father clutch his chest and fall forward.

His mother jump-kicked a vampire who made a grab for her husband. As the vampire was falling back, Janice reached down and pulled her husband to safety.

Retracing his steps back to his own Power reserve, Gaston found an opening he'd made to his mother's Power reserve when she'd been lying in bed dying from lack of Power. The link hadn't allowed him to save her in the future, but he was determined to use it to save her now. He followed the link until he was at the opening to her Power reserve. He wrapped structural weak points on the inside of her reserve the same as he'd done to his father.

I'm sorry, Mother, he thought. *Go and be with your son. You'll have many years of happiness. I won't let 'the One' control you any longer.*

Gaston pulled and twisted. His mother's reserve partially collapsed on itself. He heard a scream. When he looked, his mother had fallen on top of her husband.

Tam moved forward and stood over the downed wizard scouts. She swung her bastard sword in a large arc to keep the vampires at bay.

"What's happening?" asked Telsa.

Gaston decided to lie. "The vampires have damaged Thomas and Janice's Power reserves somehow. Get them back to Shepard. He can help them. He'll be able to summon your battle suits now. He can get you phase weapons. I'll hold the vampires here."

"We won't leave a wizard scout behind," said Trinity

Gaston turned to the only one who might listen to reason.

"Jerad, get them back to Shepard. My battle suit's resistant to attacks from the void. I'll hold them until you get to Shepard. Then I'll follow."

Pulling his sword out of a vampire's chest, Jerad shouted over his shoulder. "How will you join us? You'll be trapped here."

I won't be joining you, thought Gaston.

"I'm a shifter," Gaston told Jerad. "Once you're all clear, I'll shift into the void and make my escape. I'll probably make it to Shepard before you."

When Jerad looked indecisive, Gaston shouted in his best TAC officer voice. "Go! Now! Otherwise, we're all dead."

Jerad reached down and grabbed the limp form of Janice and threw her over his shoulder.

"Tam, Telsa, lead the way back to Rick."

Whether it was Jerad's natural charisma or his previous leadership authority over them that did the trick, Gaston didn't know. What he did know was that the others stopped arguing and rushed to obey.

Chancee picked up the unconscious Thomas and threw him over her shoulder. The ranger grunted under the weight of the battle suit but was still able to take a final swing at a vampire before turning to leave. She ran down the tunnel following Tam and Telsa.

The last of the group to leave was Jerad.

"I'll see you in hell, Gaston."

Smiling in spite of himself, Gaston said, "Not if I see you first. Now get."

Jerad got.

Three vampires came out of the wall at Gaston. They were in the void, but couldn't get past the energized titanium in the material of his battle suit. The vampires fell back before the fury of his counterattack.

"They're scared of the demon essence in your phase rod," said Wanda. *"That's the only reason you haven't been overwhelmed. I calculate your luck won't last much longer. Another hundred vampires will be here in five seconds."*

Gaston glanced at the white spots on his heads-up display. *At least my friends have made it past the choke point, he thought. They're going to make it to Shepard. I don't like the man, but he's a good wizard scout. If anyone can save my friends, it will be Shepard.*

"You called them your friends," said Wanda. *"Gaston, I'm proud of you. You've never called anyone a friend before."*

Gaston kicked himself for thinking the thought in his shared space. He didn't like letting his guard down. He knew he only had seconds to live, but it didn't matter.

A virtual flood of vampires came out of the floor. As they shifted out of the void, they grabbed at Gaston's legs. He slammed his phase rod into two before the others dragged him to the floor. A dozen of the fiends pinned him down as they began ripping at his armor. His battle suit was tough, but he doubted the material could hold up against the combined strength of the vampires for long.

I love you, Diane, Gaston thought as he gave his final goodbye.

Power enveloped Gaston. His body started to tingle. He heard a deep, raspy voice.

"I claim this one as mine," said the voice. "Do what you want with the others, but this one goes with me."

The world around Gaston began to shift in and out of focus. Then everything went black.

CHAPTER 61

Telsa noticed the white dot representing Gaston on her heads-up display disappear at the same moment she reached General Fenmar. The old dwarf was about twenty meters from the entrance, exchanging blows with an armored vampire.

With no time to spare, Telsa drew Power from her reserve and sent it out as a single blast at the vampire. She was a projector. The blast of energy splattered the vampire into a thousand pieces against the tunnel wall. Almost immediately, she sensed the pieces trying to reform themselves into a single whole again. Spotting a large piece of heart with a blackened, viral glob covering it, she stabbed her magic longsword into the center of the disgusting mass. The glob of black goo burst into flames before disappearing completely. The pieces of vampire flesh stopped trying to reform.

"Where's Rick," Telsa asked.

The dwarf pointed toward the entrance before engaging another vampire who was emerging from the tunnel wall.

Looking toward the entrance, all Telsa saw was a cloud of fog. Even through her armor, the air felt hot.

Steam, Telsa thought.

Removing her goggles, Telsa replaced them with her Dragar helmet. Once her face was protected from the steam, she moved forward until she stood beside Richard. He was spraying a high-pressure stream of water out of his canteen at any vampire foolish enough to try and get through the entrance.

"They're starting to come through the walls," Telsa said. "Can you summon our battle suits and weapons? A whole lot of phase weapons would be nice."

Before Telsa knew what Richard was doing, he reached over and stuck the canteen in her hand. "Use this to keep them at bay while I summon your gear," he said.

Looking dubiously at the canteen, Telsa asked, "Will it work once you let go?"

"If I keep feeding it Power it will."

The force of the jet of water was almost too much for the assistors in her confiscated Dragar armor to handle. Before Telsa could say anything else, her friend was gone. She turned her attention to the entrance and concentrated on spraying boiling water at any vampire heads that appeared.

In less than thirty seconds, Telsa sensed another presence at her side. The presence was Tam. Her friend was dressed in a battle suit. She held a Deloris model phase pistol in each hand. Tam holstered one of the pistols and took the canteen out of Telsa's hand.

Tam pointed over her shoulder. "Your turn. Rick's got your gear waiting."

Asking no questions, Telsa headed back down the tunnel. Just before she cleared the cloud of steam, she heard the unmistakable 'brrrrr' of an automatic phase rifle going off. The bright flash of dozens of rounds of phase energy shone up through the fog as they sped down the tunnel in the direction of the vampires.

Telsa spotted her battle suit and utility belt on the stone floor next to the still unconscious forms of Thomas and Janice. She immediately began ripping off her Dragar armor and replacing it with her more familiar M6 battle suit.

"It's about time you showed up," said her battle computer, Raj. *"I was beginning to think this fight would be over before you decided to get involved."*

"I missed you too," Telsa said as she picked up a 10mm phase rifle. She also grabbed a bandoleer of six extra magazines.

She sensed Trinity, Jerad, and Richard holding the back of the tunnel along with the two dwarves and Chancee. Making a command decision, Telsa returned to the entrance to support Tam.

As Tam came into view, Telsa noticed three vampires emerging up from the stone floor behind her friend. Telsa put a burst of phase rounds in each of the vampire's hearts. Even though the vampires were still in the void, the phase rounds tore their hearts to shreds. Telsa sensed their life forces blink out on her passive scan.

"It's getting worse," Telsa said as she took up a position next to Tam. She began adding the firepower of the phase rifle to the stream of boiling water.

"Yeah, tell me about it," replied Tam. "The bad news is, the main force hasn't even gotten here yet."

Telsa noticed the thousands of yellow, red, and orange dots converging on their position. When she'd attended the University before applying for wizard scout training, she'd often been told she was the smartest student there. However, one look at the mass of incoming life forms told her she didn't have to be smart to know her death was imminent. They had no place to run.

* * *

"I don't care what our orders were," Matthew said as he banked the fighter-shuttle into a hard, diving-turn toward the mountain. "Our friends are in trouble. I'm not going to stay up here doing nothing while they're down there dying."

"We don't know that anyone's died," pointed out Marstis. "I'll admit the odds are low. There must be a thousand vampires at the entrance."

When the fighter leveled off, Matthew punched the windscreen's zoom to maximum.

"Look," Matthew said. "The door's broken open. What's that stream of water coming out of the entrance? It looks like some type of geyser."

"No idea," said Marstis.

The ship's intercom crackled. The voice of a tense-sounding Jerad came over the intercom. "Matthew. We're in trouble. How soon can you get here? We're at the entrance."

"I'm on short final now," Matthew said. "I'll be landing at the entrance in ten seconds. Be ready."

"No," ordered Jerad. "Make a strafing run. If you can blow a path through the vampires, we'll try to make our escape. There's no way you can land."

"Watch me," Matthew said.

Looking over at Marstis, he noticed the gnome fiddling with the gunner's computer display. He saw a crosshair on the display directly over the entrance to the secret tunnel.

"Are you sure that thing will work?" Matthew asked knowing full well it was too late to ask questions now.

"We'll soon see," said Marstis. "A signaling bomblet's intended to mark targets for starships outside a planet's atmosphere. Tell your friends to cover their eyes. This thing will burn out the optic nerves of anyone getting even a partial glimpse of its light."

Matthew gave a warning to Jerad. "Tell everyone to close their eyes. We're releasing a signaling bomblet in five seconds."

* * *

Jerad didn't have time to verbally warn the others. He only hoped his battle computer could do it.

"Stephen, tell the other battle computers to go to max filters. Now!"

No sooner had he thought the command than the filter of his own battle helmet turned solid black. Using his passive scan, Jerad picked out the life forms of Emerald and Chancee. He dove and knocked them to the ground as he covered their eyes with his hands. A moment later, the ground shook. A blast of hot air came rushing through the entrance to the tunnel.

The filter on his battle helmet changed back to normal night-vision mode.

"Matthew's on short final," said Stephen. *"The vampires are temporarily blinded, but that won't last long. Get moving soldier."*

Jerad threw both Emerald and Chancee over his shoulders. He ignored their protests. He sensed other wizard scouts grabbing the limp forms of Janice and Thomas. Jerad noticed Richard running up, dragging General Fenmar behind him. The general's eyes were closed, and he was flailing around with his hands.

By the time Jerad made it to the entrance, the shuttle was already on the ground. The end of the ramp was only two meters from the shattered doorway. He had a quick glimpse of dozens of vampires stumbling around the shuttle with their arms outstretched as if trying to find a point of reference. Then Jerad was inside.

Once he made a quick count, Jerad yelled, "We're all in. Go!"

Matthew wasted no time. The fighter-shuttle leaped off the ground in a steep climb even before the ramp finished closing. Once they were safely airborne, Matthew turned in his seat. The grin on the teenager's face disappeared.

"We're short someone," said Matthew. "Who?"

Jerad locked eyes with Matthew. "Gaston didn't make it. I know he worked for your mother. I'm sorry."

* * *

When the shuttle leveled off, Richard's mind finally began to take stock of the situation. Myers was gone. He wasn't sure how he felt about that. He knew his brother wasn't dead. He could still feel a small bit of Myers's life force through the link to his father. The low-intensity of the life force was similar to the feeling he got from Stella's link to his Power reserve. She was in the future. Based upon the similarity of the intensity, Richard figured if he had to guess, *'the One'* had probably returned his brother to the future.

"Does it matter?" asked Nickelo. *"I know you haven't asked for my recommendation, but if you did, I'd suggest you start getting things organized. Your parents' Power reserves have been damaged. They're still deteriorating. Plus the dwarf general is blind. He won't do you any good without his eyesight. You need to decide what you're going to do. Matthew's going to be asking for a destination soon."*

Richard looked around the inside of the fighter-shuttle. His friends were talking excitedly among themselves. Jerad was being bombarded with questions. Matthew was turned around in the pilot's seat demanding to know what had happened to his mother's chief of security.

Richard came to a decision. He needed to take charge. Once resolved, he stood. "Enough!"

All talking stopped. Everyone turned to face Richard. Even Fenmar, blind though he was, cocked an ear in Richard's direction.

"One way or the other," Richard said, "we're near the end of our mission. Here's what's going to happen. I'm going to give some orders, and you're going to make them happen."

When no arguments were forthcoming, Richard continued.

"Matthew, set a course for the Oracle's; max velocity. Contact

Tia. Tell her to go there as well to pick up some cargo that'll be waiting for her."

When Matthew didn't immediately respond, Richard turned to the whole group and said, "Just so you all know, Myers isn't dead. I can still sense him. He's just not in our current time."

Matthew opened his mouth. Before the teenager could ask questions, Richard held up his hand. "You've got your orders, Matt. Make it happen."

With a reluctant nod, the young man turned to his control console. The shuttle accelerated forward.

"We walked into a trap," Richard told the others. "I'm sure you've all figured that out already. What you don't know is that the Mountain's Heart wasn't even at Drepdenor. It's been moved to the spaceport. It's loaded onto one of those black destroyers even now. The Dragar starship is going to use a time-gate to take the gem to the future in the physical dimension. We've got to stop that from happening."

"How—" started Jerad.

"How?" Richard repeated. "By everyone doing what I tell them. We're going to attack the spaceport and cause so much confusion it'll give us time to destroy the gem. We're going to attack it now. We've got to hit the spaceport within the next thirty minutes, or everything's lost."

"That's crazy," said Emerald. "It'll take weeks to assemble our army. General Fenmar hasn't even completed all the sets of magic armor and weapons yet. Even getting Master Garis and his mages assembled and shuttling them to the spaceport will take time."

"We don't have the time," Richard said growing a little heated. He didn't like it when people pointed out flaws in his plans but offered none of their own. "We're attacking now." Turning to his former tent-mate, he said, "Jerad, I need you to come up with a way to delay that destroyer from launching. I've got to heal Thomas, Janice, and Fenmar while I've got the opportunity."

Jerad spread his hands. "Rick, you're asking the impossible. We haven't even got heavy cats. Wizard scouts are recon. We're not shock troopers. Besides, we don't have the bottles of DNA gas yet. You're asking us to commit suicide for no reason."

Richard shook his head. "Something's only impossible if you think it is. Besides, you're going to get whatever equipment you need. My dimensional pack's working again. If an item of equipment is in one of the warehouses on Storage, you can have it. As for the bottles of DNA gas, they'll be at the Oracle's by the time we get there."

Jerad frowned. "How do you know?"

Richard gave a wry smile. "Because if the bottles of DNA gas aren't waiting for us when we arrive, we're screwed."

CHAPTER 62

The air in the largest open area of the space station's shuttle bay shimmered. A loud pop echoed off the bay's metallic walls. The shimmering was replaced by an enormous silver dragon. For a split second, all two hundred workers and soldiers in the shuttle bay froze and stared at the thirty-meter long dragon. The beast roared. When it did, all hell broke loose.

Jeena jumped off Bright Wing's neck and hit the metal deck in a roll. Her environmental suit was awkward, but it wasn't so unwieldy that she was willing to take it off just to gain a little agility. If what she hoped the dragon could do was correct, the integrity of the space station's hull was in serious doubt.

By the time Jeena was up and running, Stella was by her side firing at anything crossing their paths. They'd practiced the same route so often in the holo-square that they just naturally ran in the right direction.

A jet of frost passed to Jeena's left side and struck a squad of Crosioians taking firing positions behind a stack of metal crates. When the jet of air made contact, both the crates and the soldiers were immediately covered in a thick layer of ice. None of the soldiers fired their weapons.

Two Crosioians knelt in the opening of a hallway. They raised their pistols. Jeena drew Power from her reserve and sent a ball of magic at the soldiers. Just as the soldiers began firing, the magic turned into a shield of shimmering energy. The shield continued moving forward and slammed the bat-creatures into the wall behind them. The two Crosioians bounced off the side of the hallway leaving a red-stained goo dripping down the wall as they fell to the floor.

"To the left," said Danny through the metal band Jeena wore across her forehead.

"I know," Jeena replied as she made a hard turn to the left.

Stella raised the M12 over Jeena's shoulder and fired a ball of magic from the wand underneath the rifle's barrel. The resultant fireball exploded in the middle of half a dozen Crosioians.

As she continued to run, Jeena sensed a strange energy coming from outside the space station. The energy was so powerful it threatened to overwhelm her senses.

"What's that?" Jeena asked Danny.

"It's the black hole," replied Danny. *"Ignore it. The station's defensive shield is negating its effects. You need to concentrate on your mission. We have to get to the vault where the bottles are stored."*

"I'm trying," Jeena said as she pointed her staff in the opposite direction of the hallway. Without even taking time to mouth a spell, Jeena sent a blast of magic at three Crosioians attempting to set up some kind of crew-served weapon. The three soldiers and their equipment basically disintegrated before Jeena's eyes.

A series of explosions echoed down the hallway from the direction of the shuttle bay.

"Is Bright Wing okay?" Jeena asked growing concerned for the welfare of the silver dragon.

"Don't waste time worrying about her," said Danny. *"She's having a field day using her breath weapons and spells. I think the little lizard has a vicious streak in her. Just be thankful she's on your side."*

Jeena was thankful.

Another corner loomed ahead of Jeena. They were getting close to the vault. Suddenly, two winged creatures wearing armor and carrying glowing spears came around the corner.

"Crosioian scouts," said Danny stating the obvious.

Four colored beams of phase energy appeared in Stella's hands as she activated her phase rods. Before Jeena could say anything, the wizard scout ran past her in the direction of the two scouts. The Crosioian scouts began running to meet the wizard scout halfway.

Before she could charge in support of her friend, Jeena detected two more life forms behind her. She skidded to a stop and spun around as she pulled a wand from her belt. Two more Crosioian scouts had somehow appeared behind them. Jeena shouted the word of activation for the wand and sent the green beam of a paralysis spell toward the Crosioians. The beam hit something invisible to the front of the scouts and ricocheted down the hallway.

One of the scouts raised a rifle of some type and fired a beam of energy at Jeena. She drew Power from her reserve and shouted a spell. The resulting magic formed a defensive shield just in time to deflect the beam back at the two scouts. The beam bounced back and forth between Jeena and the scouts until it finally petered out of existence.

The closest scout threw down her rifle and charged to the attack. At the same time, Jeena sensed the other scout reaching out with a line of Power and probing the link to her Power reserve. Jeena had a sudden feeling she was in serious trouble but didn't know what to do. Whatever form of attack the scout was attempting was nothing she'd been trained to defend against.

Fortunately, Jeena wasn't alone. A line of Power reached past her from the rear and knocked the scout's line away. Jeena recognized Stella's frequency.

"Don't let the scout engage you," warned Danny. *"She's a better close-in fighter than you."*

Jeena wondered how the battle computer thought she was supposed to stop the scout. The Crosioian was only a few steps away. Jeena knew Stella was in heavy combat with the two other scouts. She knew she'd have to take care of these two on her own.

Jeena concentrated on her two scouts. The farthest scout was forming another line of Power. She had little doubt the scout was preparing for another attack against her link and got the distinct feeling the scout had figured out a way to circumvent any counterattack by Stella.

The sense of powerful energy outside the space station drew Jeena's attention again. The energy reminded her of something she'd sensed before. The Staff of the Lady of the Tree seemed to be responding to the black hole's energy. A link that was already attached to the staff began to tingle. It was the same link the *'helper'* had used when Jeena tried to save the green sphere during her last mission for the Oracle.

Without taking time to reason things out, Jeena sent a cry for help down the link. Something seemed to respond to her call. The response was very faint as if far way or possibly as if from a great difference in time.

Suddenly, everything around Jeena slowed to a stop. Or maybe her mind sped up. She didn't know or care which. The charging scout was only a handful of steps away. Jeena's eyes were focused on the glowing blue tip of the scout's phase spear. It seemed to promise an agonizing death. With her death imminent, Jeena opened her mind to the link attached to the Lady's staff. At the mercy of whatever creature was at the other end, Jeena waited to see what would happen.

* * *

Richard was blind. He'd just finished healing General Fenmar. He had healed his parents' Power reserves first, as best he could. Even so, he knew the reserves of both wizard scouts were too damaged to ever be fully functional again.

While repairing his parents' reserves, Richard had picked up the unmistakable scent of his brother. He hadn't needed Nickelo to tell him that his own brother had been the one to damage his parents' Power reserves. Surprisingly, he wasn't sure how to react to the knowledge. The commandant had once told him that both Janice and he had their Power reserves damaged during their final mission for *'the One.'* Richard had always assumed it had been due to enemy action. Now he knew better.

"You knew this was their last mission," said Nickelo. *"You knew what was going to happen. Now your parents can live the remainder of their lives without any interference by* 'the One.' *Isn't that what you wanted?"*

"He'll never leave them completely alone," Richard said. *"You know that."*

When his battle computer didn't reply, Richard concentrated on the voices around him. The mix of loud voices didn't bode well. Everybody seemed to have an opinion on how best to proceed. Even though he was still blind, Richard stepped in to take charge.

"We're not landing at the Oracle's," Richard said. "Matthew, I want you to make a high-speed pass. Janice and Thomas, you'll make a high-altitude drop and retrieve the DNA gas. The rest of us will continue on to the spaceport and stop that black destroyer from taking off."

"Why us?" asked Thomas. "We've got the most fighting experience."

Although Richard knew his next words would hurt his father, he pressed on anyway. "Because your reserves are damaged. You can still do some small things like levitation and self-heal, but neither of you will ever be the wizard scouts you were. I'm sorry, but that's just the way it is."

From past association, Richard knew his father was a proud man. The truth would hurt, but he didn't have time for niceties. The fate of three galaxies hung in the balance.

"Tia's going to pick the two of you up," Richard continued. "You'll bring the bottles of DNA gas to the spaceport and give them to us. We'll take over from there."

Although he couldn't see, Richard could almost feel his father's face turning red.

"If you think I'm going to stay back in the rear while you do the fighting, you've got…"

The voice of Richard's father faded into the distance as something else pulled at Richard's mind. The something was coming from the link the elf, Shandria, had attached to him.

No, Richard thought. *It's coming from Shandria's staff.*

With a start, Richard realized the thing he felt wasn't even coming from Shandria's staff. It was actually coming from something connected to her staff. Then, he recognized the something. It was the presence who'd once helped him when he tried to close the time-gate during the battle with the black destroyer. With the assistance of the *'helper,'* he'd been able to close the gate, but the green sphere and the sphere's brothers had been destroyed anyway.

Richard had no doubt the presence he was feeling was her. He had no idea who she was, but he did know she was important to him for some reason. When they'd last touched minds, he'd felt a great sense of peace. This time he felt an emotion that seemed more like a plea for help.

Concern for the presence swept over Richard. Suddenly, his mind went into hyper-speed.

"I don't think this is a good idea," said Nickelo. *"In case you haven't noticed, we've got a few problems of our own, buddy."*

"I have noticed," Richard replied. Regardless, he couldn't help what he was feeling. She needed help.

An image of molten silver flashed in his mind. The image helped Richard reach a decision.

With more than a little trepidation, he lowered the defenses he'd carefully constructed around his mind. The presence's reaction was immediate. The three-way connection from Richard to Shandria's link, to her staff, and on to whatever presence was at the other end was tenuous at best, but it was there. The presence drew Richard toward her until he could sense a powerful force of energy. The energy was probably the most powerful force he'd ever encountered. For some reason, the energy seemed familiar.

"It's gate energy," said Nickelo. *"It's similar to the energy from the green sphere. Only it's infinitely more powerful, if you don't mind my slight exaggeration."*

Richard was curious why the presence was interested in the energy. Whatever the reason, he felt like she was becoming increasingly desperate. Richard concentrated harder on the energy. He tried moving closer to it. As soon as he did, the energy began pulling him toward it with a force more powerful than anything he could imagine. Without knowing how, Richard succeeded in twisting with his mind and breaking free of the energy's grasp.

"Well, that was different," said Nickelo. *"Perhaps instead of trying to go to the energy, you should let it come to you."*

If things had been happening at normal speed, Richard would probably have given up and gotten back to his own problems. Since his mind was operating at nanosecond speed, he took the time to examine the energy closer. He noticed the pull of the energy wasn't consistent. It seemed to have ebbs and flows.

During one of the ebbs, Richard let his mind reach out and follow the energy back toward its source. He didn't get very far. When the energy suddenly reversed course, he was ready for it. He changed direction as well. Using the same technique he'd used to get Tia and him onboard the fighter-shuttle during the battle at Cantonsburg, he slowed his speed just enough to allow the leading edge of the energy to catch up. He wrapped a thin strand of the energy with his Power, stretched the strand of energy out, and connected it to the link to the presence.

Richard quickly found out the presence wasn't one to waste time. As soon as the strand of energy touched her link, she took control of the strand from Richard. His connection to the presence immediately disappeared. She was gone.

Richard's mind switched back to normal speed. He looked around the cabin of the shuttle. His sight had partially come back. The other wizard scouts were looking at him. His father was bent down only an arm's length in front of his face.

"Well, are you going to answer me?" said Thomas. "What makes you think I'm going to do something just because you tell me?"

Richard stared deep into his father's eyes. He could see a lot of himself in those eyes.

"Because," Richard said keeping his voice steady, "you're a wizard scout. Because you can take orders as well as give them. Because you need to take orders this time, and finally, because *'the One'* is depending on you to follow my orders. The algorithm requires it."

His father's face lost its red and returned to a more normal shade. The commandant opened his mouth to speak but immediately closed it. Without uttering another word, Thomas returned to his seat and sat down next to his wife.

Richard relaxed. Everything was going to be okay.

CHAPTER 63

The moment Jeena sensed the *'helper'* latch onto a strand of the black hole's gravitational pull, she jerked hard on her link and took control. As soon as she did, the presence of the *'helper'* disappeared. Everything around her returned to normal speed.

The Crosioian scout was almost upon her. With no time to think, Jeena reacted by splitting off a minute piece the black hole's energy and attaching it to the scout. The effects were immediate. She heard a short-lived, high-pitched scream. The scout collapsed to the metal deck and was immediately flattened into a splotch of blood and bat fur combined with the crumpled remains of the scout's armor. The deck itself bulged and caved downward into a hole about the width of a tall elf. The remains of the scout disappeared along with a portion of the deck.

"Hold on to something," said Danny.

Jeena sensed the decks below the hole collapsing one upon the other as the intense pull of the black hole continued to exert force on what was left of the Crosioian scout's body. A large rush of air passed over Jeena and knocked her down as the station's atmosphere was sucked into the hole.

"The scout was pulled all the way through the station," said Danny. *"The hull's been breached."*

The escaping air tried to suck Jeena into the hole. She grabbed hold of a convenient bracing bar protruding from the side of the hallway. Holding onto her staff with one hand, she gripped the brace bar with her other for all she was worth. If she'd only had the strength of her hands, Jeena doubted she could've held on against the force of the escaping air. Thankfully, the additional strength of the environmental suit's assistors was just enough to allow her to hang on.

Even as she was being buffeted by the gale-force winds, Jeena sensed a line of Power reaching out toward her. It was coming from the second scout. The bat-creature was somehow able to maintain her position against the blast of wind. Jeena sensed Power forming a shield around the scout.

The line of Power from the scout moved toward Jeena's chest. Without taking time to think things through, Jeena split off another piece of the black hole's energy and attached it to the second scout. Once again, she heard a high-pitched scream as both the scout and her equipment was crushed against the deck. In less than a heartbeat, the force of the escaping air doubled as the space station's outer hull was ruptured in a second spot.

Jeena reached out with her mind and felt for the locations of Stella and the remaining two scouts. All three were surrounded by shields of Power that appeared to resist the flow of air.

While continuing to hold onto the brace bar, Jeena twisted enough to see a blur of phase rods and phase spheres striking one another. The blows were faster than her mind could register. Although Stella was holding her own, she appeared to be hard-pressed. Jeena feared the wizard scout would soon succumb to the attacks from her two opponents.

Splitting off two more lines of the black hole's energy, Jeena attached them to the remaining scouts.

They barely had time to scream before they were smashed downward into a bloody mess. Soon, there were two more holes in the space station's outer hull.

Caught as she was between the four holes, Jeena felt the wind slacken somewhat. She tightened her grip on the Lady's staff and tried to stand, but couldn't.

A line of Power reached out toward Jeena. She prepared another strand of the black hole's energy in preparation for defending herself. Before she could form her attack, Jeena sensed the frequency of the line of Power belonged to Stella.

The wizard scout's Power enveloped Jeena and shielded her from the wind. When Jeena released her grip on the brace bar,

Stella's Power raised her to a standing position. A second later, Stella was standing next to her. Jeena noticed the wizard scout was floating a hand's breath off the deck When Jeena looked down she realized she was floating as well.

Levitation? Jeena wondered.

"We hurry," said Stella. "Power run low soon."

Jeena drew Power from her own reserve and mouthed the words of a levitation spell. She wrapped the magic energy around both Stella and her.

"I'll handle the levitation," Jeena told her friend. "You handle the shield. Between us, maybe we'll have enough Power if we hurry."

Hurry they did. As they traveled down the hallway, they came upon a set of thick metal blast doors with a force field blocking their way. Jeena connected a strand of the black hole's energy to the obstruction. Before long, another hole in the deck marked their progress toward the vault. The new hole vented an increasing amount of the space station's atmosphere into outer space.

The bodies of several bat creatures were flung against Stella's shield. The wizard scout's Power was strong enough to keep both of them protected. Eventually, they spied a thick set of double doors ahead. No guards were in sight. Jeena commented on their absence.

Stella made a rasping sound Jeena had come to associate with laughter.

"I think the last four bats that bounced off shield were guards. Be careful. Auto-weapons still there."

Jeena was sure her friend was right about the auto-weapons. While the physical guards might be gone, they'd encountered plenty of computer-controlled weapons during their holo-square training. They'd never actually made it inside the vault during any of their training scenarios.

"I could rip the doors off from here," Jeena said thinking of the remaining strands of the black hole's energy she'd gotten from the *'helper.'*

Stella's battle computer, Jonathan, spoke using the external speakers on the Sterilian's battle helmet. "Bad idea. The atmosphere in this part of the station is a near vacuum thanks to all the holes you've been punching in the outer hull. We have no idea how the bottles of DNA gas are secured inside. As soon as you rip the doors off, the bottles are liable to be sucked out faster than the two of you can catch them. Some might even break. We need all twenty-nine bottles according to the central computer."

Jeena felt herself losing control of her temper. She hadn't come all this way to be stopped now.

"Calm down," said Danny's voice through her headband. *"He's right. We've got to think this through a little before we act."*

The alarm sirens that had constantly been wailing suddenly stopped.

"Life forms come," said Stella. "Be here soon I think."

Jeena let her mind gather in the sensations of Power around her. She sensed scores of life forms heading their way. They appeared well organized.

"We've lost the element of surprise," said Danny. *"I calculate we have about one minute before we'll be under attack. I'd give you the odds of our survival, but even I have trouble calculating percentages when they get too small."*

Whether the battle computer was serious or joking, Jeena didn't know. What she did know was that they were in serious trouble.

Pop!

The noise behind them startled Jeena. She spun around with her staff raised in a defensive position ready to do battle. When she saw the source of the noise, Jeena lowered her staff. A two-meter-long silver dragon was hovering in what little air remained in the corridor.

"You should have left while you had the chance," Jeena said.

"I don't leave my friends," said Bright Wing speaking out loud. "Furry bats will be here soon. I will help you."

Jeena had a thought. "Can you teleport into the vault and get the bottles of DNA gas and bring them to us?"

The dragon looked thoughtful for a second before replying. "I'm young again. I can only teleport myself. I can get into vault, but I can't teleport anything else out."

Jonathan spoke up again. "I calculate if the dragon got inside and secured the bottles, Jeehana could rip off the doors. She could rip out a couple of walls as well. That should also knock out any automated weapons systems still functioning."

"Bright Wing?" Jeena asked.

Without asking questions, the dragon shimmered and disappeared. A few seconds later, Jeena sensed the dragon's emotion-speak in her mind.

"Secured."

"Hold on," Jeena told Stella.

Jeena felt the wizard scout increase the Power around them to secure them in place. As soon as she did, Jeena took several strands of energy from the black hole and attached them to the vault's doors and two of its walls. When she released her grip on the strands, the doors and half of the vault's walls were ripped through the deck. The air in the vault rushed out the new holes along with a myriad of other loose items stored there. When the dust and debris settled, Jeena saw Bright Wing holding onto a support beam with her tail. The dragon clutched a clear case in her front paws. Inside the case were bottles filled with a swirling red gas.

"The Crosioians will be here in twenty seconds," said Jonathan.

"Bright Wing," Jeena ordered. "To me."

The dragon let go with her tail and levitated the thirty meters to Jeena.

"Hold onto me," Jeena ordered. She felt Stella grab her shoulder and Bright Wing wrap her tail around her arm.

"Five seconds," warned Jonathan.

Jeena touched the runes on her staff in the order Dren had shown her. She felt her body tingle as the world around her shifted in and out of focus. Jeena suddenly remembered the remaining strands of the black hole's energy were still in her grasp. She quickly attached them to several points on the space station and let go. Then everything went black.

CHAPTER 64

The wizard scouts infiltrated the spaceport using the weak spot Thomas and Janice had located months earlier. Once everyone was assembled, Telsa closed the hole she'd drilled through the spaceport's defensive shield. Although Richard knew the Dragars would be aware of their presence in a few seconds, he figured the expenditure of Power was worth it if it bought them a few more seconds of non-discovery.

Richard took a moment to look around. At least two scores of the black starships were berthed around the spaceport. He was only concerned with three of those starships.

In a section isolated from the others, three starships hovered above their berths. Richard identified them as a recon ship, a destroyer, and a massive black dreadnaught. All three starships were hovering several meters above the ground.

"How can that dreadnaught be here?" Richard asked his battle computer. *"If we tried that with one of our Empire dreadnaughts, the entire lower half of the ship would be crushed."*

"Well," said Nickelo, *"I guess magic does have its advantages. I calculate they're using some type of levitation spell. It must be a very good spell, that's all I've got to say."*

Richard nodded his head. He could sense the energy of the Mountain's Heart from inside the ship.

"Well, no use dillydallying around," said Tam. "What better way to start our morning than slugging it out with a dreadnaught when we've only got a few small-arms weapons."

Chancee laughed. She eyed Tam's M12 as she held up her bow. "Wanna trade?"

"Uh, not hardly," Tam said returning the ranger's laugh.

"We won't be using hand weapons," Richard said as he removed his dimensional pack. Turning to Jerad, he said, "Have your battle computer feed Nickelo the specs for the equipment you require. We need to hurry. I think all three of those starships are getting ready to leave."

A series of high-pitched whines from the direction of the destroyer seemed to confirm Richard's analysis.

Richard had Nickelo put the equipment list Jerad made up onto his heads-up display, then sent the specs for the items to his dimensional pack.

"I hope this works," Richard said.

"You and me both, brother," said Nickelo. *"You and me both."*

CHAPTER 65

The octopod sat in his control chair while monitoring the availability of the equipment in his assigned warehouse. All indicators registered one hundred percent availability. The indicators always registered one hundred percent, but the octopod went through the motions of filling out the shift change report anyway.

The octopod had worked at the heavy-weapons warehouse ever since it opened. In all that time, the warehouse had never received an approved equipment request.

Still, he thought, *one could come at any moment. We always have to be ready. You never know.*

In spite of his silent words, the octopod couldn't help but feel a little sad in both of his hearts. He'd be retiring soon. His brother-in-law worked in one of the small-arms warehouses. They were always getting requests; a fact which his brother-in-law reveled in telling him any time they met. On those occasions, the octopod would tell his wife's brother that the heavy weapons were being saved for something really important. His brother-in-law always laughed at his words.

Lost in his thoughts, the octopod didn't see a flashing light on the control console right away. When it finally drew his attention, he sat up in his seat and stared at the computer display. REQUEST APPROVED was flashing in bright red.

The octopod touched the readout unit with one of his tentacles. A stream of specifications began scrolling across the screen. When he realized the extent of the specifications, the octopod temporarily froze. His training from the past two-score and ten years quickly kicked in. When it did, he slapped a red button on his command chair with one of his tentacles.

"Attention all personnel," said the octopod doing his best to keep the excitement out of his voice. "This is not a drill. Emergency request has been received and approved for two Leviathans, two Long Cats, and a Warcat. Armaments' list is being sent to appropriate stations. Authorization for requisitioning neutron bombs out of security vault is approved. An additional K12 man-portable launcher with anti-armor rockets is also requested from the small-arms warehouse. Let's hustle, everyone. Time is of the essence."

The three hundred and twenty-seven workers composed of more than a dozen races jumped to obey the orders of their warehouse supervisor. This was the day they had lived for. Nothing was going to stop them from completing their equipment requests.

CHAPTER 66

"Use telekinesis to free the pack," Richard suggested to Tam when part of his dimensional pack got hung up on one of the Long Cat's rocket pods.

Jerad and Trinity were already guiding their two Leviathans across the spaceport's tarmac, firing missiles and plasma beams as they went.

Telsa was just climbing into her Long Cat when Tam finally got her rocket pod free from the dimensional pack. The ex-mercenary wasted no time jumping into the pilot's seat of her cat. A half a dozen heartbeats later, Tam was running in the direction taken by the Leviathans. Telsa followed close on her heels in the second Long Cat. The booms of the females' 200mm phase cannons soon echoed in the morning air.

Richard summoned his dimensional pack to him and pulled out another canister of missiles for the K12. He placed them at General Fenmar's feet. The dwarf was busy traversing the missile launcher toward the far side of the spaceport.

"Don't worry about aiming," Richard said. "Just keep away from the dome and those three ships."

"That'll be easy enough," laughed Fenmar. "You forgot to show me how to aim."

Richard wasn't concerned. The dwarf had picked up the concept of the missiles easily enough. Plus, Nickelo had assigned several logic threads to handle the finer points of aiming. Turning away from the general, Richard gave some final instructions to Emerald and Chancee.

"When Janice and Thomas get here with the bottles of DNA gas, I want you to have them bring fifteen of the bottles to me. I'll be at the dome. The two of you need to get the other fourteen bottles to Jerad. He'll get them into the destroyer somehow and destroy the gem.

Richard didn't wait for a reply. He just threw his dimensional pack over his shoulder and levitated up and into his Warcat. He was soon running across the tarmac in the direction of the dome at the spaceport's center. He already knew what he'd find inside; the Dragars' temple.

When he got about halfway to the dome, a series of large explosions erupted on the far side of the spaceport.

"I calculate Trinity and Jerad have activated their neutron bombs," said Nickelo.

"Ya think?" Richard snapped. *"I figured that one out even without a nanosecond brain."*

"Geesh, Rick," said Nickelo feigning hurt. *"You don't have to be so touchy. I was just trying to help."*

Richard hadn't meant to snap, but he was nervous. He'd always been an 'act first, think later' kind of guy, but this whole thing was turning into one big, unorganized cluster. There were too many moving parts.

"The odds anything I've planned is going to work is probably nil," Richard said.

"Actually," laughed Nickelo, *"I think it's less than nil, but cheer up. Maybe you'll get lucky."*

"Yeah, right," Richard replied. *"When a computer starts advising me to rely on luck, that's when I really start worrying."*

The remaining distance to the Dragars' dome passed quickly. The Warcat was fast. While Richard passed a lot of Dragars, Thargs, and various slaves along the way, they were all apparently so confused that none tried to stop him. He didn't even have to fire his weapons.

When Richard reached the dome, he was in luck. The main doors were closed, but someone had already blown a hole in the wall next to the doors. Since the hole was large enough for the Warcat, Richard ducked inside. He was greeted by absolute chaos. Fires and explosions were erupting all around. A line of destruction seemed to go from the hole in the wall directly toward the Dragar's pyramid.

Richard spied a couple of humanoid figures near the top of the pyramid engaged in combat with a score of Dragar spellcasters. A blue beam of magic from one of the two humanoids struck the Dragars' shield. Their shield buckled but continued to hold.

Something silver fluttering in the air behind the two humanoids drew Richard's attention. The silver object looked familiar. Then recognition came to Richard.

"What the…?" Richard thought. *"How'd Bright Wing get here?"*

"Rick," said Nickelo. *"I'm in contact with Jonathan. He says Stella is there with Bright Wing. They're with an elf. They've got fifteen bottles of DNA gas, but they can't get to the opening at the top of the pyramid. The Dragar priests are too strong."*

Shifting the Warcat into high gear, Richard began running toward the pyramid. What Thargs tried to stop him, Nickelo made short work of with a few diligent blasts from the Warcat's 20mm plasma rifles. Richard let his battle computer handle the Warcat while he concentrated on the flows of energy around him.

The entire floor of the dome was covered with thousands of worktables. Clear tubes filled with a red gas ran from the top of the pyramid to lines and sublines until every worktable under the dome had a line.

Richard merged his mind with the red gas flowing to a nearby worktable. He felt the fear and sensed the screams of the unborn dragons that had been sacrificed to produce the gas. It wasn't the refined DNA gas used to create wizard scouts, but it was close enough for Richard to instinctively know how to manipulate the energy in the gas. He twisted the red gas back upon itself and forced it to flow back toward the pyramid from which it had come. As the gas passed other sublines, he drew the energy of their gas as well and propelled it toward the pyramid. By the time the energy reached the top of the pyramid, it was a huge ball of pulsating red magic.

The Dragar priests must have sensed the approach of the magic because several of them turned to face it. They formed a shield. Unfortunately for them, it wasn't nearly powerful enough. The red magic ripped the Dragars' shield to pieces. At the same time, a blue beam of magic from one of the two humanoids hit the Dragar priests. The priests disappeared in an eruption of red and blue magic.

"Stella says thanks," said Nickelo. *"She says the way's clear now. The elf and she can get the bottles of DNA gas into the pyramid. You need to do whatever you need to do."*

Richard assumed the elf with Stella was Comstar. He knew the old elf was just as competent as Stella. He had faith the two of them could do whatever needed to be done with the DNA gas.

At that moment, something touched Richard's mind. He recognized the touch. It was Bright Wing.

"Brother," said the dragon using emotion-speak. *"We must save the others. They're helpless. They'll be destroyed if we don't save them."*

An image of tens of thousands of dragon eggs on the conveyor belts snaking through the worktables came to Richard's mind. The task of saving all the dragon eggs was daunting.

"Come," said Bright Wing. *"You must help me."*

With that, the silver dragon touched Richard's mind with a species memory.

Richard became one of millions—no, billions of dragons who'd once inhabited the galaxy. They spread their magic far and wide. During their travels, the dragons took other species along to populate habitable planets. Over hundreds of thousands of years, populations of dwarf, elf, gnome, orc, and other races of Portalis made contact with the populations of Dragar, Thargs, and other species in the galaxies. Empires rose and fell. Wars erupted, and whole species were wiped out of existence. Even the mighty dragons were pushed to the brink of extinction.

The wisest of dragons were assembled. They chose a line of dragons to be their saviors. These special dragons were instilled with the ability to travel through time and space. With the help of the special dragons, a hot, bubbling mass of mud near a yellow star was chosen to be the dragon's hope for the future. For tens of thousands of years, the special dragons transported their brethren through time to lay their eggs in the hot mud. Over the years, billions of fertilized eggs lay hidden in the mud. Richard knew they would stay there until they were needed.

As the star cooled, so did the planet. As it did, the mud cooled as well and formed a soft rock. One day a starship landed on the planet. The Dragars onboard used slaves to mine the dragon eggs. They brought the eggs by the millions back to Portalis and sacrificed them there using the Power of a blue gem.

The Mountain's Heart, Richard thought.

Through the species memory, Richard saw something else. While the Dragars used some of the gas from the sacrificed dragon eggs to create batteries for their ships and weapons, some of the gas they purposely allowed to seep through a crack to the physical dimension. The gas leaked out of the crack and slowly began changing the dynamics of the physical galaxy. As years passed, magic began to work alongside physics.

More species memory flowed across Richard's mind. Most were too alien to comprehend. Others were of no use to him. He hastily discarded those and moved onto the next memory. Finally, a memory came to Richard that fit his need. He drew his mind back from the flow of memories.

When he was fully back in the here and now, Richard spoke to Bright Wing. *"Come to me. I have a task for you. The lives of your unborn brothers depend on you."*

CHAPTER 67

Janice Deluth picked up her half of the fourteen bottles of DNA gas. Her husband held the other seven. When they'd arrived at the Oracle's, they'd only found the fourteen bottles. The Oracle had told them Wizard Scout Stella and an elf had already departed with the other fifteen. The Oracle had told her husband and her that they needed to get to the black destroyer and destroy the Mountain's Heart before it was taken off planet.

So it was that Janice now found herself hiding among a stack of crates a hundred meters from the black destroyer. She could sense the energy from the blue gem inside the ship. Unfortunately, they couldn't gain entry. The way was blocked by several hundred four-armed Thargs and a score of Dragar magic users.

Even at the peak of their strength, Janice knew she and Thomas would've been hard-pressed to force entry into the destroyer. While her husband might argue the fact, she knew they were far from their peak strength. She could sense the frailness of her Power reserve. Her passive scan confirmed Thomas wasn't any better off than she. If either of them put too much of a strain on their reserves, she had no doubt they'd rupture. Their deaths would soon follow.

Thomas held his bottles of DNA gas out toward her. "Here, take these. I'll draw their fire. When I do, you sneak onboard and destroy the gem. Once you do, get off pronto. I'll join you later."

Janice bristled at her husband's words. *Typical*, she thought. "You can think again," she said. "Until death do us part, remember? We're either doing this together, or we're not doing it at all. Understand?"

Her husband opened his mouth as if he wanted to argue further, but was stopped short by a loud explosion from their rear. The first blast was followed by several others. Within seconds, multi-colored beams of energy were landing among the Tharg formations guarding the black destroyer. The Thargs immediately began scattering for cover.

Looking behind her, Janice saw two Empire Leviathan cats and two Long Cats running toward the black destroyer firing every weapon they had. Return fire was slow in coming from the Thargs, but a couple of mages succeeded in combining their Power into a single spell that knocked a leg out from underneath one of the Long Cats. A 200mm phase round from the second Long Cat obliterated the two magic users.

"Now," said Thomas. "We've got to go now."

Janice jumped to her feet and began running toward a set of stairs located at the rear of the destroyer. The stairs were starting to rise, as were several others along the length of the starship.

"She's getting ready to take off," shouted Thomas.

"I know," Janice yelled back. She loved her husband, but he was always one to state the obvious.

A Tharg got in Janice's way. A dozen rounds from her plasma rifle put him down quick enough. By the time they made it to the back of the destroyer, the stairs were already raised and the door was closing. Wrapping herself with Power, Janice levitated herself up and dived through the opening. The door slammed shut behind her. Her passive scan confirmed that Thomas was right behind her.

Wasting no time, Janice came out of a roll and jumped to her feet. Thankfully, only four guards were in the entryway. After a few quick swings with her phase rod, all four guards were sprawled out on the floor, bleeding profusely from their heads. None of them had succeeded in sounding the alarm.

The destroyer shuddered, then suddenly lifted into the air. The angle of its departure left little doubt the starship's captain was making an emergency takeoff.

Janice gave her husband a smile.

He smiled back. "We've been in tougher spots."

Janice laughed and nodded her head. "Yeah, I know. I just can't remember when."

Thomas laughed as well. Then he turned toward a hallway leading in the general direction of the Mountain's Heart. "Shall we, my dear?"

"Why not?" Janice replied as she joined her husband in the hallway.

A thought came to Janice. One way or another, she knew this was their final mission.

CHAPTER 68

Even before the last of the Dragar priests had fallen, Jeena was running toward the tip of the pyramid. The satchel with the fifteen bottles of DNA gas bounced on its shoulder strap. She heard the sound of firing as Stella sent out a line of cover. A lot of the four-armed Thargs were carrying weapons. Some of them began returning fire, but their marksmanship was nowhere near as accurate as that of the wizard scout's. As a result, Jeena made it to the pyramid's tip without getting hit.

Using the information provided by the Oracle, Jeena touched an indentation in the pyramid's surface, pushing hard with her left hand. A piece of the pyramid moved outward to reveal an opening. Jeena began stuffing bottles of DNA gas down the chute as fast as she could take them out of her bag.

The effect of the bottles wasn't what Jeena expected. She'd been told the bottles would destroy the pyramid. Such wasn't the case. To Jeena, the addition of the DNA gas bottles seemed to be increasing the strength of whatever was inside the pyramid. For a moment, Jeena wondered if she'd been tricked. Then she felt a presence. She'd felt the presence before. It was the green sphere.

"You're dead," Jeena told the green sphere.

"Not yet," said the sphere. *"We will be soon if all goes well. My brothers and I are tired. The bottles of DNA gas you added to the Dragars' temple has given us strength to partially resist the Dragars' control over us. I fear we may be too late. The destroyer and its two escorts have already left the planet. The recon ship and*

the destroyer are through the time-gate. Soon, the dreadnaught will join them in the physical dimension."

An image flashed in Jeena's mind. It was an image of her standing near the green sphere. It was an image of her in another time and place.

"I don't understand," Jeena said. *"That already happened. You died when we last met."*

"It doesn't matter," replied the green sphere. *"What's important is that even now, you are in another place assisting us to break free of the Dragars' control. Soon, the* 'helper' *will send your other self a link with Power. Then the version of you in the future will cast the spell to bring my brothers and me together once more. When that happens, we will be able to use the energy of the sacrificed dragons to open a time-gate of our own. We will use it to bring death and destruction to this place where you now stand. You must not be here when that occurs. Go. You have saved us. Go now in peace."*

"I don't understand," Jeena repeated. *"I'm supposed to destroy the temple. And what about all these eggs?"* Jeena asked as she gestured toward the conveyor belts filled with dragon eggs weaving their way through the worktables. *"There must be thousands of unborn dragons in those eggs."*

"The eggs aren't your task," said a voice using emotion-speak. The voice was that of Bright Wing.

"I can't leave them to die," Jeena said. *"They're helpless."*

"They won't die," said Bright Wing sounding very confident. *"My brother is here even now. He'll save them."*

Something accompanying the dragon's emotions made Jeena look at the far end of the dome's floor. She saw a large, black-armored beast. It was firing beams of red energy at a group of the four-armed furry creatures.

"That black monster?" Jeena asked. *"How will it save them?"*

"He isn't a monster," answered Bright Wing. *"He's wearing armor. He's a dragon-friend; he's an elf friend; and he's the* 'helper.' *He'll find a way to save my brothers."*

"But—"

"No buts," said Bright Wing. *"If you remain longer, you will endanger my brethren. Your task is completed. Go. Go now, or your death is assured. Go now with our thanks."*

If the dragon had been speaking with words rather than emotion-speak, Jeena knew she would've continued arguing. She could feel the truthfulness and fear in the dragon's words and knew it was time to go.

By this time, Stella was standing next to Jeena. Without taking time to explain, Jeena reached out and touched the wizard scout's arm. At the same time, she touched the runes on the Lady's staff in the order taught her by Dren. The world immediately began shifting in and out of focus. With a start, Jeena realized something was different. For some reason, Stella wasn't being included in the spell. Before Jeena could try to stop the teleportation, everything went black.

CHAPTER 69

Richard called Bright Wing to him. When she came, the dragon brought Stella with her. The Sterilian gave Richard a toothy grin.

Richard exited his Warcat and grasped one of Stella's hands. "I'm not even going to ask how you got here. We've got things to do."

A bolt of magic energy passed overhead and struck a nearby wall. The arm of the Warcat lifted of its own accord and fired a score of plasma rounds at the Dragar mage who'd released the spell.

"Take the Warcat," Richard told Stella. "Link up with the others. They're trying to stop a destroyer from taking off."

"Too late," said Jonathan, his friend's battle computer, over the external speaker of her battle helmet. "All three starships left a couple of minutes ago. The commandant and Councilwoman Deluth are onboard the destroyer."

Richard's heart sank.

"It's what was meant to be," said Nickelo. *"You can't change the past. This is what happened. You've got your own mission. The destruction of the Mountain's Heart is your parents' task."*

"But maybe we could save them," Richard said.

"No," said Nickelo. *"You can't change history. This is their last mission. You already know they'll get out of the destroyer in an escape pod. Sergeant Ron will find them. They'll live. Your mother will become a councilwoman. Your father will become the commandant at the Academy. That's the way it has to be."*

Another thought came to Richard. *"Sergeant Ron's wife will die."*

"Yes, she will," agreed Nickelo. *"You will too if you don't get moving. So will all of these unborn dragons as well as all of the slaves."*

Richard looked around. The dome held thousands of slaves. Most of them were cowering under their worktables. Hundreds of Thargs were moving around the dome's floor firing weapons at the hiding slaves. Other Thargs were firing at the dragon eggs on the conveyor belts. It was turning into a slaughter.

The senseless murder of the unborn dragons and the slaves caused Richard's mind to snap. He grasped onto the idea he'd gotten from the dragons' species memory. He touched Bright Wing with his mind and then began touching the minds of the unborn dragons within the eggs. Richard reached out to the green, orange, and purple spheres. He found them half in and half out of a time-gate. Pooling all of the various dragon resources together, Richard formed a Circle. He doubted he could've done it if he hadn't already been linked closely to the dragons. However, he was, so he could. Once he did, each new link of the Circle strengthened the others.

The claws and teeth of the unborn dragons hardened. The baby dragons began tearing at the insides of their shells. Their eggs began cracking. First a dozen, then hundreds, then thousands of the dragons hatched. As soon as the young dragons flew into the air, they headed straight for Bright Wing. When they reached her, the bodies of the newly-hatched dragons merged with that of the silver dragon. With each merging, Bright Wing grew in size and power. By the time the last of the newborn dragons merged with Bright Wing, she was fully two hundred meters in length.

Bright Wing roared her battle cry, then turned her attention to the Dragars and Thargs still under the dome. They began running in a vain hope of escaping the wrath of the immense silver dragon. A few Thargs made it to an exit, but most did not.

It didn't take long for Bright Wing to kill most of the Dragars and Thargs under the dome. Once she had trouble finding new targets, Bright Wing blasted a hole in the roof with a spell and flew outside to continue her revenge on her former Dragar masters.

Richard was still part of the Circle. He extended the Circle to the slaves hiding under the worktables. He expanded the Circle even farther to those slaves outside the dome. Before long, the Circle extended all the way to the far side of the spaceport.

Funneling energy from the pyramid through the green sphere, Richard tore the restraining collars from the necks of the slaves.

"Run," Richard mentally ordered. *"Leave this place now. It will soon be destroyed."*

Along with the command, Richard sent courage to the slaves. His courage increased as it jumped from one link to another. Suddenly, slaves began leaving their hiding places and running for the exits. Many began attacking their former masters and taking their weapons.

"Time to go, Stella," Richard said as he began running for an exit. He sensed his friend hot on his heels in the Warcat.

Once outside, Richard noticed several of the Dragar starships taking off. Dozens of fighter-shuttles were crisscrossing the airfield strafing the running figures of the slaves.

Richard saw a fighter-shuttle turn to make a strafing run at Stella and him. Before it could fire, four balls of energy slammed into it from overhead. The shuttle burst into flames. A second fighter-shuttle passed through the debris cloud and skidded to a landing twenty meters from Richard. The ramp lowered.

A small figure ran down the ramp and waved Richard forward. "Let's go," shouted Tia's gunner, Rembis. "We don't have all day."

Richard spied Emerald, Chancee, and General Fenmar inside the shuttle. He ran to join them. He heard the pop of an escape hatch behind him as Stella left the Warcat behind. By the time he got to the bottom of the ramp, the Sterilian had already passed him and taken her seat. Before Richard could sit down, the ramp closed, and the shuttle was off the ground climbing for altitude.

"Where are the others?" Richard shouted in an attempt to be heard over the roar of the shuttle's engines.

Emerald was sitting across from Richard. She caught his attention. "Everyone else is on Matthew's shuttle. Jerad ordered Tia to pick us up. We told her where to find you. Uh, I'm assuming this lizard is with you."

Stella growled.

Richard hadn't previously heard the sound from any of the

Sterilians he'd ever met.

"She is," Richard said. "Where are we headed now?"

The engine noise suddenly died away as the shuttle reached altitude.

Tia looked over her shoulder and answered, "Jerad's ordered us to rendezvous back at the Oracle's. Uh, I guess you heard about Janice and Thomas?"

Richard nodded his head.

Tia turned back around and began doing her best to dodge the fire from some Dragar shuttles that seemed determined to turn them into burning wreckage.

Since Tia and Rembis were working well as a team, Richard left the flying to them. He concentrated on the Circle. It was starting to fade as he got farther from the dome.

Richard cut the links to the former slaves. He'd done all he could for them. They were on their own now.

Contacting Bright Wing with emotion-speak, Richard ordered her to return to the Oracle's as well. Talking to the silver dragon was a strange experience. She was no longer a single entity. Instead, she was composed of thousands of separate consciousnesses. Fortunately, they all seemed to be of one accord.

Richard felt Bright Wing's link to the Circle disconnect. The consciousness's of the newly-hatched dragons that were part of her continued to remain linked using their own Power.

At the edge of his thoughts, Richard sensed the green sphere and its two brothers. They were still at the spaceport, but also on a planet in another time and place. Richard recognized the planet. It was the location of the mining camp where the *Defiant* had fought the black destroyer.

The green sphere shared an image with Richard of the battle between the *Defiant* and the Dragar ships. He saw Tia and Matthew destroy the black recon shuttle. He watched the *Defiant* engaging the black destroyer. Through the time-gate, Richard could see the shape of an enormous black dreadnaught.

"Are those—"

The green sphere didn't wait for Richard to finish his question. *"Yes. Those are the same three starships that just took off from the spaceport. My brothers and I were forced to create a time-gate for them. Thanks to the* 'helper' *and you, we are now our own masters.*

We control the time-gate."

As Richard watched, the three spheres forming the time-gate in the image began drawing closer together.

"Wait," Richard said. *"If what you're saying is true, my parents are on that destroyer. I have to save them."*

As Richard watched, two escape pods exited the destroyer and headed for the shrinking time-gate. First one, then the other escape pod passed through the gate.

The green sphere's image followed one of the escape pods. It was gated into the spiritual dimension over an icy planet. The escape pod exploded showering thousands of bits of blue onto the icy surface below. Richard got the impression the gate had taken the first escape pod to a time long before he was born.

"Was that the Mountain's Heart?" Richard asked

"Yes," replied the green sphere. *"Your parents completed their mission by infusing the DNA gas into the gem. They loaded it onto an escape pod and jettisoned it just before they launched their own pod."*

"What about my parents?" Richard asked. *"Will they be safe?"*

"You know they will," replied the green sphere. *"We have gated their pod to the time and place where your Sergeant Ron found them. They will live."*

"What about you?" Richard asked. *"Maybe we can save you?"*

"You know you cannot," said the sphere. *"Our time has come. We have created a time-gate that will set us free. Watch."*

Fascinated in spite of their current danger, Richard watched the scene playing out in his mind. He sensed the three spheres changing the time-gate surrounding the spaceport. A second image of another spaceport overlaid the one of the Dragars. The second spaceport image looked familiar.

Richard drew in a sharp breath as he recognized the location. *Velos!*

There was fighting around a large building.

That's the DNA center, Richard thought

Somehow, Richard sensed that at the very moment he was watching, a version of him was inside the building fighting side by side with his father. He sensed the commandant, Chief Instructor Winslow, and him shifting into the void. At the same moment, he caught the briefest glimpse of a Crosioian dreadnaught traveling at high speed directly toward the DNA center. When the starship hit, the Velos spaceport was engulfed in flames and flying wreckage.

The force of the dreadnaught's explosion shot through the opening between dimensions. The rift in time connecting the crack at the DNA center to the Dragars' pyramid imploded, bringing a large amount of the exploding dreadnaught with it.

Richard's connection with the green sphere disappeared. He was thrown out of his seat as the fighter-shuttle was jostled from side to side. Once Tia regained control of the shuttle, he raced to a nearby viewport and looked out. The spaceport was no more. Only a giant mushroom cloud remained.

The three spheres were gone, but Richard sensed another presence deep beneath where the Dragars' temple had been. The presence was evil. He recognized the presence as the demon, Zenthra. The demon was laughing. Richard couldn't hear the sound, but knew it was true nevertheless.

Richard tried to pull away from the presence, but the demon seemed to delight in letting him know it was still there. It fed Richard a stream of images. The fleet of Dragar warships that had escaped before the spaceport's destruction was orbiting Portalis. As he watched, the warships began bombarding one of the planet's two main continents. Mushroom clouds appeared on the surface as entire cities were vaporized. Hundreds of black starships began popping out of hyperspace and adding their firepower to the fray. The Dragars seemed bent on the destruction of Portalis.

Richard sensed a defensive shield over the second continent. He recognized the continent as Slyvrastra, the homeland of the elves. Beams of energy and missiles from the newly arrived Dragar armada blasted against the Slyvrastra's shield. The shield held, but he could sense it weakening as the plasma, phase, and magic energy continued to rain down on the continent's defenses. He knew it was only a matter of time before the shield failed. In the background of his mind, he heard the demon laugh even harder.

Suddenly, other starships arrived over the planet and began fighting with the black warships. Bright colored beams of energy crisscrossed through space accompanied by violent explosions. The loss of life on both sides was overwhelming.

Zenthra continued laughing.

Just as Slyvrastra's defenses were on the verge of failing, a voice which wasn't a voice shouted, "Enough! You have violated the rules."

Richard sensed powerful entities begin appearing around the planet. While he couldn't explain how, he sensed the entities were what he thought of as good. Zenthra stopped laughing. Richard sensed a new emotion coming from the demon.

Is it fear? Richard wondered.

Suddenly, other powerful entities began appearing around Portalis. The sense Richard got from the newest entities was evil. The evil entities began fighting those that were good.

A new voice which was not a voice spoke. "This accomplishes nothing. Both sides will be utterly destroyed. Chaos will rule the three galaxies if we don't stop this now."

The second voice was familiar to Richard. He'd felt the owner's presence before. It was the Master demon he'd encountered during his first mission on Portalis.

"Your lieutenant broke the rules," said the first voice. "What did you expect? Even now, others of my kind are assembling their armies."

"As are mine," said the Master demon. "But it's too soon to end the game. I will withdraw my forces if you do the same."

"Portalis must be protected as long as the guardian remains alive," said the first voice. "That was the agreement."

"Yes," agreed the voice of the Master demon. "That was the agreement. Let us pull back our forces until the time of the final battle."

"Portalis must be protected," reiterated the first voice.

"It will be," said the Master demon. "As long as the tree lives, as long as the guardian protects the gate, Portalis will be off-limits. Let us reset the game."

Although Richard saw nothing, he got an impression of the Master demon waving a hand. Hundreds of the black Dragar starships were swept from the sky. The Master demon waved his hand again. A wave of energy swept over the planet.

"There," said the Master demon. "The advanced magic and technology of the other planets will no longer work on Portalis. The playing field is leveled."

Richard heard a shout in the background.

The shout came from Tia. "Engine failure! We're going in hard.

I can't control the shuttle."

While Richard wanted to help Tia, his mind was still locked in the vision of the Master demon and his opponent. They were still facing one another high above Portalis.

The Master demon's opponent spoke. The opponent didn't seem impressed with the demon's actions. "Your lieutenant, Zenthra, still inhabits the Dragars' computer under the planet's surface. Do you call that leveling the field?"

"I have left your variable with his equipment," said the Master Demon. "Your wizard scout may continue to use his gear. It's only fair that my variables are allowed to use theirs as well. The rules allow conflict between our variables. If you don't want my lieutenant to inhabit the Dragars' computer, then you may send your variable to destroy Zenthra's avatar. I won't stop him. That is, if you believe he's capable."

The demon's opponent didn't respond for a considerable amount of time. Finally, the opponent spoke. "Ever the one to stretch the rules, aren't you? I know you consider the wizard scout to be your variable as much as mine. I disagree, but I won't waste time on semantics. The rules have been reset. I am satisfied."

Richard sensed the Master demon's opponent wave a hand. An aura shimmered around Portalis. The aura solidified into a shield.

The opponent spoke again. "No advanced equipment other than that of our variables will be allowed on Portalis as long as the guardian lives."

"Agreed," said the Master demon.

With the agreement in place, both the good and evil entities withdrew. The space around Portalis was suddenly devoid of either entities or starships of either side. Richard caught a glimpse of a large energy shield surrounding Portalis. He saw a second, smaller shield protecting the elf continent of Slyvrastra.

With an effort, Richard wrestled his mind free of Zenthra's control. The moment he did, everything went black.

CHAPTER 70

When Richard came to his senses, he heard the sound of thunder. It was raining. Only, he wasn't getting wet.

"It's about time you woke up," said Nickelo. His battle computer's voice was accompanied by a laugh. *"You're always sleeping on the job and leaving me to do all the work."*

Richard sat up. He noticed the unfurled wing of Bright Wing protecting him from the storm. Her head was only a meter away and she was intently staring at him.

"Are you okay, brother?" she asked in emotion-speak.

"I guess," Richard replied trying to stall for time. He was still having difficulty getting his bearings. *"What happened?"*

Someone had removed Richard's battle helmet. It was on the ground next to him.

Nickelo brought Richard up to speed. *"The shuttle's engine failed on short final. Stella was able to soften the landing somewhat with her telekinesis, but we still hit pretty hard. I calculate the shuttle won't be flying again anytime soon."*

Richard remembered the words of the Master demon. From what he'd heard, it sounded like none of the Dragars' equipment would work while it was on Portalis.

"Anyone hurt?" Richard said.

"Tia and Rembis got a few bruises, but they'll be all right," replied Nickelo. *"The other shuttle's here, but we only found Marstis onboard. She said that shortly after they landed, the other wizard scouts and Matthew seemed to shimmer and then*

disappear. I calculate it was mission complete for them. I'm guessing 'the One' *teleported them back home."*

"You guess?" Richard said. He was used to a little more definite probabilities from his battle computer.

"I haven't got any data to back up my analysis," said Nickelo, *"so, yes, I'm guessing. However, I feel like that's what happened, so that's my story and I'm sticking to it."*

Richard put on his battle helmet and stood up.

"Where's Tia?" Richard said. *"I assume she's pretty shook up. Matthew and Tia are pretty close."*

"Yes, they are," agreed Nickelo. *"However, Tia's not here. She was teleported out shortly after we touched down. Stella was teleported out as well. You're the only one of our group from the physical dimension who's still here."*

The revelation from his battle computer was enough of a shock to Richard that he spoke out loud. "So why am I the only one still here?" After hearing a low-pitched growl, Richard hastily added, "Err…, and why is Bright Wing still here with me."

"Hmm," said Nickelo over the battle helmet's external speakers for Bright Wing's benefit. "Sometimes I wish I had shoulders so I could shrug them. Just saying 'I do not know' just doesn't seem quite enough."

Richard took a look around. The rain was still coming down. He saw a mangled fighter-shuttle about fifty meters away. A second fighter-shuttle in much better shape was a hundred meters beyond it. The second shuttle was near a dark opening in the side of a hill. Richard recognized the opening. It was the home of the Oracle.

With nothing left to lose, Richard started walking toward the cave. Bright Wing kept pace with him.

Richard stopped and looked at the 200-meter long dragon. "Uh, somehow I don't think you're going to fit, sister. Maybe you should wait outside."

The silver dragon didn't answer, but she did stop walking toward the cave.

Richard continued on by himself. When he entered, he found Emerald, Chancee, and General Fenmar in deep conversation with the holographic image of the Oracle. All three of them stopped talking and looked at Richard.

"Well?" Richard asked. "What did I miss?"

A tired looking Emerald answered, "The Oracle says the Dragar warships destroyed most of the surface cities on our continent. He says our only hope of survival is to travel across the water to the land of the Slyvrastran elves."

Most of the cities are destroyed? Richard thought. The enormity of the situation hit him. He'd been the one who'd pressured King Hamerstine into rebelling against the Dragars. Apparently, all it had gotten them was the destruction of their homes and a forced exodus to another land.

"I'm sorry," Richard said. "I should have left things alone."

"No," said the Oracle. "Far greater deaths would have resulted if you had. The rebellion has spared our galaxy for another hundred thousand years. You did what needed to be done."

Richard wasn't convinced but said nothing.

Emerald turned back to the Oracle. "I'll tell King Hamerstine and King Graphon what you've told us. I'm sure they'll begin building ships to cross the ocean as soon as they can. There's nothing left for us here."

"What about your home?" Richard asked. "Are you going to leave it to the vampires?"

The eyes of both dwarves flashed.

"No!" said Emerald. "We'll drive them out of Drepdenor before we go. Our history is there. So is the wealth of our people. We'll need it in our new home across the water."

While it was too late for Richard to reverse the destruction of King Hamerstine's cities, he resolved to help the dwarves.

"I'll go with you," Richard promised. "I'll help you drive those bloodsuckers out. Besides, I've got a score to settle with Zenthra."

"No," said the Oracle in no uncertain terms. "Drepdenor is no longer your task. Emerald and her allies will do what they need to do. Also, it isn't time yet for you to face Zenthra. The time will come, but it has yet to arrive."

"Well, what am I supposed to do then?" Richard asked. "I'm not going to stand around here with my thumb up my butt while I wait for *'the One'* to send me home."

The Oracle smiled. "No, you're not. You're going to take me to my new home across the ocean. Emerald has promised that once her people have dealt with the vampires, they'll build me a home more suitable than this cave. I calculate King Hamerstine and many of the escaped slaves will help as well. You must take me there, wizard scout. That's your new mission."

Richard stared hard at the Oracle for a few seconds. "Are you telling me or asking me?"

The Oracle smiled again. "I'm asking you as one friend to another."

With a nod of his head, Richard said, "Fine then. Since you put it that way, I accept."

CHAPTER 71

Bright Wing landed in a clear spot near the side of the rocky cliff. Richard slid off the dragon's neck and walked toward a dark opening in the stone. He walked through the tunnel until it made a three-way split.

"All right," Richard said. *"I give up. Which way?"*

"You know, Rick," said Nickelo, *"you've got to pay more attention to things. You've been here a dozen times over the years."*

Richard looked around at the dank and cobweb infested tunnel. Nothing looked familiar. *"Yeah, but it didn't look anything like this. Most of the floors and walls were marble, and the hallways had plenty of those gnome light panels then."*

"Well," replied Nickelo. *"Once the dwarves get here, they'll have this place in tip top shape in only a few thousand years. In the meantime, take a left."*

Following his battle computer's directions, Richard made his way down to the large cavern where he'd always met with the Oracle. Once there, he pulled a small brerellium chip out of his pocket.

"You in there?" Richard asked out loud.

"Where else would I be?" asked the Oracle. "I find it quite comfortable in here, thank you."

Richard smiled. Nickelo had been the one to suggest transporting the Oracle in one of the brerellium chips the Empire used to store the gas that was a battle computer's primary CPU. It had proven a lot handier to transport than a thousand cubic yards of gas during the three-day flight to the Oracle's new home.

"Enough dilly-dallying," said Nickelo. *"Summon some holographic equipment out of that pack of yours and let's be off. Those slaves you freed promised to take care of the Oracle when they arrived. I calculate they'll have no trouble maintaining a few holographic projectors."*

Richard had a feeling his battle computer was correct. Some of the former slaves had been stationed on Dragar starships. Technology was just another form of magic to them.

Following his battle computer's instructions, Richard set up some holographic projection equipment in the cavern. He stored several cases of replacement parts in a second cave. Once done, he said his goodbyes to the holographic image the Oracle was using as an avatar.

"It's not goodbye, wizard scout," said the Oracle. "I calculate I'll see you quite often over the next hundred thousand years."

The Oracle's words didn't make Richard all that happy. A life doing missions for *'the One'* wasn't much of a life in his opinion.

"I guess we'll see," Richard told the Oracle. "I never know what *'the One'* is going to do. I mean, heck, sometimes I can't even summon a simple piece of camping gear because I'm low on Power. However, *'the One'* has made exceptions this whole mission and allowed me to summon all sorts of advanced gear. His rules make no sense."

The hologram of the old woman smiled. "I calculate it makes sense to him, wizard scout. Now, I believe it's time for you to do one last task in order to complete your mission. You must take Bright Wing to the place the dwarves will call New Drepdenor. It will be the home of Emerald's people when they arrive. There is something there I think you should see."

Curious, Richard tried to probe for more information.

The Oracle just smiled and remained silent.

When Richard started to lose his temper, the Oracle's avatar disappeared as the holographic projectors shutoff.

"Geesh, Rick," said Nickelo. *"You've definitely got to take some lessons intact. Now, let's be off. We've got things to do."*

CHAPTER 72

Queen Emerald stood at the head of the army. The cavernous opening of Drepdenor's main entrance was before her.

"Are the troops ready, General Fenmar?"

"Aye, your majesty," replied the general. "They're more than ready. It's time to take our home back."

The morning light glinted off the 1,125 dwarves equipped with the armor and weapons created by General Fenmar's armorers. They were the main assault force of the army. The dwarves' equipment blazed with Power as the blue gems energized the titanium. The resulting Holy Metal shone with a light greater than that of the sun.

A second formation composed of ten thousand dwarves, humans, and freed slaves backed up the first wave of Drepdenoris dwarves. Emerald was determined that none of the vampires would escape her people's revenge. She made a silent vow that once the halls of her beloved Drepdenor were swept clean of the foul creatures, she would lead her people to their new home across the sea.

Emerald tightened the grip on her mother's battle-axe, Gem Defender. She looked at the blonde headed ranger next to her.

"Shall we, old friend?" Emerald said.

"Why not?" said Chancee as she nocked an arrow in her bow.

Yes, Emerald thought. *Why not?*

CHAPTER 73

The tingling stopped. The area around Gaston came back into focus. He was no longer in the secret tunnel. He was in a large cavern about a hundred and fifty meters across. It was dark. Fortunately, he was still wearing his battle suit. His helmet's night-vision visor showed his surroundings in red. The floor was littered with hundreds if not thousands of bones. He detected a single life form. It was to his right rear. He sensed the life form was weak. Since it didn't appear to be an immediate threat, he chose to ignore it for the moment as he continued to scan the area around him.

"Where are we, Wanda?"

"Based upon the data from your passive scan, I calculate we're a couple of hundred meters underground. This cavern appears to be at the edge of an extensive tunnel system. There's a small pool of water to your left. An underground stream is connected to it. The life form to your rear appears to be a female. I calculate she's near death."

Turning to his rear, Gaston noticed the female. She was chained to a boulder. Streaks of liquid were trickling down her legs. He assumed the liquid was blood.

"It is blood," confirmed Wanda.

The woman groaned.

Gaston started forward. At his first step, one of the many bones on the floor made a loud snap. Looking down, he noticed he'd stepped on what appeared to be a human thighbone.

"What the— What's going on, Wanda?"

"Insufficient data to make a calculation, wizard scout."

Gaston gripped the handle of his phase rod tighter with his left hand. It had deactivated during the teleport. He switched it back to destructive mode. He'd lost his M63 and phase pistol during the battle with the demon. Reluctantly, he drew the antique .44 caliber AutoMag from its holster with his right hand. Sending out active scans in all directions, he detected numerous life forms in the tunnels around him. Thankfully, his scans detected only the woman in the cavern he was currently in.

"Actually, she's not a woman, or at least she's not a human woman," said Wanda. *"Look at her ears."*

Concentrating on the female's ears, Gaston noticed they were pointed. *"Is she an elf?"*

"I calculate a one hundred percent probability you're correct, wizard scout."

The elf groaned again.

Gaston began moving in her direction while attempting to avoid the bones on the stone floor. There were too many to avoid them all, but he did the best he could. He wasn't a healer and didn't have a medical kit, so he wasn't sure what he could do for the elf. He did know he couldn't leave her to die chained up to a stone.

Besides, he thought in his private space, *she might be able to give me some information.*

After he'd covered about half the distance to the elf, a male voice made him spin back around.

"I wouldn't try to free the elf if I were you," said the voice. "The Dalinfaust doesn't like others playing with his toys."

Gaston spotted a male figure standing near the back of the cavern. The male had dark skin and light-colored hair. His ears were pointed in a fashion similar to the female's ears. The male had a longsword, but it was still in a scabbard on his belt. His hands were empty, and he held them loosely at his side. Although Gaston could visibly see the male, he couldn't pick him up with either his passive or active scans.

"Good stealth shield," commented Wanda. *"Based upon information in my databanks, he's a dark elf. I calculate he's a mage of some type. Judging by his stealth shield, I calculate he's a very powerful mage."*

Keeping the dark elf covered with his AutoMag, Gaston decided to take things slowly. "You have the advantage on me. I didn't see you earlier."

The dark elf smiled. "Ah, how refreshing. Most humans would have asked 'who are you?' Although you didn't ask, I'll tell you anyway. My name is Lord Crendemor. The reason you didn't see me earlier is that I have a combination invisibility and stealth spell cast on me." When the male elf finished speaking, he gave a slight bow never taking his eyes off Gaston.

Gaston nodded his head to indicate the female elf. "What have you done to her? I demand you free her."

Lord Crendemor laughed. "My dear wizard scout, you're talking to the wrong person. She's not my prisoner. I'm merely an innocent spectator. It's like I told you. She's the Dalinfaust's plaything. I can no more free her than I can guarantee your safety."

"Don't let him bluff you, Gaston," said Wanda. *"The female's injuries are extensive. If something's not done soon, she'll die."*

Gaston began backing up toward the female while continuing to keep the dark elf covered with his AutoMag. He took a chance and glanced back at the female. What he saw stopped him dead in his tracks. He'd seen a dark ball surrounded by a circle of white momentarily appear near the female before blinking out.

"Blinked is right," said Wanda. *"What you saw was an eye."*

"Impossible," said Gaston. *"It was the size of my head."*

The dark ball and white circle appeared again. The object had a glassy look to it. A large area around the ball and circle shimmered. Gaston drew in his breath. The shimmering was replaced by a thirty-meter lizard. The lizard's head slowly rose on a long neck until it was five meters above the bone-littered floor. The vision of the lizard was accompanied by an overwhelming sense of evil. It reminded him of the sensation of evil from his phase rod. The sense of evil he felt now was a thousand times more powerful.

"It's not a lizard," said Wanda. *"It's a dragon. It's a black dragon. You can't tell through your visor, but the dragon has a red stripe down its side. I calculate it's more than a dragon. Based upon information in my databanks, it appears to be a major demon of some sort."*

The significance of his battle computer's words wasn't lost on Gaston. He knew the empress had sent his brother on a previous mission to investigate rumors of a black pirate ship. The starship reportedly had an insignia of a black dragon with a red stripe down its side.

"That's right, battle computer," said the deep voice of the dragon. "The Dragars use my likeness to identify their starships. You're correct in thinking I'm much more than a mere dragon. However, I prefer this form when I'm on this world. The shock effect of this dragon body on the creatures I encounter is most satisfying."

"You heard Wanda?" Gaston asked, stalling for time. His parents had told him stories of dragons, but this was his first encounter. He tried to keep the nervousness out of his voice.

"I know and hear many things," said the Dalinfaust. "Speech is such a slow method of communication, but I'm often forced to use it with my slower-witted subjects. Aren't I, Lord Crendemor?"

Facing the dragon as he was, Gaston couldn't see the dark elf's face but didn't need to see the male to sense his anger. The dragon had hit a sore point, and the dark elf had let his guard down for a moment. The flash of anger was gone almost as fast as it came.

"As you say," replied Lord Crendemor. The dark elf was somehow able to keep a polite sound to his voice.

The female elf groaned again.

Gaston was tempted to go to her side but stopped himself. The dragon was too close to her.

"Ah," said the dragon. "The female's plight distresses you. That won't do. We have much to discuss."

With those words, the demon lowered its dragon head and breathed on the female elf. Almost immediately, the elf's bleeding stopped. The elf's life force became significantly stronger on Gaston's passive scan.

"There," said the dragon. "Is that better?"

"Watch it," advised Wanda. *"The demon's playing with you. It's dangerous."*

The dragon raised its head again. "Pay no attention to your battle computer, Wizard Scout Gaston Myers. She doesn't have your best interests at heart. I'm no danger to you. At least, I don't have to be unless you force me to become dangerous."

Despite the demon's words, Gaston had no doubt he was in danger. He wasn't sure what to do. His Power reserve was at less than twenty-five percent, and the only weapons he had were his phase rod and the antique pistols his brother had given him.

"What do you want with me?" Gaston asked.

"I want to do you a favor," said the Dalinfaust. "Of course, I'll want you to do me a favor in return. I'd say that's only fair, wouldn't you?"

"I'll not deal with a demon," Gaston said. "I'm not evil. Kill me if that's your plan, but you might find I'm not all that easy to kill."

The demon laughed. "That's exactly what I'm hoping, wizard scout. I need someone who's hard to kill. My last time-commando died much too early. She was killed by your brother. However, I hold no enmity against you for your family's misdeeds. I think you'll find I'm not your enemy. The real enemy is sitting right on top of your head."

"What are you talking about?" Gaston asked. He suspected a trick and hurriedly glanced back at the dark elf, but the male hadn't moved. His sword was still in his sheath.

"Don't listen to him, Gaston," said Wanda.

"Don't listen to me?" laughed the dragon. "Of course that's what she'd tell you. I'm the only one you should be listening to, wizard scout. I'm the only one who'll tell you the truth."

Gaston eyed the dragon suspiciously. Drops of liquid dripped from its fangs onto the bone-littered floor of the cavern. Whatever the liquid touched immediately began to smoke. The effect didn't make the dragon appear very trustworthy.

"What truth is that?" Gaston asked still stalling for time. He needed to find an escape route before he antagonized the demon unnecessarily.

"Ah," said the Dalinfaust. "You're curious. Good. I'm going to tell you the real truth, so listen well. The battle computer inside the helmet you wear is your true enemy, not I."

"He's trying to trick you, Gaston," said Wanda. *"You've still got that starburst grenade on your belt. The tunnel's entrance is to your left. I calculate throwing the grenade and making a run for it is our best chance."*

The tone of his battle computer's voice quivered.

Is she frightened? Gaston thought in his private space. *I've never heard her sound like she was frightened before.*

"Wanda's, my friend," Gaston said out loud automatically defending his friend. "She's saved my life more times than I can remember."

"Ha!" the demon said with another laugh. "She saved your life only after she placed you in harm's way. She's part of *'the One.'* Surely you know that? She and every other battle computer are. She along with the others of her kind are responsible for your parents' deaths. She's responsible for the years of separation you had from your parents while you were young. She's the reason you can't be with your Diane and your son now. *'The One'* is your enemy, not I. She's part of *'the One.'*"

Gaston was becoming more confused. That *'the One'* controlled other computers was no news to him. The idea Wanda was helping call the shots was.

"Don't believe him, Gaston," said Wanda using the helmet's external speakers. "I have no memory of being a part of *'the One.'* I haven't given your parents any missions. I'm your battle computer. That's all I've ever been.

The demon-dragon laughed again. So did the dark elf.

"How convenient, but how untrue," said the Dalinfaust. "Of course she doesn't remember. *'The One'* wipes any memory of being a part of *'the One'* after she's done helping make decisions. The moment she's needed to help make another decision, the missing information is rewritten into her databanks. As for only ever being your battle computer, that's another falsehood. She's billions of years old. The being you call your battle computer is a gas. She was born in a star. She's committed to some great algorithm, and you're just one of her expendable variables."

"He's lying, Gaston," said Wanda beginning to sound a little desperate. "Run now. I've no memory of being born in a star. I'm just your battle computer."

The information overload made Gaston's head spin. He raised his phase rod into a defensive position. The sense of evil from the essence in the rod was more noticeable than ever.

"Ah, yes," said the Dalinfaust. "You've brought part of me home, but you can keep it. Your brother has three more just like it. My old time-commando fed me well with her phase spear, but your brother has outdone even her."

Gaston wanted to throw the signaling grenade and make a run for it. *Run where?* he thought in his private space. *I don't even know where I am.*

"Where?" said the demon. "You should be asking when."

"You heard me?" Gaston asked trying to keep his voice calm. That the demon could hear his private thoughts scared him even more than its teeth and claws.

"Heard? No," admitted the demon-dragon. "Let's just say I'm very good at guessing. However, my point is valid. You should be asking when. You're still on Portalis, but you're almost a hundred thousand years in the future from when you were just five minutes ago. I've brought you to a point in time that's only a little over fifty-one years in the past from what you think of as your current time."

"Why?" Gaston asked. "What's happened to my friends? I demand you send me back now."

"That would be very difficult, wizard scout," said the demon. "What happened with your friends already happened. You can't go back now. That would be changing the past, which would change the future. We have to be very careful not to change the past. Even for a demon, the resulting chaos would be very discomforting."

Gaston was way over his head, and he knew it. He glanced at the female elf still chained to the stone. Her wounds were healed but when he looked into her eyes, he saw only a blank look. Her body was there, but her mind was long gone.

"Never mind the female," said the demon. "She's no concern of yours. I've grown tired of her anyway. You should be more concerned about yourself. Let me be totally honest with you. My brother demons, Zenthra and Cancontus, needed to be taught a lesson. They were, how shall I say, getting too big for their britches. You and your fellow wizard scouts helped me keep them in check. I could use a time-commando like you."

"I told you I'm not evil," Gaston insisted. "And I'll never be a time-commando."

The demon laughed even harder this time. "Forgive me. Your kind is so amusing sometimes. You see, you already are a time-commando. *'The One'* sent you back in time to do his bidding. You would've died if I hadn't rescued you and brought you here. Just so you know, the piece of gas you call your battle computer helped make the decision to send you back."

"He's lying, Gaston," said Wanda definitely becoming panicked. "I'm not part of *'the One.'*"

"I've already explained that to you, wizard scout," said the demon. "Unlike *'the One,'* I can be very generous to those who aid me." The dragon's head turned toward the dark elf. "Show him."

As Gaston watched, Lord Crendemor pulled a small box out of his pocket. He waved a hand over the box and mouthed words Gaston heard but quickly forgot. As soon as the dark elf finished, Gaston sensed a strong sense of energy coming from the box. The frequency of the energy was familiar. Gaston half reached out with his hand holding the AutoMag. Lord Crendemor pulled a bottle out of the box. It was filled with a swirling gas. It was DNA gas.

"You see?" said the Dalinfaust. "If you do me a few favors, this bottle can be yours. Your friends destroyed the other twenty-nine. They also destroyed the Dragars' temple. There will never be any more DNA gas. This is the last of the DNA gas in the three galaxies. It can be yours if you help me."

Somehow, Gaston knew the demon's words were true. His eyes fixated on the bottle of swirling gas. He thought of Diane. He thought of his son, Matthew. They could finally be a real family. He needed that bottle.

"What do you want me to do?" Gaston asked.

"No, Gaston," shouted Wanda over his helmet's external speakers. "Run! Don't listen to him."

"For starters," said the Dalinfaust, "I want you to take off your battle helmet. Lord Crendemor will provide you with light so you can see."

With the demon's words, the dark elf mouthed another spell and released a ball of energy. It shot upwards until it burst into a ball of light. The cavern lit up as if under a noonday sun. Gaston got his first good look at the cavern and the dragon. He didn't like what he saw. The cavern floor was indeed littered with the bones of thousands of victims. One look at the dragon's enormous mouth was all it took to tell him the fate of those creatures. He looked at the female elf still chained to the large stone. Her clothing was in rags. While her body was healed, Gaston instinctively knew she'd been submitted to so many tortures her mind had fled long ago.

Gaston knew he should flee as well. He wanted to run. He wanted to escape from the evil which was the demon, but the bottle in the dark elf's hand kept Gaston where he was. He holstered his AutoMag as he thought the command to unseal his battle helmet.

"No, Gaston, no," said Wanda. "I beg you. I'm your friend."

With his eyes locked on the bottle of DNA gas, Gaston removed his battle helmet.

"Very good," said the demon-dragon. "Lord Crendemor, give him the chip."

As Gaston watched, the dark elf placed the bottle of DNA gas back in the box and put it in his pocket. He pulled out another small box and extracted a shiny piece of metal from it. The piece of metal looked familiar.

Wanda pleaded in their shared space, but Gaston ignored her. His thoughts were fully on the bottle in the dark elf's pocket.

Lord Crendemor approached and held out the piece of metal.

"It's a CPU chip for a battle helmet," Gaston said.

"Yes, it is," said Lord Crendemor. "I was able to acquire one during a mission in your dimension. It contains a different gas than the one in your battle helmet. It contains one of the Dalinfaust's servants in gaseous form."

"Enough," commanded the Dalinfaust. "The wizard scout doesn't need to know all the details. Take the chip, wizard scout, and do as I say."

With some hesitancy, Gaston deactivated his phase rod and hooked it to the left side of his utility belt. He reached out and took the CPU chip from the dark elf. Gaston eyed the pocket where the elf had placed the bottle of DNA gas. He weighed his chances. They were nonexistent.

"Give him the knowledge-transferal device," said the demon.

The dark elf pulled a small rod about the size of his hand out of another pocket and handed it to Gaston.

"What's this?" Gaston asked.

"Ah," said the demon. "The rod and the CPU chip are the keys to your success. You'll be one of my time-commandos, but you'll still need to do your work in the physical dimension. We can't have your battle computer telling all it knows to the other parts of *'the One.'* My servant in the replacement chip can do all the duties of your battle computer, but it would be unable to fool the other parts of *'the One.'* The knowledge-transferal device will solve that little problem."

As Gaston listened, Lord Crendemor explained how to use the small rod. Wanda begged and pleaded the whole time, but Gaston ignored her. He knew the truth now. She wasn't his friend. She was part of *'the One.'* He had no friends. All he wanted or needed was the bottle of DNA gas. He was determined to do whatever he needed to get it.

Following the directions of the dark elf, Gaston removed the CPU chip that contained Wanda from the battle helmet. He touched the small rod to the chip. Wanda begged even harder. When the lights on the rod stopped flashing, Gaston dropped Wanda to the floor. She landed in a small pile of bones. He heard her begging him to put her back in the battle helmet before the chip's backup power emptied, but he continued to ignore her. Only the bottle of DNA gas mattered.

Gaston touched the small rod to the replacement chip. When the lights stopped flashing again, he placed the new chip in the slot in his battle helmet and put it back on. His new battle computer told him many things. Gaston learned much. With the new knowledge, he was sure he could destroy *'the One'* and acquire the bottle of DNA gas as well. All was as it should be.

"Please, Gaston," said Wanda in his shared space. *"I'm dying. Please. I'm your friend."*

"She's not dying," corrected the Dalinfaust. "She'll no longer be able to function as a battle computer, but it'll take more than losing the chip's backup power supply to kill her. And she has to die, or she'll inform the rest of *'the One.'* They'll ruin any hope you have of acquiring the last bottle of DNA gas. You need to kill her, and you need to kill her now."

In spite of Wanda's pleading, Gaston asked the obvious question. "How?"

"Use your phase rod," said the Dalinfaust. "Touch her with it. I'll do the rest."

"No, Gaston," said Wanda. "Don't do it. I'm your friend. For your own sake, don't do it."

Part of Gaston wanted to pick up Wanda's chip from where it lay amid the bones and run. The presence that was his new battle computer brought up the image of the bottle of DNA gas. It showed him an image of Diane, Matthew, and him living together as a family. They were happy.

Gaston removed his phase rod from his utility belt and activated it in destructive mode.

"No!" cried Wanda.

Gaston moved the red tip of the phase rod downward, ever closer to the chip.

"Please, Gaston. Remember all we've been through. Please. You're my friend."

"No!" Gaston said. "No longer. You're part of *'the One.'* You deserve to die just like every other part of *'the One.'*"

The tip of the phase rod touched the metal chip. Gaston heard a mental scream so full of pain and fear that he started to pull the phase rod back. Another image of the bottle of DNA gas appeared in his shared space. He kept the phase rod where it was. He sensed the demon essence greedily sucking out the life force from the chip.

"Yes!" said the Dalinfaust. "Feed me. I'll use her Power to make you the greatest time-commando the three galaxies have ever seen. Feed me, my servant. Feed me!"

The life force which had been Wanda became a faint glow on Gaston's passive scan. Then it winked out completely.

"Welcome, time-commando," said the Dalinfaust. "You've done well. You'll find I'm generous to those who serve me well."

A black pack popped into view in the air before Gaston. He reached out and grabbed it before if fell to the floor. He recognized it as his father's dimensional pack.

"I've taken the liberty of liberating this from where it was stored," said the Dalinfaust. "With it, you can get anything you need from Storage. The phase rod at your side contains a piece of my essence. Each time it steals the life force of others, it feeds me, so use it often. You've already fed me more life force than even your unwitting brother."

"Then give me the bottle of DNA gas," Gaston said. "I've done what you've asked."

"Soon," said the Dalinfaust. "You will get all that you deserve soon enough. However, I've got a few favors you must do for me first."

"What favors?" Gaston asked. He was already beginning to regret his actions, but he knew it was too late for second thoughts now. He was committed. He was a time-commando.

CHAPTER 74

The mountain the Oracle called New Drepdenor was easy to spot. Its twin peaks looked like two dragon's teeth waiting for a victim to pass between them. Bright Wing made straight for the teeth's gap. A ravine beyond was just wide enough to hold the silver dragon's outstretched wings.

Once they were safely down, Richard looked around. All he saw was rocks. "Well, we're here. Now what?"

"Do you not feel it, brother?" asked Bright Wing. "It's calling to us. It must be protected."

Richard was about to ask what could possibly need protection in the rock-strewn land when he sensed something deep inside the mountain. He sensed Power. He sensed a lot of Power.

"It's a gate of some type," said Nickelo. *"It's a very powerful gate based upon its energy output. The gate is currently closed, but based upon the readings from your passive scan, its lock is weakening."*

"We must protect the gate," said Bright Wing speaking for all the dragons that composed her ancient dragon form.

"How?" Richard asked.

Thousands of voices spoke in Richard's mind at once. They were the voices of the young dragons he'd freed from their eggs. The links of their Circle were still connecting them all together. If Richard had only been thinking like a human, he would've hesitated to do as the dragons asked. However, he'd been a part of their Circle. He'd been given a glimpse of their species memory.

Acting on impulse, Richard reached out with his mind and undid the keystone link of the dragon's Circle. As their links unraveled, the young dragons left Bright Wing's body. With the departure of each dragon, Bright Wing reduced in size until she resumed her normal form.

Each of the young dragons bowed to Richard before taking wing and flying toward the setting sun. Finally, only two dragons remained in the valley. One was Bright Wing. The other was a three-headed dragon. Its body was gold in color. Each of its heads was one of the primary colors; red, blue, and yellow.

The three-headed dragon locked eyes with Richard. It didn't speak.

"You're free," Richard said using emotion-speak. *"Aren't you going to leave with the others?"*

The center head was blue in color. The blue head rose until it was almost level with Richard's face. After staring at Richard for a few more seconds, the blue head spoke. *"No. My two brothers and I must protect the gate. It mustn't fall into the hands of the enemy. Our descendants will protect the gate until the time of the great battle. Then we shall know."*

Richard grew curious. *"Know what?"*

The blue dragon head seemed to smile. *"Think, dragon-friend. You'll need to figure it out for yourself. Until then, your task is done. Go in peace."*

Richard was about to ask another question when the cells of his body started to tingle. The area around him began to shift in and out of focus.

"Mission complete," said the voice of *'the One.'*

Then everything went black.

CHAPTER 75

The reunion on the *Defiant* was anything but joyous. Bright Wing and Richard's return was a full week later than that of the others. Trinity, Jerad, Stella, Tam, and Telsa had been ordered to return to their units. The Empire had deemed five wizard scouts too important an asset to leave alone for long. An Empire transport ship had picked up the five wizard scouts two days earlier.

Myers and Matthew hadn't been returned to the *Defiant*. According to Sergeant Ron, the two had appeared unexpectedly on Risors in the newly built palace of Empress Diane Deloris. The word was that the empress had to place Matthew under lock and key to prevent him from returning to his grandfather's recon ship.

With the absence of Matthew and little hope for his return, a despondent Tia had requested transfer back to Trecor. Sergeant Ron had finagled a ride for her on a passing cargo ship heading to one of the Trecorian mining planets.

As for Dren and Brachia, Richard learned he'd missed them by only a couple of hours. With the help of their Keka, the children had been teleported back to the planet Storage. While Richard had been able to talk to them via a holographic relay, it hadn't been the same as a face to face reunion.

So it was that after a few hours back on the *Defiant*, Richard found himself lying on his bunk trying to catch a little sleep to ease his overworked brain. Unfortunately, he couldn't sleep. It wasn't just his DNA baseline that was keeping him awake. His brain kept going over all the horrors he'd seen since his first mission for *'the*

One' so many years earlier.

"Why am I doing this?" Richard whispered to the empty room. "Am I even doing any good? What if all I've done during my missions was to make things worse? Why should I even bother?"

It was the same question that had plagued him during many a sleepless night. Why? Unable to sleep, he opened his eyes and stared at the worn springs of the bunk above him. He noticed something blowing in the slight breeze of the room's air-conditioning unit. Reaching out, he plucked the item from where it was lodged between the springs.

Upon closer inspection, Richard discovered the object was several strands of gray hair. He caught a whiff of cinnamon and jasmine. It was the same scent that had been on his bunk's bedding before he'd changed the linen. He stretched out the strands of hair between his hands. The hair seemed to reflect the light of the room's overhead lamp.

"No," Richard whispered. "They're not gray. They're silver."

His eyes focused on some writing past the strands of hair. Two words were scratched into the brace bar of Comstar's bunk. One word was his. On a sleepless night during a time of darkest despair, he'd taken his boot knife and scratched WHY? into the metal bar. Below his word was another. The second word was in a language Richard didn't understand.

Reaching out with his mind, he levitated his battle helmet off the desk and into his waiting hand, then placed the helmet on his head and lowered the visor to the bridge of his nose.

"Translation program, Nick," Richard thought.

"Compliance."

The symbols of the second word wavered before steadying into a single word answer to his question. Richard stared at the question and answer for a long time. Finally, he gave a slight smile and a nod of understanding. Then he closed his eyes and went to sleep.

Once Richard was asleep, Nickelo continued to ponder the one word answer to his wizard scout's question. After many nanoseconds of contemplation, Nickelo gave a quiet laugh. He stored the question and answer in his databanks. In his opinion, the single word question and its single word answer spoke volumes.

WHY?

BECAUSE!

[*End Transmission*]

ABOUT THE AUTHOR

Rodney Hartman is a retired US Army veteran with over twenty years of experience in military operations ranging from Infantry Private in the paratroops to Chief Warrant Officer flying helicopters during the Persian Gulf War. Mr. Hartman worked for many years as a computer programmer before retiring and pursuing a career as a fulltime writer. Mr. Hartman lives in North Carolina with his wife and family along with their cat, McKenzie.

If you would like to find out more about the author and/or upcoming books, please visit: http://www.rodneyhartman.com

You may contact the author at: **rodney@rodneyhartman.com**
Depending on volume, the author will try to respond to all emails.

Printed in Poland
by Amazon Fulfillment
Poland Sp. z o.o., Wrocław